THE DEIFIC DOZEN

By
Brian J. Orlowski

www.AuthorMikeInk.com

First Published by *AuthorMike Ink*, 10/15/2013

www.AuthorMikeInk.com

AuthorMike Ink and its logo are trademarked by
AuthorMike Ink Publishing.

Printed in the United States of America

This book is dedicated to my wonderful mother,
Madeline, whose support and understanding knows
no limits. She continues to be my biggest fan.

And a special thank you to my wife, Anna,
who is the kindest, sweetest, and
most patient person in the universe.
She is my little alien and I'm lucky to have her.

FACT:

The Church of Scientology, a system of beliefs, teachings and rituals, originally established in 1952 by science fiction author L. Ron Hubbard, is a real organization.

Over its fifty plus years, the Church of Scientology has attracted great controversy and criticism, and has been characterized as a cult. The Church's members include many high profile celebrities, some of which are parodied in this book, but cleverly disguised so as to protect their anonymity.

All descriptions of places, architecture, documentation, and sculptures are real.

The paintings described in this book are very real, and the images of UFOs they contain are real, but subject to interpretation.

I hate to say this but Santa Claus and the Easter Bunny are *not* real. The majority of Pam Anderson is also not real, but I'm *not* complaining. Donald Trump's comb over is very unreal. I *am* complaining about that. Snoop Dogg, however, *is* real, and he's keeping it that way.

PROLOGUE

The first time Congressman Fred Stitio found himself tied to a chair was in a sleazy Burbank motel with three Latina hookers. It was his birthday and, as customary amongst his peers, he sent his wife to an all-day spa and treated himself to the carnal pleasures of prostitution for around $3000 an hour All on the taxpayers' dime of course.

They only bad thing to come of that situation was a mild case of Gonorrhea that cleared up in a few days time.

His wife got a diamond necklace that month.

The second time the good Congressman was bound to a straight-backed oak was when a hitherto unknown, Polish mafia had found it necessary to convince the Congressman to look the other way when it came to certain California import policies.

He put on his tough guy act long enough to know that it wasn't an FBI sting operation trying to uncover corrupt political officials. These chaps were the real deal. Congressman Stitio agreed to each and every demand long before the bolt cutter was placed near a single finger. He came out of that situation with soiled underwear and an envelope stuffed with twenty-five grand.

His wife got a new car that month.

This time Congressman Stitio had the feeling things weren't going to end as nicely as his first two encounters with bondage and wooden furniture. The split, bleeding lip and swollen-shut eye were a big giveaway. His tormentors had taken a break, leaving him alone in the abandoned warehouse, giving him time to think and a chance for his wounds to clot. He was beyond crying and begging, his captors were nonplussed by his appeals to their conscience. These two were dangerous; ice ran in their veins.

He looked around the warehouse with his one usable eye. There were no windows and no lights aside from the one bulb suspended above him. He sat in a circle of yellow light, as though in a force field. The bulb flickered sporadically. He hadn't any idea how long he'd been there, but assumed it was at least one day. There were several canisters nearby, spray-painted with the word, Petrol. *What's Petrol?* The Congressman wondered. *Sounds like a lubricant or something.*

He could barely remember how he got into this situation. It was all a tad foggy. He had just left a meeting with an out-of-state representative of The Commonwealth of Israel. *Whoever they are!* It was a simple meet-and-greet to show openness to all religious groups. He only half listened to their hopes for a new center in Glendale. A small group of protestors milled about the front of the Town Hall, listlessly holding signs about cults and stuff that really couldn't hold less interest for the Congressman. The last thing he remembered was getting into his Town car. He heard someone jumping up from the backseat and a wet cloth was placed over his mouth. He quickly faded to black to later awaken in this very familiar rope-and-chair scenario.

Something told him his wife wasn't getting anything this month but a knock on the door from a grief counselor out of Town Hall.

A large metal door flew open, startling the beaten and weary Congressman. He might have lost control of his bladder had he not done so a few hours ago. *It's funny how hot pee gets cold so fast.*

His kidnappers had returned.

Backlit by the doorway the silhouetted men calmly walked across the oil-stained cement floor toward him, their expensive shoes clacking on the cold, hard floor. The Congressman studied the darkened figures as they came to a stop before him. *Damn, but they looked familiar!*

They referred to each other only as Mr. Crows and Mr. Trafalgar. He hadn't really been able to see their faces in the poor lighting of the cavernous room. But the few glances he was able to steal made him think they looked like people he should know. Mr. Crows was short and lean. He had tousled brown hair that framed his deceivingly youthful face. He was wearing black on black: pants, sweater, and shoes. He had a frenetic quality to him that terrified the Congressman. Jumpy and jittery.

Mr. Trafalgar, on the other hand, was much taller and almost overweight with thick short hair, slicked back. He was much calmer, tactful, and soft-spoken. He wore a black suit jacket, white shirt and tie. He regularly had a cigarette handy; the man would accent any conversation by pulling out his pack, lighting up and blowing bluish clouds of smoke. Mr. Trafalgar did so with such cool smoothness that anyone who witnessed the man smoking would want to pick up the deadly habit immediately. *What a bad role model!* the Congressman thought.

Mr. Trafalgar spewed a plume of smoke, "Good afternoon Congressman, I hope our little break gave you time to think. Now, back on topic. We feel that you have been presented with certain information that our... organization would like to be privy to. So if you would be so kind as to relinquish said info, I'd greatly appreciate it. You catch my drift?"

Mr. Crows nervously shook behind Mr. Trafalgar, his feet shuffling, his eyes darting about. He eyed the Congressman eagerly, as though he were dinner. The Congressman thought he could see a line of drool running down the man's chin.

The Congressman spat out the collective blood and saliva that pooled in his injured mouth. "Gentlemen, I swear I have no idea what you are asking me about!" he pleaded, "Trust me! Ask anyone that knows me. I know nothing! My father *bought* me this position. I'm an idiot!"

"Liar!" screamed Mr. Crows. He jumped about, swinging his arms wildly. "You filthy, filthy liar! We know you know about the *Twelve*! What did you discuss with those bible-beating Sudafed-taking Island Pond people?"

"Sudafed?" Congressman Stitio was confused. Mr. Trafalgar also turned and looked at Mr. Crows. "Sudafed?" he asked as well.

Mr. Crows got defensive, "You know what I mean. They take medicines and vitamins and pills and stuff. Unlike us... us Thetan 7's!"

"Chill!" Mr. Trafalgar cut him off. "You've said enough." He returned his attention to the Congressman. "Continue, Congressman, if you would."

"I told you. I was half-asleep during that entire meeting. It was something about a center in Glendale. That's all! And what is this *Twelve* you keep mentioning? I don't know anything about..."

Mr. Crows leapt from the floor and landed, standing on Congressman Stitio's legs. The Congressman howled in pain. Mr. Crows crouched down, leveling his eyes to the Congressman's. "You are a dirty, dirty confused fool who's been taken in by the over-medicated media! I ought to rip your throat out!" Mr. Crows' hands reached for the trembling man's neck.

"Now stay cool, Mr. Crows." Mr. Trafalgar interrupted; he put his hand on Mr. Crows' shoulder. "We have to find out what he knows. He's no good to us dead. So just cool your jets, okay little buddy?" He scratched Mr. Crows behind the ear; the Congressman felt one of Mr. Crows' legs begin to kick.

Mr. Trafalgar led Mr. Crows down from the Congressman's rapidly numbing legs, then turned back. "We know you had a meeting with The Commonwealth of Israel, Mr. Congressman. Do you know what else they are known by? Their... aliases?"

"Their what?"

"Their agnomen, moniker, patronymic, appellation, epithet, sobriquet, eponym, autonym, cognomen, flag, denomination, nickname, designation, handle, nomen, surname, also known as also known as. Catch my drift?"

"N-no."

Mr. Trafalgar raised his voice a notch. "What else does the Commonwealth call themselves? It's really easy."

"I-I'm sorry. No, I have no idea. I never heard of them."

"The Light Brigade? Does that ring a bell? How about the Vine Community Church? Maybe the Church in Island Pond?" Mr. Trafalgar dropped his cigarette and artfully crushed it with the toe of his polished black shoes. "These are all pseudonyms of The Twelve Tribes, their real name. But you knew this, didn't you?"

"No, I swear. I never heard of..."

"Oh, I think you do. What did they want from you?" Mr. Trafalgar leaned in close. "And more importantly, did they offer you any... valuable information?"

"Like I said, they wanted to open a center in Glendale!"

"A center for *what*, Mr. Congressman?"

"I don't know... maybe recruitment? To find new members?"

"Recruitment! Yes, Mr. Congressman!" Trafalgar raised his arms triumphantly. "Recruitment for what?"

"You've lost me." The Congressman's head was spinning. He needed a gin and tonic ASAP. Hell, maybe Petrol was alcohol. He'd take a glass of that now if he could. It didn't matter as long as it helped him forget.

"Recruitment for the Light Brigade! You get it now?" Mr. Trafalgar lectured. "Let's see, what does that mean? What is a brigade, if not an army? Brigade itself is derived from Italian, brigata meaning troop, and also from brigare, which means to fight. *The Light Brigade*. And why fight for *light*, Mr. Congressman? Why build an army for a stupid light? What is this light, sir?" He pulled out the cigarette pack from inside his jacket. He gracefully placed a Marlboro between his lips and skillfully replaced the pack while retrieving the lighter with such prestidigitation that the theatrics were mesmerizing. "Why would this *army* that *fights* for the *light* change its name to the Twelve Tribes, Mr. Congressman? Why?"

"It… um… it… it has a better ring to it?" he stuttered.

Mr. Trafalgar stopped in his tracks and slowly rotated on his feet to face the Congressman. One would think Mr. Trafalgar had some training in dance with the way he spun on his feet. "You, sir, are an idiot." He began to laugh. Mr. Crows chuckled as well. The Congressman was tempted to join in the revelry but knew he was the butt of the joke. "You really don't know anything about this."

"No, no, I know nothing!" The Congressman nodded. "I had a C average in high school."

Mr. Trafalgar took a long drag. He blew out the smoke slowly while smiling.

"I told you I was an idiot." Fred Stitio squeaked.

"I now believe you." Mr. Trafalgar said. "You *are* an idiot. And of no use."

The Congressman nodded vehemently. "Yes, I tried to tell you, I did…"

Mr. Trafalgar said two words, "Mr. Crows."

Mr. Crows howled like a rabid dog and leapt upon the bound and befuddled man. Before the Congressman could let out a squeak of fear his head had been rotated 180 degrees with a sickeningly bony crack. Though the Congressman was dead, Mr. Crows continued to beat and swat at the deceased man like an enraged monkey.

"That's enough, Mr. Crows." Mr. Trafalgar commanded. "We have to leave immediately." When Mr. Crows didn't respond quick enough, Mr. Trafalgar whistled then yelled. "Heel boy!"

Mr. Crows climbed off the battered and extremely dead Congressman, but let out one last huff of hatred, like a mutt snapping in anger, at the twisted head.

Mr. Trafalgar calmly kicked over one of the Petrol canisters and watched as the combustible liquid pooled around the faceless Congressman. He dropped his cigarette a few inches away, the Petrol slowly crawled toward the glowing ember.

"Mama always said dying was a part of life." Mr. Trafalgar coolly said as he walked toward the warehouse door.

Mr. Trafalgar looked down at his companion. "Come, Mr. Crows, we have much work to do."

"And people to kill?" Mr. Crows said excitedly.

"Maybe, my friend. If we're lucky."

Mr. Crows clapped happily. "Good. I like killing."

"I know you do, little buddy, I know you do." He patted Mr. Crows' head.

And with that they strolled out of the warehouse as the petrol met with the cigarette and a lake of fire grew.

CHAPTER 1

On the eastern edge of Central Park in New York City lies one of the largest and most important museums in the world, The Metropolitan Museum of Art. Most New Yorkers, and those from nearby areas, simply call it The Met. Its location on Fifth Avenue between 80th and 84th Streets was not its first, but actually its third.

The front of The Met also, like many New Yorkers, has held more than one face. Its original look was a red-brick, neo-Gothic structure. In 1902, Richard Morris Hunt designed the current front of The Met on Fifth Avenue, giving it a central pavilion and a neoclassical façade, layered on top of the original red-brick, much like an onion. Later, wings and additions were added to the sides and back, covering the remaining red-brick, adding to its onionish layering. You can still see a portion of the red-brick within the ground floor's European Sculpture Court.

Expanding on the onion-like metaphor, the inside of the museum holds layer upon layer of sacred treasures in its seemingly endless halls and galleries. One could travel for hours without seeing every single awe-inspiring painting and artifact. In fact, if a person were emotionally sensitive to the arts, the museum might make one's eyes tear up, again metaphorically like an onion. But it is unlikely that it would make a person gassy after eating it, thereby ending any and all onion references.

Randall Teodey cursed under his breath as he fiddled with the digital camera's tiny buttons. At fifty-eight he had no real experience with modern electronics and could barely read the menu on the display screen.. He squinted at the small type, trying to decipher its meaning. *What I wouldn't do for my old Pentax Spotmatic!* He thought. *Now that creature had heft! That was a camera!*

Randall was not a gentle soul; he frequently lost his temper, yelled, cursed and belittled others. But his volatile nature did not show on his amiably wrinkled and benign face. He had a Santa Claus vibe that worked well for him, especially with the ladies down at the Dialysis Center where he went every Tuesday and Thursday. No, he didn't have renal failure or kidney problems, but it was a good place to meet women. Though his face resembled Saint Nick, the resemblances ended above the neck since he wasn't Santa fat, but his white hair and white moustache certainly contributed to the constant comparisons he received. Ho frickin ho, let's go have a drink ladies.

Randall was the curator for the Met's Arms & Armor division, an amazing and diverse collection of over 15,000 objects, from armor and firearms to edged weapons and shields. Pieces as old as 400 B.C., up to the nineteenth century, from Near East to Central Asia and from India to North America are on display. The Arms & Armor gallery sat nestled firmly between the Egyptian Art, with its larger than life Temple of Dendur, and the American Wing Courtyard, a majestic three story glass-ceilinged wonder.

It was in this very courtyard that Randall attempted to set up his makeshift photo studio. He had the small camera on a tripod and ran a wire from the camera to a nearby laptop. How he had gotten this far with all these electronic thingamajigs he'd never know. *Pure luck, most likely.* He thought. *That and determination.* He'd been at it since 5:00 a.m., because that damn photographer canceled. But the museum needed this piece on the website today. That irritated Randall as well. *The Wide World of the Web! What a dumb invention!*

Randall glanced over at the object of his photo shoot: a 15th century pistol once owned by Emperor Charles V. A stunning antique, this early multishot wheellock pistol was designed by Peter Peck, a watch maker. And the designer's background showed in the detail and mechanism of this beautiful piece of art. It was decorated with three of the Emperor's personal emblems: a double-headed imperial eagle, the Pillars of Hercules and the Latin motto "Plus Ultra". *Stunning!* It rested on a small table over a bed of black velvet. A chair sat next to the table for Randall himself. He was supposed to be in the picture as well. Though why anyone would want to see him next to this treasure was unthinkable to the curator. Armed with a camera he could barely use, he was forced to set the timer, run and sit, try and look relaxed, wait for the flash, run back, check the picture to see. No wait, his mouth looked funny. Nope, this time he blinked. Nope, he missed the chair and fell. And then do it all again. *Infuriating!* He hated this click and run technique.

Randall took a short break from the camera and spooned a mouthful of cereal into his mouth. *Thank God for Alphabits!* Randall mused. He'd had this cereal for breakfast since its inception in 1958, nearly half a century. He never tired of it, not once. Even when Post removed the sugar in 2005, he'd stuck with it. Sure, he'd protested with several futile letters, but it was habit now. No, nix that, it was more of a ritual thing. Randall couldn't start his day without it.

As Randall chewed his mouthful he balanced the bowl in one hand, and tinkered with the settings with his other hand. Without warning, the camera flashed directly in Randall's face. He stood motionless, temporarily blinded, and waited for the bright spiraling circles of light to disappear from his vision. Randall turned red with anger. The worst being that he'd nearly dropped his cereal! *Damn this infernal machine. That's the third picture looking up my nostrils!* As soon as his vision returned, he went back to setting the timer.

He hoped somebody else would show up already, that is, somebody other than the few security guys out in the lobby. It was early and Randall had arrived before his normal time to get this stupid picture out of the way. Why they couldn't reschedule the photographer or wait for their tech guy to do it?

Wait! A light bulb went off in Randall's mind, not nearly as bright as the camera's flash. *Violet might be here by now! I'm sure she knows how to work this thing.*

"Oh, who am I kidding?" Randall said aloud, his voice echoing in the empty courtyard.

Randall knew his daughter wasn't very bright. She'd barely graduated Vassar, where she seemingly majored in alcohol, cigarettes and bisexual dalliances. They had had a falling out toward the end of her high school career. She went off to college with nary a thank you. Randall was most shocked when he found out she had taken her mother's maiden name and legally dropped his. He'd have disowned her then if it wasn't for the promise he'd made his wife almost twenty years ago. Yet, she had no problem taking an allowance and having him foot the bill for college.

Randall and Violet hadn't talked much since she finished her schooling, which took 5 and a half years to complete. For many years after college, she floundered between long bouts of unemployment and pointless jobs having nothing to do with her Biology major, though some might consider her slatternly behavior a biological endeavor.

She didn't approach her father, ever, not until she was so in debt she had no choice. That was last year and Randall got her a position in the HR department, which she accepted, reluctantly. And even then, they barely spoke. Their relationship since she started at The Met was tenuous, at best. They would exchange pleasantries if they passed each other, but would never go out of their way to do so.

She usually came in early; almost an hour before her starting time. Randall was pleased to hear that, until he was also informed by one of her supervisors that it was so she could use her computer for personal interests, like Facespace or Mybook, Twaddle or Twatter, or whatever those sites were called.

Randall had been meaning to talk to her for some time now. Something had come up just this past week. He needed to sit her down, explain things, so she would understand what may happen soon. But he put it off, the opportunity never arising. It would have to be done soon. Things were getting bad; he didn't know how much time was left.

I'll do it today! He promised himself. *I'll approach her and ask her to my office during her lunch. I have to. I have no choice.*

Until then, he had to get this God-awful thingamajig working.

Randall lined up the camera, framing the pistol and leaving enough room for himself. *Why do I have to be in this Hellish project?* Enthusiasts would only be interested in the pistol, not his ugly mug. He pressed the timer and quickly moved around the camera toward the table holding the artifact.

The corner of his eye caught movement at the entrance to the courtyard, not ten feet from where he stood.

Randall froze.

A man stepped out from the shadowed doorway.

Before Randall could react, a gun roared to life. Randall felt the burn of the bullet, the searing pain in his stomach. He reeled, reaching out for support as he fell. He knocked over the table with the Emperor's pistol. His cereal fell over his shoulder, the ceramic bowl shattering, as the velvet cloth tumbled to the ground. The table, the chair, the Emperor's pistol all crashed to the floor together. Randall felt his leg kick the tripod. The man from the shadows ran out of the courtyard.

Randall knew he was fading, his thoughts turned toward his daughter. *Oh my dear Violet. I have to get you a message.* Randall attempted to move, if only he had a notepad, something, anything. He so desperately wanted to leave her a message. He looked around for anything .

As Randall's vision swam and the edges of his world darkened. He heard a small electronic whine, and then the camera's flash went off. Bright motes of light spun in his failing vision.

Infernal thing! He cursed as everything faded to black.

CHAPTER 2

Violet Sterne sat at her computer, typing frenetically on the keyboard. Had anyone else been in the office, they would immediately believe she was working determinedly on an important museum related document. A paper of such consequence that, had it not been completed within minutes, the entire building would have burst into flames, and nuns and orphans across the world would die a horrific death (as opposed to those really nice and pleasant deaths).

In reality, Violet was writing several posts for her Facebook profile and wanted them done before other employees arrived.

She knew she wouldn't get caught since no one else was in, well, except for her father who was always the first person in. *That old, early-morning grump!* But he didn't know *she* was in yet, even earlier than usual. And she liked to keep it that way. Even if he stopped by, he wouldn't know a Facebook webpage from a spreadsheet. Violet giggled as she poured out her soul for everyone to see and read.

(Ah, yes, Facebook, the subculture for the sub-intelligent. There, degenerates are able to chat freely with teenagers, and lurid pictures of your children can be viewed by pedophiles worldwide. It was originally entitled Thefacebook and created by a college nerd and a few buddies to allow fellow Harvard students keep in touch, but like a virus or cancer, its explosion of popularity with young adults across the globe brought it international attention. It grew exponentially: from the college circuit, to high schools, then businesses, and ultimately the entire planet. It dropped the "the" in 2005. In 2007, Microsoft bought a 1.6% share for 240 million. Facebook's estimated value in 2011 was over 40 billion. In 2012, Facebook went public, offering its shares at $38 apiece, and valued the company at $104 million. Its popularity still grows. Freaks, mutants, panderers, slanderers, snake oil salesmen, whores, promoters, vampires, addicts, philanderers, losers, novelists, cartoonists and drug dealers can mingle with persons, kids and teens across the globe unfettered by any adult supervision. Spammers selling illegal and misspelled versions of Cialis and Viagra can litter your inbox. Teens can discuss sexual activities and prance about in their underwear for all to see. *But at least they don't allow nudity. Thank God for that! Whew! Never mind, it's safe for your kids.* Celebrities who most likely have never even seen their own profile on Facebook can 'friend you' and make you feel like you're really tight with musicians and actors. Up and coming novelists can… well, that's perfectly acceptable. In fact, you can visit the author here: www.facebook.com/brian.j.orlowski.) *Okay, enough ranting. Back to the story.*

Violet tapped on her keyboard like a telegrapher on a speedball high. It was her third posting of the morning. She found writing and posting rather cathartic. Telling stories of a deep and personal nature and leaving it for an entire planet of strangers to read and respond to was great fun. Right now she needed to vent. This particular literary gem was about yeast infections and their negative effect on dating. Well, *her* dating to be precise. Her last date ended abruptly when she found herself itching so badly that her escort excused himself to the men's room. He never returned, leaving her to foot the bill and do the walk of shame out of the restaurant with one hand scratching her groin.

Violet didn't date all that much. It wasn't because of yeast infections or anything like that, even that was abnormal for her. And it wasn't because she was ugly. She was attractive all right, a real looker, but she carried a chip on her shoulder the size of a Buick. She grew up rather chunky. Well… okay that's being nice, she was really, really fat. In the 80's, when the fad was to wear Guess jeans, people would see the brand label on her pants and yell out large numbers, "550 pounds!" "No, wait, 2 tons!" Kids can be cruel, and sometimes funny. So that's how Violet developed her sarcastic, bitter personality. She needed a defense mechanism, and her attitude and ability to tear into anyone's weak spot made her a formidable fat kid. It was a character trait that carried over to adulthood and made her a very imposing person to woo.

Years later, Violet had become quite the hottie. She lost all of her fatness. Other women hated her because it happened without effort. She ate unhealthily, drank like a fish, chain-smoked, and never exercised. The fat seemingly melted off shortly after high school.

Now she was a stunning woman. She had long, thick, jet-black hair that framed her perfect heart-shaped face. She was tall and lean, athletic in figure without the effort of a gym membership. She captured the attention of many gentlemen, which she quickly chased away, intentionally or not. Some guys found it a challenge, thinking her looks were worth the effort to get her in the sack; they eventually got sick of being ridiculed and derided and took off angrily.

Now she was twenty-eight, working in a building riddled with dorks, dusty old men and bookworms. She didn't bother looking attractive for work anymore; though today she was a little more sharply dressed than usual. She wore a tight-fitting sweater top with a plunging neckline, her bosom bulging like rising bread in the oven. She also wore her skin-tight jeans, showing off her well rounded buttocks. She didn't know why she dressed differently today. Her only chance at a social life was when she took a break to smoke a cigarette on the massive front steps of The Met. Yes, it was illegal. But Violet didn't care, she felt it was her right. So she put up with the nasty glares and muttered comments from passersby. Not that she would meet a man smoking outside The Met, most of the smokers out there were snobbish French men, or gay, or both.

No, her last vestige of sociality was relegated to online commingling and dating websites. Hence, the almighty and vapid Facebook. Though most times when she did get a friend request, it was unfortunately from a hormone-raging, gangster-wannabe eighteen-year-old with a pimply face and hairless, shirtless photos telling her she was "hawt" and to "holla" at them. That was usually when she started thinking she needed a website for people closer to her age. She had no idea what these kids were talking about.

Violet finished her essay and posted it so all sixteen of her online friends could read it, like it, or comment on it.

She sat back and admired her profile. She'd spent weeks gussying it up with a purple floral pattern in the background. She had posted all the cool bands she liked and a list of her favorite movies. She also had posted some animated images, like a fat kid playing drums. Even though she was once fat, that little chubby kid playing the skins made her laugh every time. Maybe it *was* fun laughing at fat people. She'd have to think about that, right after she had a cigarette. She reached for her purse and threw it over her shoulder.

The sound of a gunshot echoed down her hallway. As far as she knew, only she and her father were in, besides security. The hairs on her neck stood on end. *Something really bad just happened.* Violet ran out her door.

CHAPTER 3

Violet took the large center stairs of The Met two at a time, sliding at the bottom to make a sharp left. She paused to check the security desk. It was abandoned. *Where is everyone?*

She cut through the European Sculpture and Decorative Arts section, past hanging ceramic masks with glowering frowns, and glass cases filled with pendants of turquoise and copper, and then turned left at the Arms and Armory. She stopped, looking around the gloomy area.

"Dad?" Violet called out, her voice echoing in the empty gallery. She ran by the haunting quartet of armored warriors riding their equally reinforced horses, solemnly lined up like the four horsemen of the apocalypse.

She turned left at the ghoulish parade into another hall of the gallery. Glass enclosed cases protected the displays of pistols and swords. Violet called out again. Her voice returned to her, echoing in the abandoned halls. No answer. She saw the double doors to the American Wing Courtyard propped open. She skidded to a halt in the doorway.

She gasped at the sight of her fallen father.

"No! Dad!" she screamed. Violet ran over and kneeled next to him. Her eyes welled with tears as she cradled his head. She saw the bloody wound in his torso. She felt for a pulse on his neck as Roy, one of the many security guards, ran in to the courtyard. She choked on her sobs.

"Call 911!" Violet cried. "My father's been shot!" She wanted to scream at him for not being at his post, but now wasn't the time.

Roy did a one-eighty; he was on his walkie-talkie before he was out of the courtyard.

A faint moan halted Violet's sobbing. Her father's eyes fluttered. "Violet?" he whispered. "I... I was shot... by a man. He... he..."

"Save your strength, Dad. An ambulance is on the way."

"I'm sorry… about our… our differences." His eyes were having trouble focusing on his daughter. "I have to tell… you… something."

"It's okay, Dad, I'm here. Just hang in there."

"Listen… you have to find Grant… Grant Piosto." Randall coughed, his teeth gritted from the pain. "He can… tell you… help you…"

"Who is this Grant, Dad? Why do I need him?"

"He's at the Hilton. Find him… before… you…"

"Yeah, but who is he?" she persisted.

Randall grimaced, more in frustration than pain. "Would you just… please… listen to me? Find Grant… at the Hilton…"

Violet fished around her purse. "Wait, Dad, I need a pen. You know I'm not going to remember all this."

"Gerri went to… went…"

"Gerri? What about Grant? Hold up, Dad, one person at a time. That was Grant, right?" Violet jotted down the information. "What was it? Pasta? Posta? How do you spell that?"

"P… i… o… s… t… o…" he creaked. "Gerri knows… she has…."

"Again, Dad, wait! Forget about Gerri for a second." Violet snapped as she fell behind. "Which Hilton? There are a few in New York, right?"

Randall growled, getting impatient. "The… one on… Avenue of Americas."

"Is that 5th or 6th?" She rolled her eyes. "I get that wrong every time."

"For the love of God!" Randall barked, sitting up slightly "I'm dying here! Can you just get this?"

"Sorry."

Randall slumped to the floor, his energy waning. "Grant can help… I can't keep this… a secret…"

"Secret? Dad, what are you talking about?" Violet didn't understand. "What about Gerri? Your assistant, right? What about her?"

"Gerri went…"

"Where, Dad, where?"

"You must go... go... before she... before she..." Randall's voice was trailing off. Then his eyes closed and his head lolled to the side.

"Dad!" Violet screamed. "No!"

Violet's body shuddered as she cried for her father. Years of guilt and regret suddenly piled onto her shoulders. She kissed him on the forehead and gently lowered his head to the cold marble floor. "I'm so sorry, Dad. I love you."

Violet stood up. She glanced at her father's final words. Ironically, it was on the back of her pay stub. *He got me this job. He gave me everything. And I let all this time go by without thanking him.* She read the scribbled message again. It was his last wish–his final command to her. It was obviously very serious and important to him. She wouldn't let him down. Not this time. Not like high school and college. She would find Grant whatever-his-name-was and discover this secret that burdened her father. She shouldered her purse and moved for the exit.

Roy returned, followed by Clay and Murrel–the other security guards on the morning shift.

Clay was sweet but quiet. His eyes bulged, like those big-eyed goldfish or a Chihuahua with goiter that'd been kicked in the balls a few times. He had thinning hair that was swept over his balding pate and apparently glued into place.

Murrel always smelled like hot garbage and insisted on walking by her office at least ten times a day. He was a short, seemingly mute, and incredibly hairy with a dull expression permanently etched on his face. Even now he was eying her creepily. It gave her the chills.

"They're on their way!" Roy announced. "The ambulance will be here any moment now. The police, too."

Violet weakly smiled. "It's too late, Roy. He's gone. My father's dead."

Roy placed his hand on her shoulder. "I'm so sorry Miss Sterne." Roy hung his head. Clay followed suit. Murrel reached out to hug Violet.

"Uh, no Murrel!" She jumped away like she stepped on a nail. "Thanks. Thank you, but no."

Murrel shrugged, looking dejected. He shuffled back behind Roy and Clay.

Roy asked. "Are you going somewhere? You shouldn't leave. The police will want to talk to all of us."

"Where were you guys?" Violet asked, her initial anger returning. "You weren't at the front desk! You weren't doing your job!"

Roy sighed. "After the gunshot, some guy came running through the front and ran out an emergency door. We chased him down the street. He disappeared about a block and half up 85th."

"He was fast." Clay chimed in.

Murrel nodded in agreement. Even that was creepy.

Great security. These morons can't run more than a block and a half.

"I have to go somewhere, Roy." Violet tried to explain. "My father needs me to do something. Something very important."

"But the police…"

"I will talk to them later. Tell them I'll be back as soon as I can. Right now I have to follow my father's wishes." She clutched the paper tightly in her hand.

Violet strode out of the courtyard, a determined yet melancholy look in her eyes. *Not this time, Dad. I won't mess things up again. I promise you.*

She could still smell Murrel as she walked out of The Met.

CHAPTER 4

Violet ran down 5th Avenue as the sidewalks began to fill up with the bustle of the morning commute. She agilely dodged men in starched shirts and ties and women in charcoal pantsuits. The half-awake business zombies used their briefcases and purses as an explorer would wield a machete in the jungle, cutting a swathe through the rough terrain of ambling white collars. Violet had to dodge and leap for three blocks until she finally reached her car.

She grabbed the parking ticket tucked under her windshield wiper—her third violation this month—and threw it to the ground. She opened the door to the 1985 Chrysler Le Baron. It screeched with the sound of metal on metal, way beyond the saving grace of WD40.

Violet brushed the cigarette butts and ashes off the driver's seat before climbing in. She tossed her purse onto the passenger seat, knocking empty coffee cups and food wrappers to the floor in a cascade of garbage. She jammed the key into the ignition and turned it. *Ruhr-ruhr-rhur.* The car was not in the mood.

"C'mon you pile of crap!"

It took about a dozen attempts, and a short cigarette break, before Violet was able to leave. In that time, several police cars, ambulances and even fire trucks sped by en route to the museum, lights blazing and sirens wailing. *Too bad it's all in vain. My father is gone.*

Violet pulled out onto 5th, nearly sideswiping a yellow cab. The driver cursed her in Arabic. "Stupid Mexican." Violet grumbled.

After initially heading in the wrong direction and making several left turns, including a trip down a one-way street driving against traffic, Violet arrived at the Hilton. She then realized she was at the wrong Hilton and reread her notes. She put the car back in drive and took off. *Avenue of Americas. Why do they have to give streets more than one name? It's too much!*

Violet pulled up to the front of the correct Hilton, the car coughing and shaking like a smack addict craving a score.

The valet grimaced as Violet stepped from her stuttering car. "Hello, er, I mean Hola." Violet said, seeing the Hispanic-looking young man approach her car.

He caught wind of the odor contained within the aging lemon. The funk of years of neglience. "¿Hay cadáveres en el tronco?" The valet quipped. *Is there a corpse in your trunk?*

Violet shook her head. "No luggage, I'm not staying long. But thanks." She tipped him a quarter.

He looked at the dull metal coin and forced a smile, "Da las graciasle puta barata." he said. *You are a drunken whore.*

Violet smiled in return, "Thank you. Pez bueno." she replied. *Good fish.* She ran toward the entrance.

The valet shook his head and said, "It's pretty pathetic how some of these white folk assume we don't speak English." He climbed into the rust-bucket and put it in drive. The car stalled. "Good grief."

Violet entered the lobby and paused, taken aback by the grandiose design. It was breathtaking—from the smooth marble pillars to the concentric circles of the marble tiled floor to the lights recessed in the edges of the sunken ceiling panels. It looked like the inside of a spaceship, almost like Star Trek. The newer Star Trek, of course, not the clunky cardboard sets of the original series.

Violet made her way toward the front desk. As she crossed the center of the lobby she jumped, startled. A huge metal statue stared at her with big, empty eyes. It was a warped humanoid figure, with extending arms shaped like they were cut from clay. *Jesus!* Violet thought. *It looks like ET had a baby with Gumby.* Violet shivered, not wanting to look at it any longer.

There was quite a line at the front desk, to be expected this time of morning. She had no choice but to wait. She thought about her father and all he said. It was a lot for someone to absorb, not that she knew what any of it meant. A secret? A secret that Gerri knew about? It would make sense if it were work related. But why would his assistant—the frumpy, mousy Gerri Hender—know anything about their personal lives? She had just left on vacation. Where did she go? Italy? She left a few days ago. This was all too much. Hopefully this Grant guy would be able to help her straighten it all out.

Violet was finally able to step up to the desk. She knew she was going to have trouble the minute she saw the concierge. He was stiff and snooty looking, with orange hair that looked comical yet demonic—like a tall, thin Heat-miser from those animated CBS Christmas specials.

"Hi," Violet started, trying to sound like a damsel in distress, hopefully appealing to his masculinity. "I need to know what room a Grant…" Violet paused, almost panicking. She quickly dove into her purse to produce her written notes. "Um… Piosto. What room Grant Piosto is in? Thank you."

The concierge lifted his eyes to meet Violet's gaze with what seemed tremendous effort—as though the burden of his career and life were the gravity of Jupiter. "Well, I'm sure Mr. um-Piosto is expecting you, but we cannot give out information willy-nilly to whomever asks." She could tell right away that she needn't waste her time finding one iota of masculinity in this character. His eyes immediately dropped again to his computer screen. He tapped one finger at a time, like he was playing chopsticks on the piano, but in slow motion. Violet waited, thinking he was looking up Grant's room or some kind of helpful information. After a few minutes, she realized the man had no intention on acknowledging her again. She looked at his nametag, Mr. Odieux.

"Um… excuse me," Violet coughed. "Mr. Odieux?" She pronounced it phonetically, saying Owe-dee-ucks. The concierge cringed at her ignorance. Violet obliviously continued. "Can you tell me if he is here at all? It's very important."

The gravity in Mr. Odieux's world must have doubled, because it took him twice as long for his eyes to reach hers. He spoke condescendingly, which went right over Violet's head. "Again, for those with comprehension issues, we cannot give out that information." His head dropped again, tap, tap, tap on the computer.

Violet was getting angry. Her temper had gotten her into trouble many times in the past. She did her best to keep it in check. "Please, my father was just shot and killed. His last words were to find Mr. Piosto here at the Hilton."

"You're father's dying wish was for you to hook up with a man you don't know in a hotel? How salacious." The concierge snapped. "When my pop dies I hope his final wish is that I bang George Clooney." Tap, tap, tap.

"Are you evil?" Violet blurted. "Can't you see that I need help?"

"Yes ma'am," Mr. Odieux replied without looking at her. He smiled. "I can see you need help alright." Tap, tap, tap.

"What is wrong with you?" Violet yelled. "Why are you so mean?"

"Because I put up with nitwits like you all day. I really do not have to tolerate this kind of nonsense when the rules and policies clearly dictate that I cannot dispense such information about our guests—especially to an angry lesbian with father issues. Thank you for coming to the Hilton. Buh-bye!"

Lesbian? I experimented in college but... and father issues?

"You little shit! The only reason a prancing little sissy like you can get away with this kind of crap is this desk you use as a shield. I should reach over and snap your little whiny-ass neck!" *So much for keeping my temper in check.*

The lobby practically came to a stop. A small audience gathered behind Violet. They watched as she waved her arms about at a seemingly nonplussed concierge. She stomped her foot and pounded the counter.

"Can you please call Grant Piosto's room and tell him someone is here to see him?!" she screamed. "Just that much at least? Is that so much to ask for? For the love of all that is holy!"

Mr. Odieux stopped tapping on the keyboard, looked up and nodded. "Oh, *that* I can do. Why didn't you ask for that first?" The concierge picked up the phone, dialed in a number, and hummed a show tune while they waited. Then, he hung up.

"Sorry. He's not answering." He grinned from ear to annoying ear. "He mustn't be in. Buh-bye!"

Violet whirled about and paused when she saw the group of entertained faces watching her. She huffed her way through them. "Get a life!" she growled.

She sat down on the floor near the humongous alien sculpture. *They can kick me out! I'm not leaving until I find Grant...*

17

whatever his name is. She grumbled inwardly. She looked over her shoulder at the giant mongoloid. "Shut up!" she barked at the statue.

"That's no way to talk to a defenseless golem!" a voice said. Violet looked up and saw a youthful looking man standing over her. He couldn't be older than twenty-one, twenty-three at the most. He had shaggy hair parted to the side. He wore crisp khaki pants, obviously the wrinkle-free kind with a sweater vest over a white button-down shirt. He slung over his shoulder a large, yellow back-pack . He was handsome in a dorky way— like the winner of the dork-of-the-month contest.

Violet barely acknowledged the young man. *Now is not the time for some kid to be hitting on me!*

"Sorry, junior," Violet muttered. "Move along, I'm busy." Violet crossed her arms and stared at the floor.

"Oh, I'm sorry. I thought you wanted to talk to me." he said, extending his hand. "Grant Piosto, it's a pleasure to meet you." He smiled.

CHAPTER 5

"You're Grant? Grant Pio... Piosto?" Violet leapt up from the lobby floor. "You... you look so young."

"Yeah," Grant sheepishly grinned. "I get that a lot. I'm really thirty-two. It's tough to establish credibility when you look younger than the college students you're lecturing."

"I'm Violet Sterne, nice to meet you." Violet grasped Grant's hand and shook it. She paused, glanced at her hand, and quickly let go. Her hand was soaked.

Grant turned a deep shade of red. "Gee, I'm really sorry. I kind of have Palmar Hyperhidrosis. It happens when I'm nervous... especially around beautiful women."

"Beautiful? Oh, thanks... Palmar what?" Violet fought the urge to run through the lobby looking for antiseptic gel like a man on fire looking for water.

"Palmar Hyperhidrosis. Sweaty palms. Sorry, I know it's pretty gross."

"Oh, that's okay." Violet lied, wiping her hand on her jeans. She felt the salty wetness soak through immediately. She fought the urge to vomit. *These jeans cost a fortune, now I have to burn them.*

"So, what brings you to this glorious lobby?" Grant asked. "Aside from the heartwarming and friendly centerpiece sculpture."

Violet looked over her shoulder at the monolith of bronze. "That alien looking thing? I find it disturbing. In fact, this whole lobby looks like a gaudy version of a Star Trek set."

Grant replied, "Oh yeah, it does look like a spaceship in here. They did a makeover in 2002. Cost about eighty-five million. And you're right, very mothership-ish, if you ask me." Grant looked past Violet at the huge golem. "And indeed, that sculpture, created in cast-bronze by James Metcalf is very much alien-looking. Though, the name of it escapes me. Actually, I'm not quite sure it has a name. I like it though. It moves me."

"It moves me out the door." Violet quipped.

Grant laughed at the joke. It was a genuine laugh. "So it seemed rather important that you get to talk to me." Grant nodded his head toward the concierge desk; he rolled his eyes. "Got a little heated."

"Oh, that asshole. He's got a lot of nerve." Violet glared.

"Well, concierge or not, you found me. What can I do for you?"

"Oh God, I was so upset by that stuffy guy at the counter, I nearly forgot." Violet grimaced. "My father was shot and killed a little while ago."

Grant coughed violently, choking on his surprise. "And you forgot *that*? Shot? That's quite serious." He shook his head and held his hands up, as if being held at gunpoint. "Well, I didn't do it. I hope that's not why you're here."

"No, no. He wanted me to find you."

"Shouldn't you go to the police?" Grant offered.

"No, you don't understand. His last words were to find you, Grant Piosto. He didn't have time to tell me why, but he started to say you would help me. That you would tell me." *If only I knew the Avenue of Americas he might've had time to tell me. I'm so stupid.*

"Tell you what?" Grant looked intrigued.

"I have no idea. But it was very urgent. I don't know what to make of all this. He also said that Gerri knew... something. I have no idea what though. Gerri is his assistant, Gerri Hender. And he also said he couldn't keep the secret any longer, but again I have no idea what any of that means."

"A secret? Hmmm. Sounds mysterious. And your father was who?" Grant asked.

"Oh, jeez, of course. Randall Teodey."

Grant shook his head. "Randall Teoday. Sorry, no."

"He is..." Violet paused. "*Was* a curator over at The Met. The Metropolitan Museum of Art."

"Yes. The Met, I think I've heard of it." Grant joked.

"Of course you have, I'm sorry. Anyway, did you know him?"

"Honestly, I've never heard of him." Grant said grimly. "I mean, I've been to the museum many, many times. But I don't recall having befriended anyone there. And not to brag, but I've got a near-photographic memory."

Grant looked about the lobby; it was getting more crowded as the morning developed. "Let's take a walk, it's getting loud in here. You can fill me in on what happened."

CHAPTER 6

Grant and Violet strolled along the Avenue of the Americas, the name of which she'd now never forget. Grant listened intently to Violet's account of the early morning's events. He was stunned, shocked, and sympathetic. He couldn't imagine what she was going through. It was one thing to lose your father, but to be given this extraordinary last wish, some cryptic utterances of a dying man, was something else. Grant respected her bravado and determination. He didn't know if he'd be holding himself together as well if the roles were reversed.

"First, Violet, I am so sorry for your loss." Grant said sincerely. "But even with all that you've told me, I still have no idea why your father wanted you to find me. I can honestly say I did *not* know your father. I have a near-photographic memory so I'm sure I'd remember a Randall Teodey."

Violet thought on that for a moment. "Maybe he knew of you! What is it you do for a living?"

"Well, for the most part, I am a fact-finder for a publishing house on the West side. I look up information for writers, authors and publishers," Grant explained. "Did your father have any dealings with Thales & Anaximander publishing? It's a subdivision of Yeshua Ltd."

"Who and what? A sub-what of what? That's over my head. I don't know," Violet shrugged. "We didn't really talk much." She hated admitting that. It made her guilt multiply. "But I doubt it. He loved antiquities but was never in it for the money."

"I'm a member of Mensa. Maybe your father was also a member?"

"Somehow I doubt it." Violet shook her head. "My dad was smart about what he knew—his collection, and that was it."

"Okay, I'm just throwing things out there now." Grant was trying his hardest to think of a connection. "I've also got three degrees: in art, foreign culture, and history. Do you watch TV? Maybe the game show Jeopardy, more specifically?"

"God, no!" Violet laughed. "I hate TV. Except that nostalgia channel, I like the old Adam 12 reruns."

"Okay then." *Big surprise, not a Jeopardy fan.* Grant thought. "Anyway, I was the longest running winner in Jeopardy history," Grant cleared his throat and pulled at his collar—obviously an uncomfortable subject. "Until recently, that is." *Damn you to Hell, Ken Jennings!* "But I still fail to see how your father would know me. Unless he was an avid Jeopardy fan."

"He hated television." Violet said.

"I sometimes lecture at colleges, either art history or iconography."

"Maybe. I don't know."

"How about your mother? Maybe she knows me and mentioned me to your father?" Grant was trying any angle.

"We... I don't think so. My mother isn't alive." Violet's eyes got lost in the bird poop-stained concrete. "She... died some time ago."

"Gosh, I'm really sorry." Grant said solemnly.

Violet walked in silence for a minute. She blurted out, "I thought you said you had a pornographic memory?"

"Photographic!" Grant corrected her, laughing. "Big difference!" He giggled like a little boy. He couldn't look Violet in the eyes .

"Yes, that's it. Sorry." Violet blushed. She continued. "Photographic memory. Yet you couldn't remember the name of the sculpture in the lobby."

"Well, if you recall, I actually said *near* photographic." Grant said. "I'm far from perfect. And I'm not sure I knew the name of the sculpture, just the artist."

They came to the end of the block and waited for the walk signal to beckon them. When it did, Violet took a step forward, but Grant did not move with her. She turned to look for her new companion. She almost broke out laughing when she saw Grant stomp his right foot three times before stepping off the curb. He stepped down onto the street then stomped with his left foot. Grant looked up at the befuddled Violet.

"Sorry, bit of an OCD thing." Grant hefted his bulky backpack further up his shoulder. "Had it since I was a kid."

"That's okay," Violet replied, still surprised by the behavior. "We all have our own weird little tics and quirks, I guess." *But that was a whopper! Right out of Monty Python's funny walk sketch.*

"I probably have more than most." Grant admitted. "Hopefully it won't put you off too much."

"I doubt it," Violet lied. "Who am I to judge?"

They crossed the street. Violet was thankful Grant was able to get back on the curb without any ritualistic maneuvers.

"And this Gerri Hender," Grant returned to the main topic. "She went where?"

"To Italy, Rome I believe." Violet said.

"I have to admit," Grant shrugged. "I'm at a loss. I think we best get back to the museum. The police will wonder where you've been and they'll probably ask questions. Not that I'm a big fan of theirs."

"You're not? Any reason?"

"I have my reasons." Grant's mouth twitched. "We'd better go."

Violet had already forgotten the awkward moment. "Okay. We'll take my car."

Grant slipped his backpack off his shoulder, fished around one of the many zippered compartments, and produced a cheap store-bought camera. He cranked the winder a few times, then looked up at Violet.

"Would you mind if I took a picture of you?"

Violet blushed, though she wasn't sure why he wanted to. Maybe he was a pervert and would whack off to it later. But she didn't know, so who was she to argue? "Uh, no. Go ahead." She smiled.

Grant snapped the picture, cranked the film forward, and put the camera away. He patted the side of his backpack . "Thanks. Now let's get to your car."

CHAPTER 7

Grant saw the line-up of cars and had already picked the one he hoped was *not* Violet's. Sadly, his hopes were in vain. A single tire from one of the surrounding vehicles was more valuable than the defunct rust-colored car-like thing squeezed into the parking spot. As he approached, he realized it wasn't a parking spot after all, merely a space reserved for those pesky fire hydrants. Grant sighed in disappointment at Violet's lack of respect.

Violet strutted up to the passenger's side and began sweeping garbage off the seat; some tumbled to the street, which Violet ignored. She tossed the keys to Grant, who caught them and looked at Violet, puzzled.

"You're a guy." Violet stated, as though it were law. "Don't you *need* to drive?"

Grant tossed the keys back. "I don't have a license."

Now it was Violet's turn to be confused. "No license?"

"Duh, it's New York. Most people don't even own a car."

"Oh, right." Violet ran around to the driver's side and dropped in. Grant , gingerly placed his first foot down, then slowly lowered his butt onto the seat. He then placed the other foot inside, attempting to avoid some errant rotting food. He sat motionless—his arms cradling his backpack.

Violet turned the key and was met with the expected *ruhr-ruhr-ruhr*.

"Mother fuckin' shit-face!" Violet erupted. She saw Grant's eyes bulge in fear of her verbal explosion. Violet smiled, embarrassed. "Sorry, I curse sometimes. It's kinda like Tourette's."

"I see that." Grant meekly replied.

After a few close calls, the car started. Smoke belched from the back and the single backfire sent several pedestrians ducking for cover thinking a drive-by was occurring in their expensive neighborhood.

Violet pulled out into traffic. Grant closed his eyes, overwhelmed by an amalgam of stale cigarettes, old coffee cups, hardened half-eaten bagels and muffins, and probably a few as-of-yet undiscovered species of cockroach. He jumped when he thought he felt something walk over his foot. Grant glanced down and saw no critter, but a sea of candy wrappers, empty cigarette packs, Styrofoam cups, unopened mail (including several late notices from bill collectors), and some unrecognizable viscous jelly that seemed to be growing up the center console. Grant quickly closed his eyes again and began to chant a mantra.

"Though I walk in the valley in the shadow of death, I will fear no evil…"

"What are you doing?" Violet asked, looking over at Grant.

Grant pointed forward. "Please keep your eye on the road."

Violet shrugged. Her lead foot fell onto the gas pedal.

Violet fumbled in her purse, taking her eyes off the road and her hands off the wheel. She produced a battered cigarette pack. "Mind if I smoke?"

"Actually I do," he immediately replied. "Sorry but I can't handle smoke. Makes me gag."

Violet grunted irritably and tossed the pack back into her purse.

Grant found it hard to concentrate, from the screeching of the tires, to the honks of angry drivers that Violet seemingly enjoyed cutting off, to the smell of burning oil from the engine. Grant white-knuckled the armrest and hugged his backpack for dear life. He abandoned his lengthy mantra, settling on repeating, "Please God." over and over again.

After a few near-collisions, they arrived at the museum. The car was barely in park before Grant flung himself from the lemon. He landed gleefully on the pigeon-pooped sidewalk. He stretched his arms out, gloriously enjoying the fact that he was alive, and deeply breathed in the city air. The smell of taxi exhaust and avian excrement was refreshing compared to the noxious fumes of Violet's car.

Violet realized she'd double-parked, blocking in a police car, but didn't care. She retrieved an old ticket from inside her car and placed it under the windshield. She smiled, satisfied with her scheme.

She walked around the vehicle to see Grant getting up from the sidewalk.

"You okay?" she asked.

"I am now." Grant was ecstatic. He leapt to his feet and turned toward The Met. He dug out his camera. He cranked it a few times and took a few pictures. "Very happy to be here. Very happy indeed."

Violet made nothing of it. *Probably more OCD*. She thought.

They walked up the stairs toward the entrance, which was festooned with police tape and surrounded by New York's Finest.

CHAPTER 8

Violet reached the top of the stairs, Grant a few steps behind her. He was suspiciously examining the flurry of police and EMT activity. He snapped pictures as the workers went about their duty, muffling the winding of the camera under his backpack. An officer held up his hand as they approached.

"Sorry, people," he robotically stated. "Due to an incident, the museum will not open today. You'll have to leave the area immediately." And to Grant. "And no pictures please. Stay behind the tape."

"I'm... uh, Violet Sterne. It was my father that was shot, Randall Teodey. Roy from security must have mentioned me."

"Can I see some ID, please?" the officer asked.

Violet dug through her purse, the bag bulged from excess goods and garbage. Much like her car, Grant caught the strong odor of neglect. Plastic wrappers from crushed packs of cigarettes caught in the city breeze and flew up and around the officer's head. He tried to ignore the crinkly plastic but it caught under his cap's visor. He swatted at it as though it were a gnat. Violet grumbled under her breath, making little headway in her search. Two empty containers, once keepers of "the pill", fell to the ground. They were followed by ancient, cracked M&Ms. Violet flushed red with frustration.

"I can't seem to find it." she explained. "Can't you call Roy Howard? He's the head of security. He can ID me."

The officer was on his walkie-talkie instantly, rattling off a stream of police jargon in a monotone delivery, like an auctioneer on Valium. He looked to Violet. "Mr. Howard is filing a report at the station." Just then, a burly officer stepped out of the entrance. The officers exchanged very manly and official nods. "Sir, this woman claims to be Violet Sterne, daughter of the victim."

The officer shook Violet's hand, very gently and sympathetically. "Hello Miss Sterne, I'm Sergeant Atgreens. I'm sorry about your father. Mr. Howard said you planned on returning. He showed us your company profile. I do indeed recognize you to legitimately be who you say you are."

"Okay, that's good. I think." Violet said, though that last sentence had her head spinning. "Can we go inside now?"

"Of course, Miss Sterne. But we have a great deal of questions for you." Sergeant Atgreens held his arm wide, allowing her entry. Violet went in with Grant following close behind. Grant gave the guarding officer the I'm-keeping-my-eye-on-you-buddy look as he passed—two fingers from his eyes to the officer's. Sergeant Atgreens put his hand up to stop Grant.

"I'm sorry, sir. You are not allowed in here."

Grant froze an inch from the extended limb, as though it were a weapon.

Violet placed herself between the men. "He's with me. My father wanted him here. He *stays* with me. Now please, Sergeant, can we go on now?"

Sergeant Atgreens paused briefly before leading them inside.

Violet felt chills as she approached the American Wing Courtyard again. It had been less than two hours but felt like an eternity since she'd last been there. She wrapped her arms around herself, unintentionally slowing her pace. She realized she had been holding her breath and inhaled sharply. She stepped into the courtyard.

Her father was no longer there; his supine, bleeding body was replaced by a tape outline. A pool of blood filled half the outline, showing the extent of his suffering. An officer was bagging the Emperor's pistol and labeling it. The camera had already been bagged and was on a nearby cart. The laptop was still on the railing, as of yet untouched. Another officer was taking pictures, circling the scene.

"Miss Sterne, I really need to ask you some questions about what happened here," the sergeant said softly.

"Sergeant," Violet said without looking at him. "I'd like a few minutes alone if I may. I will answer any and all questions when I'm ready."

The police officer balked, but respectfully nodded. "Of course, Miss Sterne, I understand. I'll be in the lobby." The sergeant paused, then added. "We will also be needing to speak to his assistant, a Miss Gerri Hender? We found where she's staying. It's a Hilton, in Rome, the, uh… Cava… Cavi…"

"Cavalieri?" Grant broke in. "The Rome Cavalieri Hilton."

"Yes, that's it. She has yet to respond to any of our calls. You wouldn't happen to have heard from her, have you?"

Violet shook her head without looking at him.

"There's an eight hour time difference, Sergeant." Grant spoke snidely. "It's early evening there. She's probably out on the town."

The sergeant glared at Grant for a moment. "Okay, thank you." Sergeant Atgreens waited half a beat before backing out of the courtyard. He obviously was not happy with Violet's request, but knew he needed to respect her in this very difficult situation. He kept one eye on them as he left the courtyard.

Violet turned to Grant. "Okay, we're here," she spoke to him quietly, so the officers gathering evidence couldn't hear her. "This was your idea. Do you see anything? Is this helping at all? 'Cause I'll be honest, I'm feeling a bit queasy."

"Just give me a minute." Grant said, placing a sweaty hand on her shoulder. He gave her a soft squeeze that was meant to be reassuring. Instead she bit her lip; it was the only way for her to avoid screaming as the moisture soaked through her blouse.

Grant nonchalantly circled the room, intentionally staying out of the officers' way. Grant snapped a few pictures with his camera and wound the film forward.

The officer with the camera paused, looking at Grant. "Why are you taking pictures?"

"Why are *you* taking pictures?" Grant sourly replied.

"Um, it's my job."

"Mine, too. Now please give us some privacy." Grant lowered his camera.

The officer put the lens cap on and walked out of the courtyard, shaking his head in disbelief.

Grant snuck a picture of the exiting officer and quietly cranked the camera. He He inched up behind the remaining officer, looking everywhere—the ceiling, the floor, his nails—anywhere but at the officer, until he was leaning over his shoulder. The officer sensed him immediately, "Sir, could you please not stand over me. This is an official crime scene. You cannot be interfering!" The officer stood up. He was a full foot taller than Grant.

"Oh, I'm sorry." Grant said, acting as innocent as possible. "I didn't mean to intrude." He took several steps back and feigned interest pretended with the water fountain.

The officer returned to his bagging detail until another officer stuck his head into the courtyard.

"Hey, Kumsch!" the other policeman called out. "We need a hand out here with the press!"

"Alright." the officer replied. He turned immediately to Grant. "Do not... I repeat, do not touch anything here!" He stared him in the eyes. "Do we understand each other?"

"Oh, um, yes... yes sir!" Grant said, then awkwardly saluted.

"Or I will arrest your sorry ass!" the officer said, walking away. He stopped mid-stride and pointed at Grant. "I'll be watching you." Then he was gone.

As soon as the door closed, Grant took out his camera again, "Okay, *now* we can investigate!" He looked like a kid on Christmas morning.

CHAPTER 9

Mr. Crows was standing in a hotel room, a majestic, ritzy, spacious room befitting royalty. Or uber-rich celebrities. Staying in a hotel of such caliber is nothing new for the famous actor; neither is the Scientology therapy called auditing that he and Mr. Trafalgar were now engaged in. Auditing required the use of an E-meter—short for electropsychometer. This device, designed by Scientology founder L. Ron Hubbard, is an electronic box-shaped instrument that reads changes in skin conductivity via two metal cylinders held in the subject's hands. It purportedly probes the subject's subconscious, looking for problems in their minds.

The individual reading the meter is called the *auditor*, while the hapless chap holding the cylinders is named the *preclear*. When you've cleaned your brain out of negative junk, you become a *clear*. Mr. Trafalgar studied the meter's needle, as it twitched up then down, spastically reading changes in Mr. Crows' palms.

Again, this auditing was not new for Mr. Crows. However he was entirely *naked*. Naked as a jailbird. And he wasn't sure why.

"I still don't know why I'm naked." Mr. Crows said sullenly.

"Shush, man." Mr. Trafalgar held up his hand to silence him. An unlit cigarette rested between his lips. "I'm the auditor and you're the preclear. You gotta do what I say. Trust me, having no clothes on is freeing. It makes it easier for your mind to loosen up. Just try to relax."

Mr. Crows thought on that for a second. "Okay, maybe," he sighed. "But I still don't see why *you're* naked, too."

"Dude, you're ruining the moment." Mr. Trafalgar barked. "When *you're* doing the auditing then you can decide how it's…"

The cell phone on the nightstand rang, making Mr. Crows jump, dropping the handgrips from the E-meter. He landed on the queen-sized bed, crouched, like a defensive panther. He sniffed the air for predators.

"Damn!" Mr. Trafalgar cursed. "Just when it was getting good."

Mr. Trafalgar picked up the phone and opened it. He put it on speaker so Mr. Crows could join in the conversation. "Hello?" he asked, despite knowing who would be calling.

"Greetings Mr. Trafalgar," the voice said weakly.

"Hello there, Mr. Maystyne, "Mr. Trafalgar said, his brow furrowing in concern. "You okay, boss? You sound off."

"I'm fine, Mr. Trafalgar. Do not worry about me. I trust you and your companion are well rested?"

"Yes, Mr. Maystyne, we are," he replied. "We were just auditing, too."

"Very good." Mr. Maystyne said. His smile could be heard in his voice.

"Naked." Mr. Crows grumbled as he climbed off the bed. Mr. Trafalgar smacked Mr. Crows on the back of the head. "Ouch!"

"What was that, Mr. Crows? I didn't hear that." Mr. Maystyne asked.

Mr. Crows rubbed his scalp. "Nothing."

"Anyway," Mr. Maystyne continued. "We are in need of your services again. Something has come up that may, or may not, have to do with the Twelve."

"I see. Where are we going?"

"Something has happened to a person of interest in New York. Someone with knowledge of the Twelve," Mr. Maystyne explained. "It happened at the Metropolitan Museum of Art. We fear information has been passed along that we need to intercept."

"Excellent. I will fly Mr. Crows and myself first thing."

"No, Mr. Trafalgar." Mr. Maystyne's voice took a warning tone. "*Subtlety* is the word for this mission. Not like that poorly handled Congressman situation. I need you and your partner to be discreet, remain unknown and hidden from the public's eye, and draw no attention to yourselves. Is that understood?"

"Yes, sir, it is." Mr. Trafalgar sighed.

Mr. Crows cleared his throat. "We will, uh, be killing anyone?"

Mr. Trafalgar rolled his eyes. "Forgive my partner's ebullience. He's just a little high-strung."

"I want killing to a minimum. The main target, of which her file is being sent to your Blackberry, is to remain alive. At all costs. Anyone else that gets in the way can be considered dispensable. Unless you feel information can be garnered from them. Is that understood?"

"Absolutely, sir." Mr. Trafalgar said. "You can count on us."

"You can read up on the files during your flight. Haste, my friends. And make us proud." Mr. Maystyne hung up.

"Yeehaw!" Mr. Crows cheered. He jumped up and down. "Anyone else is dispensable! That's awesome! That means killing and great fun and stuff!"

"Cool your jets, brother." Mr. Trafalgar warned. "Remember, nothing like the Congressman. We have to be a bit slicker on this one. Stay cool, y'know? Now put your clothes on and pack your suitcase. We're off to New York."

In their ritual fashion before they set out on any journey, and as high-level Scientologist clears, they thumped each other on the forehead with the palms of their hands in unison. "All Hail Teegeeack!"

They started packing. Still in their birthday suits.

CHAPTER 10

Grant circled the outline of fallen Randall Teoday; he paused after one complete revolution and walked it in reverse. He pulled out his camera and cranked it, then took a picture. Holding the camera far above his head, getting a bird's-eye view, he took another. He did this several more times, each a few feet apart. Violet was getting sick of the winding sound Grant's camera made every time he cranked it.

"They make digital cameras now." Violet blurted.

"Shush!"

"Excuse me, "Violet mumbled.

Grant dropped to the ground and placed his chin on the marble floor, getting what Violet assumed was a bug's-eye view.

Who is *this guy?* Violet puzzled. *And can he get any weirder? I hope Dad knew what he was doing when he told me to find him.*

Grant had frozen like a statue, only his eyes darting around the crime scene. He stayed that way for nearly five minutes.

Violet watched the rigid lunatic with abject fear and bewilderment.

"What are you doing?" Violet asked when she couldn't resist the urge anymore.

"Shush times two!" Grant snapped. He remained still for another minute. "Clues," he finally said. "I read this book where…"

Grant tilted his head to one side, as though listening to a distant noise, or maybe a voice in his head. Violet could only guess. She gave up hope that he'd finish the sentence.

Suddenly Grant clapped his hands and called Violet over. "We have to check out the laptop before the crime scene guy comes back." Grant whispered loudly. "If there were any pictures taken with the camera, they may already be downloaded to the computer."

"And you needed to do all those theatrics to think of that?" Violet asked, slightly irritated and disappointed. With all his odd actions and maneuvers, she expected him to get all John Edwards-ish and pull her dead father's spirit from the other side for a quick Q & A session. Instead he thinks to check the laptop. *What a brilliant guy!* she thought sarcastically. She was fidgety, in dire need of a smoke.

"Did *you* think of it?" Grant said, folding his arms.

"Well, no," Violet admitted.

"Then don't make that face," Grant chided. "I can read you like a book. Whatever helps you find out what you need, correct?"

"Yes, I guess." Violet didn't like being treated like a child. "Can we look at the laptop now?"

"Yes we can!" Grant ran to the computer.

CHAPTER 11

Mr. Trafalgar and Mr. Crows arrived at La Guardia Airport a mere two and a half hours after the phone call. They flew first class and took photographs with the pilot and crew. Mr. Trafalgar had wanted to fly his own airplane but Mr. Maystyne would not have it. He insisted on drawing as little attention to themselves as possible.

Be discreet. Their employer had said.

Upon arrival, they had a car waiting for them, a Jaguar XK convertible. They knew how to travel without drawing attention to themselves; it was only an $80,000 vehicle—not like it was a Bentley. And they also knew they had to be in disguise, so they put on sunglasses.

As they left the airport, they waved to the gathering crowds of fans and the few lucky paparazzi in the area. Cameras flashed. People called out their names. They were greeted with adoration. Mr. Trafalgar slowed the vehicle so he and Mr. Crows could pose and make sure they were taken from their best angle.

"It's good to be king," mused Mr. Trafalgar.

"Yeah, kings." Mr. Crows repeated, playing drums on the dashboard in front of him. There was no music playing, only the crazy rhythm of clowns playing bongos in his head. "We're kings."

They traveled only a few minutes when Mr. Trafalgar pulled onto the shoulder of the Grand Central Parkway.

"We're being followed," he said to his traveling partner. "We can't be followed. No one can know what we're up to."

A car parked directly behind them. Without hesitation, a man jumped out of the vehicle. He was holding a camera with a zoom lens long enough to double for an elephant gun.

The man rapid-fired pictures. He yelled comments, incendiary in nature, to get more provocative reactions on film.

"Hey, ya big Hollywood heavies! Where ya going? Smile for me, you stupid pricks! Your last movie sucked!"

The photographer gasped in shock when the camera was torn from his grip and the strap around his neck pulled him face-first into the backseat of the Jaguar.

"Get in here!" Mr. Crows growled. He turned the camera around and jammed the zoom lens into the photographer's mouth, until the man's eyes bulged. Teeth could be heard breaking from the girth of the lens and Mr. Crows' force. The man's legs kicked and flailed like a poisoned insect. He was gagging, turning a dark purple, under the crushing weight of Mr. Crows. The photographer shuddered a few times and then fell still—dead as could be.

Mr. Crows let go of the camera and sat back on the man's chest, breathing heavily. "Whew!" he yelled. "That felt gooooood!"

Mr. Trafalgar watched the entire spectacle. Once it was over, he lit a cigarette. He took a deep drag and exhaled a sexy billow of smoke.

"That was beautiful!" Mr. Trafalgar beamed. "Nice and clean, no blood. I'm proud of you Mr. Crows. Now if you would be so kind as to toss him. But make sure you remove the film first. I'd hate shots like that to show up on TMZ."

Mr. Crows popped open the camera's body and pulled out the film. He handed it to Mr. Trafalgar who proceeded to set fire to it with his lighter. Mr. Crows threw the dead photographer over his shoulder, walked to the guardrail, and then sent the man tumbling down the side of the parkway.

He hopped back in the Jaguar without opening the door, like a mental patient from the Dukes of Hazzard. "Okay," Mr. Crows was glowing with excitement. "Now *this* is an awesome start to a job!"

"It is indeed, my little friend." Mr. Trafalgar put the car in gear. "It is indeed." And they were off to The Met.

CHAPTER 12

Violet was nervous looking about the courtyard while Grant fiddled with the laptop. She was impressed with his familiarity with the equipment; he obviously knew computers and accessories.

"Do you Facebook?" Violet asked, though she wasn't sure why.

Grant looked over his shoulder at her. "No! That's for little kids and losers. Why? Do You?" He laughed derisively as he went back to the laptop.

"Uh, no!" Violet backpedaled. "No, just curious," she sighed. "Maybe I should go talk to the sergeant while you do this. It'll keep him busy. He wants a statement from me anyway. It's the least I could do."

Grant wagged his finger at her. "I wouldn't be so quick to trust the police." He stood and faced her. "In my experience, they're usually part of the conspiracy."

"Conspiracy? What conspiracy?" Violet asked. "There's no conspiracy! Wouldn't I know if my father was involved with something?" *Not really.* She thought. *We haven't talked about anything other than the weather in years.*

"If people knew about things going on behind their backs it wouldn't be called a conspiracy, would it?" Grant sneered. "It'd be called fact! Trust me. The fewer people in on our investigation the better."

"Whatever." Violet huffed, really not in the mood for yet another lecture. "Do we even know what we're investigating?"

"You're father had something important to tell you. Something that just couldn't be blurted out in the workplace, something that he needed to speak to you alone about and that required the building up of his fortitude to broach the topic." Grant paused for dramatic effect. "Obviously this is huge and not to be taken lightly."

"Whatever. My father was shot and killed. He died in my hands. I am *not* taking this lightly," Violet snapped. "Are you almost done? I'm hungry and need a cigarette."

Grant ignored the question. "So what was your father shooting with the digital camera, anyway?"

"He had to take some kind of picture for a promotional piece that the museum was doing. It was supposed to be a shot of him sitting next to a gun from the Arms collection." Violet explained.

"A pistol." Grant corrected her. "Not a gun."

"Whatever." Violet repeated. "Y'know, I'm really…"

"Okay, I've got them!" Grant interrupted, he turned the laptop so Violet had a better view. "I've found the folder where the camera automatically saved all the pictures taken by your father."

Grant opened the folder. About two dozen images were listed by date and displayed like a slideshow. Grant clicked the mouse to cycle through.

It was obvious Violet's father was getting used to the camera, taking random pictures of people around the museum. Then Randall seemed to get more familiar with the camera, specifically learning the zoom function.

"Oh!" was all Violet could manage.

At first, there were shots of women's derrieres from far away. As Randall improved, his sneakiness and photography skill, closer shots of tight jeans and shorts appeared.

"Callipygian!" Grant chuckled, his face reddening, his eyes wide with excitement. "Badonkadonk!"

"Huh?" Violet turned.

"Never mind."

Grant cycled further through the folder. The angles appeared lower as Randall attempted more direct photography of the booty; he was obviously holding the camera with his arm dropped to his side. Up came images of skirts and short dresses, trying to get a bit of an upward shot of women's undergarments. Then, Randall shifted gears. With it, came blurry images of bosoms as Randall attempted to capture the upper half of the females. The final picture of Randall's short-lived career as a photo-perv was of an angry woman's face as she swung at him with her fist.

At least they're of grown women. That was the best positive spin Violet could come up with. *He may be a creep but he's not a pedophile.*

"Um, can we… y'know… move past this stuff?" Violet's face flushed with embarrassment.

"Actually, no." Grant said. "How do we know this doesn't have anything to do with why he was shot?"

"Okay." *Crap.* He had her there. Maybe a jealous husband got wind of his activity and took revenge the old fashioned way.

"Now he's getting to the task at hand. Here are a few shots of the pistol." Grant said. "He's playing with the lighting. It appears he started in the Arms and Armory gallery and then moved to the courtyard for better lighting."

The first few pictures were of the pistol sitting on velvet cloth, alone and centered in frame. Then he backed off and took a few shots of the courtyard setup, with pistol, table and chair.

There were several failed attempts and some that were somewhat successful. But Randall never seemed to be able to get himself fully into the shot. There would be an elbow, or Randall's left eye, as he leapt into frame. This was all intermixed with accidental shots up Randall's nose, which was in dire need of a hair trimming.

Was in need. Violet reminded herself. *Was.* She smiled briefly at the humorous shots of her father's face, his look of frustration as the flash went off in his eyes. Suddenly, she missed him. Guilt hit her like a wave.

As the final image came up, Grant blocked the monitor. "You don't want to see this, Violet." he warned. "This is upsetting."

Without hesitation, Violet easily shoved him aside. Grant tumbled to the ground like a rag doll. She instantly regretted her decision to look.

Violet stifled her scream, her hand to her face. The timer must have gone off shortly after he was shot. There was her father, lying prone in a thick puddle of blood, spreading behind him like wings. He was on his side, one arm ahead of him, as though reaching. The other arm lie at his side. His legs were atop each other; he was almost leaning forward, in a sort of a flying Superman pose. His eyes were closed—his face ashen. She could feel his ebbing warmth even through the image. Tears welled in her eyes. She turned away.

"Violet, I'm so sorry." Grant whispered. "I... I didn't want you to see that."

"I had to." Violet whispered.

Grant returned his gaze to the image. He leaned in close, studying it for a good three minutes. Suddenly, he shrieked like a schoolgirl. It startled the hell out of Violet.

"What?" Violet asked.

Grant ignored her as he quickly dug through his backpack and pulled out a key chain. He removed a plastic cap off and plugged it into the computer.

"What's that?" Violet didn't like the way he was acting.

"Portable USB drive. I'm copying the image onto my key chain." Grant spoke quickly. "Gather your things. We're leaving now."

"Why? What did you see?" Violet was confused, she tried to look at the computer screen but Grant blocked it. "Why did you scream like a little..."

"Now, Violet!" Grant barked.

Violet ran for her purse, sparked by the fear she heard in Grant's voice.

CHAPTER 13

Violet knew her way around the museum, not because she worked there, but because she always had to sneak off for her several-cigarettes-an-hour habit. She was allowed to have smoke breaks, but Violet chain smoked; one cigarette an hour just wasn't acceptable. She knew every empty storage room, loading dock, forgotten nook and alternate exit—more than anyone. More than Roy, Clay and Murrel would ever know. And she'd only been working at the museum for a short time. Violet mused, as the saying goes, *necessity was the invention of someone's mother.*

Had she wanted, Violet figured she could probably make off with some pretty valuable stuff and sell it on Ebay. But that required too much effort and energy and Violet always believed the less work the better. Plus she knew she was too good looking for prison. She'd be eaten alive.

Violet and Grant had to hide a few times as security, CSI, police officers and select employees involved in the investigation roamed the hallways, looking for anything that might have been stolen or damaged.

More than once, Grant demanded Violet choose an alternate route due to phobic reactions to certain ancient artifacts. It seemed Grant was terrified of masks.

"They hide the real you!" was his defense.

Scare them back with your wet hands. Violet laughed to herself, as she led herself and Grant, finally, into a warehouse with a back exit that wasn't used very often.

Grant stuck his head out the door next to the loading dock and glanced around the empty lot. Satisfied there was no one around, he snuck down the stairs and darted across the pavement.

"We have to make our way back to your car," Grant explained as he skittered along the building's backside as nervous as a meerkat in the Kalahari Desert. "We can't let the police see us or we're done."

Hearing no reply, Grant paused and looked behind him.

Violet still stood on the dock stairs, attempting to light a cigarette with a seemingly dead Bic lighter. From twenty yards away, he clearly heard her cursing through clenched lips.

"Damn, stupid lighter! Of all the times for you to…"

Grant ran back to Violet. He whispered angrily. "Violet, what the heck are you doing? We have to go!"

"This Goddam lighter is shot!" Violet's voice echoed.

Grant ducked and threw his arms over his head as if to hide himself. As though an eagle might swoop in and claw him. He looked around fearfully and, seeing no rush of officers, stood back up.

"Violet, my dear girl," Grant started off gently. "I can empathize for your addictions, but nicotine or no nicotine we have got to get away from here. And please, for all that is holy, do not yell."

Violet shook her head. "I don't even know what we're running from or where we're running to. And I'm not going anywhere, A) without having a smoke and B) without knowing what's going on!"

"Violet, I understand your confusion," Grant explained. "I'm not sure myself. But there's something about the way your father looked in that picture… it looked… arranged. I think it was his way of sending you a message—one of great importance."

He paused to let the notion sink in. It took longer than he thought and he couldn't wait any more. "Violet?"

Violet came out of her stupor and her eyes widened. "Aha! I have another lighter in my car!" she beamed.

"No, Violet, what I said about the picture of your… deceased father." Grant sighed. "How it looked like he arranged himself. He was telling us something."

"Arranged?" Violet was befuddled. "You mean he posed himself?"

"Yes, posed, that's what I think. I didn't get to look at it long enough. But something in the picture resonated, struck fear into me. I know it means something. We have to get the image printed out so I can analyze it more thoroughly."

"There's a Kinko's down the street…"

"No, too public. Too dangerous." Grant thought for a moment.

"Um, I don't know where else you can get things printed." Violet kept flicking the defunct lighter, cursing under her breath words that Grant had never heard before.

Grant fought the urge to snatch it out of her hand and throw it. She pretty much scared him. That girl had a temper on her and could kick his ass.

Violet grasped the lighter tightly in one hand. "I hate you!" she rasped.

Then it occurred to Grant where they could go. "That's it! I know someone who can help decipher the image. Let's get back to the car immediately!"

Violet nodded. "Yes! Back to the car. I definitely remember my other lighter is in the car!"

Grant sighed.

CHAPTER 14

Grant and Violet turned the corner of The Met onto 5th Avenue. They made their way north along the museum's tremendous length attempting to get close to the entrance. They sauntered as casually as possible, blending in with the growing crowd of commuters, tourists, and vomit-stained homeless. Grant weaved, avoiding contact, as though the persons were on fire. They moved further from the building and closer to 5th Avenue, where they neared the massive front steps.

The front of The Met swarmed with black and white cars. A carnival of news vans, newspaper reporters and generally nosy onlookers had gathered behind the police vehicles, completely blocking up 5th.

A news reporter was doing a live feed for Live Action News, somebody ran into camera view and yelled out. "Bababooey!"

Violet cursed upon seeing her vehicle. She forgot that she'd parked directly behind several police cars. This was going to make it difficult to go unnoticed.

"Now what?" Violet growled at Grant. "I really, really need a smoke."

"Violet there are much bigger things at stake here." Grant reminded her. "Your father's passing? His big mystery?"

"Grant… don't mess with a smoker during withdrawals."

"It's been what… an hour?" Grant was perplexed. "You can't go an hour without…" Violet grabbed Grant by the collar. His shirt was pulled up around his face and his feet swayed several inches off the ground. Violet held him to her face.

"I repeat. Do NOT mess with a smoker in withdrawal!" Violet threatened.

Suddenly Violet was holding a rag doll.

"What the hell?" she said to herself.

Grant was entirely limp—entirely unconscious. She let him drop to the pavement with a heavy thud. She stood over him for a few seconds, fascinated by his sudden coma. She nudged him with her shoe, no reaction. She nudged harder, still none. *This could be fun.* She thought about kicking him, but decided against it. As annoying as he was, her father wanted her to find him. So the little dweeb had to be spared. She wasn't surprised when not one person paused—never mind stopped—at the sight of the crumpled Grant. Good ol' New Yorkers.

Violet patted the side of his face, gently at first, then a bit firmer. Soon she was slapping him. "Grant. Wake up, Grant. Grant! GRANT!"

Grant opened his eyes, looking groggy and disjointed. "Mom? Mom? I don't want to go to school today!" he called out. Suddenly he realized where he was. He shrank back from Violet. "Oh, God! You can smoke! You can smoke!"

"Hey, it's okay." Violet assured him. "Are you alright? What happened?"

"Oh, it's nothing. I have a touch of narcolepsy. It hits me when I get too excited or scared."

"Narcolepsy?" Violet thought about it. "Isn't that when your skin falls off?"

"That's leprosy, Violet." Grant sighed. "Narcoleptics will suddenly fall asleep in moments of extreme stress or excitement."

"Wow. Sorry, I didn't know."

His feet once again planted on terra firma, Grant smoothed his collar and breathed deeply. "That's okay, dear Violet. I must say that's quite a strong grip you have there. Now let's get your car and get out of here."

"Good idea." Violet mumbled, thinking nicotine.

"Let's just act normal. Walk casually to the car, get in and leave."

"That's your plan?!" Violet snapped.

"The best way to blend in is not to stand out."

"You're a regular Confusions." Violet said.

"You mean Confucius."

Violet put a hand on Grant's shoulder and squeezed. "Remember what I said about smokers and withdrawals. Do *not* correct me, even when I'm wrong."

"Ow! You're hurting me." Grant whined.

"Just get going," Violet growled.

Violet and Grant strolled along the sidewalk. Grant leaned in close to Violet and whispered in her ear.

"Hold my hand. It will make us look like a couple."

"You wish." Violet didn't bother hiding her disgust.

"C'mon. Think cigarette." Grant smiled devilishly.

"Uh!" Violet slid her hand into Grant's. Literally. His hand was so wet, so slimy, so gross, and so encompassing that Violet felt as though she was assisting in the birth of a calf. She swallowed the bile that rose in her throat.

"I hate you." Violet spoke out the side of her mouth.

"That's okay. Just don't look like you do."

Violet felt Grant tighten his grip, he playfully massaged her hand. She felt like she was holding a half dozen live eels. Her stomach churned. *Think cigarette.*

They reached her car. Several cops were standing about, watching the perimeter and keeping the growing number of reporters at bay. The reporters, photographers and cameramen swarmed like jackals, each wanting the best vantage point to catch absolutely nothing on film. TV reporters stood with The Met in the background, telling of horror at the museum. Photographers snapped shots of any movement near the entrance: policemen, detectives, passersby and pigeons. As the multitude of haranguers fought for sound bites from people who hadn't even seen the crime scene, Violet, the victim's daughter and star witness, waltzed behind them all, as nonchalantly as a cat burglar at an all-blind attendee diamond convention.

They reached the end of the curb, right where Violet had illegally parked her car, its bumper mere inches from a police cruiser. She stepped from the curb and was instantly pulled back by Grant.

"Jeez!" Violet yipped. "What the Hell?"

"Just wait!" Grant whispered. He proceeded to stomp his right foot before he lowered his foot to the avenue.

"For the love of God." Violet rolled her eyes.

Grant finished his routine and they sidled up to her car. The doors creaked like lurching sea ships but brought no attention over the clamor of the news crews. Violet and Grant slipped in unnoticed.

Violet fumbled about the car and excitedly found a lighter in a semi-empty sandwich wrapper. She wiped some greenish mayonnaise off the lighter onto her jeans. She threw a cigarette in her mouth.

"Can you do that once we're out of here?" Grant pleaded.

Violet glared at Grant. She bared teeth.

His hand slipped to the door handle, fearing an emergency evacuation might be in order. She dropped the lighter and reached for the ignition. "Fine!"

Violet turned the key. *Ruh-ruh-ruh.*

"Godammit!" Violet punched the dashboard.

The car turned over, roaring to life, followed by an immediate backfire.

The entire NYPD drew their guns. Reporters dove for cover. Cameramen ran toward the noise, hoping to get the best footage and maybe even get grazed by a bullet. Famous on-the-street reporter Hank "Beefcake" Knight from ABC was hiding behind an old lady, but bravely continued his live report. The writer from the Wall Street Journal immediately began scribbling notes for his unbiased story on how neo-conservatism and a free-market could have helped avoid such poorly made cars that backfired on innocent people.

Violet and Grant dropped down, hiding behind the dash. When they slowly lifted their heads back up, two dozen guns were aimed at them.

Reporters came out of hiding. Cameras clicked and flashes popped in their direction.

"Sorry." Violet squeaked and waved at the small army. *At least the car is still running.*

"Can we go now?" Grant spoke out the side of his mouth, unable to tear his eyes away from the arsenal of nickel-plated guns pointing his way.

The officers, seeing no actual threat, lowered their weapons. Violet put the Le Baron in reverse and gunned it. Smoked spewed from the tailpipe, which rattled on the coat hanger wire that held the pipe loosely in place inches above the pavement. She clipped a news van and sent the satellite dish on top of the van flying across the avenue. It landed in a homeless man's shopping cart. Later that day, he'd claim aliens gave it to him and he would be featured in the Weekly World News. A year later he'd lead a new alien cult and unsuccessfully create a mass suicide.

Grant hugged his backpack as Violet peeled out, tires screaming, cops and reporters alike confused by the spectacle but unmotivated to do anything about it.

Soon they were flying down 5th Avenue, swerving between cars, around cyclists and ignoring all traffic lights.

"So where are we going?" Violet asked, trying to steer, light a cigarette, and look at Grant at the same time.

"I know someone who may be able to help us."

"Who?" Violet asked, basking in the rush of nicotine.

"Peter Boystead."

"Who's that?"

"Can I use your cell phone? I don't have mine with me."

Violet squinted as smoke curled up past her eyes and fumbled through her purse. Her hands weren't on the steering wheel. Grant chirped in fear several times as she adjusted the steering at the last second, narrowly avoiding seniors with walkers and mothers with baby carriages.

"Here." she said, handing the smudged and filthy cell phone to Grant.

This poor, poor phone. Grant thought as he gingerly handled the DNA covered electronic device.

"I'm texting someone that should be able to help us decipher the image left by your father." Grant explained as he tapped his message into the phone.

"Why don't you just call him?" Violet asked.

"You are a person of interest to the police! Your phone may be tapped or bugged. We don't want anyone intercepting a call." Grant offered, still typing his text message.

"If it's bugged, can't they intercept your text?"

"I'm typing it in code. Only Peter would be able to decipher it, primarily because he was the one who designed the code. The kid is brilliant."

"Kid?" Violet's eyes bugged.

"I'll explain once he gets this message." Grant finished typing and hit send.

"Soh Uhx, Ibo teimt xe xec al im pibo nimaxoz cixs u sex ewjoh gsigs. Hoz zsoz houw. Zso moojz eah sowl. Fax zso xsimqz in zeno tah munoj thumg liezxe. Ze te uwemt cixs xsiz. Loxomj In zenemo cse xuatsx hea im zgseew. Equh? Co houwwh je mooj heah sowl em xsiz."

"There. He got it. He should get back to me right away." Grant said.

Violet grunted and threw her finished cigarette out the car window, narrowly missing a French Poodle being walked by a woman. Violet immediately lit up another.

CHAPTER 15

Not five minutes after Violet's less than subtle exit, a gleaming convertible Jaguar flew down 5th Avenue, music blasting from the 400-watt Alpine surround-sound audio system. Mr. Trafalgar applied the brakes at the last second, sending pedestrians, reporters and policemen scattering for cover. He parked with one tire up on the curb and stood on the car seat with his hands held wide.

"Hello fans," Mr. Trafalgar announced.

As people recognized the actor, they were star-struck and for some reason forgot they were nearly run over. "My God, it's him!" said one woman wiping the blood from her scraped knees.

"And look who's in the car with him!" said a policeman, re-holstering his gun.

"Someone get me a doctor," weakly cried one man, whose leg was pinned under the Jaguar. "And an autograph."

Mr. Crows also stood on the detailed leather seat and waved. He then back flipped out of the car. The crowd, at least those without sprained wrists from diving to the ground earlier, cheered the nimble actor's antics.

"Scene stealer." Mr. Trafalgar grumbled as he moved his less-than-nimble frame down off the seat and got out like a normal person.

Flashbulbs exploded. Pens were presented for autographs. Mr. Trafalgar and Mr. Crows made the rounds, shaking hands, making phone calls to friends and family, posing for pictures. At one point Mr. Trafalgar quickly wiped a smudge of blood off Mr. Crows' hand, a remnant of the deceased paparazzi, before it could be highlighted in a newspaper spread.

Mr. Trafalgar patted Mr. Crows on the back and faced the adoring throng of people. "Thank you, thank you so very much." he announced. "We have work to do but we want to thank you for your support and devotion. Truly we would be nothing without our fans. Thank you."

The crowd of people sighed in sadness as the famous duo turned toward the stairs of The Met. Mr. Crows jogged up the steps, taking them two at a time. Mr. Trafalgar paused halfway to light a cigarette, then slowly started back up. He reached the top and tossed away the butt. "Whew! I got to get my legs back." he breathed heavily.

An officer offered his hand. "Sergeant Atgreens gentlemen! It's an honor to meet you." He aggressively shook their hands, swearing he heard Mr. Crows growl when he touched him. "Can I ask what you're doing here? The museum is closed now. Sadly there has been a terrible event this morning and it's an official crime scene."

"Well, that's exactly why we are here, my good Sergeant." Mr. Trafalgar explained, putting his hand on the Sergeant's shoulder. "Me and my cohort here are in New York to film our latest movie. First time we're acting together in a film. It's a cop/buddy/action/comedy/drama flick. Should make a lot of money and more notoriety for the boys in blue."

"Wow! That's fantastic!" Sergeant Atgreens looked like a child meeting a shopping mall Santa Claus for the first time.

"Yes sir!" Mr. Trafalgar continued. "And what better way to learn than from New York's Finest themselves? I tell you, we are honored to portray the brave and honorable men and women of the NYPD."

"That's mighty nice of you to say!" Sergeant Atgreens blushed.

"Well, we heard what happened to the curator down here…"

"How did you know the curator was involved?" Sergeant Atgreens asked. Something clicked in his head.

"I'm me! Fame has its ear to the ground and finger on the pulse, no?" Mr. Trafalgar pushed on. "We heard about what happened and instantly ran down here to watch you guys do your thing. To see you in action. How you approach a situation, analyze it, tear it apart with your minds and piece it back together." Atgreens was mesmerized.

Mr. Crows stepped back. *Never interrupt Mr. Trafalgar when he's rolling with one of his soliloquies.*

"It's like a big, beautiful stage, cordoned off by yellow tape and surrounded by flashing lights and black and white cars. You gentlemen, bustling about, snapping pictures, interviewing people, bagging evidence, it's like a dance, a tightly organized dance of information and investigation."

"Wow." was all Sergeant Atgreens could muster, completely hypnotized by Mr. Trafalgar's speech.

Mr. Trafalgar gently took the Sergeant by the elbow, slowly turned him around, and escorted him inside as though it was the Sergeant doing the leading.

"Mr. Crows and I, we're actors, simple entertainers in need of guidance. I ask you, where can two regular thespians, looking to do justice in our performance of New York City police officers, go to other than to the men themselves? Straight to the source, to the fountain of courage, to the collective pride and honor that is known as the NYPD. Really, we are here to learn from the masters, to learn from the source. We're here to learn, Sergeant Atgreens..." Mr. Trafalgar paused for dramatic effect. "...from *you*."

Sergeant Atgreens' mouth was agape. He was on the verge of tears. He slowly roused himself from his stupor and could not erase the smile that was tattooed on his face. "Gentlemen," he finally managed to stutter. "Feel free to look around and watch us in action. If you have any questions, ask any of us and we will answer it for you. And find me and I'll personally see to it that you're taken care of."

"You are a generous and wonderful benefactor of the arts, Sergeant." Mr. Trafalgar gave him a hug. "Hollywood thanks you."

Mr. Crows grunted his agreement. His hands were in his pockets and the toe of his shoe was digging an imaginary hole in the tiled floor.

Sergeant Atgreens reached for his walkie-talkie and thumbed a button. He spoke energetically into it. "This is Sergeant Atgreens, general announcement troops, from here on Mr. Trafalgar and Mr. Crows have a carte blanche ticket to any and all aspects of today's crime scene. They're here to learn from the best! So boys, polish your badges and show them how it's done." He clicked off and replaced his walkie-talkie. He looked up, beaming, prepared to spill his guts. "Guys, let me tell you what took place here this morning."

He held his arm out showing them the way. His two guests followed, one of them paying attention, the other wishing he could pummel the sergeant to a bloody mess.

CHAPTER 16

Violet was lost in thought as she ran red lights and flipped the bird at cabs and pedestrians alike. Grant stayed quiet, his eyes were closed and his lips were moving in silent prayer.

He's a weird one, all right. Violet mused. She thought about this morning's events and the crazy path it had forced her to travel. What could her father have been trying to tell her? Could it have been about her mother? Violet hardly remembered her, just a ghost in her memory. Even the last night with her mother was like a dream. Her father never discussed her mother. Especially the last night. Violet wished she could remember what happened. She wished she had the nerve to force her father to tell her what happened. Too late for that now. Violet was getting into a funk. She needed to think about something else. Suddenly Grant spoke up, as if reading her mind.

"Where did you say Gerri Hender went on vacation?"

"Italy. Rome, I think." Violet was happy for the change of subject.

"I think I may know the meaning behind your father's pose."

"What is it?" Violet couldn't hide her interest.

"I don't want to say yet," Grant held up his hand. "Not until Peter looks at the image. He'll either confirm or contradict my theory."

"Okay." Violet sighed with disappointment. "So tell me about this kid."

"Peter is an exchange student from England. He's been living with a family on the West side for some time now."

"How old is he?" Violet asked.

"He's fifteen. A brilliant kid. I met Peter Boystead at a lecture I did on variable translations of Nostradamus' quatrains and whether or not he predicted Paris Hilton's sex tape." Grant said.

"Paris Hilton's sex tape?" Violet laughed. "You have got to be kidding."

"Surprisingly I'm not." Grant continued, nonplussed. "When it comes to Nostradamus many people believe you can retroactively read anything into his predictions. His quatrains were partisan at best, specifically from all the sundry English translations that are available. By taking a current event, one could potentially discover that Nostradamus *seemed* to have predicted it, or at the very least, alluded to it. But the event has to occur first and then one can then look back at the quatrains to find clues. But no one has ever predicted an event before it happened using any of Nostradamus' works."

"What's a quatrain?" Violet asked.

"It's a poem with four lines. It's the most common stanza in all poetry. Nostradamus wrote 941 rhyming quatrains and one non-rhyming."

"But Paris Hilton?"

"There are lines that one might think suggests an heir, with blond hair, and sex acts. But really it's all interpretive." Grant explained.

"Like what?"

"Hmmm, let's see. A few of the lines being bandied about were

> '*At night the last one will be strangled in bed,*
> *Because he became too involved with the blond heir elect*'
> and
> '*The Greek lady of ugly beauty,*
> *Made happy by many suitors*'. You know, stuff like that."

"Paris Hilton isn't Greek, is she?" Violet asked.

"Nope. But she dated that Greek billionaire guy for a while. You can create almost anything out of Nostradamus' jibber jabber."

"Sounds like horse shit to me." Violet shook her head.

"Well, that's why you're best to leave this kind of stuff up to us academics." Grant said condescendingly.

"Just because I've had a smoke doesn't mean I won't pop you one!"

"Are you hitting on me?" Grant joked, fearful of being hit.

Violet laughed. "You're not my type, but thanks anyway."

"So anyway, Peter is a child prodigy. He's a phenom on all things iconic and symbolic. The kid blows me away when it comes to symbology. We've remained in touch via the Internet since we met at the lecture. If anyone can help decipher your father's message, it's Peter."

Grant heard a beep and noticed Violet's cell phone had lit up. He flipped it open. "Peter got the message. He said to stop by; he'll be waiting for us."

"Where's he live?" Violet asked. "I hope you know you're way around the city, because I sure don't."

"Yes, don't worry. Make a left up ahead." Grant pointed. "Oh, here's your phone back," he said, handing the phone to Violet. She reached for it and forgot about his sweaty palms, and to expect the extreme sliminess. She screeched in disgust, shaking the phone trying to get the alien slop to dislodge from her phone. The phone slipped from her hand and flew out the window.

"Shit!" Violet screamed as it shattered on the pavement. "Don't you have towels in that freaking backpack?!"

"Don't hurt me!" Grant cried, pushing himself as far from Violet as he could.

CHAPTER 17

Sergeant Atgreens had walked the two actors through the majority of the crime scene investigation, holding back on little, if not none, of the delicate and highly classified information involved in the shooting. Mr. Trafalgar feigned awe and acted as though he were shocked and surprised at the events. Randall Teodey's shooting was nothing compared to the violence and destruction he and Mr. Crows' dealt out on a regular basis. Mr. Trafalgar listened intently and absorbed the information, tossing aside the irrelevant portions, and memorizing anything he felt Mr. Maystyne would consider pertinent to their cause.

The threesome was standing in the American Wing Courtyard at the scene where Randall's body had lain. Now, middle of the day, light poured in from the glass ceiling, filling the room with effulgent beams of sunlight.

Officer Kumsch was still bagging evidence; he briefly looked up, paused in surprise, and then nodded his admiration to the pair of A+ celebrities. He immediately returned to the business at hand.

"So, tell me," Mr. Trafalgar began after Atgreens had finished his macabre tour. "Where is Miss Teodey now? If she is so pivotal to the case I imagine you'd have her giving a statement."

"Oh!" Sergeant Atgreens seemed to awaken sharply. "You're right! I left her here not twenty minutes ago. And it's Miss Sterne, Miss Violet Sterne. Seemingly her and Mr. Teodey weren't that close."

"Do you know if Mr. Teodey said anything to Miss Sterne? Maybe gave her some documents or something."

"As a matter of fact the head of security, Roy is his name, spoke briefly with Miss Sterne. He said that Randall did tell her something. Something important. So important she ran out." Sergeant Atgreens continued to spill everything he knew. "But she did return a bit later, I asked to get a statement from her but she was shaken up. You know how these women get."

"Oh, yeah," Mr. Trafalgar said. "They get crazy when their dad gets shot."

"Exactly." Atgreens rolled his eyes. "I was planning on grilling her good. You boys would have loved to see me pulling information out of her."

"You have no idea."

"Where the Hell could she have gotten off to?" Atgreens looked at Officer Kumsch. "Hey, where did the Sterne broad and that queer she was with go?"

Officer Kumsch looked up, shrugged, and went back to his labeling.

"Thanks a heap." Atgreens grabbed his walkie-talkie. "Hey people. Keep an eye out for Miss Sterne. She's MIA. If you find her detain her or bring her right to me. Make that a priority." He turned it off and looked apologetically at Mr. Trafalgar. "Crap. We'll find her. There's no way she got past the boys out front."

"I'm sure you're right, Sergeant." Mr. Trafalgar offered. "Would you mind terribly if Mr. Crows and I were to wander around alone for awhile?"

"Alone?" Sergeant Atgreens looked saddened.

"A fly on the wall thing. You know, blend in, go unnoticed, watch your men at work without... well, without you. You are the big gun here."

Atgreens puffed up slightly. "Well, yes. Fly on the wall. Of course." He smoothed his uniform. "I will be out front should you need anything, just ask."

"Thank you Sergeant."

They watched as Atgreens made his exit, strutting out of the courtyard. He practically clicked his shoes and turned on his heel when he turned the corner.

Mr. Trafalgar turned to speak to Mr. Crows, who moments before stood quietly to his left, but was now missing. "Um, Mr. Crows?" He looked around and almost choked when he saw his counterpart having snuck up behind Officer Kumsch and his hands inches from the officer's neck. "Hey!"

Officer Kumsch looked up, startled. Mr. Crows paused pre-strangle. He looked over at Mr. Trafalgar with an 'I got caught' look.

"Officer Kumsch, would you mind allowing us some time in the courtyard alone?" Mr. Trafalgar abruptly asked.

"Oh, uh, sure." Kumsch nodded. "Very honored to meet you Mr. Trafalgar." He trotted out of the courtyard

"Honor is all mine," he lied as the officer ran past. As soon as he knew Kumsch was beyond hearing range, he turned back to Mr. Crows. "Mr. Crows, what did I tell you about leaving my side?"

"I'm sorry. I couldn't help it. I needed to hurt someone." He made his way back to his partner in crime. "All that blathering the Sergeant was giving us. Blah blah shot. Blah blah evidence. It was driving me mad." Mr. Crows looked up at his friend. "You're not going to hit me are…"

Mr. Trafalgar swatted Mr. Crows on the head. He dropped to the ground and curled up like a scolded dog. Mr. Trafalgar leaned over and gently mussed Mr. Crows' hair. "Now get up and get that bagged laptop over there. Atgreens said the old man was using it when he was shot." Mr. Trafalgar pulled out a cigarette and lit up. He looked around and spoke to himself. "Lots of old junk in a place like this. Probably rude to smoke." He laughed as he took a drag and exhaled a noxious cloud.

Mr. Crows finished violently tearing open the carefully bagged laptop, plugged it in and powered it up. He fidgeted nervously and circled like a caged animal as he waited for Windows XP to load up. He barked at the laptop, "Hurry up!"

When the computer was up and running Mr. Trafalgar tossed his cigarette somewhere near 18th century muskets and sidled up to the computer. He lost no time finding the folder containing the pictures previously discovered by Grant. He smirked when he saw the numerous images of women's body parts. "Interesting." He froze at the last image. He stood back, analyzing it. He knew it was something Mr. Maystyne would want to see.

"Did you find something on the magic lapbox?" Mr. Crows asked.

"Yes I did, little buddy. I most certainly did." He opened up the wireless network connection and went to his Gmail account. He attached the picture and emailed it to Mr. Maystyne's account; evilbadguy@gmail.com.

"Now we wait." He stood back and crossed his arms. This job was really getting interesting.

CHAPTER 18

Violet skidded to a stop outside of Peter's exchange family's two-story brownstone. She completely blocked in a bus stop with her bumper slightly touching the bus stop sign. Grant hit a No Parking sign when he opened his door; the door opening less than a foot to allow himself and his backpack out of the car. He grunted as he forced himself through. He popped out, falling onto the backpack like an overturned turtle. He felt like the car had just birthed him.

Violet stood on the curb, smoking and waiting, offering no apology for the inconvenient and illegal parking job.

"You know you parked illegally, don't you?" Grant said as he pushed himself up off the urine-scented sidewalk.

"Well we're not going to be here long, are we?" Violet huffed.

"You're really not getting this whole quest-for-your-father's-secret, are you?" Grant's shoulders slumped.

"You want me to throttle you again, don't you?"

"Can we stop talking in questions?"

"Fine with me." Violet tossed her cigarette. "Let's get going Harry Potter."

"Hey! Be nice."

Grant slung his backpack over his shoulder and climbed the steps to Peter's brownstone. He briefly perused the list of occupants and pressed the button next to 'The Greeksteks'.

"The Greeksteks?" Violet laughed.

"They're the foster family. Nice people. Don't be rude."

Violet shot him an angry look. "Like I would be, you dork."

Grant sighed. "You're right. I don't know where I get these crazy ideas."

The door swung open and a chubby kid, about fourteen years old, stepped out. He was wearing a dark blue blazer over a white button-up shirt. It was buttoned to the top and the boy's generous jowls spilled over. It looked very uncomfortable. He was shiny, too, with a sweaty sheen that reflected the midday sun. He was, however, only wearing his underwear, Scooby-Doo boxers. Violet tried not to laugh.

He held out his hand to Grant, offering a pudgy sweaty handshake. "'Ello there, what!" Peter spat in a loud Cockney accent. "Welcome to me flat. Well, me foster folk's flat at least, right then."

Grant and Peter shook hands. Violet got nauseous thinking of the two slimy, sweaty paws exchanging salty fluids. Fingers wrapped around each other, palms rubbing. It was like gay hand-model porn.

"And look at this lovely lassy!" Peter stuck out his hand. Violet could see the glossy sausage fingers, wiggling like some sickening snake mating ritual. She felt her stomach twitch, agitated with acid.

"Sorry, no. Can't do it." Violet shook her head. "Nice to meet you, Peter. I don't shake hands." She coughed, her throat burned.

"It's all right, love. Nothing personal taken, what." Peter trudged back into the building. They followed him to the end of the hall. He opened the door to the apartment; he held his arms wide open. "Come in, make ye'selves comfortable. Would ye like a spot of tea, then?"

Grant pulled his camera out and cranked it a few times. He snapped a few pictures of Peter. "No tea for me, thank you."

Violet just shrugged her shoulders.

"Ah, still with the camera, eh Grant me boy?"

"Yes, Peter, still with the camera."

"I bet he's taken a few of you, then what, little lady?" Peter led them through the living room and up a small flight of stairs. "Right then, let's 'ave a look at what you brought me. Me computer's in me room. Well, not my room, it's the Greekstek's cheeky boy. But it's got lots o' fun stuff in it." He led them to a door, slathered in posters of space scenes, like the Space Shuttle, Neil Armstrong, Apollo 13, even a poster of Albert II, the first monkey in space.

Peter opened the door and Violet couldn't hold back a chortle. It was a nerd's paradise. Everything that would make a kid not cool, any interest that would make you a social outcast, any hobby that would make girls turn you down and boys steal your lunch money, was in this room. Dungeons and Dragons paraphernalia, Star Trek posters and models, actions figures from every science fiction movie ever made, a diorama of the solar system hanging from the ceiling, a chess set (which wouldn't be too bad, but the pieces were all characters from the Lord of the Rings movies), computer games and cheat books, and plush Star Wars characters. The nerdish list went on. And on. And on. Peter noticed Violet eyeing the room.

"Come on in, love. Sit on me bed there, what. It's an eyeful me room is. Don't be scared of nothing here. Except me." He winked at her.

Violet saw an exceptionally abused Playboy magazine peaking out from under Peter's bed. He ran over and kicked it back under the bed, like David Beckham kicking a winning goal. He turned back, his face flushed red.

"So what 'ave ye brung me, Grant me boy?" Peter abruptly changed the subject.

Grant dug out his key chain hard drive and handed it to Peter. "Pop this baby in. There's an image on it you need to see."

"Well, I hope the image has great jomblies." Peter joked.

"Don't be crass, Peter." Grant admonished, turning bright red and trying not to giggle. "There's a lady present."

"What's jomblies?" Violet asked.

"Never mind." Grant said. "It's a British thing."

Peter inserted the USB drive into the back of his PC. It opened a folder on the desktop containing only one item and he double-clicked on the image. The computer opened the image and filled the screen.

"Bloody 'ell!" Peter cried out. "Piss in me pig-snacks!"

CHAPTER 19

After several minutes of hand shaking, picture posing and generous thanks from the officers of the NYPD, Mr. Trafalgar and Mr. Crows made their way back to the Jaguar. Mr. Trafalgar slid in behind the wheel, dug out a cigarette and lit up. Mr. Crows hopped into his seat and sat with his arms folded. He was obviously upset.

"What's bugging my little monkey?" Mr. Trafalgar asked.

"I hate waiting." Mr. Crows whined.

"I know you do. But we have to get our orders from Mr. Maystyne. I'm sure that pic we sent him will get things going."

"And you never let me drive."

"Because you run over things. And people! You can't always do that, little man."

"That last guy I ran over I took to the hospital. Access Hollywood told everyone I was a hero!" Mr. Crows argued. "I've saved many people, you know!"

"Because you were the one to put them in jeopardy in the first place!" Mr. Trafalgar laughed, coughing on his smoke. "You may fool the media, little buddy, but you ain't fooling me. You dig?"

"Whatever." Mr. Crows sank in his seat. "I should be allowed to drive at least once in a while."

"Not in the city. Maybe next time we're out in the country."

Mr. Crows looked around. He saw the signs for Central Park. "Hey, can I go chase squirrels while we wait?"

"No, we stay right…" The Blackberry in Mr. Trafalgar's jacket beeped. He reached in and took it out, popping it open.

Mr. Crows jumped up and down in his seat. "What is it? What'd he say? Who do I get to whack?"

"Easy, little man!" Mr. Trafalgar opened his email account, questionablystraightduo@gmail.com. He had received an email from Mr. Maystyne. It read:

Stay put for the moment. Whereabouts of target unknown. Will contact you as soon as information comes in.

Mr. Trafalgar read it aloud for Mr. Crows, who sank even deeper into his seat and depression. "Aaw! I hate hate hate waiting!" He kicked his feet like a petulant child. "*Now* can I go chase squirrels?"

Mr. Trafalgar started up the Jaguar; he put it in reverse and drove backward up 5th. He stopped in front of one of the many entrances into Central Park.

"Go ahead." Mr. Trafalgar offered, he held up a finger warningly. "But don't wander too far. Do NOT hurt any people. And I don't want any blood on the leather in my car. Dig?"

"Rules. Rules. Rules." Mr. Crows sighed. He jumped out of the car and scampered off into the park. He was up a tree in seconds.

CHAPTER 20

"The Creation of Adam!" Peter exclaimed.

"I knew it!" Grant said.

"What's a pig-snack?" Violet asked.

"I could recognize this bloody image anywhere!" Peter paused. "But dare I ask, dear Grant. Who is this poor chap and is he…?"

"That, um, is Violet's father." Grant bowed his head. "And sadly, yes, he was shot this morning."

"Oh, my. My most sincere condolences Miss Violet." Peter stared longer at the image on the screen. "How terrible."

Grant stepped forward. "After he was shot, Violet had a chance to talk to him. He had some secret, a very important secret that he wanted to share with Violet. He didn't get to tell her though before he… passed on. So we don't have much to go on." Grant pointed at the computer screen. "But when I saw this, a picture taken moments after he was shot, I knew that he was trying to send us a message. It has to be."

"I agree," Peter said. "You made the right call there, Grant."

"What is the Creation of Adam?" Violet asked. She stayed on the other side of the office, not wanting to be near the image.

"My dear, the Creation of Adam is one of the most famous frescoes ever painted. It resides on the ceiling of the Sistine Chapel in the Vatican. In the last moments of your father's life, he recreated the figure of God as depicted on the Sistine Chapel ceiling, painted by the great Michelangelo Buonarroti himself!"

"Michelangelo has a last name?" Violet asked, her brows furrowed. "I thought Michelangelo was his full name. Like Cher or Madonna or Da Vinci."

"Da Vinci?" Peter looked at Violet, puzzled.

"Ugh, Da Vinci. Can we not mention him, please? And yes, Michelangelo has a full name." Grant said. "His complete name is actually Michelangelo di Lodovico Buonarroti Simoni."

"Good show! Well done. Not too many people can pull that out of their bums." Peter said to Grant. "But back to the Creation of Adam."

"I've seen a picture of the Sistine Chapel before. Is that the picture of God pointing at Adam?" Violet asked. "Where they're flying or something."

"Exactly. Here let me show you. I will pull up images from the Web." Peter turned to Violet. "Don't worry, dear, I'll hide the image of your father."

"No. Leave it up." Violet swallowed hard. "I have to deal with this."

Peter opened Internet Explorer; it defaulted to his home page, which was a porn site. It was embarrassingly titled lubedlimey.com.

Violet cringed at the sight, but she could hear Grant chuckling. *God, this guy acts like a little schoolboy sometimes!* Peter gagged in embarrassment and quickly typed in Google.com.

"Ahem. Here we go." Peter stuttered. He did an image search for Creation of Adam and a litany of thumbnail pictures popped up. Peter clicked on one, making it larger. "Look, the similarities are incontrovertible!"

"Amazing," Grant whispered in awe.

"Fantastic," Peter agreed.

"It's exact," continued Grant.

"Unmistakable," Peter said.

"I don't see it." Violet said.

"What?!" Peter and Grant both asked.

"Violet, look at the way your father is lying on his side, leaning forward, one arm extended. His legs back, his other arm at his side. Even his expression matches that of Michelangelo's God."

Violet did her best to see the picture of her father and treat it as it were just another painting, like the Creation of Adam next to it. She avoided her father's eyes.

"Well, maybe. He sort of looks like Superman flying, too."

"Hardly." Grant disagreed. "Undeniably, that's the Creation of Adam. Tell me Violet, was your father religious?"

"No. Not that I know of." Violet said. "He never discussed religion with me. But then again, we didn't really speak about anything much."

Peter thought for a moment. "How about your mum, then?"

"She died when I was eight. I don't remember her much. And my father refused to talk about her."

Grant put his hand on Violet's shoulder. "Again, I'm sorry, Violet."

"Thanks." Violet said, staring down at the wet palm on her shoulder. She resisted brushing his hand off of her. Luckily he didn't keep it there long.

Peter was leaning forward, squinting at the image of Violet's father. Suddenly he bolted upright. "Hold on! What's this? I think I've found something else!"

CHAPTER 21

"I think I see something in the upper corner." Peter said excitedly.

Grant nudged Violet. "What time is it?" he asked.

Violet huffed and looked at her watch. "It's 11:30. Why?"

"I've got pills to take. Thanks." Grant then nudged Peter. "Do you have water?"

"In the fridge, Grant me boy." Peter said without looking away from the computer screen. His nose was practically touching the monitor. Violet wouldn't allow herself to imagine how much DNA was on that screen and keyboard.

Grant jogged out of the room and returned a minute later with a bottle of water in his hand. He squatted down in front of his backpack.

Violet watched with dismay at what was clearly an addled person.

Grant rummaged through his backpack and pulled out a pill tray. It was divided into seven days, with compartments for morning, noon, dinner time and night. Grant opened the noon compartment on Saturday and dumped out a half dozen pills, each a different shape and color. He scanned through them, picked out one and placed it in his mouth. He took a swig of water then swallowed. His lips moved as he counted to fifteen. Grant then scanned his pills until he's found the next one and repeated the procedure.

"Why don't you just pop 'em all in at once?" Violet asked impatiently.

Grant held up a finger, warning her to wait. He swallowed the second pill and counted to fifteen again. He then looked at Violet. "Because they can't be taken that way. They have to be taken in a certain order."

"Why?"

"Because they have to be. That's why." Grant snapped.

"Did your doctor say this or is this all you?" Violet smirked, poking the side of her head. "Is this just more of your OCD thing?"

"Go talk to Peter." Grant grunted, then returned to scanning his pills.

Violet decided it was best to ignore him. *Freak.* she muttered in her head.

"I've got it!" Peter declared. "Gather round, mates! Another clue!"

Violet and Grant stepped closer and looked at the monitor. Peter had zoomed in on Randall's spilled cereal. The Alphabits were scattered across the floor, soggy from sitting in milk for so long. "I thought this was something but it took me a few minutes to figure it out. Look at that."

"What are we looking at?" Violet asked. "Cereal?"

"Not just cereal. Alphabits. Spilled right at the tip of your father's finger, he's clearly pointing at it." Peter explained.

"And?"

"Look at the letters. Right here." Peter circled the letters with his finger on the monitor. "See the letters, M, D, V, I, I, and I?"

"And?"

"Good God, woman. It's the Roman Numerals for 1508!"

"And?"

"The year Michelangelo was commissioned to paint the Sistine Chapel!" Peter waved his hands about enthusiastically. "This seals it! Your father was definitely trying to convey to us something about Michelangelo."

Violet was squinting, shaking her head. "Wait a minute. You see 1508?" She pointed at the screen. "They're hardly in a row!" She pointed out other letters. "Using that line of logic I can see *POOP* up here!" She pointed a little lower. "And this says *SNOT!*"

Grant chuckled at the words like a schoolboy. "She said poop." he mumbled.

"Does that mean we have to find Michelangelo's snot-covered poop?!" Violet was screaming. "You two are insane!"

Grant's eyes were tearing from holding in his laughter. *Snot-covered poop.* It was all he could think about.

"My dear, Violet, there is no need to get dramatic. We are merely trying to help." Peter said soothingly. "Let us think for a moment. Had your father ever been to the Sistine Chapel?"

"I don't know? Where is it, in New York?"

Peter stifled a laugh. "It's in Italy, dear, Rome, Italy."

Grant jumped up from the floor. "Wait a minute!" he yelled. "Violet, didn't your father say something about his assistant, what's her name, Gerri Hender right? Wasn't she going to Rome?"

"Well, yes, he did say something about that." Violet said, thinking back. "He didn't finish the sentence but he said 'Gerri went to…' and that 'I must go…' and that was it. I mean, *I* know she went to Rome but he didn't actually say to go to Rome."

Peter stood up, shaking with excitement. "That seals it. It's too coincidental to be a coincidence! Think about it Violet. Your father posing like God in the Creation of Adam, pointing at the Roman numerals for 1508, mentioning his assistant, who's coincidently in Rome, and that you must go. It does add up. Seemingly your father was aware of something that Miss Hender was up to in Rome. Something involving the great Michelangelo. But what?"

"Michelangelo is part of many theories and mythologies." Grant said, stumped. "The entire Sistine Chapel is riddled with inside jokes and mysteries."

"What was your father photographing, Violet?" Peter asked.

"I don't know. A gun of some kind." Violet looked to Grant.

"A pistol." Grant clapped his hands. "Is it in the image?"

Peter returned to the computer and examined Randall's final image. The pistol was lying on the floor, just below his feet. Peter zoomed in on it.

"Dear God, I know this pistol!" Peter exclaimed. "Correct me if I'm wrong but is this not the pistol of Emperor Charles V?"

CHAPTER 22

Mr. Trafalgar sat on the door of the Jaguar, smoking as always. He watched people as they meandered past. He had signed at least two dozen autographs and had posed for a sundry pictures. He was getting restless and wondered if lunch at Nobu would be against his order to remain incognito. *I mean, jeez, I'd wear sunglasses.*

He sucked on the cigarette and sighed. He heard the patter of feet and Mr. Crows came skittering out of the park. He stopped and stood next to Mr. Trafalgar. "Hey, boss. Thanks for letting me play out there."

"No problem, little buddy." Mr. Trafalgar reached into his pocket and retrieved a Kleenex. He wiped at Mr. Crows' chin. "You have a piece of squirrel on you."

"Thanks" Mr. Crows said. "Did we get our next order?"

"Not yet. Getting a little tired of keeping my jets cooled, you know?"

A man in a business suit strutted by sporting a fine leather briefcase and Rolex watch. He sniffed the air and saw the cigarette dangling from Mr. Trafalgar's mouth. "Disgusting." he muttered, just audible enough to be heard.

Mr. Crows was off in a flash, but Mr. Trafalgar's hand was on his shirt collar and dragged him back. "Easy there!" he yelled.

Mr. Crows barked furiously. "Let me at him! He can't talk to us like that! We're kings! I wanna kill him!"

"Please sit, Mr. Crows, we are on a job and people are looking at us. Subtlety, remember? Besides, we can only kill in the line of duty."

"Man, this sucks."

"Tell me about it little buddy, tell me about it. I'm getting hungry." Mr. Trafalgar said through clenched teeth. He rubbed his generous belly.

Mr. Crows' eyes bulged. Normally when Mr. Trafalgar was hungry, cigarettes tided him over. But when he got hungry-hungry, watch out. Even Mr. Crows knew not to get in the way. "We best get you some eats, boss. I might be able to get another squirrel."

"That's okay, killer, I can deal."

CHAPTER 23

"Okay, my dad was taking pictures of a gun." Violet said, looking at the relic in the photo. "What's the big deal?"

"It's a *pistol*." Grant said.

"You tell me that one more time I'll throw you out the window." Violet growled.

"Jeez. Sorry."

Peter pulled up information of the gun off The Met's own website. Sure enough, there was the pistol and a paragraph describing it. "Indeed, it is *the* very pistol!"

"So what does that mean?" Grant asked. "What does that have to do with Michelangelo?"

"Maybe nothing directly. But indirectly it may have much larger implications." Peter was speaking rapidly, his excitement growing. "Violet, you're father may have been privy to, and bearing the secrets of, one of the most shocking theories in all of Christianity."

"My dad?" Violet laughed.

"What theory, Peter?" Grant asked.

"The Twelve." Peter sat back and grinned. "Surely, you're heard of The Twelve?"

"Of course, but Peter, are you sure?" Grant was awestruck.

"As sure as my mum's got a big bum!" Peter said as he typed into the computer looking for more information on the pistol.

"What the Hell is The Twelve?" Violet asked.

Grant stepped in. "Twelvists as they like to be called are purveyors of a radical concept in Christianity that Jesus Christ himself was given information as a gift from extraterrestrial beings."

"Wait, what? Aliens?" Violet shook her head. "You guys are off your rockers!"

"This isn't as crazy as it sounds, Violet." Grant continued. "Since the beginning of recorded history man has reported and documented encounters with spacecraft and otherworldly beings."

Peter chimed in. "It's true. Even before Christ's existence himself. As far back as primitive man, there have been cave drawings of saucer-shaped objects in the sky. And of smaller humanoids interacting with man."

"Cavemen?" Violet was incredulous.

"From the Kimberly Ranges in Australia to the Nazca lines of Peru. Everywhere. The rock carvings of Val Camonica in Northern Italy show fantastic samples of humanoids and technology, all of which is dated 8,000 BC. Images and symbols of aliens and their technology have been presented to us over the eons."

"Even the Bible itself has references that many interpret as interactions with UFOs and aliens." Grant said.

"Aliens." Violet grunted. "Get real."

"We don't have time for that now, Violet, but trust me, it's all very true." Grant interjected. "Getting back to the pistol, Peter, what does that have to do with The Twelve?"

"It was designed in the mid 16th century, shortly after Michelangelo completed his work on the Sistine Chapel. It was designed by Peter Pech, a watchmaker. Look at the inscription here, Plus Ultra, it was Emperor Charles personal motto, translated it means 'More Beyond'."

"Like space travel." Grant whispered.

"That's weak." Violet muttered.

Grant shot her a look. "Go ahead. What else?"

"It also has Charles personal emblems, a double headed eagle and the Pillars of Hercules."

"So?" Violet had had enough; she sat on the edge of Peter's bed. She was thinking of going outside for a smoke.

"Hercules. He was known for what, Grant?" Peter looked expectantly at Grant.

"The Twelve Labors of Hercules!" Grant exclaimed.

"Precisely." Peter clapped his hands.

"Pech. Why does that sound familiar?" Grant asked.

"I'm very glad you asked," Peter nodded his approval. "A Pech is a mythological creature of Scottish lore. They were tiny in stature, strong and intelligent. They were thought to be the builders of many of the stone megaliths of ancient Scotland."

"Sounds like aliens to me." Grant couldn't hide his enthusiasm.

"The name is also related to picts or pixies. Which also mythological creatures, all of which could be potentially explained by alien phenomena. These creatures are in every legend of every culture, along with aliens." Peter turned to Violet. "See, Violet, this is all part of a message your father was sending to you. This has to do with the Twelve! He left you an iconic image suggesting he knew of this sacred and most infamous mystery. Michelangelo, which the name itself has twelve letters, 1508, Plus Ultra, the Pillars of Hercules, Pechs, they are all interconnected. Perhaps your father *was* a Twelvist. Or even more, perhaps he was one of the enlightened. A carrier! Perhaps he possessed a twelfth of this most holy information himself, a scholarly descendent of Christ!"

"A twelfth?" Violet said from the edge of the bed, sitting up a little straighter. "Is there money in this?"

"No, but much more. Twelvists believe that Jesus dispersed the information given to him amongst his disciples. Breaking it into twelve sections, or portions, whatever. That's why there were twelve apostles. Nobody knows exactly how this information was written or stored or how it was represented. Each apostle carried their piece, protected it, and when they felt their time was near an end, passed it on to a worthy heir."

"Protect it from who?"

"Whom." Grant corrected her.

Violet shot him a look. Grant cowered.

Peter jumped in. "This information is said to cover all things. Broken down it is applicable to science, nature, finance, weapons, medicines, and even life itself. In the wrong hands it could conquer all life or destroy the world. In the right hands it could create Heaven on Earth."

"So why didn't Jesus use it himself? You know, to make the world better." Violet had actually rejoined them, temporarily forgetting about the cigarette.

"The aliens felt Jesus was the right person to give it to, but," Peter pointed to a crucifix hanging from around his neck. "It's pretty clear that Jesus felt we weren't ready for it, considering how that poor chap's story turned out."

"Yeah, I guess so." Violet sighed. She felt weird, she wasn't used to thinking. Her brain was hurting.

Grant decided to chime in. "So you see Violet, we think it's quite possible your father was an heir to a portion of this information. And after he was shot, he had no choice but to tell you in any way he could. He had to pass on the legacy."

God, if only I let him talk, Violet flushed with regret.

"So what does Gerri have to do with this?" Violet asked.

"Maybe she was one of the, um, bad guys? So to speak." Grant said. "Maybe she was spying on Randall, trying to learn his secret from the inside, by working for him. She was able to divulge what she needed to know from him and, well… " Grant didn't finish the sentence.

Peter mulled it over. "Well, she obviously didn't shoot him if she left two days ago, but then again, isn't that the perfect alibi? She finds out what she needs, and then has someone else kill him while she goes off to Rome. This way Randall can't stop her and she doesn't get blamed. It's perfect!"

Grant was pacing, his hand on his chin.

"So she's going to get this big Jesus secret?" Violet asked, angry at the thought.

"Not the entire secret." Peter said. "The first of twelve. According to Twelvists, the information is hidden in twelve separate locations. Hidden across the planet. Thereby making it nearly impossible for one man or organization to find them all."

"So what's the big deal if Gerri finds one of them?"

"It is speculated that at each location, there is a clue that leads to the next. A person of great intelligence, skill, and cunning would be able to start at one location and find the rest."

Peter was as excited as a kid on Christmas morning, but this time it was Christmas with aliens. "She is in Italy right now stealing what is rightfully yours, Violet. She has to be stopped!"

"Then it's decided," Peter turned back to the computer. "You two are going to Rome and catching her and reclaiming your birthright!"

"What?" Violet shook her head as if she was punched. "Wait, what? I'm not going anywhere!"

"Violet, you have to." Grant pleaded. "Don't you see? This is what your father wanted. This is why he wanted you to find me. Somehow he knew I would be able to put it together for you. This is your father's last will and testament."

Peter smacked a few keys. "There! I went to Travelocity. I always liked that little British gnome guy in the commercials."

Grant turned away. "I can't look! I'm scared of gnomes!"

Peter chuckled. "And again, such a coincidence, we talk of Pechs and their involvement and here we are getting help from said creature. Okay, I've got two tickets from JFK lined up. So, er, who has a credit card? I'm not allowed to have one."

Grant stuffed his hands in his pockets. "I don't travel with plastic. I only have, like, twenty bucks on me."

Grant and Peter both looked at Violet.

"Shit." Violet stomped her foot. "Shit. Shit. Shit! Fine!" Violet dug through her purse. "I've only got like a few thousand left on this card then I'm maxed. So make sure it's coach!" She handed the beat up card to Peter.

Peter looked at the card; it was a Victoria's Secret credit card. He showed it to Grant. They giggled ferociously. Peter smelled it.

"Oh, you two are gross!" Violet shouted. "Just buy the damn tickets."

Grant placed his hands on Violet's shoulders. "Don't worry, Violet. We'll find this Gerri Hender and your father's secret. I'll see to it!"

"Get those slugs off me. I'm going outside to smoke." Violet pushed Grant and stormed off, mumbling to herself. *This is so going to suck.*

CHAPTER 24

Mr. Trafalgar sat at Nobu eating his third salmon steak. Though he wore sunglasses, he'd been inundated with fans and photos. So much for lying low. Mr. Crows sat with his head on the table. Occasionally he'd lift his head just enough to thump it back down on the table and make the glassware rattle.

"I'm bored." Mr. Crows said to the floor.

"Patience, little man. We'll hear from Mr. Maystyne soon."

"Not soon enough." Mr. Crows pouted.

As if on cue, the Blackberry beeped. Mr. Crows flung his head up.

"Is it him? Is it him? Is it him?"

Mr. Trafalgar put out his cigarette in the remainder of his steak. Though there was no smoking in the restaurant, kings were allowed exceptions. The nice young couple at the table next to them coughed fitfully from the smoke, but gushed when Mr. Trafalgar asked, no actually stated, that they wouldn't mind if he smoked. They shook their heads and blushed that a celebrity had talked to them.

"What does it say? What does it say? What does it..."

Mr. Trafalgar smoothly opened the Blackberry and swatted Mr. Crows in one fluid swing. "Chill."

He read the email aloud. "It says;

My inside man had just informed me that Miss Sterne has booked two tickets to Italy leaving from JFK in one hour. Air Italia. Intercept them at the airport; they must not leave the country. Do not, I repeat, do not kill her. That goes twice for you, Mr. Crows. I've attached a photo of Miss Sterne that my source provided me. Memorize It! Find her! End of message.

"Here she is, Mr. Crows." Mr. Trafalgar held the blackberry so they could both view the image. "She's a cutie."

"She looks tasty." Mr. Crows salivated.

"You heard the boss. No killing, that goes double for you!"

"Aww, man." Mr. Crows fumed, then brightened suddenly. "At least we get to see the big silver airplanes!"

"Yes, we do buddy.   And you know how much I like airplanes." Mr. Trafalgar agreed.

"Yeah, 'cause you're a pilot." Mr. Crows beamed proudly.

Another smack to the head.

"Ow!" Mr. Crows cried.

"I'm a captain! I have the uniform and hat to prove it. Now come on and let's go. We have a mission."

They thumped each other on the forehead with their palms.

"All Hail Teegeeack!"

CHAPTER 25

Violet returned from her smoke break looking pale. "Are you guys sure I need to do this? This is all unreal."

Grant handed back Violet's credit card, but not before sniffing it. "Violet, trust me. We are on the trail of one of the greatest mysteries ever. The truth behind Jesus' relationship to aliens."

Violet wiped the card off on Peter's bed spread. She returned it to her purse.

Peter swiveled around in his chair and retrieved papers being spat from his printer. "All right, then, what? Here are ye tickets, lad and lassy. Ye got an hour to get to the airport and board."

"An hour? I have to pack!" Violet cried.

"No packing. We go as is." Grant explained.

"Easy for you to say, you walk around with your life in your stupid sack like a homeless guy!" Violet swatted the backpack.

Grant giggled. "She said sack."

"God, you're so immature. Do you have to giggle at any word that could have a double-meaning?" Violet reprimanded.

"I find double entendre funny, thank you very much." Grant said defensively. "And this is a rucksack, Violet, not a sack." He giggled again as he spoke the word himself.

Violet scowled. "I really don't care what you call it. Can we go now?"

"You're all set." Peter beamed, handing the tickets to Grant who then put them in his backpack. He pulled the zipper shut with a loud, snooty, "Humph!".

Peter held up his hands. "Now you two get along, yes? This is a great journey you're going on here. A mystery the likes of which must be taken very seriously. The fate of Christianity, nay, the entire world, lies in your hands! So please, for all that is Holy, just get along."

"Fine." Violet glared. "But I am stopping by my apartment. I can't get out of the country without my passport, can I?"

"Very true." Peter said. "But be quick. Our foil Gerri Hender has quite a lead on us and you must stop her. Grant, you have your passport on you I hope?"

"Is the gnome gone?" Grant asked.

"Yes, he is." Peter said closing the web page.

Grant turned around and patted the side of his backpack. "I never leave home without my passport. Let's go."

Violet sighed heavily as she followed Grant out the door. She stopped when Peter called to her.

"Oh, dear me. Violet, wait, I nearly forgot!" Peter rifled through a bookcase littered with folders, papers and books. He pulled out a Star Trek folder. "This, my dear, is all the research I have on Twelvists. This includes all things on the Twelve and anything else considered to be involved. It will make good reading on your long flight. I did a book report on the subject a few years back. I think it will help you to understand the gravity of your venture."

Violet accepted the folder. "Thanks." It was smudged, smeared, dog-eared, and stained with a horrifying rainbow of unattractive colors. She handed it to Grant. "Here. You hold this for now." She turned and walked out the door, without even a thank you.

Peter winked at Grant. "She's a wildcat that one! Have fun in Rome, if you know what I mean. Nudge, nudge, wink, wink!"

From the stairway, Violet yelled out, "I heard that you little British pervert!"

CHAPTER 26

Fifteen minutes later, Violet screeched to a halt in front of her apartment building. Grant was curled up in a ball on the floor of the car, no longer disgusted by the collective filth and detritus it contained. He figured rolling around in garbage was better than seeing what was actually taking place outside the rusted juggernaut's windows.

"You can get up now." Violet muttered as she forced open her car door.

Grant slowly climbed up, giving his heart some time to slow down. He stepped out of the car and gasped. *Did she drive to a third world country?*

"Are we still in New York?" Grant whimpered.

The sounds of sirens, screaming, gunshots, and for some reason, chickens squawking assaulted his ears. To his left was a faded chalk outline of a poor soul who was at the wrong end of what had to be a bazooka, considering the amount of brownish dried blood stains on the pavement. Rorschach patterns of urine and other fluids decorated the sidewalk where hopscotch boards would be if this were a Norman Rockwell painting. Grant tripped over a wadded nest of police tape. He kicked at it and it only wrapped around his ankle tighter, like an angry wad of spaghetti. A homeless man approached Grant and spoke in gibberish, the man's breath attacking Grant's olfactory senses and causing waves of nausea and temporary blindness.

"O-Qua Tangin Wann. Qua Omsa Lagee Wann," the man said with a heavy slur, leaning in far too close to Grant for his comfort. Being on the *same planet* was far too close for Grant's comfort.

Violet was at the top of her building's steps waiting for him. "Come on, wussy boy. We don't have much time."

Grant ran as fast as he could, his feet barely touching the ground. He leaped over a puddle of urine with the radioactive hue of

Prestone antifreeze to get to the steps. Cigarette butts and flattened wads of gum decorated the cement steps like fetid confetti.

Violet opened the main door to her building and Grant leapt inside, his imagination making him feel as though a bullet was flying toward him. He tripped over a few poorly closed trash bags and fell onto the stained vinyl tiling. He rolled onto his back and looked at Violet with wild eyes. "Where in God's good name are we?"

"Get up Grant. It's not that bad around here." She stepped over him and entered the stairwell. "I thought you were a New Yorker?"

"I am! I swear, but…" Grant quickly got to his feet and scrambled to catch up with Violet. "Don't leave me alone!"

Grant caught up to Violet on the third floor. She was unlocking her door, a cigarette dangling from her mouth.

"Isn't this a no-smoking building?" Grant asked.

Violet ignored him and swung open the door. She flicked on a light and cockroaches scattered, a black blanket of insects breaking up and taking cover under the mountains of garbage and dirty laundry. Grant stood paralyzed in the doorway. His hands were sweating cats and dogs, even more so than usual. He quickly dug through his bag and placed a doctor's surgical mask. He peeled his eyes off the toxic floor and scanned the room. His eyes bulged at the spectacle.

He swallowed hard as he saw a variety of female undergarments. Bras, panties and lingerie-type things he didn't recognize were hanging from lamps, cabinets and some kind of bungee chair hanging from the ceiling. Pink and purple lace, leather, pleather and vinyl, nylon and mesh in a variety of colors. It was like a brothel had exploded.

He couldn't help it but a rhyme began in his head. *Bras and panties and lingerie, oh my! Bras and panties and lingerie, oh my! Bras and panties and lingerie, oh my!*

"You coming in?" Violet barked from the bedroom. And then. "Why are you wearing a mask?"

"Uh, um, I'll wait in the hall," he squeaked. Grant turned from the door and plastered his back against the hallway wall. He forced his mind to think about baseball, car crashes and his grandma's unfortunate issues with drool.

Violet was running around, throwing items in an overnight bag. She ran from the bedroom to the kitchenette, grabbing a variety of misplaced items. She threw in several packs of Marlboros. "Yes!" Violet exclaimed as she held up her passport, once she had dug it out from a drawer filled with Soap Opera Digests. As she ran around the apartment, she kicked up a dust cloud of cigarette ash in her wake from her un-vacuumed floor. She paused as she passed her phone.

"Hey, I've got messages. A bunch of them." Violet called out to Grant. "It could be important!" Just then the phone rang, Violet reached for it.

"Do not answer that!" Grant screamed. He ran into the room and jumped in front of Violet. "It could be them!"

"Who's them?"

"Them! The bad guys! If you answer it, they'll know where we are!"

"If they thought I'd return to my own house, wouldn't they have just staked it out?" Violet stood with her fists firmly planted at her sides.

Grant thought on that for a second. "Wow. Good one. But all the more reason we have to get going, and fast! They could be on their way here."

The answering machine kicked in for the incoming call. A gruff voice belted out of the tiny speaker. "Miss Sterne, this is Sergeant Atgreens, I need to speak to you immediately concerning your father's…"

Grant pressed the mute button. He pointed at the answering machine and the flashing number of messages. "Holy crap! That makes twelve messages! You don't see this all lining up? We are on to something majorly cosmic here."

"You are insane!"

"Well, you wouldn't have come this far if you didn't believe in some of what you're hearing. Doesn't the number of messages mean something to you *now* that it didn't mean before? Signs, clues, portents, they're everywhere. Trust me; you don't want to listen to these messages or let the police get their hands on you. No one can be trusted. Now, we have really got to leave."

"Fine I've got pretty much everything, let's get…" Violet looked around. Grant was already in the hallway. "Going?"

"Just making sure the coast was clear!" Grant's voice echoed from the hallway.

CHAPTER 27

It had taken them almost half an hour to get to Terminal 1 at the John F. Kennedy International Airport. Violet cut off a cab and skidded to a stop in a no-parking zone. Several cars honked in anger, cabbies flipped the bird, and people dove out of her way. The car belched smoke and rattled for half a minute after Violet turned it off.

"Where'd you learn how to drive?!" yelled an irate man with a thick Irish brogue.

"Go back to France you jerk!" Violet called back.

Grant was curled up in a ball as Violet threw open his door. He fell to the ground in a heap. He was muttering something about evil incarnate.

"Get up, Sally. We've got a flight to catch." Violet slung her overnight bag over her shoulder and marched into the terminal.

Grant slowly got up. "You're just going to leave your car here?" But Violet was already gone, the glass sliding doors having closed behind her.

Grant caught up as Violet waited on line at the Alitalia Airlines baggage claim. "I'm a little nervous flying," he said. Grant opened his tray of pills, pulled out two Xanax and swallowed them. "You know they say flying is safer than driving? I don't believe that. You can survive a car crash. When a plane goes down, it's bye-bye."

"Don't be silly. What did you take?"

"Xanax. The first crash at JFK, known as Idlewild at the time, was December 8, 1954. Twenty-six people died. In 1960, 127 people died in a DC-8 that went down. In 1962, there were two crashes, killing over a hundred people. Then in 1965…"

"All right! I get it. What are you, Rain Man?" Violet looked at the obviously nervous Grant. She smirked. "You know I thought I saw some shady looking Hindus getting on board our flight." she lied.

"Oh, man." Grant threw two more Xanax back. "That's very racist, by the way."

But it'll keep him quiet, Violet thought.

"Did you know that JFK airport is 12 miles south of lower Manhattan?" Grant beamed. "The connections continue."

Or not. Violet frowned.

Violet patted Grant's backpack. "Better get out those tickets before you zone out on me."

"I'll be fine." Grant argued. "I know my meds."

"Give me my ticket at least."

"Fine." Grant unzipped a pocket and produced one of the printed tickets.

Violet snatched it from his hand. "Thanks."

It was finally her time to check in her bag, she approached the main desk. "Hi, round trip to Rome." Violet said, holding out her ticket and passport.

"Any baggage you'd like to check in?" the woman behind the desk asked.

"Just him." Violet joked, pointing at Grant. The woman didn't laugh. Violet sighed. "No, just bringing this." Violet held up her overnight bag.

Violet turned to Grant, who was standing a few feet behind her. "You know you can check in *with* me." Violet offered.

"No, you go ahead." Grant said. "I figure you can go have one more smoke before we take off while I check in. It's going to be a long flight."

Violet was shocked. "Hey, you're right. Thanks, Grant. I didn't think of that."

"No problem. It's more for me than you. You're a bear when you don't have your nicotine."

Violet growled but was interrupted by the woman behind the desk. "Everything is in order, Miss Sterne. You can go to Gate 11. Please enjoy your flight."

"Thank you, I will." Violet said. She gave Grant a light hip-check as she walked by. "I'm going outside. See you at Gate 11."

"Sure thing, boss."

Violet stood outside and puffed angrily on her Marlboro. She watched as a tow truck backed in to take her car away. *Who cares? A piece of junk anyway. It'll cost less getting it out of impound than paying for parking here.*

She finished her cigarette and lit another one with the ember of the first. There was a cigarette disposal container next to her but she tossed the butt on the ground anyway. A man grimaced his displeasure as he walked by.

"Blow me." Violet spat. Violet turned the other direction and jumped, Grant was standing behind her.

"Jesus Christ!" Violet screamed.

"Not quite." Grant slurred. "But we be looking fer him!"

Oh, great. He's stoned. Violet cursed. She grabbed Grant by the collar. "We've got to get you on the plane before you pass out."

They lucked out and there was no line at the security check. Violet emptied her pockets, stepped through the metal detector, and was quickly frisked by a security officer. She was clear and allowed to collect her things. She turned back to Grant. *Now was the challenge.*

Grant hesitantly placed his backpack on the conveyor and stepped up to the metal detector. He surveyed the gateway as though it opened to Hell. He slowly placed his foot forward then pulled it back, like a slow motion hokey-pokey. He closed his eyes and stepped through.

The alarm beeped and red lights flashed. He was swarmed immediately. He was frisked, patted and in some ways molested. A large security guard asked him to empty his pockets, holding out a tray. Grant smiled weakly and began rummaging through his khaki pants. He produced a metal Spider-man keychain, several arcade tokens, a tuning fork, a ball bearing, a Star Trek dog tag, and a few trinkets that Violet didn't recognize.

Grant shrugged and stepped back through the gateway. He stepped back through and cringed, but no alarms rang.

He smiled at the large security guard. "Can I have my things back?"

The guard handed him the key chain, dog tag and tokens. "That's it."

"Um, ok."

Surprisingly his backpack made it through the x-ray without a hitch. Violet grabbed him by the arm. "All right, let's go."

By the time they had reached the gate, Grant was a stumbling heap. Violet handed the man at the gate her boarding pass. She looked back at Grant, who was looking at the ceiling high above. "Grant, get out your boarding pass."

"Huh?"

"Grant, get your pass." Violet tensed up.

"Passes are nice." Grant mumbled.

Violet grabbed his backpack and threw it to the ground. She found it underneath a thick sediment of doodlings, textbooks and nudie mags. *Geez, no wonder this thing weighs a ton.* She stood up and handed the man Grant's pass.

"Okay, you're all set to board." the man said.

Violet shoved Grant down the tunnel and onto the plane.

CHAPTER 28

A brilliant, expensive Jaguar pulled up outside of JFK International Airport moments after a rusty cheap car was towed away. The car pulled into the same no –parking zone that Violet had. The doors swung open and out stepped two men in ponchos, bushy moustaches and big colorful sombreros. They looked like Mexican Revolutionaries… with the exception of their $600 dollar patent-leather shoes.

Mr. Trafalgar looked twice as tall with the tremendous sombrero on his head, Mr. Crows' hat, however, was ill fitting and constantly slid over his eyes. They both looked ridiculous.

"Okay, little buddy." Mr. Trafalgar came around the side of the car to join his cohort. "We're looking for Alitalia Airlines at Gate 11."

"Si." Mr. Crows replied in a stereotypically racist version of a Hispanic accent, much like the infamous cartoon character, Speedy Gonzalez.

"Huh?" Mr. Trafalgar looked at him puzzled.

"Si, amigo."

"Cool it with the Spanish." Mr. Trafalgar took a drag from his cigarette, part of his bushy moustache burned from the ember, the hairs curling up and melting. "We just have to be inconspicuous. The costumes will hide us; we don't have to speak in Spanish. You dig?" Mr. Trafalgar tossed his smoke and calmly patted at the smoldering moustache. "Mr. Maystyne says we haven't been discreet enough. We have to blend in, disappear into a crowd." His hand continued smacking the big bushy moustache, until the clouds of burning plastic dissipated. When he was confident he wasn't in jeopardy of burning up, he headed into the airport. "We have to be invisible."

"But I like speaking Spanish." Mr. Crows said, following close behind. "I'm in character!"

"Yeah, but I don't speak Spanish and have no idea what you're saying."

"Lo ciento." Mr. Crows replied.

Mr. Trafalgar smacked him, knocking his sombrero off.

"I'm sorry! I'm sorry!" Mr. Crows cried, picking up his hat. He mumbled under his breath. "Pendajo."

The airport had filled considerably and crowds of people were now in various stages of crowdedness; they were swarming, walking, running, lining up, checking in, arguing, looking suspiciously at anyone with skin not white as linen, and making phone calls complaining to loved ones that their flights were late. The two Villanistas stood in the center of the herd of travelers, with only Mr. Trafalgar tall enough to see over most of the people. Mr. Crows occasionally jumped in an attempt to see, but accomplished nothing more than looking silly with his big moustache bouncing and fanning out with each leap.

"We need someone to give us some directions." Mr. Trafalgar said. "I can't see any signs for Gate 11."

"I can't see anything." Mr. Crows said.

"Hey, here comes one of those guys in a golf cart. He's gotta know where we have to go." Mr. Trafalgar pointed, which was useless for Mr. Crows.

"Does he work here?" Mr. Crows asked.

"No, the guy just likes to drive around airports in a golf cart, you moron."

"Sorry."

Mr. Trafalgar made his way through the throngs of people, his poncho fluttering like a cape, on an intercept course with the golf cart man.

The baggage handler looked up and saw the over six foot tall bandito flagging him down. He slowed down. *Oh, now what the Hell is this?* he thought. *It sure as Hell ain't Halloween.*

Mr. Trafalgar caught up, breathing heavy. He placed his hands on his knees and held up a finger, signaling 'Wait a minute.' He wheezed for a few moments and then straightened up. His face was flushed. Mr. Crows caught up and stood behind him. The baggage handler was surprised, seeing two identical loons.

"Thanks for stopping." Mr. Trafalgar said, with no hint of any accent. "We're lost and were hoping you could help us. We need to find Gate 11. We have a 3:00 flight."

The baggage handler nodded. "Oh, sure. It's that way." he said pointing over his shoulder; he then looked at his watch. "You better run, otherwise you'll never make it."

Mr. Trafalgar's eyes bulged out of his head. *Run? Oh crap.* "Come on, brother. Give us a lift. I can't run. Look at me."

"Sorry, *brother*," the man sarcastically replied. "Policy. I can't give anyone a ride."

Mr. Trafalgar thought for half a moment. "Mr. Crows."

Mr. Crows leapt, nearly as high as he is tall, letting out a blood curdling, "Ayayayaya!" and landed on the man in the cart. He took him off the cart in one swift move and dragged him into a nearby men's room. Mr. Trafalgar got himself comfortable in the driver's seat and waited for the ruckus to end. He whistled loudly when it went on too long. Mr. Crows came bounding out of the bathroom; he had a torn swathe of the baggage handler's uniform in his mouth. He hopped into the cart.

"Let's go!" Mr. Trafalgar announced, gunning the cart and rapidly hitting the horn. He beeped and sped along, nearly wiping out two dozen teenagers on a school trip, he took out a nurse pushing a man in a wheelchair that then went on to roll down a ramp and into a Burger King trashcan, and he sideswiped a fat lady, intentionally stealing the burrito she was eating.

"Now this is fun!" Mr. Crows yelled out.

"It sure is, little buddy!" Mr. Trafalgar agreed, scarfing down the burrito.

"Arriba! Arriba!"

"Don't make me hit you again."

They arrived at the security check for Gates 11-16 and Mr. Trafalgar decided not to stop. He toppled the man with the metal detector wand. Soon security was on high alert for two crazy Mexicans in a golf cart. Police were called and the United Nations was notified.

By the time they reached Gate 11, the doors to the tunnel had been closed. Mr. Crows scrambled for the door, Mr. Trafalgar running much slower and chewing on his food a few feet behind. The man at the gate stepped in their way.

"I'm sorry but you cannot…"

Mr. Crows had taken him down by pouncing on him; he had the man's throat in his mouth. Mr. Trafalgar caught up and swatted him on the nose. "No!" he scolded. "No biting the man!"

Mr. Trafalgar threw open the door and ran down the tunnel, he stopped short of the fifteen foot drop to the tarmac. The plane was nowhere to be seen.

"Damn it!" he cursed, kicking the side of the tunnel. He pulled out a cigarette and lit it. Mr. Crows stood next to him, grimacing.

"What now?" Mr. Crows asked, not looking his partner in the eyes.

Mr. Trafalgar began walking back up the tunnel. He dug inside his jacket and pulled out his Blackberry. "I tell the boss we screwed up again and hope he doesn't hang us for this."

"Man, we're supposed to be kings." Mr. Crows pouted. "How could this get any worse for us?"

They stepped out of the tunnel and back into the terminal. The cocking of several dozen guns echoed throughout the evacuated section of the airport. Security, policemen, and SWAT surrounded them. A man with a megaphone yelled out to them.

"Put your hands in the air! Lie down on your stomachs!"

CHAPTER 29

The plane had taxied to the end of the runway and was waiting for the go ahead from the tower to take off. Everyone had settled in and was preparing for a long flight. Grant restlessly fidgeted in his seat, much to the dismay of Violet. *What is taking so long?* she thought. *We've been sitting here for almost half an hour.*

The speakers overhead crackled and the voice of the pilot filled the cabin.

"Okay, everybody. We apologize for the delay, seems there was a disturbance in the airport but everything is okay now. We will be taking off in three minutes. Thank you for your patience and choosing Alitalia. Buono Italiano!"

"Thank God!" Violet hissed. She was nudged and elbowed by Grant one time too many. "Jesus, Grant would you please stop moving around?"

"I'm shorry," Grant slurred leaning in too close for Violet's liking. He was definitely doped up from the Xanax but his fear of flying was more powerful than the drugs. "I'm jush a bit nervoush. I can't get comforb... comfotle... comflor... comfy!"

Violet pushed him away. "Just try, please?" She turned away and looked at the folder in her lap. As soon as they were in the air she would spread it out on her tray and delve into it. *Was there really something in all this claptrap? Could her father really have been a protector of some ancient secret? From Jesus no less?* Violet never even believed in Jesus. Violet never really believed in much of anything. Except shopping. But she'd never really had enough money to practice that religion as much as she'd have liked. But she always felt there *had* to be some kind of higher power. *You can't really say all this, this world they lived in, was a quirk of fate. A scientific accident that made man crawl out of the Pacific ocean a few million years ago? Or something like that.* Violet never really paid attention in High School.

She looked up briefly as the flight attendant had begun her pre-flight routine. The flight attendant went through the motions with the zest and energy of a glassy-eyed zombie. Oxygen masks, floatation devices, vomit bags, bathrooms, and sadly, absolutely no smoking. She spoke each part in English and then Italian. When she was done she said, 'Graci!' and returned to her seat and buckled up. Violet heard the engines roar and they lurched forward.

"Oh, Lord." Grant mumbled. "Thish ish it."

The plane turned onto the runway, paused, and the pilot gunned it. Soon they were speeding along at hundreds of miles an hour. They felt a few small bumps. The plane shook. Grant groaned.

Violet shook her head as Grant hyperventilated. He pulled his backpack from under his seat and clung to it like a scared baby monkey clings to its mom. He began a slurred mantra, different from the one he'd done in Violet's car.

"I thought you passed out if you're scared." Violet asked.

Grant peaked out from behind his backpack. "It'sh more of a shudden thing. Not jusht an overall fear thing."

The plane left the ground, the G-force kicking in. Grant puffed his cheeks. "I don't feel sho good."

"So you mean like something shocking?" Violet smiled. "A scary shock?"

"Yesh."

Violet leaned over Grant and looked out the window. Her eyes widened, "A piece of the wing just fell off!" she yelled, just as they hit turbulence.

Grant opened his mouth to scream but his eyes fluttered and his head dropped onto his backpack. He was out cold.

Violet sat back, amused and happy that she'd have a while to herself. She noticed several people glaring at her. They muttered disapproval and shook their heads. She shrugged. *Fuck 'em if they can't take a joke.*

CHAPTER 30

Mr. Trafalgar and Mr. Crows stood with their arms held up high. Mr. Crows was making a low growling noise like a guard dog ready to attack.

"Don't do anything. You'll get us shot." Mr. Trafalgar softly warned his partner. He cleared his throat and spoke to the wall of firearms trained on them. "We're actors! Famous ones!"

Mr. Trafalgar and Crows slowly removed their hats, moustaches and ponchos.

A SWAT sniper looked through his scope and recognized them immediately. "Hey, they're telling the truth!"

With a chorus of sighs, the entire room instantly relaxed. The guns and rifles were uncocked, re-holstered and a round of applause grew. They crowded around the two celebrities like children to the ice cream man.

The swarm of officers yelled out as they met the Hollywood couple.

"Wow. What a performance!"

"You guys are great!"

"We cleared the entire airport because of you! Awesome acting!"

"Fantastic. I'm a huge fan of yours!"

"I'm being paid double overtime to meet you!"

"God bless you celebrities!"

"Pose with my Glock!"

Mr. Trafalgar lowered his hands and waved like royalty. "Yes, thank you. We appreciate it. Thank you." He shook hands, posed for photos and signed 9mm cartridges. "Yes, you've all been Punk'd. Mr. Kutcher is just outside that window. Great fun. Yes, we were wonderful."

Mr. Crows begrudgingly did the same. He forced his big white smile, hugged smelly strangers and talked on their cell phones to

Brian J. Orlowski

family members, wishing them a happy birthday or anniversary. In the back of his head he'd already snapped everybody's neck, twice.

Mr. Trafalgar was smiling for a photo when his Blackberry beeped. He excused himself from the two men hanging on him. "I've got to take this." He looked at the Caller ID, it was Mr. Maystyne. *Damn, he must have heard already.* He answered the call. "Yes, sir. I'm sure you heard what…"

Mr. Trafalgar's eyes bulged from the geyser of cursing pouring through his phone. "But I…"

"Yes, but…"

"But, sir, I…"

"Yes, sir." he hung up.

Mr. Crows sidled up to his taller counterpart. "Was he mad?"

"Very much so, little buddy."

"What are we doing now?"

Mr. Trafalgar smiled. "My personal jet is being flown out for us even as we speak. I'll fly us out to Italy myself. So we gotta stay cool and lay low. We can't bring attention to ourselves."

"Gotcha!" Mr. Crows agreed.

They wandered back to the throng of fans and stood for more photos.

CHAPTER 31

Hours into the trans-Atlantic flight, Violet found herself consumed with the notes Peter had given her. At first she glossed through them, sipping on her vodka tonic, feeling as interested as when she sat in Algebra class, or History, or English. Or even Sex Ed, of which she had already known far too much and subsequently ended up correcting the teacher on more than a few things.

But as she flipped through the pages, some hand-written, some printed from the Internet, and some photocopied from sundry newspapers and magazines, Violet saw a pattern take place. What she initially saw as hogwash, or bullshit as she preferred to call it, was starting to make sense.

She glanced over at Grant. He'd been asleep the entire time and she saw no sign of him waking at all soon. *Thank God.* She winced when she noticed the waterfall of saliva running from his gaping mouth. It flowed over his chin and pooled in his collar. She looked away before she got nauseous.

She returned her attentions to the folder. It was amazing. There really may be something to this Twelvist hoopla.

The Twelvist theory was not a new one; it had been around for millennia, long before Christ had even walked the earth. Twelvists point out the importance of the number twelve in a vast collection of documents culled throughout history. Twelve shows up in science, music and language, not just religious texts.

Violet skipped ahead, she was amazed each time the magical number appeared in historical religion. She was reading more words, and faster, in this one flight than she had in all five years of college. She flipped page after page.

The religious connections were endless. They didn't adhere just to Christianity, but traveled across time and continents. Judaism, Ancient Greek, even Buddhism.

The Ancient Buddhists' teaching repeatedly divided teachings, thought processes and beliefs into twelve sections. First is the Twelve Nidanas; also known as the Twelve Links of Causation or the Twelve Links of Conditioned Existence. Within that teaching lays the Twelve Domains. Also The Four Noble Truths, which are Dukkha, Samudya, Nirodha and Marga, when broken down into their resulting actions, are actually twelve distinctive courses of action. There is also the Upanisa Sutta in the Samyutta Nikaya, in which the conditions not for suffering but for enlightenment are given. Again, there are twelve in total. Even the great Buddha himself is known for his Twelve Great Deeds. Buddhism is a shining example of the power of the number twelve. Like western civilization, Asian culture also divides its zodiac into a twelve year cycle.

Twelve appears throughout the Bible, in both the Old and New Testaments. In the Old Testament, the biblical Jacob had 12 sons, who were the progenitors of the Twelve Tribes of Israel. There were, of course, the twelve apostles. And in the Book of Revelation 12.1, there is a reference to a woman wearing a crown of twelve stars. In Christian religion, there are twelve lesser prophets and twelve traditional sybils. There are also the twelve stones and the twelve princes. And who could forget the Twelve Days of Christmas?

In Shi'a Islam, there are twelve Imams. These twelve early leaders of Islam are—Ali, Hasan, Husayn, and nine of Husayn's descendants.

The Roman Empire ruled using the Law of the Twelve Tables.

Eastern Orthodoxy observes 12 Great Feasts. In Ancient Greek religion, the Twelve Olympians were the principle gods of the pantheon.

And of the most discussed and fought over twelves in all history was the Mayan calendar, which mysteriously ended on 12/21/2012. This day, which was the last Mayan cycle on the calendar, was a cycle of 144,000 days. A multiple of twelve.

Some Twelvists argued it wasn't the end of time, or the end of days, but the date when mankind would be ready to receive *the gift*. Whatever that gift may be, either information or enlightenment, immortality or the secrets of the universe, it was given to Christ who then divided it into twelve equal parts. It was this gift that many believe would be imparted unto mankind.

Violet sat back in awe. *It couldn't be.* she thought. Not that she didn't believe there was a chance that this theory may be true, she'd always tried to be open-minded to new ideas. Actually that was a lie. She was entirely close-minded to pretty much anything. But she wasn't biased in her disbeliefs, which she felt was a backwards form of open-mindedness. What couldn't be was that her father, and now she herself, were carriers of this great and holy honor. That she, Violet Sterne, could possibly be part of anything of such potentially great importance.

It was mind numbing.

Overwhelming.

Inspiring.

She needed a cigarette.

Violet was suddenly distracted by kissing noises. She looked over at the comatose Grant. He was fondling his backpack and puckering his lips, kissing at the empty air. Violet nearly gagged. She took the napkin from under her drink and draped it over his face. At least she wouldn't have to see him.

She sighed. It was criminal to make smokers suffer through such a long flight without a smoke break. *Insufferable.* And the bathrooms were close. So close. Maybe no one would notice just one cigarette. One. Little. Smoke.

CHAPTER 32

"Yes, sir. I understand." Mr. Trafalgar repeated for the fifth time. "No, I get it now. When have we ever let you down?" He grit his teeth as he listened. "Okay, I mean recently. Other than today." He threw his cigarette to the ground. "Okay, yes, that one was rather messy. Yes, very bloody. But it turned into a huge positive when they thought it was a publicity stunt. Mr. Crows' box office numbers jumped big time!"

The two actors were standing on the tarmac. One of Mr. Trafalgar's private planes, a Boeing 707, taxied toward them.

"What's he saying?" Mr. Crows pranced about. "Which box office numbers?"

Mr. Trafalgar pushed Mr. Crows aside and listened to his employer. "Okay, consider it done. My plane is here. We'll be in Italy in less than eight hours."

The plane stopped and the engines whined down. Mr. Crows ran about the plane, waiting for the door to open, like a dog excited to take a car ride. Stairs were driven up to the plane and the temporary pilot stepped out. Mr. Crows ran up the stairs knocking the man aside.

The man righted himself and walked down the stairs. He shook hands with Mr. Trafalgar and said, "She's all yours. She flew smooth."

"Thanks, have her fueled immediately. I told the tower to stop all other flights and clear the runways for me. They listened, of course."

"Yes, Mr. Trafalgar." The man said then thumped Mr. Trafalgar on the forehead. "Hail Teegeeack!"

Mr. Trafalgar returned the gesture. "Hail Teegeeack!"

CHAPTER 33

Violet had snuck into the bathroom, sucked down a cigarette in record time, and returned to her seat, giddy as a schoolgirl. *I did it!* She thought. *That was so easy.* She planned on having another in half an hour if not sooner.

A flight attendant tapped her shoulder. "Scusi." The woman said.

Violet frowned, the jig was up.

"Excuse me, miss." The flight attendant repeated with a thick Italian accent. "We have been told that you were, ah, smoking in the bagno, the bathroom." She wagged her finger. "No fumare. There is no smoking. We will let it slide once, but to do it again, you will be arrestato when we get to Rome. Comprendere?"

Violet fumed, but she knew she was beat. "Yes, I understand."

The flight attendant nodded, smiled, and walked away.

Vaffanculo! Violet thought. She was proud to know how to curse someone out in almost any language. Well, at least she got one cigarette in, and they were almost halfway to Italy. How was she going to kill another four hours? She thought about rifling through Grant's backpack and taking a few Xanax herself. She had unfortunately hit her limit on in-flight drinks and was allowed no more alcohol, no matter how much she pleaded.

Back to the books! She thought and dug out the folder on The Twelve.

Grant mumbled something and Violet turned to look at him.

"Did you say something?" Violet asked.

Grant was looking at her, but not really. It was more through her. He mumbled another string of nonsense and smiled. His lips were wet with drool.

He's sleepwalking! Violet chuckled. *Well, actually sleepsitting. This could be entertaining.*

Grant rattled off another line of gibberish and suddenly reached for Violet's breast. Without hesitation she punched him in the nose. Grant's head flew backward, smacking into the cabin wall with a loud thud.

"Ow!" he screamed, drawing the attention of the surrounding passengers.

"It's okay!" Violet announced. "He's just having a nightmare."

Grant rubbed his nose with his sleeve, leaving a long smear of blood. "I'm bleeding! What just happened?" He looked shocked.

"Must've been quite a nightmare." Violet said. "Do you remember any of it?"

"I was, um…" Grant blushed as he vaguely remembered his dream. He wouldn't meet Violet's eyes. "I don't remember what I was dreaming," he lied.

"Oh, okay. It wasn't dirty, was it?" Violet played with him.

"What?" Grant stuttered. "N-no! Who me? No! I don't remember!" Grant looked at the pile of papers spread out on the tray in front of Violet and quickly changed the subject. "Oh, I see you've been reading Peter's Twelvist folder."

"Huh? Oh, yeah. It's actually pretty interesting stuff." Violet started flipping through the pages. "I never realized how much the number twelve is referenced in the Bible. Not to mention all the other religions."

"And it's not just religion." Grant pointed out. "Nature, science, music. There are signs of Twelvist theories in all aspects of life."

"Like what?"

"Well, aside from the obvious twelves that we all know and use every day." Grant waited for a response.

Violet stared at him blankly.

"You know. Twelve inches in a foot. Twelve months in a year. Twelve zodiac signs. Two twelve hour sections to a day. Twelve items in a dozen. The twelve step program. Twelve members in a jury. In chess, there are twelve ways of arranging the queen so she cannot be captured." Grant explained. "Twelve ounces is the perfect pour for beverages, like soda and beer."

"Oh those things. Yes, of course." Violet nodded. *Mmmm, beer.* She'd kill for a beer right now. Or twelve.

"Okay, good. Then maybe you also know of the epic poem of Twelve Labours of Hercules. There are also other literary works, such as The Twelve Caesars, written in 121 AD. There's been The Twelve Dancing Princesses by the Brothers Grimm and, of course, Twelfth Night by William Shakespeare."

"Um, yeah. Never read any of those."

"That's okay. But you should read them when you get the chance. They're fantastic."

"I'll get right on it."

"Getting back to twelve. Did you know that there are twelve orders of soil? In music, there are twelve notes or tones before the series repeats itself and twelve major and twelve minor keys as applied by the twelve tone equal temperament. The Chinese use a twelve year cycle called the Earthly Branches. Did you know the minute hand on a clock moves twelve times as fast as the hour hand? It's the number of levels in judo. There are twelve pairs of ribs in almost every human. And twelve men have walked on the moon."

"Jeez, I had no idea!"

"Few people do. If you really dig into cultures and religion, science and nature, you'll find endless connections to twelve. Which is why Twelvists believe that the information given by the aliens has permeated throughout this planet and shows up in almost everything."

"But they gave it to Jesus, and he has kept it hidden. How could it permeate throughout the world if it has been kept under lock and key?"

"Well, you'll learn more about that when we get to the Sistine Chapel. But I'll tell you this, what they gave Jesus were the secrets to everything. But what they gave us, the world, was done long before Jesus walked the Earth. So portions of this information, tidbits were leaked, either purposely or by accident, and it all played a role in the advancement of mankind and civilization."

"Wow. That sounds deep." Violet rolled her eyes.

"Still a doubter?" Grant shrugged. "You'll be a believer before this is all over."

"I'm learning. And trying to keep an open mind." Violet conceded.

"You know, I'm surprised Peter didn't give you his favorite book. Now that would have opened your eyes to it all."

"You mean this one?" Violet pulled the crumpled, dog-eared novel from her purse. The book depicted Jesus on the cover looking skyward with his hands held toward the Heavens; a beam of light was lowering the number twelve unto him. The book was old, published in 1987.

"Ah, yes. He did." Grant exclaimed. "Now that is one great read! It's an oldie, but a goodie!"

"I thought it was a joke." Violet looked at the cover. It was called *Holy Twelve, Holy Crap* by Don Brawn.

CHAPTER 34

The Boeing 707 flew over the Atlantic, high above the rough seas below. Mr. Trafalgar sat in the cockpit, smoking his cigarette and flicking the ashes on the floor. He exhaled a large cloud of smoke.

Mr. Crows was a terrible co-pilot. He couldn't sit in the seat very long, he always needed to get up, stretch, jog in place or scratch himself.

At one point, Mr. Crows wouldn't stop touching buttons and playing with switches. When he almost hit the emergency fuel dump button, which would have released their fuel and emptied their tanks, leaving them to forcibly crash their plane in the middle of the ocean, Mr. Trafalgar had had enough.

"Get out!" Mr. Trafalgar screamed. "Dude, you're killing me here!"

"What?" What'd I do?" Mr. Crows curled up, fearful of a flying backhand.

"You don't hit that unless we're going to crash! If you had dumped our fuel we'd never make it to Italy! We'd have just coasted into the Atlantic."

"I didn't know!" Mr. Crows cried. "I'm sorry. I'm fidgety."

"Just get in the back." Mr. Trafalgar threw his cigarette at him. "You're driving me crazy. Just go in back and stay out of trouble."

"Fine." Mr. Crows pouted and slinked away. He intentionally slammed the cockpit door behind him.

"Who does he think he is?" Mr. Crows mumbled to himself as he dragged his feet along the plush carpeting of the cabin. "We're both Thetan 7's." He dropped himself onto one of the several leather couches that surrounded the room.

Mr. Crows found a remote control on a mahogany coffee table and began pushing buttons. "Can I press these buttons?!" He yelled out, though there was no way Mr. Trafalgar would be able to hear him.

After flipping through many channels at breakneck speed, a loud, bright, obnoxious group of four men in Star Trek-like uniforms filled the screen. They held instruments and sang songs that appealed to three-year-olds and ruptured eardrums of anyone above ten years of age. Within minutes all was forgotten and Mr. Crows clapped his hands, giggled, and jumped about on the couch to the silly music and funny noises provided by The Wiggles.

CHAPTER 35

"Tell me about this Don Brawn guy." Violet said, realizing they still had two hours to kill.

"Well, not much to say other than what's in the book. The man is a recluse now. His theories and research weren't received very well back in 1982." Grant explained. "Some claim there was a conspiracy against him by the Catholic Church, that they'd bribed the media and had him blacklisted or negatively reviewed."

"Did they?"

"No one knows for sure, but what Mr. Brawn wrote about, if true, would be very damning of the church, and would show that they'd been lying and covering up things for centuries."

"You mean aliens and The Twelve."

"Yes, and much more. His theories went further back, like I said before, to the beginning of man on earth."

"Are you saying they were here before us?"

"They made us."

"What?" Violet laughed. "Are you nuts?"

"Maybe. But what about the missing link? What was that leap in evolution? Where is that one step where primates became hominids? Why can't we find that segue in our lineage? We find fossils of this, fossils of that, we've found everyone that's partied on this planet, but there's that one guy missing. Who is he?"

"I don't know. But you're saying he was an alien?"

"We don't know. I'm not saying they boinked some apes to help evolution. But maybe they did come down and tinker with what was here. Maybe they saw where everything was going and knew we needed a push in the right direction. With their technology, they could have influenced our development."

"That's bullshit."

"That's what you and alot of people would say. But there's a lot of folk that think to the contrary."

"Where's the proof? What do you base this cockamamie stuff on?"

"Well, the book you're holding is considered the Twelvist's Bible. Don Brawn is the pioneer in this belief." Grant took the book from Violet's hand and flipped it around to show the back cover. A scholarly looking man, in his mid-forties sat at an expansive oak desk. He had on a tweed jacket with the stereotypical elbow patches. He was surrounded by shelves of books, assorted papers and a large globe. One was to assume this was to add to his image as a purveyor of noteworthy information. "It's a shame that more people didn't take him seriously. The man could have revolutionized modern religion."

"And he's a hermit now. We could have used him on this little trip of ours."

"You're not kidding." Grant thought for a moment. "I think he lives in the Los Angeles area but I'm not certain. I'm sure it's on the Internet somewhere. You can always find everything on the Internet."

Violet briefly thought about those pictures someone had taken of her in college. She flushed red and quickly put it out of her mind. "So what was his theory about the beginning of man?" she quickly asked.

"That God and the angels as mentioned in the Old Testament were actually aliens." Grant stated.

"And what makes him think that?"

"The evidence can be found throughout the Old Testament. There's references and descriptions of aliens in almost every scripture."

"Of the Bible?"

"Yes, indeed."

"What about the New Testament?"

"Well that's even more plentiful. That's a Twelvist's dream when it comes to references that support their beliefs. It's chock full of hints and clues."

"This is so overwhelming."

"Well, we have nearly two hours of flight left. I'd suggest you dive into Mr. Brawn's book. How fast can you read?"

"Um, well." Violet looked away. "Not great."

"Well, give it a whirl. I won't bother you." Grant dug into his backpack and produced a PSP; he connected headphones to it and plugged then into his ears. In minutes he was playing the latest Call of Duty, shooting, running, and blowing things up. "Go ahead, I'll be busy with this!" he said too loudly.

Violet sighed and opened the book. She promised herself that she'd read as quickly as she could and really try to absorb it. Ten minutes later she was asleep.

CHAPTER 36

Violet awoke to the sounds of an announcement, first in Italian and then English.

"Dare il benvenuto all'Italia. Speriamo che lei ha piaciuto il suo volo." And then. "Welcome to Italy. We hope you enjoyed your flight."

Damn! Violet looked out the window. They had already landed and were pulling up to the terminal. It wasn't dark out yet, but the sun was on its way out. She could see the lights of Rome in the distance. She looked at her watch. According to her watch it was almost midnight. *Holy shit!* she cursed. *I slept this whole time? And why didn't Grant...*

Violet looked over and saw Grant entirely out. He was drooling again. The PSP was lying limp in his hands, the screen blank, presumably from dead batteries.

Violet smacked him in the side of the head.

"Ow! Dang!"

"Another nightmare?" Violet asked. "You should stay awake. It'll hurt less."

Grant groggily looked about. "Oh. Are we here already? That went fast."

"Yeah, and you let me fall asleep!" Violet shook Don Brawn's book in his face. "I didn't get to read this!"

"How far did you get?"

"I didn't get past the introduction."

"Well you looked so cute sleeping I didn't want to disturb you. Besides, I can fill you in on everything as we go." Grant stretched his arms and yawned. "Plus I have the feeling we're going to be needing all the sleep we can get." He looked out the window. "Ah, Fiumicino International Airport. What a site!" Grant dug out his camera and took a photo through the window.

"Fumi-what?" Violet was looking at her boarding pass. "It says here the Leonardo da Vinci International Airport."

"That's what some call it. I, for one, do not."

"Isn't he a famous artist or…"

"Hey! Don't get me worked up." Grant stuffed his PSP into his backpack. "I don't get in the way of you smoking and you don't talk about… that guy."

"Wow. Whatever… freak."

The plane had stopped and the 'unbuckle your seat belts' light flared accompanied by a loud *ding*. The flight attendants quickly assumed formation and opened the door. People began bustling out of the cabin like cattle.

The flight attendants repeated the practiced routine to each departing customer. "Ringraziarla per volare con noi. Speriamo di vederla ancora." And then. "Thank you for flying with us. We hope to see you again."

Violet sat eagerly in her seat as the aisle filled with people. She tried with all her might to be patient. *I'm a stranger in a strange land. Must be nice to the natives.* she told herself. Twenty-five seconds later. *Screw that!* Violet pushed her way in front of an elderly man, she knew she was within thirty yards of a having a cigarette. She could taste the freedom!

Grant smiled meekly at the old man, who grunted in dissatisfaction. Grant humbly apologized for his traveling companion's rudeness. "Spiacente sono brutto," he said. The old man cracked a huge smile, nodded and laughed. Grant nodded and laughed with him. *Phew! Good thing I know the language.* Grant thought.

Violet tore through the tunnel until she reached the concourse. A smile split her face. Everywhere she looked she saw a beautiful sight. Ashtrays. Ashtrays filled to the brim with grey, crushed, burnt-out cigarettes. Everywhere people were smoking. Violet was sure she heard a choir of angels. She held her hands to the heavens. "Thank you!"

Grant stepped out of the tunnel and onto Italian terra firma. He dropped to one knee, drew a circle on the ground with his finger five times, brought it to his mouth and kissed his hand, then let it go like a dove. He stood up and smiled. "I'm ready!"

By the time Grant reached the concourse, Violet was sitting in a chair smoking her second cigarette. She looked up at him and smiled, like a heroin addict who just had their fix.

"Italy is awesome!" she squealed in delight.

"Most people are taken in by the art, the culture, the people or the food. For me it's the history and the architecture. For you… it's because you can smoke almost everywhere."

"That's right." Violet beamed.

"That's sad." Grant corrected her.

"Hey, isn't that artist guy you like from around here. What's his name? Oh yeah, Da Vinci!" she laughed.

Grant crossed his arms. "Not funny. We had a deal."

"Yeah, lay off my smoking."

"Fair enough." Grant looked around. "We have to look for money exchange."

"Why? American dollars don't work here?" Violet asked.

Grant shuddered. "You're kidding, right?"

"Leonardo da…"

"Okay, shut it!" Grant turned and walked up the concourse. "C'mon." He had a very serious look on his face Violet had never seen before.

Violet caught up to the scuttling Grant. "I'm sorry. I was just kidding." She nudged him. "Really. I am sorry."

Grant stopped dead in his tracks and turned to her. "We are here on a very important mission that your father, your recently deceased father I might remind you, sent us on. If Peter and I are right, we are onto something very serious and potentially dangerous. I am here purely out of the goodness of my heart and I would appreciate a little respect!"

Violet was frozen. She hadn't seen such seriousness or passion in the man before. She suddenly felt very stupid, and childish.

"I'm sorry, Grant. Really. I've never really been anywhere and I guess I get carried away. Really, I am sorry."

Grant paused. "Fine. Apology accepted." He smiled. "Hug?"

"No chance."

"Thought so." Grant went back to surveying mode. "Okay, once we exchange our money we need to find transportation from here to Rome. Not to mention it's getting late. We'll need a place to stay for the night. Hey, there's what we need." Grant scrambled up to the exchange window.

"Stay for the night?" Violet asked, then followed Grant as he ran toward a booth. "Aren't we just doing our thing here and going home? Hey, wait!"

The woman behind the counter smiled as Grant approached. "Quanto lei amerebbe scambiare?"

"Oh, um." Grant hesitated. "No, we're not hungry. We would like to exchange American dollars for Euro."

The woman stared at Grant for a moment, then spoke with a thick accent. "I said, how much would you like to exchange?"

"Oh, yes! Of course!" Grant chuckled. "I knew what you meant." He patted his pockets and then turned to Violet. "Can I have that credit card again?"

"Damnit! I knew it." Violet stomped the ground as she dug into her purse.

CHAPTER 37

Mr. Trafalgar had radioed in that he and Mr. Crows were arriving. The airport was shut down within minutes. Commuter planes were ordered to circle the airport indefinitely. The larger 747s, loaded with tourists and weary travelers, were rerouted to not-so-nearby Ciampino Airport in southern Rome.

Fifteen minutes later, they were welcomed at their gate; crowds of fans gathered and showered the two with flowers, kisses and screams of marital proposals. Some women were also joining in.

"Okay little man." Mr. Trafalgar said. "We gotta be quick about this. Our objective landed a little while ago. We gotta find 'em before they leave the airport."

Mr. Trafalgar and Mr. Crows obliged the swarm as long as possible, before losing them by taking an employee-only elevator and ducking into a bathroom.

Minutes later, two very unfeminine nuns strode out of the men's room, one tall and fattish nun alongside a shorter psychotic-eyed nun. Their long black habits and gowns were flowing behind them. They also wore Ray-Bans.

People stared at the odd looking sisters but no one recognized the famous duo beneath them.

"See, little buddy?" Mr. Trafalgar whispered. "I told you these cool outfits would work, didn't I?"

"I feel like a moron." Mr. Crows growled. He scratched at his groin like a baseball player in the ninth inning on a hot day. "And I don't understand why you made us wear bras and black stockings underneath. No one can see that! We could have kept our street clothes on!"

"You gotta get into the role, brother. Besides, I thought you looked kinda cute in them. A sassy nun!"

"I don't get you, boss."

"I know little buddy."

They trolled the airport for ten minutes, around baggage claim and car rentals. It wasn't until they neared the Euro Exchange that Violet had caught Mr. Crows' eye. She was standing angrily with her arms folded.

"Is that her?" he yelled.

Mr. Trafalgar kicked his diminutive partner. "Quiet! You don't want her to hear you." Mr. Trafalgar stared at her for a moment. "Yep. That's her buddy. Good job." A man returned from the exchange window and spoke to her. "I see the mystery man is still with her. He don't look like much."

"I could kill him now!" Mr. Crows growled.

"We have our orders. No killing. We follow them. It looks like they're heading outside."

CHAPTER 38

Grant and Violet exited the airport. It was even darker now and the lights of the airport and distant city twinkled brilliantly in the purple and orange twilight of Rome. Grant again had his camera in hand and was clicking and winding like a maniac. Violet fumed that Grant had 200 Euro in his pocket and she had to dig deeper into her limited well of credit.

"200 Euro should be enough to get us to Rome, into the chapel, and back." Grant said. "Plus a nice lunch. Oh, and a souvenir!"

Violet growled. "We are not eating. We are not getting you a knickknack. We are taking any money that's left and trading it back for American dollars."

"Okay, you're the boss. But we'll be here a while, we're going to need to eat." Grant sighed. "But I bet you'll spend it once you run out of smokes."

"It's my money! I'll get smokes when I want to." Violet said. "You're lucky I let you buy me that English to Italian book."

"Well, you're going to need it. I'd hate to think of us getting separated and you not able to communicate with anyone. Rome is a big and confusing city. You'd get swallowed alive by this place."

Grant scanned the front drive, as cars and taxis picked up and dropped off dozens upon dozens of tourists. "Okay, we have to get a taxi."

"How do you say taxi in Italian?" Violet asked.

"Taxi." Grant answered.

"Oh."

Grant flagged down a taxi. A tiny white car that one would expect fifty clowns to get out of drove over to them. It screeched to a stop and they climbed in.

The driver looked over his shoulder, briefly at Grant, but smiled as he scanned Violet up and down. He spoke in a smoky voice. "Dove lei vuole andare la bella signora?"

Violet blushed and giggled, she knew just from the tone of his voice she had just been complimented.

"Scusi." Grant cleared his throat. "Le sue puzze di automobile di piedi." *Your car smells like feet.*

Violet was politely escorted from the car by the sizable driver. Grant, unfortunately, was handled with much less care. The burly man lifted Grant by his neck with one arm and tossed him to the pavement. "Americani stupidi! Nessuna classe! Uscire dalla mia automobile!" The driver bellowed with rage. He hopped back in the taxi and sped off.

"What the Hell did you say?" Violet screamed.

Grant dusted himself off and straightened his collar, looking much like Rodney Dangerfield. "Nothing bad. Must be a different dialect than what I was taught."

Violet waved her arm at another taxi. "This time I'll do the talking."

Another small car pulled over for them. Once inside Violet pushed Grant aside and leaned toward the driver. "Excuse me. We need to go to Cavalieri Hilton in Rome. Yes?"

"Si, bella donna, si! Cavalieri Hotel." The driver nodded and put the car in gear.

Violet shoved Grant again. "Now how tough was that, Mister I-speak-Italian?" she mocked.

"I do speak Italian." Grant defended himself. "It must be a regional thing."

"Whatever. Just keep your Italian to yourself."

Grant mumbled under his breath. "Keep your Italian to yourself." he mocked.

"I heard that."

Forty-five minutes, thirty-two kilometers, and a whole lot of no-talking later, they arrived in central Rome. The driver spoke to his passengers in broken but easily understandable English. "This is the heart of Rome. Soon we pass the Vatican and then we get to Cavalieri. Ten more minutes, si?"

"Grazi." Grant said. "Il suo fungo è malato come il papa." *The pope is sick with fungus.*

The car swerved and skidded to a halt. The driver turned around to face Grant. "Il papa?" His eyes were filled with rage.

Oh crap. He did it again! Violet smacked Grant in the side of the head which caught the attention of the driver. "Shut up! What did I tell you?" She quickly flipped through the book while Grant rubbed his battered ear. Violet pointed at a phrase in the book. "Sono spiacente! Sono spiacente." Violet said, pronouncing it poorly but well enough for the driver to understand. She added, "Per favore." Violet quickly ran through several more pages until she found what she wanted. She pointed at Grant. "Mentalmente svantaggiato." *Mentally retarded.*

The driver paused and thought about that. Then a huge smile broke out and he laughed heartily. "Si! Mentalmente svantaggiato. Si, si!" He stopped laughing abruptly and pointed a finger at Grant. "Disgusta per insultare il papa."

"Amo delle rane." Grant meekly replied. *I love frogs.*

The driver laughed even louder. "Svantaggiato! Si!" Soon he was driving again.

Violet glared at Grant. "Last warning."

CHAPTER 39

The odd pairing of nuns had ghosted Violet and Grant from a safe distance. They watched at the first failed attempt to get into a taxi. Mr. Crows laughed as the taxi driver tossed Grant about like rag doll. Mr. Trafalgar was tempted to intervene when it looked like the driver was going to kill Grant and possibly Violet, but everything worked out. The nun had re-holstered her .45 hidden beneath her gown. Violet then hailed a second taxi and soon they were successfully off to Rome.

Mr. Crows jumped about. "They're getting away!" he cried.

"Nothing to worry about," Mr. Trafalgar motioned behind them. "Our car just pulled up."

Parked near the curb, just outside the exit, surrounded by a dozen gawking onlookers was a 2011 Ferrari 612 Scaglietti sparkling in the morning sun.

The two nuns walked up to the car and a man handed Mr. Trafalgar the keys. In his own voice he thanked the man. "Thanks brother."

"You're welcome, Mr. Tra…" The man quickly stopped as Mr. Trafalgar froze. *Crap! I almost gave him away!* "Um, er, Miss… Nun… Nun-sister-lady!"

Mr. Trafalgar stuck his finger in the man's face. "Not cool! I'm undercover here!"

The crowd watched as the two sisters climbed into the vehicle, not sure what to make of the odd sight.

Seconds later, the $165,000 car revved its engine and peeled out onto the road, the nuns' habits blowing in the breeze.

CHAPTER 40

The taxi drove around the majestic circular driveway in front of the Rome Cavalieri Hilton Hotel. The white marble statues were stark against the lush green grass and trees in the landscape of the hotel's entrance. Violet was wide-eyed and she was entirely speechless at the grandeur and beauty.

Grant took pictures with his camera.

The driver stopped at the front doors and a doorman in a white jacket, gloves and hat opened the door for Violet. She stepped out and smiled at him, he was a really good-looking guy. She blushed but was quickly annoyed when Grant popped out and snapped a photo of the doorman. "Graci!" Grant chirped.

"Doesn't that thing ever run out of film?" Violet asked.

"My camera?" Grant tilted his head. "Oh, there's no film in here."

Violet was dumbfounded. "What?" she screamed. "There's no goddam film in there? Are you insane?"

"No, I am not." Grant acted insulted. "My film is in my head. I take pictures with my mind. I just use this to frame out my images."

Violet hesitated half a second. "Give me that freaking thing!" she barked and lunged for Grant's camera.

Grant stepped sideways and held it at arm's length. "Hey! No!" He screeched and hid behind the doorman.

Violet didn't even try to go around the doorman, she went through him. The three toppled to the ground and tussled for half a minute. The taxi driver got out of his car, ran to the other side and quickly closed the passenger door, got back in and took off.

Violet climbed out of the pile, camera in hand. "Aha!" She yelled triumphantly and proceeded to throw the camera to the ground. It shattered into several dozen pieces.

"No!" Grant cried, still twisted up in the doorman. The doorman shoved Grant off of him, stood up and brushed down his uniform. There were smudges and scrapes all over his once pristine jacket. He placed his marred hat back on his head.

"Scandaloso!" he grumbled.

Violet smiled proudly, turned and walked into the entrance of the hotel.

Grant picked up the pieces of the camera and followed her. He frowned at the doorman. "Spiacente." he said correctly.

"Non parlarme!" The doorman replied.

Grant caught up with Violet at the Reception Desk. She'd obviously already found an English speaking employee.

"Yes, that's Miss Gerri Hender. I'm not sure what room she's in." Violet explained. "I know you can't tell me what room, but if you can call her room and tell her Violet Sterne, that's me, is here to see her, I'd very much appreciate it."

"Un momento." The woman behind the desk said. She typed into a computer for a few seconds. "Si. Yes. Miss Hender. You want I should ring her?"

"Yes, please. That'd be great." Violet beamed.

The woman picked up the phone and tapped in the necessary digits. She put the receiver to her ear and waited. A few moments later, she put the phone down.

"I'm sorry, but Miss Gender is not in her room." She placed a pen and paper on the counter. "You can leave a note if you wish."

Violet cursed under her breath. She turned to Grant. "What good does a note do? I can't leave her my cell phone number! You saw to that!"

"I didn't drop it, you did." Grant defended himself. "Besides, probably wouldn't use it here anyway. Roaming charges would kill you."

"So what do we do? We're not staying anywhere."

"Violet, be realistic. The Sistine Chapel has been closed for hours. It doesn't open again until around 9 tomorrow morning." Grant offered. "Look, it's late as it is and whether you like it or not, we're staying overnight here in Italy. So, we might as well accept that."

Violet sighed. "I guess." *This sucks.* She didn't want to be trapped in a room with Grant. "I'll leave Gerri a note and she can meet us at the chapel tomorrow morning." She turned back to the counter and jotted her note. She slid it back to the woman behind the counter. "Thanks very much," Violet said and turned back to Grant, who quickly snatched the note from the woman.

"We don't want Gerri to know we're here. She might run." Grant admonished.

"What are we going to do, surprise her and tackle her?"

"We'll jump off that bridge when we come to it." Grant said.

Violet sighed in frustration. "Fine. How far is the Sistine Chapel? We can find someplace to eat between there and here. Someplace cheap!"

Grant smiled. "We can walk to the chapel from here. Well, it's really late but we should be able to find a place to eat and stay. Besides, we're in Rome! We can walk, and there is so much to see along the way. It will be quite exciting and edifying."

"I don't know what edifying means, but you're not getting in my pants." Violet warned him as they walked out of the lobby.

"Wouldn't think of it." Grant said.

CHAPTER 41

Violet and Grant walked the cobblestone streets of western Rome, pausing at restaurants and outdoor cafes looking for cheap eats. As they passed the quaint eateries, the aroma of fresh Italian cooking filled their nostrils and set their stomachs to rumbling. Violet paused to look at the menu; she then salivated over a steaming plate of fettuccini, rather rudely, as it was on a table between a young couple about to dive into it. They sniffed at her derisively and mumbled something about tourists. Violet was about to hurl some American insults at them but Grant dragged her away.

"Let's not get into anything, Violet." Grant pointed to another café. "Did you know this establishment here is a Vicentino restaurant?" Grant explained.

"Smells good." Violet frowned, thinking about digging into her money so she could try some of the regional food. *It smells so damn good!* "Isn't there a diner somewhere around here? A nice cheap diner?"

Grant ignored her. "Vicentino coincidently enough is also the name of famous Italian composer Nicola Vicentino. He was a music theorist during the Renaissance. He has been followed closely by twelvists." Grant said as they continued down the winding street.

"Jeez." Violet huffed. "Does everything connect to the twelve?"

"Not everything." Grant said. "But a lot! You see, Nicola was such a visionary that many speculate he had to have had some knowledge of, or exposure to, a portion of The Twelve. It was his research into the keyboard layout of the archiorgano and of playing music in meantone temperament that lead to today's standard equal temperament, which divides octave into… can you guess how many equal parts?"

"Gee, um, twelve?" Violet said sarcastically.

"Very good, Miss Sterne. Yes, twelve equal parts. You see, twelve is the number of pitch classes in an octave. As I said on the plane, there are also twelve major keys and twelve minor keys. This is all part of the twelve tone equal temperament."

"Fascinating." Violet said dully.

They strolled past street cafes where tables with brightly colored tablecloths and sturdy canvas umbrellas shaded locals, old and young, as they sipped their afternoon aperitifs or spuntinos. They passed pastry shops, art exhibits, and a colorful flow of passersby, tourists, nationals, scenery and beautiful architecture.

Violet felt a wash of romance hit her, something she'd rarely felt. In fact, any kind of emotion other than anger and impatience was new to her. The power of the streets of Italy was working their magic. She glanced over at Grant. He was talking to a potted plant and shaking one of its fronds in greeting. *Damn, why him? Why couldn't I have been stuck here with Colin Farrel? Or Colin Firth? Hell, I'd take Colin Mochrie!* The air of romance dissipated like a soda belch.

Violet lit a cigarette and waited for Grant to finish whatever OCD routine he was running through. Suddenly her eyes widened in shock as she watched him reach into his backpack and retrieve a camera. A whole camera. Not a broken one. Not the old one put back together. But a new, shiny, exact duplicate of the one Violet herself shattered into a million pieces. Grant took a few pictures of the plant then returned to Violet's side.

"Where the hell did you get that?" Violet barked.

"What?" Grant looked around.

"The camera."

"Oh, um, that, I always carry a spare." Grant shrugged, his face reddened. "Or two. Sometimes more. Please don't smash them all. I promise not to get carried away with it."

"Fine. Keep it out of my face though." Violet looked down the street. "Can we just pick a place that looks inexpensive and eat?"

"Let's walk a few more blocks. I'm sure we'll come across something." Grant pointed westward. "Isn't this wonderful here?"

Violet's brief flood of romance was long forgotten. "Yeah, great. Let's keep moving." She stomped off down the cobblestone street.

"Jeez, you're a romantic." Grant mumbled as he fell in behind her.

Half a block behind them, two dark and flowing figures stepped from behind a column. The large nun tossed a burning cigarette to the ground; the diminutive nun shook nervously and chattered to himself.

"How's this place look?" Grant said. They had walked for another five minutes and approached a classic looking trattoria. It was decorated with columns, similar to the Pantheon, and sat nestled in a small piazza. Inside, they could hear the clinking of utensils and the cadence of pleasant Italian conversation.

"Looks expensive." Violet said warily, she subconsciously clutched her purse tighter. "Can you tell how much the food is here?"

"A few Euro. Who cares!" Grant stood aside the door and waved her in. "We're in Rome. Let's eat some native cuisine."

Violet growled as she walked inside, but no more than her stomach was. "Fine. But for every dollar over ten bucks, I'm punching you in the nose."

"You're such a lady." Grant laughed as he followed her inside.

Violet looked about the room as they waited in the foyer. She looked at dozens of tables that hosted couples, friends and families while they dined in the rustic but elegant trattoria. She pretty much expected to see tables with red and white checkered tablecloths, accordian music playing in the background and waiters with big bushy moustaches and bow ties. Instead of her stereotypical expectations, she marveled at the dark mahogany wall trim, brass highlights and textured stucco walls. The tables were beautifully decorated with yellow flowers, crystal ware and candles. The leather clad straight back chairs matched the dark wood tone of the walls' trim. The air was pungent with spices and baked goods. It was remarkably better than her Americanized vision of Italian restaurants.

A waiter quickly approached them and smiled widely. "Dare il benvenuto Al Canile. Lei è una bella coppia. L'americano, no?"

Grant nodded. "Si. American. Do you speak English?" The waiter nodded and turned to lead them to their table. "I do speak some English. Please, come with me." They followed the waiter, who pulled out Violet's chair for her.

The waiter's smile never vanished, even when talking. It was as though a stroke had permanently frozen his face into a Cheshire grin. "Shall I get you a drink? Vino?"

"Yes, please." Violet was suddenly smiling as widely as the waiter. "A drink, any drink, would be great."

"And for you?" The waiter asked of Grant.

"Water, please. I can't drink alcohol. Mixes with my meds."

"You're a real party." Violet said under her breath as the waiter shuffled off.

Grant either did not hear her or chose to ignore her. "So, what are you going to have?" he asked.

"I don't know," Violet said, scanning the menu. Her brow furrowed. "It's all in Italian. Why do they do that?" she said, frustrated.

"Because they're Italian." Grant replied.

"God. I don't know what anything is. Can you tell me?"

"Sure. What are you looking at?"

"What's zuppa?"

"Soup."

"Nah. What's pesce?"

"Fish."

"Nah. What's pasta fagioli? That's funny." Violet asked, saying the word with a hard G. Fag-ee-oh-lee.

"That's bean soup. And has nothing to do with alternate lifestyles. It's not even pronounced that way! It's pronounced fazool. Or fa-sool, depending on who you ask."

"Nah. Not in the mood for bean soup. What's…"

"Violet," Grant interrupted, a bit too loudly. "Why don't you tell me what you're in the mood for and I can find it on the menu?"

"Sheesh, Grant, don't get pissy. I will." Violet smiled wickedly. "You're such a little fagioli."

Grant grimaced. "I told you that it didn't mean that and it's not pronounced that…"

The smiling waiter returned, Grant stopped mid-sentence. The waiter placed their drinks on the table. "Are you ready to order?" He bowed slightly. "Need more time?"

"Yes, please." Violet said.

The perma-grin waiter nodded and trotted off.

"What are you in the mood for?" Grant asked.

Violet took a sip of her wine. "Aaaaah. That's more like it." She savored the drink before replying to Grant. "Do they have hamburgers?"

"Hamburgers?!" Grant was astonished. "Violet Sterne, we did not come thousands of miles to a foreign country to eat burgers!"

"Don't reprimand me. I'm not a child."

"Why don't you ask for a mac and cheese, Wolfgang Puck?" Grant barked. "Or maybe we could have found a McDonalds and gotten you a Happy Meal!"

"Okay, settle down. Did you need to take any pills? You're awfully cranky."

"What time is it?" Grant said.

Violet glanced at her watch. "5:30," she answered.

"No, no pills, I have time before my next round of meds. Thank you very much." Grant shook his menu at Violet. "Food? Any ideas?"

"Fine. No hamburgers. Can I just get some pasta in like a sauce?"

"You're in Italy!" Grant laughed. "Pasta in sauce is what they do best."

"Cool. I like that Chef Boyardee stuff."

The Cheshire waiter returned before Grant began crying. "Are you ready now?"

"Yes," Grant started. "She will have penne a la vodka."

"Vodka? Nice!" Violet squealed with delight. "Get my party on!"

"Relax, drunky. It's used in the sauce and the alcohol is burned off in the cooking. You can't get drunk off of it no matter how much you eat."

Violet pouted.

Grant returned his attention to the waiter. "Now. I would like the pasta fusilli con melanzane and the orecchiette con broccoli. But in the fusilli, can you not use garlic? I'm allergic. Oh, and no pepper. Or oregano." The waiter was scribbling furiously. "Oh, and leave out olive oil, use canola oil if you can. That would have made my skin get a rash. And when you make the orecchiette, can you leave out the heavy whipping cream and use margarine instead of butter. And again, no garlic, pepper or olive oil. Thanks." Grant closed his menu.

The waiter, still smiling but obviously forcing it, cursed under his breath and turned on his heels. "Si."

"Yep. I can see you're really enjoying authentic Italian cuisine." Violet quipped.

"That's as good as I can do. Trust me, you wouldn't want to be around me if I ate the wrong things." Grant took a sip of water. "So, where are you and I sleeping tonight?"

Violet almost choked as she sipped her wine.

Outside the restaurant, two nuns stood across the street. Though the sun was setting, they kept to the shadows. The tall nun smoked like a chimney. The short nun was watching a young couple strolling down the cobblestone street, he was salivating. And not because the female was attractive. Nor the male.

"Can I go run around?" Mr. Crows asked.

"No can do, little man," Mr. Trafalgar said. "We have to keep an eye on these two. We don't want them giving us the slip, we'll never find them again."

"Fine." Mr. Crows pouted. "But I'm hungry. And some of these Italians look yummy. Roasted, toasted, boiled and boasted."

"That doesn't make sense." Mr. Trafalgar said through a cloud of smoke.

"It's my rhyme." Mr. Crows swatted a fly and ate it.

"Dude," Mr. Trafalgar shook his head. "You got issues."

Thirty minutes later, Violet forked another mouthful of penne, wiped her mouth on her arm, then sat back. "Whoo! I'm stuffed. This was really good!" She burped, then laughed. "Sorry. Not used to eating so much."

"That's okay. We all have bodily gasses sometimes. Some more than others." Grant politely wiped his mouth with his napkin then placed it back on his lap. "Well, mine was very good as well. I'm glad we got to have this meal together. I think it helped ease some of the tension." Grant pulled out his pill tray.

"I'm not sleeping with you, Grant." Violet blurted. She had downed several glasses of wine. Grant's last count was four.

"Wasn't what I was talking about. I meant the tension of the mission." Grant replied, nonplussed. "And for the record, I don't want to sleep with you."

"Of course you do."

"No, I do not."

"Bullshit."

"Can we talk more about the significance of the number twelve?"

"Oh God, Grant. Can't you give that a rest? I'd rather go back to talking about sleeping together."

"Why? Are we sleeping together?" Grant perked up.

"No chance in hell."

"Fine, back to twelve."

Violet crudely called out across the restaurant. "Waiter. Mas vino, por favor! More wine!!"

"Violet, you're speaking Spanish." Grant sighed.

"Whatever. It's all the same. Now go on and give me more twelve crap."

The waiter with the cemented smile returned with Violet's fifth glass of wine. He barely stopped moving to drop it off. Violet grabbed the glass and slurped down half of it.

"Now, you have to realize the power of the number twelve and what it represents to Twelvists." Grant explained, ignoring Violet's poor behavior. He had lined up his medications and took them one at a time with water. He closely monitored his watch in between each swallow."I've already pointed out how it shows up in nearly every aspect of life, from measuring time to weight to quantities. Twelve just works."

"Why?"

"There's a reason we don't use the metric system, because it's flawed. You see, with tens, you can only divide in tenths, fifths and halves. But with the magic number twelve, you can divide by not only halves, but twelfths, sixths, quarters and thirds. It has more prime factors. "

"That's fascinating." Violet said dourly and took another swig of wine.

"Many think that twelve is a newer method of measurement, developed by our modern-day clock-watching society. But it's not. It was organized by the oldest human civilization in written history, the Sumerians."

"Are those the big fat Chinese guys that wrestle?"

"No, Violet," Grant felt his stomach drop. "Please listen. This is all important for your father's cause. It was the Sumerians' duodecimal system for commerce. And it continued to be used by later civilizations. The Romans adopted it in their system of fractions."

"Oh, math! Jesus Christ, I hate math!" Violet said loudly. Several patrons glanced over angrily at Violet. She didn't notice their glares, or the portraits of the son of God on a few of the walls. She did, however, finish her glass of wine. Instead of putting it back down, she simply elevated it as high as she could and called out. "Oh, smiley waiter! Mucho mas vino, gracias!"

Grant sank in his seat, covering his face with his hands. "Maybe we should go."

Violet put the glass down, none too happy. "Fine! Can't let a sister have a little vino, now can you, Grant?" She waved her hand around in the air. "Check, please!"

The waiter appeared so quickly, with check in hand, that Grant could only assume the man was more than eager to have them leave. "Si. Thank you." He handed it to Grant.

"Oh, gimmee that!" Violet snatched it from the waiter's hand. She slapped her credit card on top of the check and shoved it back to the waiter. Somehow, his smile remained. If the waiter hadn't had a stroke before this, he might this evening if Violet stuck around. He ran off with the card, dying to rid their restaurant of the bawdy Violet.

"Okay, what else, smart-guy?" Violet's speech was a tad slurred.

"Ugh. Okay, we then have to understand the religious ramifications of twelve. If I'm repeating myself, let me know, but there's the Twelve Tribes of Israel, the twelve disciples, twelve stones, twelve princes, twelve books of the minor prophets in the Hebrew Scriptures, and the list goes on. Twelvists believe, in fact they are positive, this all leads back to twelve being magical, or transcendent, or a number with more significance to our lives and where we come from."

The waiter returned with the check and cautiously placed it in front of Violet. She quickly scribbled a signature and stood. "Grant, let's go. These people are rude!" She turned and stormed out.

"I'm sorry, I'm very sorry." Grant said as he quickly got out of his chair. "She's never like this, really!"

The waiter's smile finally broke. "Get out," he rasped.

Grant ran out the door, never looking back.

Violet had wobbled half a block down the Via Giulio Cesare by the time Grant had caught up. At least she was sort of in the right direction.

"Hey, Violet. So what's the plan?" Grant said excessively merrily. "We should really find a place to crash for the night. We have a long day tomorrow."

"Fine, Grant, I'm tired."

"Hey did you know, this street we're on, called Via Giulio Cesare is named after Julius Caesar? And it was Caesar that established the Julian Calendar, breaking it up into 365 days and 12 months, with a leap day added every four years."

"Fascinating." Violet turned a corner. She saw bright lights on a building and smiled. "That's great, Grant, how about we stay at this place?" Violet pointed to the building next to them. "Looks nice."

Grant blushed. "Ahem, Violet, that's a strip club." They seemingly had wandered into a section with many bars, clubs and lower-end eateries. Still not a bad neighborhood by any means, but Grant marveled that something so polar opposite to the catholic beliefs could be so close to the Holy City itself.

"Ooh. They have them here? That's cool." Violet walked further along the side street. "How about here?" She pointed at another building.

"Much better." Grant nodded as he sized up the small, three-story hotel. *Not much, but better.* Grant opened the door and gestured for Violet to enter.

Once inside, Grant withdrew his hasty judgment of the two-star hotel. He knew it was a two-star because the management had a few framed newspaper and magazine clippings framed on the foyer wall. They were obviously proud to have received the double rating. But as far as budget places went, this one was as quaint and homey as he could imagine. The foyer was narrow, but with a plush carpeting that met the fine oak paneled walls. A man sat behind a counter, he greeted them with a smile.

A few minutes later, Grant had gotten them a small room with a single bed. He wasn't trying anything, it was all they had. Violet had wandered around the small lobby and eventually dropped into a chair. Her head was on her chin, eyes open. The lights were on, but everyone home was in a coma.

The manager behind the desk shook his head as he watched Grant struggle to lift the taller, heavier Violet. She eventually got to her feet and he led her to the stairs.

"Great." Grant hissed. "Two flights up."

Several more minutes and dozens of bruises later, Grant got Violet into the room. She fell face first on the bed. Within seconds, her snoring reverberated within the small room.

Grant looked about. It was a really nice looking room despite its small size. It had cream colored walls, terracotta floors and dark walnut stained furniture. It could have been someone's comfy den. And for the price, it couldn't be beaten. He sighed. Too bad he was going to have to sleep on the floor.

Grant grabbed one pillow from the bed and tossed it on the floor. He attempted to retrieve one of the two sheets on the bed from under Violet's dead weight. It wasn't happening. There was no way he was getting a blanket.

He sighed for a second time and lay down on the hard, uncomfortable floor. *This is no way to see Italy!*

CHAPTER 42

In the morning, Violet lifted her head off the drool-soaked blankets beneath her. Half of her face was red and indentations from the folds in the blankets had left their mark. "What..." She cringed, her head was thumping. "What happened?" She said to no one in particular.

Grant poked his head from out of the bathroom. "You had a bit much to drink, Miss Lushy-pants," he said chipperly.

Violet suddenly sat up straight, she felt herself, and relaxed slightly upon feeling all her clothes were still on her. "I didn't... we didn't..."

Grant laughed. "It wasn't easy!" he lied. "You were very amorous last night. I could barely keep you off of me."

"What?! Really?!"

"No." Grant laughed again. "You got drunk. Got very rude. Then you passed out. Relax, I slept on the floor. It was very uncomfortable."

"Thank God." Violet breathed out finally.

"Gee, thanks."

"Sorry." Violet frowned. "I have a habit of waking up next to guys I barely know when I drink wine. I've been trying to break that habit."

"Well, lucky me. You broke it." Grant chuckled.

"My head hurts." Violet rubbed her temples.

"I figured it would. I put out some aspirin for you and a glass of water." Grant was tying his shoes. "Pull yourself together. Sun has been up for a while. We've got to get to the Sistine Chapel pronto."

"Ugh." was all Violet could muster. "Where's my cigarettes?"

Nearly half an hour later, Grant and Violet, accompanied by a massive crowd, wandered into St. Peter's Square in Vatican City. At

Grant's urging, Violet tossed her cigarette and promised not to smoke anywhere near the Vatican.

Violet spun about slowly, in awe of the sights, the architecture, the statues, the sheer magnitude of the courtyard.

"Impressive, isn't it?" Grant whispered, soaking it all in himself.

"It's amazing."

"See the obelisk?" Grant said, pointing to the large, tapering monument in the center of the square.

"The what?" Violet looked about, confused.

"The obelisk. That tall, red marble tower." Grant waved his hand toward the giant needle. "It was moved into the basilica in the 13th century by Emporer Caligula. Obelisks were predominantly Egyptian architecture, adopted by the Romans, who were infatuated with them. Obelisks symbolize Ra, the sun god, and the shape is supposedly a petrified ray of *aten*, or sundisk."

"Okay. And what does that mean?"

"In Egyptian mythology, Aten, also known as Aton, is the creator of the universe. Their sun god. I find it funny, and coincidental, that the Vatican would have a monument in their city that represents a being from the stars. A space traveling deity. Christianity has a way of keeping close ties with aliens."

"Freud said monuments like that were giant penises." Violet joked.

"Freud was a mental patient." Grant replied. "Come on. Let's make our way to the chapel."

The two approached the Basilica of St. Peter. A mammoth feat of architecture, an outstanding feature in the Roman skyline, and one of the largest churches in Christianity.

Violet pointed to an inscription above the main entrance. "What does that say?"

Grant squinted at the façade. "It says, 'In honor of the prince of apostles, Paul V Borghese, a Roman, Supreme Pontiff, blah blah blah'."

"Blah blah blah?" Violet looked at him.

"I have trouble with Roman Numerals."

"Borghese. That sounds familiar... hey, wasn't that guy on The Bachelor?"

"Yep. Sad how far the royalty fall, isn't it?"

They stepped into the shadow of the basilica, climbed the stairs and stared up in awe. The columns towered over them, the dome of the basilica, or cupola, was like a majestic mountain of marble and brick.

"They say the dome was designed to resemble a UFO." Grant whispered.

"What?! A UFO?" Violet laughed. "Don't be ridiculous."

A few tourists nearby looked in their direction.

"Quiet." Grant shushed her. "Some people are sensitive around here to talk like this. Just look at it. The roundish shape, the portholes. It is said that it was supposed to be Michelangelo's homage to alien spacecraft and was initially to be a hemisphere. But he died before the dome was put up, so the architect Giacomo della Porto finished the dome. He changed the shape slightly. Some say to emphasize the alienish appearance. It is actually a paraboloid in shape. Meaning it has upward thrust. Tell me it doesn't resemble a UFO at all. You can't."

Violet tilted her head and considered it. "Well, maybe."

That was all Grant needed. "These things are out there, Violet. You just have to be open to them. Hopefully we'll get up into the dome after the chapel if we have time, it really is something to see. Now I wanted you to see St. Peter's Square and the Basilica, but to get into the chapel we have to go around." Grant led the way out of St. Peter's and led Violet three blocks to the entrance to the Vatican Museums. They waited in line and when their opportunity came up, passed on a tour guide. After a short wait, and an 11 Euro entrance fee for each, Violet and Grant stepped into the Vatican Museum. The hallways were mobbed with tourists and Grant and Violet pushed their way past dozens of people who were enjoying and in awe of the hundreds of ancient statues, frescoes and paintings. Grant didn't pause for any of the sights, Violet struggled to keep up with him, her heels clicking on the tile floor and stepping on the occasional toe. Finally, they came to the entrance to the chapel.

A few steps into the Sistine Chapel Violet gasped.

"Oh my." was all she could muster.

"That's the standard reaction." Grant was smiling.

The artwork of Michelangelo Buonarroti loomed overhead, over 5000 square feet of color, movement, emotion and dynamic imagery. The fresco spanned the full width and length of the majestic room, 40 by 130 feet. Violet spun in circles, attempting to absorb the maelstrom of paint suspended over 60 feet above her. Grant placed his hand on her arm, fearing she might become dizzy and fall.

"Oh, look!" Violet chirped, pointing at the Creation of Adam painting and not even noticing his clammy, wet hand on her. "There's the picture we were looking at in Peter's apartment."

"Yup." Grant nodded. "That's one of nine scenes of the Genesis. They run the length of the room down the center. The triangle-shaped paintings that follow the border of the ceiling are called pendatives."

"Shhhhh!" A guard nearby hissed.

"Sorry." Grant whispered back, he turned to Violet and pointed to signs posted on the walls. "There's really not supposed to be any talking. And definitely no pictures or video. We'll have to be super-extra quiet."

"Oh, okay," Violet barely made a sound. "There's so much happening up there. I don't know where to begin looking. All those figures."

"Over 300 figures were painted." Grant explained. "He was hired just to do 12, there's our favorite number again. There's so many ways to tie Michelangelo in with the twelvist theories." Grant led her to the end of the room. The only fresco done by Michelangelo that was on a wall rather than the ceiling stood before them. "I want to give you a bit of insight into Michelangelo, the way he thought, and the way he liked to incorporate secrets, messages, and inside jokes into his paintings. This is The Last Judgment, it captures the moment before Jesus Christ casts his verdict on mankind."

"It's amazing." Violet whispered. "And kinda scary."

"Well, it was also very controversial at the time. Originally there was a bit more, well, skin showing to say the least. All those nicely draped swatches of cloth were not there at first."

"Really?"

"Yep. In fact the Pope's own Master of Ceremonies, Biagio da Cesena, said it was shameful and not fit for a papal chapel but for a bathhouse."

"That's not nice."

"No, it wasn't." Grant continued. "And a campaign by Cardinal Carafa prodded the papacy to cover up the nudes. So another artist was hired to brush on loincloths and hide the naughty bits."

"Wow. It's weird to think that someone could do that to something painted by Michelangelo."

"Well, in the long run Michelangelo had his revenge."

"How'd he do that?"

"Well, see that guy there with the knife in one hand," Grant pointed toward the middle of the large fresco. "And the skin of some poor sap in the other hand?"

"Ick." Violet grimaced. "Yes, I do."

"Michelangelo felt so betrayed by the comments of Carafa and da Cesena that he painted his own face on the skinned person. It represents how he felt he was treated."

"Good for him."

"And even better," Grant continued, pointing toward the bottom right corner. "See that guy with the serpent twisting around him?"

"Yep. Who's that?"

"The face is of Biagio da Cesena himself. The big-mouthed complainer."

"Wow. That's awesome."

"Michelangelo used art to express his own feelings. He even would go above his client's wishes, which was unheard of beforehand. And he always infused his own ideas secretly into his work if he couldn't obviously include them."

Grant again steered Violet through the crowds of people. They stopped midway and Grant pointed upwards. "Here we have 'The Fall and Expulsion from the Garden of Eden'. On one side, Adam and Eve reach for apples from the Tree of Life while the serpent looks on, on the other side, they are cast away by a cherub with a sword."

"It's beautiful." Violet said, then looked at Grant. "Okay, I'm catching on. What's hidden in this image?"

"Some say, and Twelvists agree, that it's his signature. You'll notice that the way it's laid out, it creates one huge M."

"Hey, it does."

"But not just any M, an M written in uncial script." Grant explained.

"What the Hell is uncial script?"

"Uncial script was a common form of script used in the 3rd to 8th centuries. Predominantly by Latin and Greek scribes. But the interesting thing is that the word uncial most likely came from uncialibus, which means that when properly written the letters occupied one-twelfth of a line of a manuscript. There's that magic number again!"

"Amazing how everything seems to go back to that number." Violet furrowed her brow. "I hate to say it, but I may actually be buying into this nonsense." Before Grant could reply. "Maybe! And it's a *big* maybe!"

"It's enough for me." Grant smiled.

"Okay, show me more."

"Aside from his inside jokes and signature, Michelangelo also was a fanatic for human anatomy. Let's take a few steps back and I'll show you the granddaddy of all of Michelangelo's anatomical infusions." Grant held his arms wide at the fresco above. "Here we have 'The Creation of Adam' as you are now very familiar with. What you see is God, in all his greatness, surrounded by angels, giving life to Adam."

"I can see why you thought my father's pose resembled this. It was exact!"

"Shhhh!" Another guard warned.

Grant and Violet lowered their voices again.

"Now, notice ovoid drapery that encloses God and his traveling companions."

"Okay."

"What does it look like?"

Violet growled. "You know I'm not going to guess. I don't do well with guessing games. So just tell me! I can't find one word in a search-a-word puzzle!"

"Okay. Sheesh. Experts all agree that it is actually a mid-sagittal of the human brain." Grant beamed.

"A mid-what?"

"Mid-sagittal. It's the brain cut in half. The drapery is obviously the outline of a brain. The angels help make up the folds of the many lobes. God's feet, along with others, make up the cerebellum. The chap just below God, his leg is the spinal cord. The guy in front of the chap makes up part of the temporal lobe and his arm is the hypothalamus. It's all there. And it's irrefutable."

"That's gross."

"See, now Twelvists agree that it is the mid-sagittal of the human brain, but they disagree with what experts think is the reason Michelangelo painted it. Some experts claim that it was Michelangelo's belief that God was an invention of the human mind."

"And, of course, the twelvists have a different theory," Violet added.

"Indeed, they believe it was Michelangelo's way of saying that we were brought here, or created, by a higher intelligence."

"Yeah, that would be God."

"Nope. He was telling us it was aliens." Grant paused, waiting for Violet's outburst, which surprisingly didn't happen. "Not only is this telling us that God was a higher intelligence, but he traveled here in an ovoid shaped craft, with passengers, of which there are eleven, and God would make twelve."

"So that's a brain, a spaceship, and twelve aliens?"

"Yup."

Violet sighed. "Okay, what's next?"

"Okay, right next to the 'Creation of Adam' is the 'Creation of Eve'. Now this is pretty cool. In it God is creating Eve, and her form seems to spring from Adam's supine body. God commands her forth as though he is breathing life into her. The interesting thing is if you look at God, his robe has a strange shape to it, and when compared to the human lung, it's a match."

"A lung?"

"Yup. And the tree that Adam is tied to is a bronchial tube."

"Oh, that wiggly part?"

"Yes, the, um, wiggly part. On the other side of the 'Creation of Adam' is the 'Separation of Land and Water'. Again, Michelangelo's sense of anatomy combines with his sense of humor. The drapery that surrounds God is in the shape of a kidney. Do you see it?"

"Um, I don't know. What's a kidney look like?"

"It looks like a kidney bean." Grant rolled his eyes.

"Oh, really?" Violet was surprised. "Is that why they call them kidney beans?" She stared at the fresco a few moments. "Okay, I see it. But why is it a joke?"

"Separation of Land from Water. Duh. What does a kidney do?"

Violet glared at Grant. "I honestly have no idea."

"Really?" Grant was shocked. "I mean, really? Okay then. Your kidneys process a couple hundred quarts of blood a day and sift out, or separate, waste and water. So in the fresco, God is flying in a kidney, doing what a kidney does, separating."

"Oh, but what does this have to do with the Twelve?" Violet asked.

"Nothing. But it's fascinating stuff. It lends credence to Michelangelo's ability to infuse secret information and knowledge into his works of art. We also have a heart and aorta in one fresco over there and a humerus bone and socket in another."

"Isn't the humerus bone the funny bone?"

Grant buried his head in his wet and slimy hands. "I'd laugh if I thought you were kidding." He said into his hands. He fought the urge to cry. He looked back up at Violet, his face slick with palm-slime. "Now let's stop looking up and start looking down." He took several steps backward. "What do you see?"

Violet shrugged. "I don't know. A bunch of floor tiles. A design of some kind."

"Indeed. But do they remind you of anything?"

"No."

"Anything that planes might spot."

Nothing.

"While flying over a wheat field."

Nothing.

"In Europe mainly, but also all over the world."

Still nothing.

"Concentric circles. A greenish-brown hue."

"Concentric? What's that?"

"Circles! Crop circles, Violet, crop circles!" Grant burst.

"Shhhhh!" The guard wagged a finger at them.

"Oh, yeah! I do see it." Violet spun around, looking at the several repeated circles, the ring upon ring, the squares with circles inside them. "It does look like crop circles! A whole bunch of them!"

"Well, coincidently, this style is called Cosmatesque, its etymology, or word source, is named after Cosmati, which was a group of marble craftsmen in Medieval era Italy. Now what, pray tell, does Cosmatesque and Cosmati sound like?"

"Cosmetics?"

"Okay, I was hoping for Cosmos but you're still on track. Cosmos and Cosmetics are derived from the same root, kosmos, which originally meant order and arrangement. Pythagorus was the first to use the term cosmos in reference to the arrangement and order of the entire universe. Twelvists have long felt that Pythagorus was privy to a portion, if not more than one portion, of the Twelve."

"Who's Pythagorus?" Violet's eyes were blank.

Grant fought off yet another urge to cry. "Perhaps we should get back to the matter at hand. We should stop looking at the ceiling and see if Gerri Hender is wandering around here somewhere."

"Oh, that's right!" Violet's eyes widened. "I nearly forgot why we were here." She glanced around the chapel. There were nearly thirty people wandering around, pointing, oohing and aahing, standing with mouth agape in awe. There were also two odd looking nuns finding interest in the tiled floor. "I don't see her here."

"Okay, well we have to assume she came here and found what she was looking for or she has yet to do so. Either way, we have to find out what's here."

"Well, how the Hell do we do that?" Violet looked perplexed.

"I'm not sure. As far as I know, we are the first to begin such a quest. No one that has looked for The Twelve before has been successful. At least as far as I've heard." Grant paced in a circle. He rubbed his hair with his wet hand and it stood up in the back, giving him an Alfalfa-ish hairstyle. "Michelangelo would have placed clues to the hiding spot in his paintings as a cryptic message to those in the know of the Twelve, but meaningless to anyone who weren't aware of the Twelvist ways."

"Well if folks for centuries haven't been able to discover it," Violet spun around, looking. "Then how are we?"

"Oh ye of little faith," Grant pointed to his chest. "They didn't have me!"

"Great, we're doomed."

Grant ignored Violet and let his eyes roam the ceiling. Images, shapes, potential signs and clues formed in his mind. He began doing numbers in his head. "Okay, where's the twelves? There's eight spandrels and four pendatives. That's a twelve."

"What are those?" Violet asked.

"That's the triangular shaped frescoes. The characters painted within the spandrels are not known and continue to be a point of speculation." Grant continued counting and searching. "Now of the characters along the perimeter there's seven prophets and five sybils. Again, that's twelve."

"Does that mean anything?"

"I don't know. In Catholicism, there's twelve lesser prophets and twelve traditional sybils. But Michelangelo only included these certain ones. I'm not sure if that's relevant. Okay, there are also only twelve sloping surfaces. Now there are fourteen lunettes and on each one is an ancestor of Jesus."

"Boy, this could take forever," Violet fidgeted, not finding any of this interesting. "You'd think that if Michelangelo wanted us to know where the secret thingy was, he'd have simply pointed it out." Violet began rummaging through her purse, looking for a piece of gum.

"Please be quiet, Violet, this isn't..." Grant froze momentarily, then dashed off toward one end of the chapel.

Violet watched in dismay. "Little weirdo, where's he going now?" She hesitantly followed him. Violet caught up with Grant at the foot of Michelangelo's Last Judgment, his neck was craned backward, looking up at the fresco.

"Violet, remember when I said that Michelangelo included himself in the Last Judgment?" Grant said. "Well, I think you were right!"

"I was?"

"Look up at the flayed skin. Remember?"

"Ugh, yes." Violet turned away.

"That's Michelangelo. He painted his own face on it. And look where his fingers are pointing."

"And?"

"I think you're on to something. He's clearly pointing. I'd say downward." Grant's eyes followed the path that Michelangelo's fingers pointed. He paused at the cluster of angelic trumpeters beneath the hanging skin. There were only eleven in the group. They were holding two books, one for good deeds and the other for evil. Grant didn't think that held any meaning for them. He followed the path some more. It came down on top of the head of Charon, the ferryman of Hades. Grant thought about the character, its meanings and background. As far as he could remember, there were no connections to the number twelve. Grant continued following the path down, past Charon's boat, past the land mass at the bottom, and then finally off the fresco altogether. Grant cursed under his breath. *Dammit! I thought for sure it had to be in here somewhere.*

"What's the matter?" Violet asked, seeing Grant's look of unhappiness.

"I just figured you were right. It has to be here."

"What has to be here?" Violet asked.

"The secret location of a portion of the twelve! Why do you think we're here?"

"Don't get snippety," Violet smirked. "Did you think it would be in the painting itself? I mean, if this thing is a whole code and a whole lot of information, wouldn't it need to be on paper or something?"

"I guess you're right," Grant said, refusing to look away from the wall. "And he certainly wouldn't bury it in the wall, at least not under his painting. He'd never allow anyone to simply destroy his work looking for the secret." Grant followed the path of Michelangelo's fingers again. "Unless…" Grant moved toward the altar beneath the tremendous fresco. Though people were not allowed to touch the altar, Grant went to its side and looked behind it. Violet followed.

"This altar is where they lay the pope after he's passed away. The cardinals pick the next pope in this room as well. This is a very important and sacred place. The Vatican has made many changes to the sacristy and altar area in the past, but the floor here is original. Michelangelo could have hidden it here without anyone accidently discovering it. If it's anywhere, it'll be hidden beneath the tiles." Grant whispered.

"We can't just start digging in here!" Violet's eyes grew wide. "They'll throw us in jail or hang us."

"We have to. If we don't, Gerri Hender will. And she's one of the bad guys."

"Then how do we do it?" Violet folded her arms.

"You'll have to create a distraction. Go to the other side and take off your clothes or something." Grant said matter-of-factly.

Violet stood unblinking.

"No, really," Grant urged.

"Uh, gee, no chance." Violet scowled. "You go do it and I'll dig. How about that? You like the idea now?"

"Shhhhh!" A guard a few feet and several tourists away hissed in their direction. He recognized them as having been shushed before and began approaching them.

"Great, now we're doomed." Grant said.

Violet sighed. "Fine. I'll handle this. But you better be right or I'll kill you."

"Watch the cursing, we're in a chapel."

Before the guard could reach them entirely, Violet began moving toward him at an angle, trying to draw the guard away. The guard followed Violet, who flipped him the bird. "Get bent, Frenchie!" she called out.

The guard began clapping, which at first Violet thought was applause. She then realized it was how guards warn tourists to be quiet. And it also alerts the other guards. Soon three other guards began working their way through the crowd toward Violet. She looked for the nearest exit and, upon seeing one several meters away, began shoving people aside.

"Wow! She's got balls." Grant said proudly. The dozens of tourists were all watching the spectacle of the mad woman shrieking and shoving her way through the crowd. Grant dove behind the altar where he was pretty much concealed should any tourist *not* be watching Violet's spectacle. He dug around his back pack and pulled out a Swiss Army Knife. He aligned himself once again with Michelangelo's fingertips and breathed in deeply.

"God forgive me." He then jabbed the large blade between tiles. Surprisingly they gave way easier than he'd have thought.

Violet saw the trio of guards converging on her and started getting scared. She really didn't want to spend the night in jail, especially in a foreign country. For all she knew they'd cane her or sell her on the white slave market. She didn't know much about Italy, but she always heard to stay out of trouble when traveling.

She was getting closer to the exit, elbowing and pushing past angry and cursing tourists. She certainly wasn't making any friends. One tourist tried to be a hero and attempted to hold Violet until the guards could reach her. That poor dope landed on the ground with a bloody lip.

"Scusi!" Violet said sarcastically.

Violet made it to the door just as two of the guards were upon her. "Oh, I'm so going to Hell," Violet said as she grabbed an old woman and pushed her into one of the guards, who heroically caught the frail woman.

The other guard, nostrils flared with rage, leapt on Violet. They wrestled briefly but Violet grabbed the velvet roping used to cordon off the tourists and removed the brass hook on the end. She swiftly swung the heavy metal hook up and between the guard's legs. The guards eyes bulged, nearly falling out, and he collapsed, curled up like a pill bug.

Violet made it to the exit and ran outside. She stopped a few blocks away, where she couldn't be seen but could keep an eye on the exit for when Grant made it out. If he made it out.

The first cigarette was used to light the second. The second was used to light the third. And so it went as Violet chain-smoked, waiting, praying that Grant would make it out okay. She figured if they caught Grant, after all that Violet had just done, they'd draw and quarter the poor guy. *Whatever that meant.* Violet just knew it wasn't good to be drawn and quartered.

"Hey, Violet!" Grant called out.

Violet spun about. "Grant! You're okay!" She ran to him. Violet's arm went out as she was about to hug him, but stopped.

Grant frowned.

"Anyway," Grant ignored the rude gesture. "We did it!" Grant held up an obviously ancient iron box. He opened it and showed it to Violet. Inside were scrolls. It was partially rolled up but looked to be many, many pages.

"How'd you get out?" Violet asked. "I've been watching the exit for an hour."

"There are other exits," Grant explained. "There just not supposed to be used by the public. Luckily I know this place pretty well. I made my way back into the church and then the square. And then…"

"Okay, great, whatever," Violet said. "Let's look at what we came for!"

"Geez, you don't have to be rude." Grant gently removed the scrolls and handed the box to Violet. He then slowly unfurled them. They looked at the first page.

1540

Liberato dal marmo, lo stoico ed il freddo
Giovane David guarda verso vecchio
Nella mia casa di nemici mente
Sopra la spalla del Madonna vola
Nello squillo dorato che la verità è liberata
Dove lo sguardo fisso della madre conduce

LE11.36.7   PR25.11.5   GE8.9.5   GE49.6.9   DE13.18.22
JE26.11.19 EX2.12.16 EP1.9.7   PS87.6.12   JE28.1.38   GE6.9.10
RU2.8.13 EX10.6.4 JU9.51.32 AC5.7.6 GE23.6.21 JE25.1.11 PS2.7.16
IS36.4.22   DE17.4.19   EP3.16.5   NU8.19.47   IS6.11.14   JE44.3.34
GE4.3.5   PR20.22.10   PS81.4.2   EP3.18.10   GE1.20.15   JE33.11.25
HE5.11.17   AC1.1.16   AC4.11.11   PS7.12.4   EC2.19.17   GA6.3.9
GE30.1.23   EP3.19.2   DE1.14.18   GE12.1.8   JE50.10.5   NU1.1.24
JA5.11.15   EX5.4.21   DE15.1.11   PR30.23.17   IS5.11.16   GE9.21.6
NU2.5.4 LU11.54.9 PS8.5.16 JE4.3.15 GE9.5.38 HE12.1.21 DA2.23.2
JE29.21.29 PR18.6.11 GE31.18.20 DE34.4.7 DE17.18.26

Ricetta LE13.17
BA56

"My God! Look at all this stuff!" Grant shrieked.

"What is all that?" Violet asked, looking over his shoulder.

"I'm assuming most of this is a code of some sort. Probably a Bible code. It would take a while to decipher that." Grant pointed to a different spot. "This first part is in Italian. It's a poem of some sort." Grant read the poem aloud in Italian and saw Violet's look of despair. "Don't worry, since it's in Italian I can translate it."

"Yeah, I'm going to trust your Italian after seeing you talk so well to the locals." Violet crossed her arms. "Go ahead."

"Thanks for the vote of confidence." Grant sneered. "Anyway, roughly it goes like this;

> Freed from marble, stoic and cold
> Young David looks toward old
> In my enemy's home does it lie
> O'r the Madonna's shoulder they fly
> In gilded ring the truth is freed
> Where the mother's gaze does lead

Catchy! And it rhymes." Grant said proudly.

Violet shook her head. "Madonna? As in the singer? Are you telling me that Michelangelo predicted Madonna? That's amazing!"

"No, my dear, sweet, clueless Violet." Grant hung his head. "*The* Madonna. The Virgin Mother of Jesus Christ. Mary Magdalene. That's the Madonna."

"Oh, jeez. Sorry I'm not all book smart and geeky as you." Violet took out another cigarette. "At least I've been laid," she mumbled.

"What'd you say?" Grant shot Violet a look.

"Nothing."

CHAPTER 43

Sister Trafalgar quickly grabbed for his Blackberry from under his gown. He quickly typed in a message to Mr. Maystyne.

"What are you doing?" Sister Crows barked. "They found something! We have to kill them and find out what they know! Or at least just kill them!"

Sister Trafalgar flicked Sister Crows' nose. Sister Crows yelped.

"Stay frosty, little man. They're not getting far." He placed the Blackberry back inside his gown. "If the bossman wants us to move in, then we'll move in. Until then, we watch and follow."

Sister Crows stomped on the ground. "I'm getting fidgety!"

"Hey, they're moving. Let's go."

"When we get outside," Sister Crows pleaded. "Can I at least run around the courtyard? I have to let off some steam."

"For two reasons, I'm going to say no." Sister Trafalgar warned him as they kept pace with their targets. "The first being, you'll probably jump someone."

Sister Crows shrugged. He had him there!

"The second reason is, what kind of nun runs around in circles in St. Peter's Square, you moron?"

Sister Crows frowned. "Sorry."

CHAPTER 44

As they walked out into St. Peter's Square, Grant continued reviewing the poem, trying desperately to both translate it and decipher it. His head was spinning.

They descended the steps from the basilica and within minutes Violet had inhaled half her cigarette. "So what do you think? Can you read it?"

"Yeah, I'm pretty sure. It starts out with freeing from cold marble, but that could mean anything. Michelangelo always said that his sculptures were always there and that he simply freed them from the slab. The second line suggests the sculpture is in front of his enemy's home. Hmm, his enemies."

"Okay, who were his enemies?" Violet tossed her smoked-to-the-filter Marlboro to the ground.

"Whoo boy, well there were plenty of other artists who really didn't care for him. But I really wouldn't consider them enemies. Except maybe…"

"Da Vinci?" Violet smirked.

Grant growled. "Yes, him. Anyway, I know Michelangelo referred to nature as the enemy. But somehow I don't think that's it."

They walked out of Vatican City and found themselves again walking the streets of Rome. Grant thought aloud, his brain running at a hundred miles per hour. His eyes darted side to side. They walked in no particular direction. Violet strolled beside him, smoking of course, interjecting very infrequently.

"Enemies. Who's the enemy of Michelangelo? Who did him wrong?" Grant swirled his fingers in the air, like he was using a floating, invisible abacus. "His father beat him. The younger Medici chased him from Florence. There was Savonarola. Bramante and Raphael supposedly screwed with him. Oh, and the Counter Reformation and the Popes involved with that! And of course da Cesena, Carafa and Sernini and what they said about his Sistine Chapel frescoes. Arg!" Grant held his head in his hands; he then threw his hands skyward. "I can't say for certain!"

Violet patted his shoulder, avoiding Grant's swinging, wet hands. "Stop pushing yourself so hard. You'll never think of it like that." She paused and Grant whimpered. "What about the other lines? You're stuck on the one, move off of it and come back later. Maybe the other lines will help make that one more sensible."

Grant froze, and then abruptly dug out the paper he had scribbled the poem on. He looked at Violet. "You're right. Sorry. I get a little, er, obsessive."

"That's okay. I'm starting to know you a bit."

"And like me?" Grant's eyes lit up.

"Don't push it. Get back to the poem, Romeo."

"Romeo! Ah, Shakespeare. He was a Twelvist. He wrote frequently of angels, and travelers from on high. He wrote Twelfth Night. Sonnet 144, which is a multiple of twelve, is all about angels. And, ironically, Sonnet 12 uses your name, Violet."

"That's great, Grant. Get back to our little poem problems."

"Jeez, sorry. Just trying to educate you more about our quest here."

"Educate me later." Violet lit up another smoke. "I'm getting hungry."

Grant returned his attention to the poem. "Okay. Over the Madonna's shoulder it flies. I mean, there's Madonnas in art, literature, and history all over Europe, never mind Italy. It could be anywhere."

"What about the Davids?"

"We just saw his fresco of David beheading Goliath back in the Sistine Chapel."

"Okay, but it suggests there are two. Is there another David?"

Grant stomped around animatedly. "Are you kidding? Of course, there's Michelangelo's David sculpture. It's considered to this day the single-most recognizable piece of art today."

"So is he talking about them? Is one old and the other young?"

"Well, yes. He created the David sculpture before he painted the chapel."

"Where is this statue?" Violet asked.

Grant pondered that for a moment. "It's at the Accademia Gallery in Florence, Italy. They built a special tribuna just to house it."

"Is it possible that's our next location?"

"I don't know. I guess it could be." Grant suddenly jumped up and down. "Yes, yes, it could be! It was founded in part by the Medicis. Though originally supporters of Michelangelo, they were eventually the cause of his exodus from Florence. They could very well be considered enemies."

"So, they lived there? That was their home?"

Grants face fell. "No. Dammit!"

"Was that gallery there when Michelangelo was alive?"

"Actually, no. It was founded the year he died. I highly doubt he was overly aware of it."

Violet tossed her cigarette and crossed her arms. "So, if he sculpted David so long ago, and the Macadamia Gallery…"

"Accadamia."

"Whatever. If the gallery was created after the David was sculpted, where was it before that?"

Grant's eyes shut, then his face broke into a huge grin. He ran over and kissed Violet. She immediately threw him to the ground, fist raised for a strike. He leapt back up and screamed with joy. "Violet, you are brilliant!" he said as he wiped gravel from his rear end. "It makes sense now. He's referring to his newer fresco of David looking toward his older sculpture. The statue of David was originally commissioned for the Overseers of the Office of Works of the Duomo in 1501. Upon nearing completion, they held a meeting as to where it would be held. The meeting consisted of several famous folk, including Botticelli and your Leonardo da Jerky. It was decided that it would stand before the Palazzo Vecchio in Florence. The Palazzo Vecchio was home to Cosimo de' Medici in the mid to late 15th century."

"So that's where we have to go? Florence?" Violet asked, she could feel her credit card aching from inside her purse.

"It has to be! Carved from cold marble. From young David to old. Home of my enemy." Grant skipped in a circle. He whipped out his camera and took a picture of his dancing feet.

"And what about the Madonna?"

"I'm not sure. But it has to have something to with where the next twelfth is. We'll figure that out once we get there!" Grant continued prancing and skipping.

Violet looked around. "You keep dancing, Ginger Rogers. I'll hail a taxi." She shuffled down the winding street toward a busier avenue half a block away. Grant followed, whirling and pirouetting.

CHAPTER 45

The Blackberry beeped and Sister Trafalgar pulled it from beneath his flowing black gown. He flipped it open.

"It's the boss," he announced to his diminutive partner.

"What's it say?" Sister Crows nervously hopped from one foot to the other, appearing to be in serious need of urination.

Sister Trafalgar read the email aloud. "It says;

Keep following them from a safe distance. Do not come in contact with them at any cost. They are following a known path. We hope for more discoveries to follow. And please remind Mr. Crows to take a Valium and not attack anyone, including innocent bystanders. Contact me when any new events occur. End of message.

Sister Crows let out a ferocious growl. "Godammit!" he yelled. Several pedestrians looked in shock at the expletive-spewing Sister. "Why does he have to always say such bad things about me?"

"Because you randomly attack and kill people." Sister Trafalgar said matter-of-factly.

"And take a Valium? Ha! I'd sooner drink bleach than take pills and become one of the mindless drug-warped zombies of Middle America!"

"Okay, cool it." Sister Trafalgar inhaled a lungful of tar and nicotine. "Don't get on your pill popping tirade again. All right? Now, we can't afford to lose them and one of us has to get the car. But I don't trust you not to jump on them the first chance you get. So you have to go grab the car while I stick with them. Can you do that?"

Sister Crows whined. "Yes."

"Good. Get going, dude. I'll see you in five."

Sister Crows was still mumbling under his breath as he ran off to retrieve the car.

CHAPTER 46

Violet was waving and finally caught the attention of a taxi. As it swerved to pick them up, Grant was digging into his bag and removed his pill tray.

"What time do you have?" he asked.

Violet glanced at her watch, pulling her eyes way from the massive amount of pills in Grant's tray. "It's, uh, 2:30."

"Thanks." Grant quickly counted out four pills and threw them into his mouth.

The taxi stopped and Violet started to climb in but then hesitated. She turned to Grant and grabbed his collar. "Do NOT talk. Do NOT make conversation. Do NOT do anything that gets us tossed out of the car. Understand?"

Grant shrugged her off. "Duh. Yes, I understand. Sheesh!"

They climbed in and Violet leaned forward toward the driver. "Um, Palazzo Vecchio? Florence? Por favor?"

"Si, Palazzo Vecchio in Firenze. Ciò costerà abbastanza un lotto." The driver smiled and nodded.

Violet looked at Grant. "What did he say?"

"He said 'Yes, Palazzo Vecchio. It will cost alot.'" Grant looked out the window, not wanting to get involved for fear of extermination. "I thought you said don't talk."

"To him." Violet barked. "Do we have enough?"

Grant glanced at the driver. "Quanto?"

"40 a 50 Euro," he said.

"You get that, boss-woman?" Grant said facetiously.

"Yes, I got it." She looked back to the driver. "Okay. Si."

The driver turned around and put the car in drive. Soon they were bouncing along twisting cobbled streets, winding narrow paths, and up and down steep hills surrounded by historical beauty.

After about fifteen minutes, Violet started feeling good. Grant was quiet, they were on their way, and it seemed like there really was a big secret here. Her father *was* part of something great and ancient and beautiful. A purveyor, as Grant had called him, of information passed down from Jesus Christ himself. Violet never really got into religion. She dared say she'd pretty much despised it. All that guilt. *Who needed it?*

But now? Who knows? Maybe she'd start attending church when all this was through. Maybe her life would improve and she wouldn't be such a lost sheep with a penchant for losers with drug problems and gonorrhea.

She glanced over at Grant, who was still staring out the window. *Good, stay that way.* she thought. If he's asleep then we may make it through one full cab ride.

She looked closer. Wait. Is he breathing?

Violet reached over and nudged him. His head flopped toward her and she shrank back in terror. He was the worst color of green she'd ever seen.

"Grant, are you okay?" she asked.

He mumbled a few words before rousing himself. "I don't feel so great. Are you sure you gave me the correct time?" He was drooling on himself. Actually it was more of a foam.

Violet re-checked her watch. "Yeah. Of course I'm sure. Why?"

"Did you reset it for Greenwich Mean Time?"

"Green what? What the Hell is that?" Violet's eyes bugged out.

"We're in a different time zone, Violet. You have to reset your watch when you travel." Grant moaned.

"Or what?" Violet was puzzled. "Okay, I had the wrong time. What's the big deal? Did you have to watch Judge Wapner, Mr. Rainman?"

"Violet, I can't overlap certain pills. There are drug interactions. Some not so great." Grant wiped the drool from his chin on his sleeve.

Shit. Violet cursed in her head. *I knew this was going too smoothly.* She started to actually feel bad. She hoped she didn't really mess him up.

Grant started rattling off facts, apparently he was slightly delirious, and slurring his speech. "Did you know that there are 24

Standard time zones subdividing the Earth? They are known as Lunes. 24! That'sh a multiple of twelve," he laughed. "Looky looky, Darrel found a cookie! Another ekshample of how twelve ish the all meaningful number! Whoo hoo!"

Violet grabbed Grant by the face and turned him toward her. "Seriously, Grant, are you going to be okay? Do you need a hospital?"

Grant shook his head. "No, I'll be fine. Jusht woozy. I'll probably jusht shleep the whole ride."

The driver couldn't help but notice Grant's odd behavior. He looked in the rearview at Violet. "È bene? È malato?"

Violet was visibly upset and concerned. She also wasn't sure what the driver said, but had a good guess. "I don't know. I hope so."

Grant sprang forward and tapped the driver on the shoulder. "Ehi, l'amico. Vado al sesso questa donna!" he sloppily yelled.

The driver laughed and nodded. "Buono per lei. Desidero che sia stato!"

Violet was surprised. Not only was Grant *not* insulting the driver. He was making him laugh. He wasn't getting them tossed out and left by the side of the road. Whatever he said, it was funny. Maybe Grant was better off doped up!

Then Grant vomited down the back of the driver's neck.

CHAPTER 47

Sister Trafalgar watched as Violet and Grant climbed into the taxi and after a few minutes of conversation, started off. Within seconds he heard tires squeal and their Ferrari skidded around a corner and screeched to a stop next to the tall nun. Tire smoke filled the air as Sister Crows jumped out of the car and ran around to the passenger side.

"Am I in time?" Sister Crows asked.

"Sure are, little buddy."

"You drive. I know you want to." Sister Crows hopped into the passenger seat.

Sister Trafalgar paused as he slid behind the steering wheel. He tilted his head and stared at his friend. "Okay, what did you do?"

"Huh? What do you mean?"

"You're being real nice-like. Like you did something wrong." Sister Trafalgar continued to stare as he pulled on the seat belt, trying to get it around his extensive girth. "Did you run over anyone?" he grunted.

Sister Crows attempted to help and started tugging on the seat belt. He lost his cool and growled at the safety harness. He jerked at it angrily. Sister Trafalgar slapped his hands away.

"I'll get it! Let go!" Sister Trafalgar inhaled sharply, sucking in his stomach. With a loud heave he managed to drape the seat belt around him and click the belt into place. He looked back at his partner. "So?"

"I didn't run over anyone! I swear!" Sister Crows was sweating.

"Then what did you do, little man?" Sister Trafalgar lit up a smoke. "I know you did something."

"I may have knocked over one... or three people," he mumbled.

"Three? Is that it?"

Sister Crows smacked the dashboard in front of him. "Damn. Okay five. But nobody died!"

Sister Trafalgar leaned back and put the six-figure car in gear. The tires screamed and smoke billowed as he tore down the rustic street. "Good boy." He smiled.

CHAPTER 48

Violet stood over the green-tinted, vomit-splattered, and now black-eyed Grant. He was conscious, barely, and he was prattling on like a drunken man in the gutter. The driver, standing over Grant, was a little more than miffed now that puke had dribbled down his back, probably all the way to his ass crack. He was less than gentle with Grant when showing him the way out of the taxi. Now they were in the middle of nowhere, stranded, again.

She looked around, they were about twenty minutes outside of Rome, with no nearby establishments, at least not as far as she could see. She saw beautiful mountains, rolling hills covered in green, scattered trees draped with vines, and old fences leaning randomly. It was a gorgeous sight, and she would have been breath-taken had it not been for the seriousness of the situation. There were a few signs and as best she could tell they were on a road or something, called Via Salaria.

She was tempted to leave Grant and look for help but she didn't feel right doing that. Despite the fact that this was all his fault. *What do I know about time zones?*

A few cars drove by, and a couple had actually stopped for her, seeing such an attractive young woman waving them down. But they immediately sped off once they saw Grant and assumed they were drug addicts looking to hi-jack a car or possibly worse.

"Dammit!" she screamed out for no one to hear. Except Grant.

"Amen, sister!" Grant burbled. "The Via Salaria was created most likely before even Rome. It was for salt trade. It is 242 kilometers, which when divided by twelve is twenty point one shix shix shix shix shix shix and sho on! Which means absolutely nothing!" He rolled around giggling, and then was out cold.

I'm in trouble. Violet sank to the ground and hung her head.

The squeal of tires lifted her head. About a quarter mile away she saw a shiny sports car speeding toward her. She lifted herself off the ground and approached the road. *Oh, well. I have to keep trying.*

Violet lifted her hand and waved as the car crested the hill before her. It slammed on the brakes thirty yards from her and skidded to a smoky halt, directly next to her. The tinted, passenger-side window lowered itself.

Violet gasped upon seeing who was inside the ridiculously expensive car. Two nuns. Two very unattractive nuns. Wearing sunglasses. *Now there's something you don't see everyday!*

They both lowered their sunglasses, all cool-like. The nun directly in front of her, in the passenger seat, had an odd, beady stare to her. She was most likely Italian, with a prominent nose. But those eyes… And the larger nun behind the wheel was all smiles, but the size of a bear. A cigarette dangled from her mouth. *She's my kind of nun.* Violet mused.

"Well, hello there little lady." The nun behind the wheel said in a deep, very unfeminine voice. She tossed a cigarette out the window. "Are you stranded? Or lost? Can I offer you a ride somewhere?"

Violet couldn't believe her luck. Nuns! How safe could that be? This was the luckiest thing that could have happened. "As a matter of fact, yes, I am lost and stranded. Myself and my friend over there." She pointed at the heap that was once Grant. "He's not well. A bit under the weather."

"Oh, my." Sister Trafalgar feigned sympathy.

"You speak such perfect English!" Violet exclaimed. "I am so lucky."

"Lucky indeed. So, where are you headed? We can give you a ride as far as we are going."

"The, uh, Palazzo Vecchio?" Violet said.

"Holy coincidences! We're going to Florence!" The nun lied, giggling like a schoolgirl. She nudged Sister Crows next to her. "Why don't you be a good little Sister and help put this little lady's friend in the backseat."

Sister Crows shot Sister Trafalgar a mean look, then turned and forced a very painful smile for Violet. "Of course." he said through gritted teeth.

He opened the passenger door and stepped out. He followed Violet over to Grant and the two of them dumped him into the back seat of the car like a bag of laundry. Sister Crows then went to sit in the passenger seat, but was stopped by Sister Trafalgar.

"No, no, no little Sister." He pushed her back out. "You stay in back with the poor man under the weather. The little lady can sit up front with me."

Sister Crows grumbled angrily as he climbed into the back seat. He glared at the unconscious pile of Grant with intense hatred.

Violet dropped into the passenger seat and closed the door. She looked over at the nun behind the wheel of the Ferrari. She couldn't help but notice the slight five o'clock shadow. *Poor thing,* Violet thought. Bad enough she's large as a house with a face like a man, she's also got some serious facial hair. No wonder she became a nun. "Boy, I sure am glad you guys, um, nuns came along. I thought we were in trouble."

"Oh, it's our job, you know, serving the Lord and helping others." Sister Trafalgar chuckled. "And you're perfectly safe with us. Now you best put on your seat belt." The nun put the car in gear and stepped on the accelerator. "Because this baby flies!"

Violet's jaw dropped as the car hit sixty miles per hour within seconds. She quickly grabbed for her seat belt.

CHAPTER 49

Violet peeked through one eye, and even that one eye was only slightly open, as Sister Trafalgar sped through back roads and highways at incredible, if not entirely illegal, speeds. Violet caught a brief glimpse of the speedometer and could have sworn she saw 120. Violet would have loved to have enjoyed the scenery, the quaint towns they were passing by on their journey north, but it flew by so fast it was all a blur. The wonderful mountains, the historic towns, the herds of sheep, nothing was seen for more than a second.

Sister Trafalgar hummed merrily and smoked the entire time. Occasionally glancing over at Violet and smiling, a large cat-ate-the-canary smile. Actually the cat-cooked-sautéed-ate-regurgitated-and-re-ate-the-canary smile.

I'm very appreciative that these nuns picked me up. Violet thought to herself. *But I'll be glad to have my feet on solid ground and see the ladies off.*

"Is everything okay, dear?" Sister Trafalgar asked.

"Hmmm?" Violet was roused from her thoughts. She would still only open one eye. "Oh, yes. I'm fine. You certainly like to drive, well, speedy."

"Makes me feel alive, like I'm flying. Does it make you nervous? I could slow down if you want."

"Um, maybe a little." *But not too much, I just want to get to the Palazzo.*

The large nun shifted down. She gave Violet another of her creepy smiles. "So what's waiting at the Palazzo Vecchio, if I may ask?"

Violet shrugged. "Nothing much." She didn't want to insult the Sister by talking about God being an alien from another planet. "Just touring Italy. Seeing the sights."

"I see. So where were you two coming from? Rome?"

"Yes, we did. We went to the Sistine Chapel. It was beautiful." Violet saw no harm in sharing that much. Just don't say anything offensive.

"Ah, yes, the chapel. A beautiful place." Sister Trafalgar laughed. "We've been there, I don't know, maybe twelve times." She heavily emphasized the twelve and waited for a reaction.

Violet was too scared to pick up on the nuances of the Sister's conversation. She was barely able to concentrate. Her heart was pounding. "Oh, that's nice," was all she could muster.

In the back seat Sister Crows was staring at the still sleeping Grant, salivating. The little nun's hands flexed uncontrollably. Grant's neck was calling out, 'Please choke me! Please kill me by snapping my neck!' The repetition in Sister Crows' head was intolerable. He wasn't going to be able to fight off the urge much longer.

Up in the front, Sister Trafalgar continued to try and get Violet to slip and reveal something. "Did you see anything interesting at the chapel? Find anything that was, I don't know, some kind of a revelation?"

"The entire place was interesting." *I don't know what a revelation is so I'll leave that alone.* she thought. "It was breathtaking to say the least. I wish I could have taken pictures."

"Why, did you find something to take a picture of?" The nun blurted.

Violet was surprised by the nun's persistence. "Duh, yeah. The whole place." Violet laughed. "It's truly an amazing place."

Sister Trafalgar was getting frustrated. The girl just wasn't going to give anything up. He was going to have to be patient and see what happened in Florence. As he fumed over his inability to retrieve any information, Sister Trafalgar glanced in the rearview.

Sister Crows was strangling Grant.

Grant's face was turning a deep shade of purple. Sister Trafalgar quickly looked over at Violet and saw her eyes closed. He reached back and swatted Sister Crows in the side of the head, the car swerved violently, entering the opposite lane. Cars coming in the other direction honked and crashed, swerving off the road into ditches. Violet screamed as Sister Trafalgar regained control of the vehicle.

He turned to Violet and smiled. "A poor little animal wandered onto the road. We can't hurt any of God's creatures, can we?" he giggled.

"I guess not." Violet was shaken, but nodded her agreement. She fought to regain her breathing.

Behind them, Sister Crows whimpered, rubbing the side of his face. He looked at his partner in the mirror and bared his teeth.

Suddenly Grant awoke, his face now only slightly red. He lurched forward and yelled, "We're on a religioush quesht!!!" Then passed out again.

Violet smiled at the nuns and weakly laughed. "Ignore him. He's had a bit too much of this country's fine wine."

CHAPTER 50

They slowed a little once they entered the city of Florence. But only a little. The Sister still drove maniacally through the crowded streets, they flew over the Ponte Vecchio, a bridge that spans the Arno, a large, slow-moving river that dissects Florence. Crowds of people jumped for safety and pigeons took flight to avoid being squashed beneath the screaming Ferrari.

Minutes later, they came to a screeching stop in front of a tall, gothic palace.

"Here we are!" Sister Trafalgar announced gleefully.

Violet opened her door and shakily exited the car. She gave herself a minute to get her land legs back. As she did, Sister Crows climbs from the back and began dragging the semi-conscious Grant out. She helped the nun and sat Grant on the sidewalk. Sister Crows hopped into the front seat and closed the door.

Violet leaned into the car and smiled at the nuns. "I can't thank you enough. You g.. I mean, ladies were life savers, really."

Sister Trafalgar waved it off. "Think nothing of it, dear! Just another day in our line of work. You take care of your sickly friend there and enjoy your vacation here."

Violet looked over her shoulder at Grant. A woman walking down the street dropped a Euro in his lap and frowned, feeling bad for the homeless man.

"We'll be okay." Violet said. "Thanks again."

"Take care." And the nuns were gone in a squeal of burning rubber.

Wow. Didn't think I'd survive that. Violet sighed. She returned to Grant and helped him up. She lightly pat his cheek, hoping to awaken him. "Grant. C'mon Grant. Wake up."

"Huh? What?" Grant slurred, his eyes only opening half way.

"We're here. At the Palazzo Vecchio. We did it, Grant. How do you feel? Can you walk?"

"I'm hungry," he mumbled. "I feel better but I'm real hungry."

Violet thought about it for a moment. They certainly couldn't afford to eat. Not monetarily, or even time-wise. She quickly routed through her purse and found an old sandwich bag of trail mix. It was probably very stale but it would have to do.

She poured what was left of her breakfast from yesterday into her palm and held it up to Grant, who munched on it like a horse from a feedbag. She patted his head. "There you go, good boy, there you go."

A short while later, Grant was feeling better and was able to stand on his own. "I'm really sorry about that. I have to be real careful when it comes to mixing my pills."

"I can see that." Violet smiled. "Are you okay enough to go on?"

"Yeah. I'll be fine." Grant mustered up strength to laugh. "What are we waiting for? Your heritage awaits." He stood up and waivered a little.

Violet appreciated his feigned strength and put an arm around him. Together they shuffled toward the Palazzo.

CHAPTER 51

Just past the entrance the Ferrari took one turn and screamed into a parking spot near the back of the Palazzo.

Sister Crows tore off his habit and threw it against the dash. "We had them!!" he screamed. "We could've tortured them, killed them and dumped them in that big river back there!"

Sister Trafalgar calmly lit a cigarette. "Mr. Maystyne wants us to find out what they know first. He thinks they are on the path. Secondly, we have to make sure they haven't shared any information with anyone."

The shorter nun shook visibly. "I'm itchy. Real itchy. I need a fix!"

Sister Trafalgar unlocked the passenger door. "Go ahead. I'll give you one minute. Two tops. But hurry, we have to get in there and see what they're doing."

Sister Crows threw open the door and was off like a feral animal, sniffing down a victim.

"Damn! He should have put his habit back on." Sister Trafalgar sighed, then laughed to himself. "That boy's got problems." He looked in the mirror and adjusted his own habit.

CHAPTER 52

"There's the statue of David," Grant said. "Well, a copy at least. The original, as I said earlier, is at the Accademia Gallery."

"Wow, it's beautiful." Violet's eyes were wide. "Why'd they move the original?"

"Well, the marble that Michelangelo carved it from was a rather poor block. It was porous marble, and they felt exposing to the elements any longer would contribute to its degeneration. So in 1873 they moved it. Did you know, the slab was quarried 40 years before Mr. Buonarroti ever layed chisel to it? And two other artists attempted to carve from the stone but eventually gave up. Only Michelangelo could free such an exquisite statue from that block."

"It's a good thing they did. It's amazing."

"Indeed. Now we better get inside. I don't know when they close."

Violet and Grant entered the Palazzo, but not until Grant borrowed more of Violet's money to pay the admission fee.

Worst date ever. What kind of guy makes the woman pay every time? Violet groaned to herself. Well, maybe not the worst date ever. There was that one guy that puked up a tapeworm.

Upon entering, they found themselves in a medium sized courtyard. They gazed about, admiring the impressive stonework, the intricately carved columns and the fountain in the center. Violet cooed over the sculpture in the fountain.

"Look, it's a boy with a fish! What's it called?" Violet asked.

"Boy with a fish." Grant replied, scratching at his collar.

"Very funny."

"No really. It's by Andrea del Verrocchio. Simply titled 'Boy with a fish'." Grant nudged her along. "We have to get inside. From what I hear, there's a lot of rooms in this place and we don't even know what we're looking for."

"Yes, mother." Violet frowned as she tore herself away from the fountain.

Once out of the first courtyard, they had to pass through two more. Each as impressive as the one before. All decorated with powerful columns, stone carvings, and statues. Grant plowed ahead, weaving in between tourists.

"Grant, slow down." Violet called to him. "This isn't a marathon."

"Violet, this place closes in about an hour. I overheard one of the other tourists saying that. It'll take a miracle for us to search this entire place and find what we came for in that amount of time. So if you don't mind, can you please stop gawking and get back to our mission?"

"Jeez," Violet grimaced. "Do you have an anti-cranky pill in that backpack of yours?"

Grant didn't answer, but stepped further into the building. Violet shook her head as she followed behind him.

Violet's scowl disappeared as soon as she entered the first room.

"Holy..." was all that she could say.

The Salone dei Cinquecento was an immense hall measuring over 8000 square feet. Large frescoes covered the walls, towering over them. Every footstep echoed inside the cavernous room.

"The frescoes in here were originally done by none other than Michelangelo himself, and, that *other* painter dude." Grant scowled. "Then later it was redesigned by Giorgio Vasari and his pupils, they depict some of the major military skirmishes of Florence. There's no Madonna in here. We have to keep moving." Grant paused briefly to point out a large marble statue. "Genius of Victory by Michelangelo."

It looked to Violet like two gay guys getting it on.

Violet fell in behind Grant again as he whirl winded through the hall. Grant was practically dashing as he scanned the Palazzo's several rooms, rooms that were smaller in size but not lacking in decor. Statues, frescoes on the walls and ceilings, maps, tapestries, even furniture decorated with gems, they all flew past. Violet kept pace but was frustrated. She was really starting to appreciate art and architecture, even, she dare say, history. She was used to Grant rattling off facts when they were looking at something. It was a different Grant, a more serious one. Also an itchy one, he was constantly scratching, at his neck, his chest, even his butt a few times.

They passed through another room and into another. Grant skidded to a halt.

He suddenly ran up to a small statue. "Madonna and child!" he said, studying the piece. It was about ten inches high, the figures were a light brown color, only the Madonna's cloak was painted with color. It sat on a dresser. Grant stood with his nose within inches.

"Not what we want," he declared and took off again.

"Are you sure?" Violet called after him.

"Yep! It was made after Michelangelo. There's no way he'd know it was here." His eyes darted about like a maniac. "Besides, there's nothing flying over her shoulder."

Another three rooms passed, one with cabinets decorated with bronze and what looked like tortoiseshell. The next with tapestries telling stories of hunting. The next with green walls and frescoes of Moses.

"This looks familiar." Grant said as they stumbled into yet another room. "Some of the other rooms I haven't seen in books. But this room I know. This is the Chapel of the Signoria. It is dedicated to St. Bernard, and before you laugh, not the dog."

Violet rolled her eyes. "Like I would have said that." *I didn't know St. Bernard was anything* but *a dog. It's a real person?* She admitted to herself.

"The frescoes on the walls here are by Ridolfo Ghirlandaio." Grant took several steps further. "Aha! The next room." And Grant was off again.

"Sala dell Orologio," he announced. "Also known as the Hall of the Lilies."

"Ooh. I like lilies." Violet smiled, looking around for the flowers.

"Don't look for actual lilies." Grant said, pointing up. "It refers to the fleur-de-lys design in the ceiling." The ceiling was a honeycomb of relief. Framed in gold polygons, the flower shaped carving sprouted from a field of deep blue.

"Floor de what?" Violet stared, mesmerized by the amazing pattern.

"It's a variant of the Latin fleur-de-luce or flower of lights." Grant smirked. "And yes, you guessed it, it is suggested the flower of lights is a reference to UFOs, since many spacecraft have been reported as looking like blooming flower-shapes bathed in light. And the pattern above you, with the flower in the field of blue, is supposed to appear to be them floating in the sky."

"Okay. What does that all mean to us?"

"It means we're close." Grant spun and returned to the hunt. "The next room, the Stanza del Guardaroba!"

CHAPTER 53

Sister Trafalgar stood outside, leaning on the Ferrari. He checked his watch again and cursed under his breath. "That irresponsible little…"

Sister Crows came bounding around the corner. He ran up, obviously scared, and quickly began a rambling apology. "I'm very very very very sorry but I was at a café and there was this guy and he was really annoying, acting all snooty, I think he was French so I just had to…"

Smack!

"I gave you two minutes, you took eight. That is unacceptable. But I don't have time to deal out your punishment." He pulled out Sister Crows' habit and threw it at him. "Put this on. We have to see if they found anything."

Sister Crows replaced his habit. "I'm sorry, boss."

Sister Trafalgar reached for Sister Crows, who immediately cringed, expecting to be hit. The hit didn't come.

Sister Trafalgar wiped at his little friend's chin.

"You got a little dead French guy on your lip."

CHAPTER 54

"There she is!" Grant screamed, gaining the attention of all the other tourists. He ran up to a wall and lifted his arms in reverence. "The Madonna!"

Violet caught up and stared at the large fresco held in a golden frame. It was a beautiful image of the Virgin Mary, kneeling on a hill over two infants. Violet had no idea who the children were, she thought maybe it was Jesus or some other religious kid.

Grant shook excitedly. "I knew I'd seen this before! I'm such an idiot for not remembering! This image is so important for ufologists across the globe. It completely ties Mary in with aliens. The next twelfth has got to be around here somewhere!"

Violet stepped in. "First thing Grant, quiet down, everybody's staring at us. Secondly, how does this tie in anything? It's a beautiful painting, really, but where's the connection? What are you seeing that I'm not?"

Grant took a few steps away from the fresco, he placed a slimy hand on Violet's shoulder and led her further away.

"Just look at it. It's called the Madonna with Saint Giovannino, painted sometime in the 15th century."

"Sometime?"

"It's not really known. Nor the artist. But some speculate, based on the style, it was a student of the Lippi school. Some of the Lippi pupils were Ghirlandajo and Botticelli. Fillipo Lippi himself was commissioned to do work here at the Palazzo but it never happened. So we will probably never know who painted it." Grant had his cheesy grin on again. "But," he said with flair. "The artist was definitely in on some key alien knowledge. If not a protector of the Twelve himself."

"Again, why do you say that? What am I missing?"

"Look closely."

"I am." Violet was getting impatient.

"What's going on around her?"

"Nothing. Two babies on the ground, she's kneeling over them. There's a tree and some mountains. A river or ocean or lake, there's water."

"And?"

"Oh for Christ's sake Grant just tell me. I'm obviously too stupid to find it myself." She planted her hands on her hips.

"Look in the sky. Over her left shoulder."

"Yeah, I see that. Wait." She squinted, then took a step forward. "What is that?"

"You tell me. Look closer."

Violet tilted her head left then right, she glanced back at Grant. "Are you serious? Is that a…"

"Yes, it is."

"Holy shit!" Violet barked, soliciting angry and disapproving stares from the others in the room. She lowered her voice. "It's a UFO?"

"Yup," Grant beamed proudly, as though he were the painter himself.

Violet stepped up closer. Sure enough, flying in the sky over the Virgin Mary's shoulder, far back in the horizon, was an ovoid object hovering in the sky. It wasn't just a round shape, like a cloud or something simply bumpy, like a meteor. It had the classic elements of a hubcap flying saucer, a sectionalized top, fatter middle, and thinner bottom. And this was long before hubcaps existed. It was on a slight angle, as though either taking off for the heavens, or coming in for a landing. It looked almost as though there were protrusions from it, like several antennae. And it was glowing with an aura of yellow. *Un-freaking-believable!* Violet was in awe. A UFO, painted over Mary's shoulder, over 500 years ago.

Violet looked next to her, Grant had joined her for the closer examination.

"This one is very hard for non-believers to explain. There's nothing you can write it off as other than a glowing solid object in the sky." Grant pointed. "And it gets better. Look on the side of the hill there. What do you see?"

"Hey! It's a guy, standing there with his dog." Violet's voice was getting more and more excited. "And they're looking at it! He's covering his eyes, as though he's got the sun in his eyes."

"Or the glow from the space craft is that powerful," Grant added.

"Even the little doggie is looking up at it." Violet turned to Grant. "This is unbelievable, Grant. This is so much more than just seeing a brain or liver in a painting. This is a solid object flying a hundred years before man took flight."

Grant snickered. "Four hundred. But who's counting?"

Violet leaned in close and whispered. "Okay, I'm blown away. But now we're going to have to find the hidden reli-whatever, right?"

"Reliquary. Yes."

"How? There's quite a few people milling about. I can't cause another scene like I did last time."

"We're going to have to kill time. According to the poem, it should be hidden in the frame where her eyes are looking. But that's going to draw a lot of attention if I start breaking that open. This place closes in less than half an hour. We have to hide somewhere until it either thins out or closes."

Violet gritted her teeth. "I don't want to get locked in here overnight or anything like that. I think it'd creep the Hell out of me."

"Don't worry. I won't let that happen. Now let's find someplace to be scarce."

CHAPTER 55

The two nuns were allowed entrance into the Palazzo Vecchio without paying the entrance fee. Nor were they searched, not that people are searched at the Palazzo, but in this case they should have been. Two Glock 9mm pistols, fitted with silencers were carefully hidden beneath their flowing gowns.

The man at the front told the Sisters that they were closing in a little while but he'd wait around so they could take their time.

"You're such a sweet, nice man." Sister Trafalgar said in his falsetto, scratchy pseudo-woman's voice. "*Graci.*"

They quickly made their way through the courtyard. The crowd had thinned considerably and it was easy to scan areas, see that their prey wasn't there, and then move on. Sister Trafalgar lit up a cigarette once they were inside the main building of the Palazzo. The few tourists that remained stared in disbelief as the audacious nun puffed on her Marlboro. "Disgraciado!" they mumbled in his direction.

Sister Trafalgar ignored them, shooting them a venomous glare, which made them retreat quickly. A man approached, with the intent look of someone ready to give a lecture on proper etiquette. Sister Trafalgar raised his robe, showing his hairy, thick man-legs and his gun resting in a garter belt. The man quickly exited.

Sister Trafalgar turned to his little partner. "Get their scent yet, buddy?"

"I think I do." Sister Crows said, sniffing the air. "Follow me." The nun took off, scampering through the galleries and hallways of the Palazzo.

CHAPTER 56

"What time is it?" Grant asked Violet.

She looked at her watch. "I still haven't adjusted it, but my watch says 5:58."

"Okay, good. We should be able to get out of here in a few minutes."

The two had found an adjoining room with several closets, smaller side rooms, and even a large chest capable of fitting two adults. Grant suggested hiding in the chest but Violet, knowing that Grant would want nothing more than to be stuck in a box, lying prone, indefinitely with or, even worse, on her. No way! So she suggested one of the closets, choosing the largest one she could find, after peeking in most of them.

Grant rubbed at his eyes. "Man, it's hot in here isn't it?"

"Not really." Violet shrugged.

"I feel like it is." Grant was now raking his nails across his cheek, like a dog with fleas. "I'm itchy and my stomach doesn't feel too good."

"Maybe you're due for more of your pills?" Violet offered.

"No. Not until seven." Grant put his hands on his stomach. "Gosh, I'm swelling like a balloon."

Violet cracked open the closet door and peered out. "The room's empty. Should we venture out?"

Grant's face distorted with discomfort. "Yeah. I think I need to walk this off."

The two crept from their hiding spot and made their way back into the Stanza del Guardaroba. The Palazzo was eerily quiet, no one was in sight. Violet checked the adjoining rooms.

"I don't see anyone," she whispered.

"Good," Grant moaned. "Let's make this quick."

Grant shuffled up to the painting of the Madonna, without his standard enthusiasm, and took out his Swiss Army Knife. He followed the Madonna's eyes and drew an invisible line to the point of the frame she appeared to be looking.

Grant turned to Violet. "Go keep watch at the door and make sure no one wanders up this way."

"Yes, boss." Violet replied. She walked across the room and poked her head out.

Grant felt around the frame, then behind it, looking for an opening. It was thick, heavy, and wouldn't come apart easily. So he dug in. Through much grunting and groaning, Grant managed to pry an edge of the frame back.

"Need any help Hercules?" Violet quipped, calling out across the room.

"No," Grant panted. "And keep it down. I've almost got it."

"Don't damage what's in there." Violet added.

"I won't! Now let me work here." Grant returned to his struggle, too stubborn to show any weakness in front of Violet. Eventually the frame bent enough and something fell from inside and clattered on the floor. "I did it!" Grant said. He went to put the knife away but the blade was bent. He couldn't fold it back. He shrugged and put it back in his back pack.

Violet scurried back to Grant's side. She picked up another iron box. Again, once opened, layers of ancient papers were curled up. Grant watched her as she unfurled them. It was remarkably similar to the first one.

1830

Vicino ai cieli' il viaggiatore fa la conoscenza risiede

Su alto, il padre ed il figlio il mondo che guidano

Un'abbazia rinata da un progetto del Papa

In Perusia dove hanno ricostruito il tempo

PS51.17.5 EP3.13.12 GE27.1.40 DE28.68.9 IS5.4.1 IS6.2.28 AC7.7.12 EX9.1.12 EP2.1.2 DE1.28.40 IS2.22.7 NU6.4.10 LE17.9.14 DE5.1.28 GE27.18.14 PS87.6.12 EP6.1.10 IS5.25.42 EX23.7.6 LU6.9.3 EX9.7.26 PS37.1.2 DE31.5.25 RU3.14.28 PS84.11.19 LE19.4.8 LU16.4.6 PS42.8.19 GE27.30.12 EX18.3.21 GE26.9.16

RU1.13.25   DE3.4.9   PS66.6.16   RO12.18.10   IS24.1.11   GE13.4.19
EC1.10.11   IS56.10.3   GE26.27.21   GE31.18.15   GE33.9.6   DA12.2.6
LE4.2.33   RO16.23.10   PS58.9.5   LU6.26.9   EX30.5.4   PS4.7.8
EX21.11.17   PR17.27.2   PS16.8.6   PS4.8.15   RO16.7.23   DE33.29.1
NU2.12.3   LE20.2.1   PS92.1.8   DE30.20.23   PR21.6.2   DE31.22.4
DE29.20.31

    Ricetta LE2.13
    TH90

"Hmmm. This one is kind of easy, I think." Grant beamed, obviously proud of himself. "I know where we're going next."

"Do tell." Violet frowned. "So what's it say?"

"It pretty much says,

> Near the heavens' traveler does knowledge reside
> On high, father and son, the world they guide
> An abbey reborn by a Pope's design
> In Perusia where they did rebuild time"

"Okay, and you know where we're going?"

"Well, Perusia isn't around anymore. It's now known as Perugia."

"Wow, big name change. Go ahead."

"Anyway, the only abbey in Perugia that was reborn would be the Church of San Pietro. In 1398 it was practically burned to the ground in a rebellion. But Pope Eugene IV brought it back after years of neglect. And this reference to rebuilding time must refer to the clock tower. It had partially collapsed and was rebuilt in 1483."

"So we're off to Perugia. Do you know how to get there?"

"Not really." Grant's stomach rumbled violently as he reviewed the poem.

Violet looked at him in surprise. "Wow. I heard that. Are you going to be okay?"

"I don't know. This usually only happens when I eat peanuts," His cheeks puffed as he swallowed a belch. "Or any tree nuts. Or milk and eggs. And shellfish." He sighed. "Oh, and wheat."

"Jesus, is there anything you're not allergic to?" Violet asked.

"Yeah, soy." Grant said. "I don't get it. I haven't eaten since this morning. What could have caused this?"

Violet's eyes bulged. *Oh crap.* She forced a smile. "Well, er, Grant. Remember when you were kind of out of it earlier?"

Grant nodded his pale face. "Yeah. Why?"

"Well you were so sick, I thought food would help."

"Yeah. And?"

"I, well, I sort of fed you trail mix."

"What?!!" Grant shrieked. "Are you insane?"

"How was I to know?" Violet defended herself. "I was trying to help. How was I supposed to know you were the most allergic guy in the world?"

Grant grabbed his backpack. "Okay, okay, okay. Let's not panic." He was ranting, practically to himself. "Trail mix of all things! Not only did it have peanuts, but probably sunflower seeds. And raisins!" He paused and looked at Violet. "Don't tell me it had Chex in it?"

Violet nodded.

"Good grief!" He returned to fishing around his bag. "Wheat! That's all I needed!"

"Are you going to die?" Violet placed a hand on Grant's arm.

"Maybe!" Grant withdrew a packet from his backpack. "Aha!"

"What is that?"

"It's my auto-injector. Also called an epi-pen, it's full of epinephrine." Grant smiled, his face all red and bumpy. "I keep a few of these on hand just in case." He opened the plastic packaging and pulled out a needle, which he promptly uncapped and jabbed into his thigh.

"How long until you're better?"

"Depends," Grant's watery red-rimmed eyes glared at her. "On how much I ate."

"It was only a few handfuls." Violet pouted. "Grant, I really am sorry. I was trying to help. I had no way of knowing. Please forgive me."

He grabbed his stomach again. "Not to gross you out but I think I need to release a little internal pressure. If you know what I mean."

Violet stared blankly. "No, I don't."

"You know, let off some air." Grant's pale face was reddening with embarrassment.

Blank stare.

"Toot? Pass wind?"

Nothing.

"Fart, Violet! Ah may have to fart. You know wit dat means, dint you?"

"Oh! Fart! I got it!" Then Violet tilted her head, her brow furrowed. "Um, Grant. What's happening to your speech?"

Grant looked back at her confused. "Why? Whas wong wit mah spish?" Suddenly he realized what was happening. He felt around the inside of his mouth with his finger. "Ah, giddimit! Mah tunk is awl swollen! Jeshish fuggin kistmash!"

"My god! That's awful. Will this go away?"

Grant shrugged. "Awl be awite. Ah hewp. Da epinefern wull halp, bot it well tik a wahl."

"I'm really sorry, Grant." Suddenly a door opened a few rooms away, and hushed talking could be heard. Violet looked at Grant. "Somebody's here!" she whispered. "We better hide!"

"Uh-kay." Grant stood up, his bloated tongue hanging from between his equally swollen lips.

Violet led them back into the room of closets. They returned to their original hiding place. Violet left it open a crack so she could see who, if anyone, came into the room. Grant dropped to the ground, holding his stomach. Violet cursed her luck. *Why me? Why me? What did I ever do?* She frowned. *Never mind. I've done plenty wrong. But why now?* She glanced back at Grant. At least it was dark in the closet. She didn't have to look at his face for a few. It really was breaking out in a rash and swelling, it was kind of freaking her out. *Big baby. It was only trail mix.*

The sound of softly placed footfalls broke her train of thought and she placed an eye to the crack of the door. She could sense someone back in the room where they found the Madonna. A shadow crept into the doorway to that room. She held her breath.

The flowing robes of a nun filled the doorway. A tall, portly nun, with a hand gun.

No way! Violet's mind screamed. *The nun from the car!*

Sister Trafalgar glanced around the room then returned to the Stanza del Guardaroba. He was whispering to someone out of view. Violet was pretty confident it had to be the short nun.

I should've known it was too coincidental. And weird! But why? And who are they? Violet heard Grant moan and she swatted him. "Shhh! There are nuns with guns out there."

"Wha?" Grant tried to speak. "Nunth wit gunth?"

"I'll explain later. We have to be real quiet." Violet slowly closed the closet door all the way. Better to hide and be completely in the dark than have them potentially see the door open a crack.

Sister Trafalgar found the reliquary, and realized it was empty. "Dammit!" he growled. He let out a slight whistle and seconds later, Sister Crows scampered into the room. "They're here. I know it. They couldn't have gotten past us." He leaned in close. "Find them. Don't kill them, not yet."

"But Mr. Maystyne, he didn't want us to interact. He wanted…"

"I am making an executive decision here." Sister Trafalgar said. "We can't afford to lose them and they've already found two of the twelve! Now you… go… fetch!"

Sister Crows smiled viciously. "You got it!" And he was off, sniffing the ground in the Stanza del Guardaroba.

Sister Trafalgar spoke aloud, hoping his prey could hear him. "Hello, my friends. It is we, your nun friends. We came back; you forgot something in the car we wish to return to you. Do you not want it? It looks so valuable."

Violet couldn't believe what she was hearing. The nun was calling for her to come out. *This is bizarre! Nuns don't do this. Do they?* Violet didn't really know much about the Catholic Church, but nuns with guns? Unless they weren't nuns! Suddenly, it made sense. Sort of. Violet heard Grant's stomach howl like a distant wolf. *Get it in control Grant!*

Violet suddenly froze. Beneath the doorframe she saw a moving shadow and heard the shuffling of feet. She also heard… was that sniffling? Did they have a bloodhound out there?

Violet jumped when a noise escaped from Grant. *Fweeeeeeep.* It wasn't loud, but startled her nonetheless. *Good lord. Now is not the time, Grant!*

The sniffling of the supposed dog came closer, then moved away again. Violet let out a sigh of relief. And in his own way, so did Grant. *Fwap.* That one was slightly louder. Violet reached over and whispered in Grant's ear. "You have to hold it in! Can you please do that?"

Grant could only moan, his stomach gurgled like a clogged bathtub drain.

We're doomed. Violet shuddered.

"Excuse me, sister?" The security guard called out. He was standing in the doorway of the Stanza del Guardaroba and he looked at his watch. "They informed me that you were allowed to stay but we are shutting down in a few. I have been sent to see you safely out."

Sister Trafalgar considered shooting him there and then but thought better of it. That would only bring more and that would most likely compromise the entire situation. He shot a look over at Sister Crows, who was crouched in the next room, aware of the guard and already salivating at the opportunity to strike.

"Of course, my good man," Sister Trafalgar said. "That's very kind of you." He quickly gave Sister Crows a few simple hand gestures, telling him to stay, find, fetch, and no kill.

Sister Crows nodded and Sister Trafalgar walked off with the guard. *Such a good little trained doggie.* he mused.

CHAPTER 57

Grant moaned, a little too loudly. Violet cupped her hand over his mouth then recoiled in terror.

"What the?" Violet shivered at the touch of Grant's puffed up face. In the dark she could only see his outline at best. "Grant," she whispered, keeping her distance. "I know it's not easy but you have to be quiet."

Grant shifted slightly. A squeak escaped from beneath Grant, like air from a deflating balloon. *Fweeeeeeeeee!*

Grant spoke and Violet could hear his fat lips flapping. "Ahm twying," he cried. "Mah tunny huts ant ah cand huld it mush logger."

"Well, try Grant." Violet listened at the door. "I don't hear anything. Maybe just let out a little. But keep it quiet."

Violet heard Grant shift, lifting one butt cheek off the ground. A short squeal echoed in the closet. *Wheeeeeet!* Followed quickly by two short raps of gas. *Ffft. Ffft.* Grant giggled.

Violet glared at him but the look was wasted in the dark. "Keep it down, Grant, or else they'll…" Violet caught a lungful. "Dear God," she cried. "That's awful."

Grant giggled even more. "Dorry, ith kinda fonny."

Fweeeeeeeeep!

Violet swung her head about, trying to find untainted air to breathe. "Lord! It's like road kill in the July sun!" She actually giggled a little herself. "This is torture, Grant, stop it!"

Fwap! Fwap!

Grant was chuckling hysterically now, his shoulders bouncing as he held in his laughter as best he could. "Ah cand hep it!" His releases were getting stronger and more powerful, and with it more volume.

Bwaaaaaap!

Violet could tell he was reaching a crescendo. "Grant, hold it! Squeeze your ass together or something!"

Bwap! Fweeeep! Bwap-bwap!

"Oh, Gahd!" Grant cried. "Ahm gonna loosh it!"

Violet was in tears, she had her shirt pulled up over her mouth and nose. Her head was buried in her arms and she was laughing hysterically. She repeatedly smacked Grant on the arm, her muffled voice crying. "Stop it! Stop it! Stop it!"

"Ahm not gonna meck it!"

Violet tried to sound threatening through her own laughter. "Don't you dare let go or I'll…"

Bbbbbbrrrrraaaaaaaaaaaaaapppppppppppppppptttttttt!   *Brrrt!*
Fweeeeeeeeeee!

Just then the door was flung open. A hand grabbed Violet and dragged her out before she could make a sound.

CHAPTER 58

Sister Crows had one arm around Violet's neck and the other arm had a large, serrated, gleaming knife at the end of it. He held it up to Violet's throat. The nun was far shorter than Violet, by several inches, and Violet briefly considered attempting to fight him. But the look in his eyes seemed to lack a soul, plus the ten inch blade, made her reconsider.

"Hey, other guy, come out or the bitch gets it!" Sister Crows warned.

"Bitch?" Violet rasped. "That's not nice. What kind of nun are you?"

Sister Crows leaned in real close and whispered in Violet's ear. His voice ran shivers of fear down her spine. "Talk again without me asking and I'll gut you like a fish. I'll cut you open and show you your guts. Understand?"

Violet nodded vehemently.

"Hey, other guy. If I have to ask again you're girlfriend's blood will paint every wall in this room!" Sister Crows fidgeted nervously. "It's bad enough I have to stand around this place with you... freaks. You pill popping mutants. In this robe, in this place of your so-called religion. I don't like this weird, religious, Tylenol-infused contact with you people. And on top of all that not be able to kill anyone. I'm not a happy camper! Other guy, answer me now!"

"Hodd on!" Grant called out. "Ahm commin!"

"Was that English?" Sister Crows asked. Then he caught a whiff of Grant's expulsions. "Holy shit!" he cried. "That smells so awful! Like a diseased corpse in an oven!" Then to Violet. " What's going on in there, girlie?" When Violet didn't answer he shook her like a rag doll. He was strong for his diminutive size. "I asked you a question!"

"He's having some sort of..." Violet thought about it. There was something about his demeanor that showed fear. He was obviously nervous about something. Violet thought she'd give it a try. "He's… he's alot worse since you last saw him."

They heard shuffling from inside the closet. Grant was getting up off the floor.

"Worse?" Sister Crows asked, taking half a step back. "You said he had too much to drink!"

"I lied. We needed the ride. In reality, he's… well, he's mutating." Violet lied. "He's caught some kind of virus."

"V-virus?"

"Yes, it's terribly contagious. I probably have it. It's called… um, Sagdab's Disease. No one knows where it comes from. Some suspect space."

"Space." Sister Crows said with awe. "I like space. But not space disease."

Violet could feel the nun shaking as they watched the entrance to the closet. Suddenly a hand was placed on the door frame. It was red, puffy, and covered in ooze.

"Don shoot." Grant murmured. "Ahm commin aht."

Grant exited the closet, Sister Crows and Violet gasped in unison. Violet couldn't believe her eyes, or her luck. Grant HAD mutated. His entire face was swollen to twice its normal size. His eyes were practically shut. Drool cascaded freely over Grants inflated lips. Grant's skin was a mottled pink and red with splotches of stark white, a sheen of sweat covered him. He was more alien looking than Violet had ever seen in any movie.

"Holy… shit… holy… shit." Sister Crows repeated. "Keep him away!"

Violet jumped on the opportunity.

"Grant, you're not well." Violet honed her acting chops. "You have a serious contagion. You have to stay away from us." She could feel the nun's grip faltering slightly.

"Ah am?" Grant looked about, confused. "Ah tawt ah had gash?"

Do NOT ruin this Grant you idiot. "You're delirious, Grant. The virus has moved into your brain and is now eating it. And you're scaring the nun here. So approaching us would be bad, mostly scary, but bad."

"Okee, Vahlet. Ahll stee awee." Grant retreated to the closet.

"No, Grant." Violet wasn't getting through to him. "You're touch alone can transfer the alien virus. So you really should stay away. Especially from the nun here."

"Ahm leavin! Jeeesh." Grant started to turn away. "Ahm veddy cunfoozed." He glanced at the nervous Mr. Crows, then it dawned upon him. "Oooooh! Ah gaht du. Okee, heer gowsh."

"What is he saying?" Sister Crows whimpered. "Keep that bag of Jell-O away from me! Or so help me, I'll cut him in two!"

"You don't want to do that, Sister."

"Why not?"

"He'll explode, and then you'll get him on you, in your lungs, your eyes. You'll definitely be screwed then."

Grant took a shambling step toward them, he spoke with a weird exaggerated gurgle. Which was entirely unnecessary considering his current condition. "Vahlet, ah need hep. Hep me! Hep me! Ahm becummin an aleeyon."

"No stay away, Grant. You're diseased, a big balloon of alien pus and... and manure! Ready to burst at any moment. Stay away!" She faked a scream.

Grant was almost on top of them, reaching with a puffy, sweaty hand.

"Ahhh! Xenu help me! No!" Sister Crows cried. He quickly used Violet as a shield and shoved her into his grip. As soon as Violet landed in Grant's arms she screamed at the top of her lungs.

"Nooooo!" Violet shrieked. She doubled over, feigning pain. "Arg! I can feel it in my blood now! It's eating me! Eating me!"

Grant let her slide to the floor as she continued her charade. He took another few steps toward Sister Crows. "Ah need to eat peepel! Ah need to eat brainsh!"

Sister Crows turned and ran without hesitation. He had pulled his habit over his face to shield himself from breathing in any space zombie dust. They heard him screaming as he slammed every door behind him.

Grant turned to Violet and tried to smile. The smile didn't work by any means, his face too swollen to control his lips and cheeks "So howd ah do?"

Violet dusted herself off as she stood up from the floor. "You did great, Grant, once you knew what I wanted from you."

"Dorry. Ah can hahdly breeve. You were veddy convindin when you toushed me, actin ahll sick."

"Oh, yes. Acting. Thank you!" Violet rolled her eyes. There was hardly any acting. It was revolting enough looking at Grant, but when she landed in his swollen slimy arms, she could practically feel the fake virus eating through her skin. That wasn't any acting, it was pure revulsion. "Come on. We have to find another way out of here before they wise up."

"Letsh go." Grant slurred.

Violet took the lead and tried several doors until she found one with stairs leading down. Grant stomped and stumbled behind her, half blinded by his swollen eyelids. Violet wanted very much to help him but he was way too gross to touch. Every now and then she'd look back and ask him if he was okay. He would nod, try to smile, and release a cascade of spittle down his chin. Every step forced out more butt-air.

Eventually Violet stumbled upon a large, dusty storage room. Metal shelves lined the long room, labeled boxes and packages filled the shelves. Dust swirled in their wake. It was predominantly dark save the few scattered bulbs suspended above.

"This looks like some kind of archive." Violet said, mainly to herself. She was scared for her life and really wanted out of the Palazzo. "Hopefully it'll have a back door or dock or something." She prayed she was on the right track.

"Ah dink mah tung ish goin down." Grant said, sounding better.

"Good, now keep your eyes open for…" Violet grimaced, looking back at Grant's puffy face and nearly swollen shut eyes. "Sorry. Just stay near me."

"Dash okay."

Violet almost tripped over a stack of small boxes stacked next to a door. On the door was written; *Caricamento. Allarme di sicurezza. Non aprire.* "Can you read this?" Violet asked.

"It sez, 'Loading. Thecurity alahm...'"

Violet threw open the door without waiting for the finished translation.

"'...do not open.'" Grant finished.

Alarms exploded above their heads and shattered their eardrums. They dashed through the door into a back alley and out into the street.

"Where to?" Violet asked.

"I dunno." Grant shrugged his swollen shoulders.

"Shit." Violet looked around. Suddenly, a shiny, red, expensive looking object caught her eye. "Hello sweetheart. Who do we have here?" Violet stepped up to the Ferrari and looked back at Grant. "It's the nun's car!"

"Hah do you know?" Grant asked.

Violet was only somewhat surprised. After all, Grant was completely out of it. "You really don't remember?"

Grant shook his head.

"I'll explain later." She smiled wickedly. "Ever hotwire a car?"

Grant's eyes would have widened had he been able to. "Whah?!! No!"

"I'll show you."

CHAPTER 59

Sister Trafalgar was talking to the guards near the entrance, smoking a cigarette and flirting, when Sister Crows came running out of the first courtyard of the Palazzo. His eyes were wild with fear, sweat poured from his forehead, and he ran up to the larger nun and wrapped his arms around Sister Trafalgar's leg.

"What the Hell?" Sister Trafalgar cursed, then looked at the guards realizing his bad language. "Oh, pardon me. What in the name of the good Lord?" He reached down and pet the terrified nun on the head. "What happened in there? Did you find, um, what you were looking for?"

Sister Crows would not lighten his grip on Sister Trafalgar's leg, nor would he look up. He trembled violently as he spoke into his robe. "Diseased! That's what he is! The little one, he's diseased! And he tried to kill me with it! It's a space virus. A zombie from Mars! Oh, I didn't know what to do!"

Sister Trafalgar was utterly confused. *What the Hell is he talking about?* He looked at the guards. "You'll have to excuse him, er, her!

"What is wrong with the Sister?" The first guard asked, his eyes narrowing suspiciously.

Just then alarms began ringing throughout the entire Palazzo. One of the guards tipped his hat to the nuns then ran into the first courtyard. The other guard quickly got on the phone. Sister Trafalgar was relieved that he could leave without any more questions. Not that he'd have any problems shooting them all but he didn't want to make messes unless he had to.

Sister Trafalgar led his shaking partner away from the entrance and walked down a side street next to the Palazzo. The alarms continued ringing in the background.

"Hey, little buddy. What's wrong?" he asked. "What'd they do to you? I'll kill 'em if they hurt you!"

"He was so... mutated!" Sister Crows cried. "He was an alien!"

Wow! He's more screwed up than usual. "I'll get you back to the car. We'll figure out what happened. Hang in there little guy."

Sister Trafalgar was practically carrying his friend when he turned the corner to the back of the Palazzo.

"Mother fucker!!" he screamed at the sight of a missing Ferrari. Several pedestrians looked in shock at the profane nun. He glared back. "Mind your own Goddamn business you frigging guidos or I'll kill every one of you!" He pulled out his gun. People scattered in all directions.

He tried to regain his calm. "Now how am I going to explain this to the boss?"

CHAPTER 60

The loud grinding of gears echoed through the streets of Florence and crowds stopped and stared at the butchering of a $165,000 car.

"I didn't know it'd be stick!" Violet screamed over the noise. The car bucked and stalled. A small car beeped behind them. Violet stuck her head out the window and screamed at the driver. Her guttural bellow terrified Grant.

"I'm trying here! Do you mind?!! Scusi!!!" Violet slid back into the seat and put the car in neutral. "God, the nerve of some people."

Grant said nothing, despite the fact that his tongue was doing rather well.

Violet dug in her purse, looking for a smoke. She glanced over at Grant, whose swelling had gone down greatly, but he still wheezed a bit when he breathed. *I can wait until we get out of the car. I need this guy, I can't kill him.* She put her purse aside.

Twenty minutes later, outside of Florence, Violet finally had gotten the hang of a stick shift. They were speeding along at 20 miles per hour, permanently in first gear, but moving nonetheless.

Violet spoke loudly over the whining of the engine. "So I guess we should get to an airport?"

Grant nodded. "If my translation of the poem is correct, no. We're off to Perugia, which is only a little more than a hundred miles from here. We have to get to the Church of San Pietro."

"A hundred miles? God help me! We're going to need directions." Violet pulled into the first Petrol Station she saw and hopped out. The car shuddered before it finally quieted down. Violet only hoped it would run again when she started it up. She left Grant in the car, not only because his appearance was terrifying, but he'd probably say something to offend the station attendant. On her way in Violet noticed a rusty old car next to the station. She trotted up to it and peered inside. "Yes!"

Grant watched Violet with curiosity as she dashed about the front of the station before disappearing inside. "What is she up to?"

Violet reappeared a few minutes later, map in hand, and walked up to Grant's window. "Get out," she said.

"Why?"

"Because we're not going another mile in this thing. We're trading down."

Grant shook his head. "Uh-uh. You mean that old Fiat over there? No way. That thing is like thirty years old at least. I'd rather cruise along in first gear the rest of the way then go anywhere in that."

Violet grabbed his collar. "Use your head. Not only can we go faster in that but the nuns, if that's what they were, might be looking for their car. And if they have connections with the *polizia*, then we're screwed. Plus, it's an automatic, which I can drive, so we won't blow up on the highway! *Capisce?*"

Grant nodded his lumpy head. "Well put. I accept your argument."

Soon they were speeding down the highway doing 25 miles per hour. Grant kept to himself, studying the map that the station attendant was kind enough to draw out the route to Perugia.

Violet and Grant chugged along winding roads, through rolling green hills full of lush grass and vineyards. The sun was high and strong and saturated the landscape in brilliance. Violet sighed. This would be such a wonderful vacation if the situation wasn't so awful.

"Hey Violet," Grant said, clearing his throat first. "Can you tell me more about your mother?"

"What about her?" Violet wasn't thrilled to have her tour of the scenery disturbed.

"I don't know. Whatever you remember? Maybe it's connected somehow?"

"I don't know much Grant, it was so long ago. What little I remember about her was that she was sweet to me."

"What about near the end?"

"I sort of remember the night she left. I used to tell my father what I remembered but he would just say it was a bad dream."

"Tell me about it."

"Okay, but it sounds a little nutty." Violet couldn't believe she was going to share her memory with a sweaty little nerd like Grant. "It was night, very late. I had already been in bed but I woke up because I saw all these lights. They were coming through the window, under my door. And I heard talking, chattering, like on a radio." Violet paused as they slowed to pass a herd of goats. "So I walked out of my room, and I could barely see with all the light. But I remember men, at least I think they were men, with big eyes, and I saw my mother, floating. They were taking her. And I cried out to stop them but my father grabbed me and took me back to my room. And I called after my mother and she just floated out the front door. My father locked me in the room and wouldn't let me out until the lights were gone." Violet wiped at a tear in her eye. "And that's what I remember. Told you it was crazy."

"Wow." Grant was stunned. "I'm really sorry. But that is… so cool!"

"What?" Violet was aghast. "How dare you!"

"Violet, that was a classic example of an alien abduction!"

"Get real. You're an idiot." Violet spat. "Did you eat lead-based paint chips when you were a kid?"

"Think about it, Violet. It all makes sense. We know there's a connection between Mary, Jesus and aliens. We're not sure what that is yet but it's there. We also know the connection also involves Twelvists, which you father apparently was. Why is it so hard to believe that your mother was abducted? What if, because your father was a protector of a portion of the Twelve, your mother was taken for good reasons?"

"What possible good reason could aliens have to take my mother?"

"I don't know. They're beyond us intellectually. Maybe she had an illness and they could cure her. Or maybe they thought they could learn from her. Maybe your father traded her."

"For what?" Violet growled. "You know, I may be buying into some of this alien and Jesus crap but don't push your luck. Do me a favor and don't talk for a while."

"Okay. Sorry." Grant sank in his seat.

A short while later they arrive in Perugia. Grant perked up after such a long silence. "Did you know that Perugia first appeared in history, as Perusia, and was one of the twelve confederate cities of Etruria?"

"Of course, Grant, who didn't?" Violet said sarcastically.

Grant shot her a look. "I was just pointing out historical facts about the places we're traveling to and their connection to the number twelve. No need to be smarmy."

After asking a polite older woman for directions, Grant and Violet arrived at the Church of San Pietro. There was no fee and was open to the public. Violet was thankful that she didn't have to shell out even more money.

Grant and Violet gazed upon the building, soaking up the beauty of the two story church. The golden hue of the sunlight poured in over the gilded columns and pews, glinting off the inlaid furniture and sacristy. They walked among the rows and rows of polished oaken pews and stood before the wooden choir. Grant pointed to the collection of paintings that lined the walls beneath the overhang of the second floor.

Grant ran up to a painting. "This here is a Raphael, and that is a Vasari! Man, this church alone is like a museum. This place is gorgeous!"

"So what should we be looking for this time?" Violet asked, not as enthralled by the paintings. Not that they weren't beautiful, but she was hungry and overwhelmed. And she hadn't had her cigarette. How long had it been? She'd never gone this long without a smoke. She'd have to double-up when they got out of the church.

"Well, the poem mentions a father and his son, so most likely that'd be God and Jesus. And this thing about heavens' traveler, I'll assume like the prior painting, it's going to be a UFO."

"How about a satellite?" Violet asked.

"A satellite? Doubtful." Grant said without looking at Violet.

"No, really," she continued. "How about an actual satellite?"

Grant turned and saw where Violet was looking. Across the church, a fresco stretched from floor to ceiling, surrounded by a golden frame. In the painting; two holy men stood in front of an altar, looking up at a cloud, upon which sat God and Jesus, and between them… an exact replica of a 1960's era satellite.

"Sputnik!" Grant exclaimed.

"Sput-what?" Violet asked.

"Sputnik was a series of satellites in the fifties and sixties, from Russia no less," Grant's excitement grew as he stared at the fresco. "And what we see between God and Jesus is a ridiculously dead-on depiction of a sputnik satellite."

God and Jesus sat facing each other with the satellite between them at their feet. The sphere, made of polished metal, showed lines as though from welded metal and had a lens in the lower left portion of the sphere. From the top of the satellite, two antennae sprouted, and each antenna was firmly held in the grasp of both God and Jesus, as if they were directing its course.

"B-but how could that be?" Violet was amazed. "When was this painted?"

"Its exact date is unknown." A voice from behind them. "But it was roughly painted around 1600 AD."

Violet turned around, startled. Grant let out a small shriek. A man stood behind them, no more than five feet tall. He wore an old three-piece suit that was sullied by time and disregard and was held together by threads in some spots. He had a wide smile, filled with neglected teeth, and framed by long, gray beard. He bowed slightly and waved a pleasant salute.

"Who are you?" Violet demanded.

"Please, we must speak in hushed tones." the man said. "There are those that would destroy all that we believe in."

"Okay, who are you?" Violet repeated, slightly softer.

"I, like you, am a protector of secrets and pursuer of the truth. I spend my time, lingering here, at the Glorification of the Eucharist, helping those that share our beliefs in their pursuit."

Violet turned to Grant. "Was that bullshit or what?"

Grant shook his head and stepped toward the man.

"Why should we believe you? What do you know?" Grant asked.

"You stand before a fresco, painted centuries ago, that clearly shows the Lord and his child holding a space satellite. I think what we all share is the relationship between Christianity and our friends from beyond the stars."

"He's a nut!" Violet blurted.

"Now hold on." Grant reprimanded her. "So you know of the Twelve?" he asked the little man.

"Indeed." He smiled. "Allow me to introduce myself, my name is, or was, Prince Shozich. I was the ruler of a small Lithuanian province until my knowledge of the twelve and the untruths of Christianity forced me from my seat and a relative took my throne. I was locked up, called insane."

"See?" Violet gnashed her teeth.

Prince Shozich continued. "I feigned clarity long enough for my family to regain faith in me. And at first chance, I left my homeland. And I have been searching for the truth for nearly a decade. I fell on hard times and spend my remaining days here, helping those that share the search."

"Prince Shozich," Grant didn't hide his excitement. "So it is all true! Then you know that somewhere here is a reliquary, with a poem, a code, and a clue to the next portion of the Twelve."

"Sadly, my boy, it was discovered months ago. By a gentleman who did not give his name. And I aided him, not knowing myself that I sat upon the information of which you speak. He found it and took it. I fear he was not one of us, a good guy as you would say, but searching for selfish reasons."

"Did you catch any of it? Did he say anything of what it said?" Grant begged.

The Prince closed his eyes, appearing pained, then sighed. "He spoke into a phone when he read what he'd found. He read a poem, the verses of which I'll never get correct, not from memory. But the few lines I remember are,

> *The virgin's wisdom comes down from above*
> *Her fate is guided by our savior's dove*

I'm afraid that's all I remember of the poem."

"Anything else?" Grant asked. "A set of four or five numbers preceded by one or more letters?"

"A few numbers I think. I think it was a 5, then a 1, and then another 1. I think there was an L before them. Then the person on the other side spoke, I assume, since the man waited and listened. And then the man said the National Gallery. I'm sorry, but that's all I can recall."

"That's more than I hoped for." Grant said. He turned to Violet. "Still a non-believer? He gave a partial poem. Knew there was a code in there."

"I guess." Violet shrugged. "I'm still not a hundred percent."

Grant turned back to the Prince. "Where was the reliquary, if you remember?"

Prince Shozich waved his hand toward the wall to the right of the fresco. "It was around here. The man broke into the plaster of the wall. After he left, the caretakers saw the hole, blamed me and removed me, then repaired it."

Grant sighed. "I can't thank you enough, Prince Shozich. You have really aided us on our holy quest. Is there anything we can do to return the favor?"

The Prince shook his head. "Stay true to the search, believe in our friends from beyond the stars, and hold to your beliefs no matter what anyone says."

"Thank you, Prince, we most certainly…"

"And, if you would be so kind, I have not eaten in days. A few dollars would go a long way in an old man's life."

"I knew it." Violet rolled her eyes. "Here comes the scam."

"Violet, don't be disrespectful! Prince Shozich has really helped us." Grant flashed his eyes angrily. "If he wasn't here, we wouldn't be able to find the next location and the next twelfth."

"Fine, you pay the man!"

Grant crossed his arms. "I absolutely would. I would give this man more than just a few dollars if I had it. He's worth it! His information was invaluable."

Violet grabbed her purse from her shoulder. "I hate you, you know that!" she said as she pulled out a few Euros and pushed into the awaiting palm of the Prince.

"Thank you, dear." the Prince said, bowing slightly.

"Go take a shower." Violet muttered.

The Prince, unaffected by the comment smiled. "Young lady. I know that you do not believe in me, nor do you trust me. But trust me when I tell you…" The Prince grabbed his chest and screamed. "Ahhh! They're shooting at us!" The Prince stumbled backward, knocking into several pews.

Grant hit the deck and crawled underneath Violet. Violet kicked Grant for his cowardice. "What shot?" she screamed. "I didn't hear anything?!"

"It's a silencer!" Grant cried. "I'm pretty sure I heard it. Hide, Violet!"

"They're here! Run!" The Prince shouted.

"He's a nut! There's nothing going on!" Violet yelled.

The Prince pulled himself up from the pew, screaming and covering his head. He turned and ran for the exit, calling to Violet and Grant. "Run, my friends. Get to cover. It is them! They are after us!"

Grant jumped up and grabbed Violet's hand. "We're getting out of here!"

"Grant, I really don't think that…" Violet was being dragged, she fought but Grant's fear was stronger than her fearlessness.

They exited the church and scrambled down the stairs. Violet was still trying to protest but Grant wouldn't hear it. The Prince was nowhere to be found. Eventually Violet slipped free of Grant, thanks to his sweaty palms. She stopped dead in her tracks.

"Grant, I'm not going another step. There is nobody shooting at us!"

"Violet, I don't know why you've become such a doubting Thomas, but is it worth your life to find out your right or wrong?" Grant was crouched down beside the Fiat, looking around for a gunman.

"Grant, that man was a con artist or a crazy person or something. But he wasn't a Prince and no one was shooting at…"

A loud bang echoed throughout the courtyard of the church and Violet screamed. She leapt over Grant and climbed into the Fiat, it was started and moving before Grant could even close his door. They raced away from the church as quickly as possible.

A few blocks away, a young man made a second attempt at starting his car, only to have it backfire and stall again.

CHAPTER 61

Mr. Crows had caught a pigeon and had just finished stuffing it into his mouth. One little, orange foot protruded from his mouth, it was still kicking. Blood trickled from the corners of his puffed cheeks and white feathers stuck to the red rivulets. More feathers floated about, clinging to his hair.

"I was hungry." Mr. Crow's speech was muffled by the mouthful of bird.

"You are strange." Mr. Trafalgar cringed. He took a few steps, taking his nun's habit off. "Well, we don't need these costumes anymore."

"I kinda liked wearing a dress." Mr. Crows said, feathers shooting from his mouth when he spoke.

"Who doesn't, little buddy?" Mr. Trafalgar agreed. "But we were figured out. We can change back to our civvies now."

"Awww. Okay, I guess." Mr. Crows wiped the smears of blood on his sleeve. He began taking off his black gown where he stood.

"Whoa, whoa!" Mr. Trafalgar intervened. "Have some decency. We can't just get all naked in the middle of this quaint town. We have to change somewhere." He looked down the street and saw a gas station. "I'm sure they have a restroom. We can change there."

The two nuns swished down the street and into the gas station parking lot. Mr. Trafalgar pointed. "Over there. Let's go."

Once inside the men's room, they began stripping out of there garb. Mr. Crows was out of his costume in a flash, being the nimbler of the two. It was cramped in the small bathroom and Mr. Trafalgar's large frame made it difficult for him to maneuver. He grunted as he attempted to pull down the zipper in the back of his gown.

"Hey, peanut, give me a hand. My zipper is stuck."

Mr. Crows, still in his tighty-whities, squeezed behind Mr. Trafalgar and began tugging on the zipper. He growled as the stubborn zipper wouldn't budge. "It won't give, boss," he said. "Can't you just pull the gown over your head?"

"I guess I'll have to." Mr. Trafalgar started pulling the gown upward, he wrestled with the cloth as it fought past his midsection. "Give me a hand."

Mr. Crows grabbed hold of the gown and was pulling it up. He grunted and groaned, trying to force the material over his large friend's torso and shoulders.

"I can't quite…" Mr. Crows said breathlessly.

Mr. Trafalgar's face, if it had not been covered by the dress, was flush red as he wiggled and wormed, trying to free himself. "I can't breathe," he rasped.

"Just hold still." Mr. Crows ordered.

"I'm trying."

"Just… wait."

"I'm dizzy."

"I've almost got it!"

"Arrg."

"Oomph!"

They were standing, butt to groin in a spooning position, with the gown over Mr. Trafalgar's head, both men in their underwear, grunting and wriggling, when the door to the men's room opened.

They froze.

The man in the doorway hesitated, pretty positive he knew what he'd walked in on. He said a quick prayer in Italian and turned to leave.

Mr. Crows was on him before the door closed.

Ten minutes later, Mr. Trafalgar and Mr. Crows exited the men's room, back in their black-on-black attire. Back in the men's room, hidden in a stall, were the remains of the poor bastard that walked in on them.

Mr. Trafalgar puffed on yet another cigarette and warily eyed his Blackberry. They had nothing to do now but wait and Mr. Maystyne was going to be really pissed with them for screwing up.

No big deal. Mr. Trafalgar thought. *We'll get them. We always do.* He smiled evilly at the thought. He knew he'd have his revenge.

CHAPTER 62

Violet drove the car recklessly through Perugia. "I still say that guy was a complete loon."

"I know you do," Grant said. "But he had a great deal of information. Our quest would have ended if not for him."

"Okay, so where to?" Violet steered the car with one knee while digging through her purse. Wrappers and assorted detritus spilled onto her lap.

"I think we have to get to the National Gallery in London, England."

"London?" Violet screamed. "Are you frigging nuts? You know how much that'll cost me? We'd be lucky if there's enough room on my card for that!"

"It has to be done, Violet." Grant stated. "Can't you see how important this all is? Can't you see we're traveling a path that countless others have attempted? We have found two twelfths on our own! The guy that beat us to the church here didn't even accomplish that. Here we are, two young people, never having done anything like this, and we've made so much ground. We can't give up because of money. This goes beyond money. This is an ancient mystery, this is life changing, this could be huge! You want money? What if we make this into a book? How much would that make? And then a movie? Talk show circuit? There's your money!"

That got Violet's attention.

"Okay, fine." she said. "But I get top writing credits!"

"That's okay with me." Grant shrugged. "Can you write?"

"Write? Any idiot can write a book." Violet walked to the car. "Especially about aliens and Jesus. A monkey could do that."

They needed to get to the Pisa International Airport. They had already driven recklessly out of Perugio so that they were closer to Pisa than to the airport in Florence. Besides, the creepy nuns were back there somewhere. Grant thought about the nun he'd seen. He was positive he was right and he knew he had to tell Violet.

Grant decided to break his silence. "I think I know who's after us. It dawned on me back at the Palazzo. I recognized our pursuers."

Violet was shocked. "You do? Who?"

"Celebrities. Big name actors. Scientologists."

"Scientists? Why? What do they have to do with all this?" Violet was confused. "Do they need to study us?"

"No, not scientists, scientologists. Don't tell me you've never heard of Scientology?"

"Okay, I won't tell you."

Grant sighed heavily. "Wow. Well, where do I begin? It's really not an easy thing to explain without going in depth."

"Well, try. I'm useless if you don't give me the Reader's Digest version. Or better yet, Cliff Note it."

"Scientology is a religious philosophy created by science fiction author L. Ron Hubbard. Its name basically translates as 'a study of knowledge'."

"Science fiction author?"

"You got it. Trust me, it gets weirder." Grant scratched at the fading lesions on his neck. "Anyway, over the years, this belief has grown and gathered quite a following. Not only with the everyday Joes of the world, but celebrities. The teaching is pretty secretive, and unless you dedicate yourself to it, and move up its ranks, and pay a lot, you really can't know everything that goes on behind the closed doors of the Scientology Centers."

"Where are these centers?"

"Well, the first one was in Camden, New Jersey back in 1953."

"Ha! Jersey. That says it all!" Violet laughed.

"You got that right. But now there are centers across the United States, and even in several other countries. And with celebrities joining in, and expanding public awareness, it's still growing."

"What does it teach?" Violet swerved to avoid a sheep.

"That depends on who you ask, really. Devout members tell you it shows you how to expand your mind. Clear it of negativity, past mistakes. It claims it can free people from addictions, depression, mental illness and even homosexuality."

"What? Homosexuality? Don't tell me that's a curable disease?"

"No. But there's some fringe mentalities believe that. So anyway, Scientology claims that through their auditing methods, wherein a higher ranking member, or thetan, guides you through the process and helps you achieve awareness of your spiritual self and have more effectiveness in this material world. This process is called auditing, nothing like what the IRS does. They use a simple electronic device, called an E-meter, to detect your body's 'electric resistance' in a one-on-one communication with a trained counselor. Auditing can take a few minutes or several hours and depends on the level you're at."

"Okay," Violet interrupted. "That stream of words bounced off me like bullets hitting Superman's chest."

Grant laughed. "Funny that you mention Superman."

"Why's that?"

"Because he's just as tied into this as Scientology and the Twelve."

Violet groaned. "Jeez, the shit keeps getting deeper.'

"He's an alien. Much like the ones who contacted Jesus and the ones who L. Ron Hubbard claimed to help found Scientology. Bear with me," Grant said. "It all comes together in the end. Trust me."

"It better." Violet fumbled about her purse. "Do you realize it's been hours since I had a smoke?"

"Actually, yes." Grant smiled, his face practically back to normal. "See how easy it can be when you replace nasty habits with education and travel?"

"Education and travel my ass!" Violet spoke through the cigarette between her lips. "How about guns, knives and killer nuns?"

"Well, that too." Grant chuckled.

"How long until we get to Pisa Airport?" Violet blew clouds of smoke out the window.

"About twenty four minutes." Grant traced his finger on the map.

"Tell me more about this Scientology. And who these celebrities are."

CHAPTER 63

Mr. Trafalgar exhaled smoke angrily and kicked Mr. Crows yet again. "You stupid, stupid, whiny little dog! What in Xenu's name were you thinking?"

Mr. Crows yelped and scampered a few feet away, he looked up at Mr. Trafalgar with big, baleful eyes. "I'm sorry! But you should've seen him. He was bloated and slimy and all alienish!"

"Of all the people in the world, of all the actors like us who have made crappy alien movie after crappy alien movie, we should know that shit like that doesn't exist!" Mr. Trafalgar tossed his cigarette at Mr. Crows, who dodged it skillfully.

"Don't say that! That's blasphemy against the story of Xenu!" Mr. Crows looked around as though they would be struck by lightning for such a comment.

"I'm not talking about Xenu! Of course he's real! I'm talking about other aliens, the ones people see flying around in saucers in the skies now, or read about in the rags, or the ones in our stupid movies." He pointed his finger at Mr. Crows. "I would never blaspheme the story of Xenu!"

Just then Mr. Trafalgar's Blackberry rang, causing him to stiffen in fear. He retrieved it from his pocket and checked the ID. "Damn. It's Mr. Maystyne!"

"Whew!" Sighed Mr. Crows. "I was afraid it was Xenu."

Mr. Trafalgar attempted to kick his partner again, but Mr. Crows rolled away and landed on all fours several feet out of reach. Mr. Trafalgar growled. "You idiot. Xenu doesn't contact people. Especially not on a Blackberry! Now be quiet!" he answered the Blackberry, he was visibly nervous. Not the same, calm and collected snooty actor he had been a day ago.

"Y-yessir?" he stuttered.

Mr. Crows could hear Mr. Maystyne screaming despite his ten foot distance. He cringed at the thought of what their employer was saying.

After what seemed like an eternity, Mr. Trafalgar hung up the Blackberry and returned it to his jacket pocket. He immediately lit up another smoke. He now held two lit cigarettes. He tossed the shorter one to the ground.

Mr. Crows took a few steps toward his partner. "Well, w-what did he say?"

Mr. Trafalgar sighed a plume of smoke. "We're still employed, for one thing."

"That's good."

"Yep. It is. And he said we weren't going to be killed for losing them, attempting to capture or kill them, or letting them get away with two portions of the Twelve."

"Not being killed is real good." Mr. Crows smiled.

"He did say, however, that we'd be in for the auditing of our lives when we got back to the center. I guess it could be worse."

"Dead is worse." Mr. Crows agreed. "Much worse."

"Okay little man," Mr. Trafalgar checked his watch. "Our new ride should be here any minute now. What we have to do is pull ourselves together. Remember, we are a team. How many missions have we done for the cause before?"

"Many."

"How many have we failed?"

"None.

"That's right, peanut. And we won't fail this one. So let's pull ourselves up by our boot straps and see this thing through. You with me?"

"Hail Teegeeack!" Mr. Crows cried.

"Hail Teegeeack!" Mr. Trafalgar agreed. They thumped each other in the forehead with exuberance. "Damn straight!" Mr. Trafalgar fixed his jacket, looking cool. "That's right! We bad!"

CHAPTER 64

"Okay, that's the airport ahead. The Pisa International Airport." Grant pointed. "I think we have to stay left here. Left! Left!"

"I heard you," Violet shot him a look. "Relax!"

Violet turned the car into Pisa Airport Italy.

"This airport is also known as the Galileo Galilei International Airport." Grant explained as Violet cursed at the crowded connecting roads that intertwined around the airport. "Now Galileo was an interesting character."

"Yeah, yeah, yeah, let me guess. He was also a Twelvist or even a protector of a Twelfth himself?" Violet spat.

"Why, yes." Grant beamed. "You've heard of him?"

"Nope, never." Violet tried honking the car horn at a passerby but growled when she discovered the horn was inoperable. "It's just whenever you mention someone, gee whiz, they're connected!"

"You don't have to bite my head off." Grant pouted. "This is your legacy, not mine. I'm only trying to help and educate."

Violet found a parking spot and pulled in. She turned off the car. "Sorry, Grant. You're right. I'm just stressed, and a little hungry."

"It's okay. So anyway, Galileo was considered himself a contactee by the aliens. Not only did he preserve the Twelvist ways, and prove much with his astronomy, physics and mathematics, but some felt he had insider information from our friends in the sky themselves. How else would he be the first to argue the heliocentrism and geocentric theories of his peers and predecessors. He was..."

Violet cut him short. "Though I apologized, Grant, it wasn't an invitation for more lecturing. Right now we need to get tickets. Tickets that I'm obviously footing the bill for. And food, which stands to reason I will also be picking up that tab. So let's please get inside, buy some tickets for the next available flight and get some grub. Is that okay with you?"

"Sorry, Violet." Grant opened his car door. Upon exiting, he noticed the sign in front of their parking spot. It read, 'Parcheggio riservato. Vigilare soltanto'. Grant leaned back in. "Uh, Violet. This parking is reserved for…"

"I don't care, Grant. It's not like we're coming back for this car anyway."

"Good point."

Violet slammed her door shut and marched toward the airport entrance. Once inside she turned to Grant. "Find a ticket booth. Get us tickets. Don't screw it up." Violet handed him her credit card.

"Where are you going?" Grant asked.

"Food," she grunted and took off.

Grant called after the disappearing Violet. "Don't get anything with peanuts. Or dairy. Or wheat!" He looked around for a ticket agent.

Violet walked for what felt like miles, and finding no food court, settled on a snack machine. She was thrilled to see that American junk foods predominantly filled the vending machine. She stuck in several Euro, not even concerning herself with the proper amount. She was so damn hungry!

Once she was satisfied she'd picked enough things for herself, M&Ms, Fritos, Doritos, Little Debbie snack cakes, and potato chips, and a Diet Snapple, she decided to grab something for Grant. *What couldn't he eat? Peanuts, I know that much.* She couldn't remember the rest. Violet stared at the wall of munchies, not sure what contained what. *Hell, I'll just buy everything I can and he can pick out for himself.*

Grant had no trouble getting tickets for London. There were a few flights with stops in Spain and France but he wanted a more direct route. So he took a slightly later flight that directly landed them at London International Airport in about two and half hours. *That should make the wicked witch happy.* he grumbled. He turned to walk in the direction she had run off in and was surprised to find Violet behind him, arms laden with crinkly plastic bags of snack foods.

"Oh my," was all Grant could muster.

They found their way to Gate 115, even though they had an hour and a half wait and plopped down for an impromptu picnic. Violet dropped the twenty-odd packages in the seat between them.

Grant began picking through the pile. "Nope, not that. Nope. Oh God, not that! Nope. Nope."

Violet stuffed her face happily, munching and crunching with glee. She could practically hear her arteries clogging but she didn't care. She washed every mouthful down with the Snapple. "Anything?" she said with her cheeks full of Devil Dogs.

Grant lifted out one sole item. "Uh, yeah."

Violet looked at it and felt terrible. "Lifesavers? That's awful."

Grant sighed. "It'll have to do."

CHAPTER 65

Mr. Trafalgar snapped shut the Blackberry. "We got them!" he announced.

He and Mr. Crows had been standing by their new ride, a 2011 Maserati Quattroporte Executive GT. Mr. Trafalgar had been disappointed that the car was only worth $115,000, but it would have to do.

"What did the boss say?" Mr. Crows asked.

"They just booked two tickets to London. We're to catch up with them there."

"London?" Mr. Crows frowned. "That's in England, isn't it?"

"Yes, my little monkey, we're going to England." Mr. Trafalgar opened his Blackberry and dialed. "I'll have my plane brought here to the Florence Airport and we'll be there in a few hours."

"I hate the English. They squirted water on me!" Mr. Crows grit his teeth. "It took everything I had not to rip that guy's head off!"

"I know, little buddy. But hopefully we won't be there very long." Mr. Trafalgar hopped behind the wheel of his new car and ordered his plane brought to him.

CHAPTER 66

Grant and Violet boarded British Airways Flight 112, direct non-stop to merry old London. They had no luggage to check, just carry-ons. Violet took her purse with her to her seat and Grant brought his bulky backpack.

"Shouldn't you store that above?" Violet asked.

"No way I'm letting go of this!" Grant declared. "You never know when I'll need stuff inside of here."

"They're going to ask you to stow it above, Grant. You might as well just do it now before the plane gets all crowded."

"Forget it." Grant pouted.

"Well, you may as well take your Xanax now." Violet offered. "Though you really don't look too nervous, for once."

"I'm actually fine." Grant smiled. "I think I'm going to give this a whirl sans medication."

"My big brave hero." Violet joked.

A flight attendant approached them and leaned down conspiratorially. "Sir, you will have to stow that bag overhead," she said softly in a thick Italian accent. Her ample bosom looked as though it was struggling to free itself from the confines of her uniform.

Violet looked at Grant, who couldn't remove his eyes from her chest.

"Sir?" The flight attendant repeated.

"Huh? What? Oh, yeah. Sure." Grant jumped up, smiling wide. He pushed past Violet and quickly shoved the back pack into the compartment. He sat down, short-breathed, and grinned happily at the flight attendant. "There we go!"

"Thank you, sir." The attendant smiled back. And then quickly left.

"Have you never seen boobs before?" Violet scowled. "That was the most pathetic display of patheticness I've ever seen!"

"Boobs?" Sure, boobs, plenty." Grant was flustered. "Of course I have. I've seen tons of boobs. Lots. More than one at the same time! Pair, I mean. More than one pair. Of boobs that is. Yes, of course. Love them boobs. Yep. Boobs."

Violet's eyes widened as realization dawned upon her. "You are a virgin!" she said a bit too loudly.

"No I am not!" he argued.

"Wow! You are a freaking virgin." Violet laughed. "Have you even kissed a girl? No chance you've been to second base if boobs do that much to you."

Grant spun in his seat and faced the window. "I am *not* talking to you."

"Well kick my ass and call me Phil. A virgin! A thirty-something year old virgin. Well, I'll be." Violet sat back as Grant continued to ignore her. *At least I'll get some peace for a while.*

An hour into the flight, and several screwdrivers later, Violet had become quite buzzed and more than a little bored. She glanced over at Grant, who had fallen asleep shortly after she emasculated him. He was again making his weird little noises.

She suddenly pushed his head into the window, the dull thud echoed in the cabin of the plane. He awoke with a start.

"What the?" Grant rubbed his forehead. "What was that for?"

"I'm bored. Talk to me."

"Fine. You don't have to hit me. You're so violent."

"So tell me more about this Scientology." Violet said, ignoring him and sipping her screwdriver. Violet had actually pocketed a few small bottles of vodka when the cart the flight attendant was pushing stopped briefly next to her. She had since been adding to it when no one was looking. It probably now contained less than 1% orange juice. "What makes you think they're after us."

Grant sat back in his seat. "I'll tell you why I think they're after us after I tell you about L. Ron Hubbard."

"That's fine." Violet poured more vodka and OJ down her throat.

"L. Ron Hubbard was a science fiction writer who once said, according to Reader's Digest, 'If a man really wants to make a million dollars, the best way would be to start his own religion'. So in 1952 Mr. Hubbard created his own philosophy and in 1953 birthed his 'applied religious philosophy' of Scientology. Like I said, after over fifty years, it has developed into a center of controversy, both lauded by celebrities and criticized by academics."

"Anyway, the background of Scientology is pretty turbulent. Over the years, Mr. Hubbard has been kicked out of countries, criticized by governments, ridiculed by religious scholars, and has been accused of harassing critics and exploiting members."

Violet laughed. "Then why are there so many members?"

"That's a good question. Many speculate that members are brainwashed or something similar. No one knows for sure because so few deserters have come forward with insight to the inner workings of Scientology. It is said that they sign waivers and legal papers that keep them from talking. And of the few who have, they have been character assassinated in the press. So there is no definitive proof as to the goings-on within Scientology's walls. But there is a great deal of information culled from L. Ron's books, some assorted documentation leaked from the training, and whispered tales of Mr. Hubbard's crazy history of the universe."

"Tell me about that." Violet said.

"Okay, but in L. Ron Hubbard's own words, 'Your mind is completely unprepared for what is about to happen to your reality…' The information given here is for Scientologists who have reached Level 3 out of 8, which is needed to find their inner thetan. What is revealed beyond Level 3 is not known to the general public." Grant smiled. "It all has to do with the thetans. Thetans are immortal spirit beings, not a physical body, nor a mind, nor anything relatable. It is the essence of awareness and one's identity. Hubbard created the term, or his wife did, from the Greek letter theta, which means 'the source of life and life itself.' These spirits are beyond ancient, and have God-like powers. They've been so beaten down through the eons that they now reside in all of us. And it is Mr. Hubbard's Scientology that can help release them. Get ready for a mind-altering flashback."

(Author's note: Not much of this is able to be proven to be the actual thoughts of L. Ron Hubbard, but through some minor research and tomfoolery this is the closest thing. This really is what Scientology appears to be based on. There is no way for me to know for sure what the full story is since I am not a pre-clear, or a clear, or a thetan of any kind. I'm not a thetan 7 nor am I a lowly thetan 1. I'm not even a vegan. Or a thespian or a lesbian, but boy would I love to be. Anyway, back to our story)

Wavy lines, wavy lines, as we travel back in time to the beginning of the poor thetan's existence. These troubled souls are the high-school nerds of time and space, forever being picked on, abused, tested, tortured and destroyed.

In the vast darkness of space, a quadrillion years ago, the Godly thetan is awakened by loud snapping noises and a flash of blinding light. Flying by, a chariot races through the sky, pursued by a cherub playing a trumpet. All at once, the thetan is thrust into darkness. This is only the beginning of the trials and tribulations that have tested the thetans.

Several million years later, a brass dog appears. It sits patiently, staring at the thetan. When the thetan traveled too close to the brass dog, the thetan would be caught in an electric field and sucked into the dog's mouth. It would then be shot out of the rear of the dog. Yes, the ass. Then all is dark again.

A trillion years later an aircraft, exactly like a Douglas DC-8 airplane, hurtles through space. The thetan finds himself suspended, motionless, trapped in front of the aircraft door. He is assaulted by explosions from the doorway and he is again cast into darkness.

Soon, the thetan finds himself in a glade. On all sides of the glade stand tremendous stone heads. The heads spew white energy at the thetan. Pelting him relentlessly.

The thetan is then captured and held in a force field and hypnotized into thinking he is someone else. His spirit leaves and inhabits a new body.

Invaders from Helatrobus arrive and stick the thetan into a large amusement park. Gorillas roam the park, some of them live, some of them mechanical. The park is run by the Hoi polloi, who blasted the thetan with electricity and explosions. The Hoi polloi wore pink-striped shirts and sleeve garters, like carnival barkers. They rode around in rollercoaster cars. Monkeys kept the Hoi polloi company.

Shortly after, mechanical bears were introduced. They were called The Brotherhood of the Bear. They were excessively violent.

The thetan was then presented with two visions of Heaven. The first was beautiful and looked just like Busch Gardens in Pasadena. The second was a mess. All plants are dead, the town in ruin, no saints or angels. In the bad Heaven there is only a gardener and an electrician hiding in the bushes. They would occasionally jump out and scream.

Soon the planets would become surrounded by radioactive clouds and the Helatrobans would attack with orange bombs. These bombs would yell out confusing statements like, 'Who's there?' 'Look out!' and 'Hark! Hark!'.

The thetans on the planet would be captured by a capsule that shot out bubbles. These bubbles would suck the thetans into itself and return to the capsules. The capsules would then join with an aircraft.

More recently, thetans were placed in a train station and were forced to board a British railway-like coach. They were tortured with blinding white energy.

And then...

Then came Xenu!

75 million years ago Xenu was the galactic ruler of all the planets in this part of the universe, this included Earth, at the time called Teegeeack. There were 76 planets total in his reign, and each planet had 178 billion people. They were grossly overpopulated and Xenu wanted to get rid of them.

With the assistance of renegades from the Loyal Officers, Xenu called in billions of people for tax inspections, but tricked them. He actually gave them injections of alcohol and glycol. The people were paralyzed. Xenu put them onto space planes, again like DC-8s.

The space planes took them to Earth (Teegeeack), and the paralyzed people were stacked around the bases of volcanoes. When they were done stacking them, H-bombs were lowered into the volcanoes. Xenu then detonated the H-bombs and killed everyone.

This destroyed the bodies of the people, but remember, the thetans had taken residence inside those bodies, and they were released. The thetans were blowing around in the nuclear winds and Xenu used special electronic traps that captured all the souls in electric beams that were sticky, like fly paper.

The captured souls were gathered on electronic ribbons and taken to huge cinemas where the thetans were to spend their days watching special 3D motion pictures explaining what life should be and other confusing things. They were also shown false pictures and were told they were God, the Devil and Christ. This was called implanting.

The thetan souls were so confused by this that after the cinema, the souls thought they were all the same person. They were clustered in groups of a few thousand. These clusters went on to inhabit the few people still living, which is why, according to L. Ron Hubbard, we are all filled with these thetan clusters. And in order to be a free soul, we must remove all these thetans from inside of us. And Scientology is the way to do that. The only reason we as people believe in God and Jesus and the Devil today is because of the films we watched 75 million years ago.

Xenu himself was finally overthrown by the Loyal Officers and was locked away in a mountain on one of the 76 planets. He is still alive today, trapped there by a force field powered by an eternal battery.

This is the sad and tortured story of the thetans.

Wavy lines. Wavy lines. Back to present day.

Grant took a deep breath. "And now you know the basic history of the universe. At least according to one L. Ron Hubbard."

Violet's eyes were wide with a myriad of emotions; shock, amusement, shock, disbelief, and shock. "Are you... fucking... kidding me?!!" she said a little too loudly.

Grant was taken aback by her more than usual gruff language and unnecessary volume. "Uh, no, I'm not, um, kidding you."

"That's what all these people are following? That's their religion? That's Scientology?"

"Well, there's more to the teachings and construct of the philosophy, but that's the general history, yes."

Violet sucked down the rest of her drink. She spotted the flight attendant and called her over. "Can I have another screwdriver, please?"

CHAPTER 67

Miles above France, a Boeing 707 arced through the sky. A very irritable Mr. Trafalgar smoked in the cockpit, while an unhappy Mr. Crows sulked on the floor behind his larger friend. He was sitting with his legs crossed and his sad face planted in his hands.

"I don't like England," Mr. Crows mumbled.

"I know little peanut," Mr. Trafalgar said, tired of hearing it. "You've already said that a dozen times."

"I don't know why anyone would go to England," Mr. Crows sighed. "They're all a bunch of big dummies with bad teeth."

"Now that's not nice, buddy. They're not all dumb. And there are a few with decent teeth. I think."

"And the weather is stupid and they talk all funny."

"Listen, you and I both know why you don't like England. And while you're with me no one will spray you in the face with water. Okay? We're not going on a junket. We're not doing any interviews. We're going to go in, grab the girl, and leave."

"Can I kill that bloated freaky guy she's with?"

"I believe you can, my cute little monkey." Mr. Trafalgar lit up another cigarette with the dying ember of the previous one. He tossed the used smoke away, regardless of where it landed. "I'll double-check with the boss but it's okay with me. Does that make you feel better?"

Mr. Crows sat up a little. He forced a smile. "Yeah, I guess."

"That's a good buddy. Now pull yourself together, we're landing in an hour."

"Okay. But they still have terrible teeth."

Shortly after, Mr. Trafalgar and Mr. Crows were briskly climbing down the stairs from the Boeing. A stretch limo waited on the tarmac.

As the driver of the limousine held the door open, Mr. Trafalgar spoke on his Blackberry. "You have them in sight? Okay, good. Yes, I know where that is." He hung up and stepped inside the limo. Mr. Crows bound in after him and jumped around on the leather detailed seats.

"Wow, I love limos. These are some bouncy seats, too! Whooo!"

"Sit down, Mr. Crows." Mr. Trafalgar ordered.

Frowning, Mr. Crows complied.

Mr. Trafalgar poured himself a martini and placed out a bowl of water for his partner. Mr. Crows lapped up the water noisily.

"We'll be on them in no time." Mr. Trafalgar sipped his drink and smiled.

Mr. Crows smiled happily at his buddy, lines of drool hanging from his mouth like a Bulldog.

CHAPTER 68

Violet and Grant deplaned at the London International Airport without incident. Violet scurried off in a hurry to have a smoke. Grant shrugged and followed her outside.

"You know, one of these days you might really want to analyze this slavish relationship you have with smoking," Grant offered.

"What do you mean?" Violet glared at him.

"Well, look at yourself." Grant pantomimed a frenetic Violet. "Ooh! Gotta run, I have to smoke. Oooh! Hurry up, I need a cigarette. Ooh! Gotta get one more in."

Violet gave Grant a little shove. "I'm not like that."

"You're right," he agreed. "You're worse. The way you run around, totally enslaved by this habit. And for what? It doesn't fill your stomach, or quench a thirst. It holds no nutritional value. It feeds a cyclical addiction."

"It feels good to have one." Violet argued.

"Yeah, because you created an addiction to it. If you never had one, you wouldn't miss the feeling, you wouldn't be here. So the only reason it feels good is because the one prior to it wore off. It's an addiction to nothing but an addictive chemical."

"My head hurts. I don't want to talk about this anymore." Violet smushed out the cigarette on a brick wall. "We have to find a taxi. How do you say taxi in British?"

Grant looked sharply at her. "Are you serious?"

Violet shoved him again. "No, this time I was kidding. Come on. Let's go." Violet took off through the flurry of travelers, airport workers, and cars to find a taxi.

"She's coming around." Grant smiled to himself. "Oh, yeah. She's digging me."

A tiny, black taxi pulled over for Violet and she waved for Grant to hurry up. Grant trundled up and tossed his backpack through the car door.

"Where to, then?" The driver asked.

"The National Gallery." Violet said. "In London."

"I know where it is, love. It'll be about twenty minutes" He waited for them to get comfortable then started off.

Grant leaned toward Violet. "This is called a hackney carriage. These are officially licensed cabs serving the area within the M25 motorway. The drivers have to pass a test called 'The Knowledge' to demonstrate they have an intimate knowledge of London streets."

"What does this have to do with the Twelve?" Violet asked.

"Funny that you ask. I didn't think it had any but, they say the test for 'The Knowledge' usually requires at least 12 appearances to pass the test."

"That's weak, Grant." Violet shook her head. And stared out the window at the London landscape. "You're reaching now."

"Yeah, probably." Grant sank in his seat. He grumbled to himself. "You try and piece together a three thousand year old puzzle."

The taxi driver took them on a winding journey through the streets of London. Each street was a brief glimpse as they spent no more than half a mile on any one road. Violet was in awe of the buildings, the sheen of water on the streets from the omnipresent drizzle, the forecourt gardens. London was someplace she'd never even considered seeing in her life, and now that she was here, she was thrilled.

Violet noticed the street post as they took a turn. She looked at Gant. "Whitechapel. Why does that sound familiar?"

"The Whitechapel Murderer." Grant said. Or better known as Jack the Ripper."

"Oh, yeah. That'd be it."

"Also at one time the home of the Elephant Man."

"Gee," Violet snickered. "No twelvists?"

"Well, we're not sure but some claim George Bernard Shaw was a follower."

"Who?"

"Don't worry about it."

The driver left Whitechapel and sped the tiny black car through the gray brick and stone canyons of London. They took so many short, little roads; Braham, Aldgate, Queen Victoria, White Lion. Violet laughed to herself, she couldn't believe they named a road after an 80's hair band. She almost mentioned it to Grant then decided against it. It was probably not so and would only make her look more stupid than usual.

Ten minutes in and Violet started to feel good about their situation. They were thousands of miles away from Florence where they'd left the killer nuns, who turned out to be killer celebrities, and Grant seemed focused and in no way on the verge of upsetting the driver. Maybe they'd get out of this unscathed and successful.

"So you never did tell me why you think those crazy Scientologists are after us?" Violet asked Grant.

The car screamed to a stop. "Oi! Lady, I'm a Scientologist and some of me best friends are Scientologists. So don't go knocking off on me beliefs."

Violet was taken aback and slightly irritated. "You mean you worship aliens that blew up H-bombs on Earth a trillion years ago? With flying chariots and cherubs? Are you freaking kidding me?"

The driver stared her down hard. "I don't know about any bombs or chariots you stupid American twat. What say you get out of me cab?"

"What say you suck on my…" Violet was cut off as Grant pulled her out of the taxi.

"It's okay, Violet. We're only a few blocks away." Grant tried his best to hold her back. She was strong! "Come on, Violet. Let it go!" he yelled as the car took off.

Violet calmed down a bit and turned to face Grant. "Can you believe that guy? What a wack-job!"

"Violet, you have to be careful what you say about religion when you travel abroad. You never know who you might offend."

Violet shot him a nasty look. "That coming from a guy who's had us kicked out of two cabs already." Violet kicked the ground and dug out a cigarette out of her purse, she paused, looked at Grant again, and put the smoke away. "So now that we're hoofing it to the gallery, you can tell me why you think Scientologists are after us."

Grant led the way along Upper Thames Street. "Well, I recognized the nun with the knife. At least I'm pretty sure I did."

"You knew the nun? What are the odds?"

"Pretty good odds that we all know *of* him, at least. *He's* a very famous actor, and a renowned Scientologist. And a part-time nut."

"He?" Violet squinted; trying to process what Grant was getting at. "He? Actor?"

"You mean you're not familiar with Thom Crows?"

Violet stopped dead on the sidewalk. "Thom Crows? *The* Thom Crows?"

"The one and only."

Violet pictured the maniacal nun in her head. The face *did* seem familiar. Something about the nose and the big teeth. "You know I'd say you were crazy, but now that I think about it, I can sort of see it for myself." She shivered. "Wow. Thom Crows. I always hated most of his movies." She laughed.

"You and plenty of other people." Grant laughed with her.

CHAPTER 70

Trafalgar Square was the new home of The National Gallery of London in 1832. Its pedestrian accessibility was the optimal choice to create a museum of broad art-historical scope and works of consistently high quality. It has remained there since, and it, combined with the beauty and richness of Trafalgar Square, is a shining jewel in London's crown.

"Hey, this is really beautiful." Violet said as they strolled through the square. She gazed up at the 185 foot column in the center. "I can't even see what's on top of that thing."

"That's Admiral Horatio Nelson. It's to commemorate his win at the Battle of Trafalgar in 1805 wherein he defeated Napoleon." Grant explained.

"Not a twelvist?" Violet joked.

"Don't think so, but you never know." Grant laughed. "Though, aside from Mr. Nelson, there are twelve other statues atop plinths in the square. The twelfth was regularly changed to new, commissioned artworks. I've heard rumors of that twelfth plinth's occupants being a secret message to twelvists."

They strolled through a cloud of pigeons that exploded and took flight, only to return in a cluster behind them.

"Not supposed to be pigeons here," Grant muttered, terrified of imaginary falling meteors of poop. "They were banned because of all the damage they caused."

"How do you ban birds?" asked Violet.

"Get bigger, hungrier birds."

"Ew."

Ahead of them lay the National Gallery, a very intimidating building with an entrance surrounded by columns, its facade decorated with relief sculptures and the roof topped by turrets and a large dome.

Grant pointed to the dome. "Okay, here we are again, looking at a dome that supposedly represents a UFO."

"Again?" Violet sighed, looking at it. "Yeah, okay. I see all the portholes running around it. I see the upward thrust of the dome. Blah, blah, blah. Anything else?"

"Well, Miss Snotty-pants, there is." Grant pointed to the other side of the square. "There is a sculpture of the dome's designer and architect, Filippo Brunelleschi, on the other side of the square here. It was carved by none other than Donatello himself."

"Donatello?" Violet rolled her eyes. "The ninja turtle?"

Grant grimaced painfully. "Violet, did you even attend school? Never mind. Donatello is a famous artist. Anyway, the sculpture has Filippo staring up at his own dome. It is rumored because he is waiting for it to take flight, as he had dreamed it would."

"Is he really over there staring up at the dome?"

"Yes, he really is." Grant nodded. "Others say he is staring into the sky beyond the dome, waiting for visitors from the stars."

"Hmm. If we have time I'd like to see that."

"It's a deal." Grant said, and turned toward the stairs of the National Gallery.

As they walked up the stairs, Grant pointed toward the columns. "You'll notice there are twelve huge columns protecting the entrance."

"Of course there are." Violet smirked.

A few dozen yards away, two men, wearing thick rimmed glasses with bushy moustaches attached, strode inconspicuously through the crowds of tourists and pedestrians. The two Groucho Marx lookalikes kept a safe but close distance. One smoked, the other fidgeted and salivated on himself.

"Don't get too close, little guy," Mr. Trafalgar whispered. "We can't afford any more mistakes. Mr. Maystyne will have our heads."

"Sure thing, oh obese leader," Mr. Crows grumbled.

"What was that?" Mr. Trafalgar snapped.

"Nothing." Mr. Crows adjusted his dollar store plastic glasses and moustache.

"Don't fiddle with our expert-level disguises."

"Yes, your heftiness." Mr. Crows eyed a warbling pigeon.

"You are so going to get the e-metering of your life when we get home!" Mr. Trafalgar wagged a nicotine-stained finger.

"Sorry." And with that, Mr. Crows subtly and violently stomped on a pigeon. A sickening, wet crack followed by a small explosion of feathers.

"Good show, old bean," a man called out. "Those sky vermin are the worst!"

Mr. Trafalgar held Mr. Crows back, struggling to wrap his hands around the Englishman's neck. "Easy, killer," Mr. Trafalgar calmed his smaller friend. "He was complimenting you."

Mr. Crows relaxed and shook off his urge to kill. "I can't understand these foreigners."

"So what are we looking for again?" Violet asked. "Sorry, I'm not good at puzzles and poems and whatnot."

"That's okay." Grant said. "From what I can figure, it has something to do, again, with the Virgin Mary. And a saint. And odds are, an alien or flying saucer. It'll most likely be in a painting, maybe a sculpture or piece of architecture."

"Well, that narrows it down," Violet said.

"Don't worry, we'll know it when we see it." Grant waited next to the ticket booth. "Ahem. I'm still a bit short on cash. So, um."

Violet looked up at the sign. "It's free! What are you talking about?"

Grant wagged a finger at her. "It's donation based, Violet. We don't just waltz in here and soak in the culture and art and sights for absolutely nothing. It's contributions that keep these places alive! Shame on you!"

"Shame on me? Easy for you to say, you haven't spent one nickel since we've left New York." Violet rummaged through her purse. "How much? I've got like 8 Euro in here. Will that ease your conscience?"

"I guess."

Violet slapped down the bills and pushed Grant out of the way. "I hope you sleep better now."

"I most certainly will. Thank you."

Violet and Grant wandered through the gallery. They followed the course of traffic with the dozens of other attendees shuffling along, gathered in groups to admire the paintings hung sparsely on the walls.

"Maybe we should split up." Violet suggested. "This place is a little big."

"It's not that big." Grant replied. "Besides, you'll probably get lost.'

"Me?" Violet was shocked. "You'd have an allergy attack. Or overdose on Benadryl. Or explode from dust consumption. Or see a loose M&M and curl up into the fetal position."

"Ok, fair enough. But I still think we should stick together." Grant admired a Botticelli. "We're not in a rush and there's so many great works of art here."

Violet paused in front of a framed painting. "Um, Grant."

Grant moved on to Raphael. "Ah, Raphael. Now his stuff was inspiring."

"Hey, Grant."

Grant was peering closely at another painting by Cezanne.

"Grant!" Violet screamed.

Every person within hearing range stopped and stared. Grant turned around.

Violet was flushed red. "Sorry, everyone," she squeaked. "Grant, come here."

Grant sidled up to her and she stepped aside, revealing the painting that had caught her attention.

"Oh!" Grant froze. "Great job, Violet. I'd say that fits the bill. It's the The Annuciation, with Saint Emidius."

"You've heard of it?" Violet asked.

"Yeah, I have. I've seen a few textbook images of it but never with any great detail. But it makes sense now. The painting was finished sometime around 1430 by Carlo Crivelli and it depicts the annunciation of the Virgin Mary from the Gospel of Luke. It shows the Archangel Gabriel appearing to Mary and informing her that she'd conceive a son from divine intervention through the Holy Spirit."

"She looks like she's in pain." Violet said.

"In this painting, yes, she does. Usually, Mary's enlightenment is depicted by a dove descending from the heavens. But Crivelli chose to depict a beam of light, a ray, zapped from a spherical shape in the sky. Albeit there is a dove in the beam, it still isn't the typical depiction. And with Mary doubled over, grabbing at her chest, she looks more like she's being shot by an alien beam than receiving holy blessings."

Violet pointed toward the object in the sky. "It's hard to tell if that's a solid object or a circular pattern of clouds."

"Well, if you look real close, it is several rings of clouds, almost swirling, like a crop circle. But there are several passengers, as it were, little angel-heads peeking out from the rings, as though riding within the circle. Any way you look at it, it's more of a depiction of UFO activity than angel activity."

"What does that say?" Violet asked, noticing the Latin words beneath the painting.

"Libertas Ecclesiastica is supposedly translated as 'Freedom of the Church'. Some say it means 'Freedom *from* the Church', suggesting that the cover-up of the aliens/God relationship needed to be revealed, as this painting does."

"Okay, so it's safe to say we found the next location." Violet glanced around. "Where would we find the reliquary?"

"Hey, you said it right." Grant said excitedly. "Reliquary!"

"Hey, I did!" Violet beamed proudly.

"Well, most of this wall appears to be newer, very well maintained." Grant got as close to the wall and painting as he dared. "And this painting hasn't always been here, as far as I can recall."

"Maybe the frame again?" Violet offered.

"I would find that doubtful, only because this was originally painted on an altar piece, but was later transferred to this frame." Grant tilted from one side to the other, trying to see behind the painting.

"But it has to be attached," Violet joined him in his search. They looked like skittish squirrels, moving, pausing, tilting their heads, moving, then pausing again. "How else would later generations find the portion of the Twelve. Unless the portion was also moved after the fact, like the painting was."

"I guess we have no choice but to find out." Grant reached for the painting.

"Hey, wait!" Violet blurted. "Don't you think that thing is wired with alarms?"

"Yeah, most likely." Grant replied. "Well, if either of the poems give an indication, it would be hidden in the portion of the frame where Mary is looking." Grant leaned as close as he dared. A few other spectators looked at him admonishingly. He stood up, eyes wide. "Violet, it's here," he whispered.

"What?" Violet replied "How do you know?"

Grant began to point, then withdrew his hand. "There's a hairline crack, it forms a perfect rectangle in the section of the frame that Mary is looking."

"Okay, now what?"

"I think I can open it without disturbing the painting," Grant dug out his bent knife. "Just make sure no one is looking."

Violet turned around and blocked Grant's hunched form from passersby. If anyone got too close, Violet would scowl and give them nasty looks. One person didn't take the hint and Violet had to get verbally abusive. "Beat it you pasty Brit!" She feared she was drawing too much attention and security would be called. But then finally Grant stood up and whispered.

"I got it!" He took Violet by the hand and moved them away from the painting. "I was able to pry open the compartment, take out the box, and put the faux cover back. No one will know unless they look real close."

"Great," Violet looked at the small iron box. "Smaller than the others. Let's see this thing."

Grant quickly opened the box and unfurled the first scroll.

1865

Un deposito un sostanzioso nord dovuto che sta in piedi,

Il settimo offerto con le mani generose,

Il regalo più benedetto ricevuto dal figlio,

E la conoscenza scintilla da tre a un,

Dove il raggio dorato mira e mostra,

Fa il bisogno nascosto segreto è stivato.

EC4.4.12   IS18.1.9   DE32.13.10   GE49.1.24   RU4.7.8
LU13.22.10 AC20.24.10 IS9.10.8 AC20.31.16 RO1.8.10 IS1.16.19
PS40.10.3 IS15.1.14 RO6.19.13 DA9.21.31 NE8.8.23 EC6.9.14
HE9.23.1 PS49.1.3 EX34.7.16 NE2.2.19 IS3.6.26 RO9.16.4 NU7.5.9
NU11.15.8 NE7.24.5 DE15.13.17 AC7.42.40 GE26.6.1 NE8.12.19
RO16.22.3 GE40.14.2 EP6.5.6 PS147.1.6 PR6.26.3 AC23.15.26

LU8.13.25   AC3.22.24   DA10.9.3   IS49.4.11   PR17.7.8   EP5.16.3
GE21.14.22   IS43.9.19   PS98.8.12   LU11.22.5   GA5.21.13   AC2.26.2
EP1.19.18   JE23.18.25   GE21.10.7   HE8.2.6   IS6.9.6   RO15.30.26
PR6.1.9 LU5.23.4 RU4.8.7 IS63.1.3 DE31.26.3
     Ricatta LE17.13
     MT109

"Wait, this one makes perfect sense, I know where this one is! We have to get to Cambridge."

"Massachusetts?" Violet asked.

"Sorry, no. We're not leaving England just yet. Cambridge, England. That's a pretty short trip away."

"Thank God, 'cause I can't afford any more flights." Violet said, relieved. "How are you so sure?"

Grant pointed to the first two lines of the poem. "This here says that due north is a large repository and this refers to the seventh with generous hands. That can only be the 7th Viscount Fitzwilliam of Merrion!"

"Of course," Violet rolled her eyes. "How silly of me not to see that."

"Anyway, it's telling us that the next location is in the Fitzwilliam Museum."

"Wow. Are you kind of savant?" Violet joked. She turned to lead the way out. "Let's hit the road Jack and…"

Violet looked about the room and then tilted her head. A rather odd looking person drifted through the crowd. She watched, smiling at first, mainly because of the ridiculous glasses-nose-moustache disguise the man wore. It took a few minutes for realization to dawn on her. Suddenly she recognized the famous face beneath the cheap disguise.

"Hey, Grant." She prodded Grant with her elbow. "Isn't that guy that actor? What's his name? What's he doing here?"

Grant turned to look. "Where?"

Violet didn't answer, instead she froze. True recognition kicked in. Yes, it was the famous actor, but an actor she'd met already! She suddenly realized that the famous face was remarkably similar to that of the killer nun driving the car.

"Oh shit." Violet whispered. "Grant, that's Jon Trafalgar! And he was the second nun! I recognize her, er, him from the car ride."

Grant didn't wait to spot the celebrity in the crowd. He grabbed Violet's hand and pulled her into another room and down a corridor. "It makes sense that he's working with Thom Crows. They're both major Scientologists."

Mr. Trafalgar didn't notice Grant and Violet's escape until it was too late. He had them in his sights, but then they were gone. He plunged into the crowd, pushing aside students and little old ladies with his bulk. "Get out of my way, mortals!" he yelled. He scrambled about the room, looking through doors and down hallways. He'd lost them. "Damn!"

Violet huffed and puffed, trying to keep pace with the agile and quick Grant. "But really, Jon Trafalgar and Thom Crows, aren't they a bit above hunting people down with knives and murder and stuff?"

Grant didn't slow at all. "Violet, who knows what Scientologists put in their heads behind closed doors? These guys might be so brainwashed that they'd do anything the Scientology organization asks."

Violet and Grant found themselves again leaping down steps in a desperate attempt at escape. They ran across the square. "Hey," Grant said, though breathing heavily. "Did you notice that this square shares the same name as the maniacal Scientologist behind us?"

"I really, really don't care, Grant." Violet wheezed. She was really regretting the more than ten years of smoking.

"Quite a coincidence," he breathed heavily. "Just saying."

"Keep moving."

They exited the square and found themselves on the main thoroughfare. Violet waved her hand and called for a cab. A little black car flew from across the street and skidded to a stop in front of them. Grant opened the door and they jumped in.

The cab driver wore a wide brimmed hat pulled down low to his eyes. He also sported thick framed sunglasses. His face was mottled with an uneven length beard, it was patchy on his face, as though hurriedly glued on. "Where to mateys?" He asked in an accent that was a cross between English and possibly French. Maybe a southern drawl thrown in. He didn't turn to face his fare, instead keeping his face forward and his hands tightly gripped on the steering wheel.

"Cambridge, please. And we're in a hurry!"

"Right-oh, hibbety-jibbetty, and all that!" The driver gunned the little vehicle and took off. In an alleyway, just a block away, two tourists discovered the broken and dead body of the taxi's real driver.

CHAPTER 70

Mr. Trafalgar smiled as he calmly walked through the square. His own ride, the stretch limo was just a block away. He had watched as Grant and Violet took refuge in the cab driven by Mr. Crows. *Perfect!*

He rounded the corner and the driver of his limo was waiting with the door open. Mr. Trafalgar climbed into the back and poured a fresh, cold Martini. He took a sip, breathed deeply, and sat back. He reached inside his jacket for the Blackberry.

"Now I'll call the boss and tell him we've got everything under control. Then we'll see what he wants us to do next." He took another sip as the driver started up the limo. "Life is good." Mr. Trafalgar said, dialing the Blackberry.

CHAPTER 71

Mr. Crows drove like a madman. He never really got the chance to drive, it was always limos and town cars and bodyguards. And especially when on a mission with Mr. Trafalgar, who always had to be in charge. So when the rare opportunity arrived, Mr. Crows took advantage of it.

He remembered back to when he filmed the race car movie, they kept insisting on a stunt driver. What a rip-off that was! Just because he kept hurting people, accidentally running into or over stunt drivers, a few cameramen, a make-up artist, a stand-in, and a few people on line at craft services. Well, that and he would simply keep driving even after they yelled 'Cut!' a few dozen times. But it wasn't his fault. They should have cleared the set!

But at least now he was in charge, he was the big man, and taking full advantage of it. He pretty much forgot he had passengers. In fact, he had almost blanked out entirely when the rage took over and he saw so many potential targets on the roads. Dogs, cats, children, even a mother pushing a stroller. The urge was powerful, but he resisted. *I've got to focus!* So instead, he drove really, really fast.

Mr. Crows had careened through almost a dozen short side streets before exploding onto the M11 North. His tires left macadam and caught air as he tore up the on ramp. With over forty miles of road ahead of him, the sky was the limit. Mr. Crows pushed the little cab as much as he could, switching lanes randomly, occasionally using the opposite lane to pass while oncoming cars honked and swerved angrily. He fought back the overwhelming urge to cackle maniacally, it always felt good to do that when he was causing mayhem.

I like cackling, and driving fast is fun, too! Mr. Crows thought to himself. *So is strangling. And pudding. And sleds on a snowy hill. And strangling.*

Violet had had about enough. She held onto the door handle for dear life. Grant was curled up with his backpack like a frightened pill bug. Violet had been sliding from side to side, her and Grant bumping hips, it didn't take long before it really started to hurt. Violet grabbed the top of the front seat and leaned forward. Her lower half swayed as she held onto the driver's seat for dear life.

"Hey!" she yelled to the weird little man. "Why the hell are you driving like this? We didn't tell you to speed. Can you please slow down?"

"Oh, me so sorry, little lady, I don't-a mean to a-scare you fine mateys." Mr. Crows rattled off in his terrible accent that seemed to switch from Cockney to almost Jamaican. "I will slow down so much-a more for you, eh?"

"Thank you." Violet grunted, before she returned to the back, she asked one more question. "Exactly where are you from?"

"W-who me?" Mr. Crows stuttered. "Oh, I'm from the, er, north of Wales. Yes, that is me, from Wales."

"Oh, okay." Violet replied, not knowing where Wales is never mind what a person from Wales may sound like. "Where is Wales?"

Panic hit Mr. Crows like a hardened cow patty. "Er, Wales, is um, just north of the, uh, southern tip of, um this here place. But more eastward."

"Oh," Violet accepted the explanation. "Just slow down, okay?"

"Si, me lady." Mr. Crows said, inside his mouth he was biting his cheek violently. The taste of blood assuaged his need to stick his fingers into her trachea and free the warm, red geyser held within. "Will do! Righty-oh!" Mr. Crows eased off the accelerator, putting the speed to just above the limit.

Violet sat back and turned to Grant, his face was pushed into his backpack. She pulled him into an upright position. "Grant? You okay?"

"Please tell me we're there." Grant asked, his face had imprints of zippers and strings from his backpack. He looked like he was stitched together.

Violet swallowed a laugh, looking at him. "No, but I asked him to slow down. By the way, where is Wales?"

"Oh, well Wales is on the western coast of the United Kingdom." And upon seeing Violet's blank stare, added, "It's part of England."

That could sort of worked with what the driver had said. Maybe. Violet had never looked at a globe in her life. *I hate knowing countries and capitals and all that geology stuff.* "What kind of accent do they have?"

"Well, if you've never heard it, it's a little odd. A bit harder to understand than a thick British accent. You'd probably have a hard time understanding it."

"I'll say." Violet agreed.

CHAPTER 72

Cambridge was a fairytale landscape, replete with majestic cathedrals and castles. Towering spires topped the stone and brick marvels of churches, museums and schools. Historical architecture surrounded the travelers as the little black taxi sped along.

Even Grant had to lift his face from hiding within his backpack to take in the scenery. Violet stared wide-eyed, again, in awe of wondrous worlds she never knew existed, nor expected to see.

"Grant, this place is wonderful," Violet spoke in a hushed tone.

"Cambridge is an old university town." Grant spoke, not taking his eyes off the passing buildings. "After thousands of years of war, occupations by the Romans, Saxons and Vikings, it wasn't until 1209 that students fled from Oxford and created the first university here. Then it was called Peterhouse." Grant chuckled at the name. "Then came King's College Chapel, an amazing example of English gothic design, and you can see parts of it in the skyline there." Grant pointed.

"Most of the buildings here are hundreds of years old, you can see the more modern additions here and there," Grant continued. "Which I think are a stain on this landscape. Ahead you can see the Fitzwilliam Museum, our destination. A very neo-classical building, it resembles many of the buildings in our country's capitol."

The cab zoomed along Trumpington Street and eventually screeched to a stop in front of the museum.

Violet stepped out of the cab and took a moment getting her land legs back. She steadied herself on the side of the taxi. Grant stepped out and fell to the ground. He tried standing, then fell again. He looked like a newborn fawn walking for the first time.

"C'mon Bambi," Violet said, helping him up.

Violet leaned back in and handed the driver his money. "Um, thanks. I think," she said, then closed the door.

"You-a so welcome, love!" the driver called out, sounding like an Italian chef with a slight British accent. "Hasta la vista, baby!" The cab fishtailed as it sped away and took the first corner. Violet could have sworn she heard a woman scream but wrote it off as the taxi's tires screeching around another corner.

Grant finally found his footing, holding onto a sign post, and wiped the sweat from his brow. "Thank God that's over."

"You're not kidding." Violet agreed. "C'mon, let's get in there. The light is fading and I'm guessing we'll have to find somewhere to sleep."

Grant perked up at that. "Er, yes, we, uh, should. Find. Place to, uh, sleep." He didn't think he'd get a second chance to spend the night with Violet.

Violet, being used to predators and the crosshairs of men's attention, did not miss Grant's sudden awkwardness and enthusiasm. "Don't get your hopes up, Einstein, just like last time, no chance for you. Separate rooms. Worst case, separate beds. Worst worst case, you get the floor."

Grant nodded. "That's fine." His face was a bright red.

They turned to the museum and stared up. It was a huge, intimidating building. Its massive columns, relief sculptures, carved stone floral patterns on the ceiling of the entrance, crenellations, almost forced one to fall backward looking up at it all.

Violet was relieved, upon entering, that there was no entrance fee, nor were there donations expected, that she saw. Luckily, Grant was still too flustered by the second chance of them rooming together for him to get into a tirade of supporting the arts and museums. So they simply strode in.

The lobby in the main entrance was a two story marvel of sculptures, marble stairs and railings, tiled floor and, completely out of place, a circular, glowing information desk in the middle of it all. Grant looked at Violet, who knew exactly what he was thinking. It did look like a UFO. She nodded, hating how much this stuff turned up everywhere.

There weren't many patrons at this time of the day. There were maybe half a dozen people wandering about within view. Violet was sure they'd have to move quickly before the museum closed.

Grant grabbed a pamphlet and rifled through it, looking for anything that might give them a direction to start. He as reading through the names of artists and artisans.

"Well, we know it has something to do with baptism. And again, the Madonna, which is a very recurrent theme. And... whoa!" Grant slapped his head.

"What? What is it?"

"The poem said to look for art! I thought they had simply been referring to artwork. A sculpture or painting. But they might have been referring to Aert De Gelder!"

"A guy named Art? Who is he?"

"Don't know. I haven't heard of him." Grant admitted. He shrugged.

"Holy crap!" Violet lifted her arms as if in exultation. "Did my ears deceive me?" She looked up to the ceiling. "Did you hear that Lord? Hello Jesus? Is everyone getting this? Mark this day on the calendar! Make it a federal holiday! I'm taking this day off, every year, for the rest of my life! Grant-didn't-know Day!"

"Okay, okay! Let it go." Grant muttered. "Hey, I don't claim to know everything. Just a whole lot."

Violet patted his shoulder. "You'll be okay," she said condescendingly. "I'm sure that took quite a bit to admit. Today, my son, you are a man."

"Anyway," Grant pushed her hand from off his shoulder. "He has a painting here, coincidently titled 'The Baptism of Christ'. He'd be in the Dutch section. Room 15 on the first floor." Grant headed for the steps.

"Isn't this the first floor?" Violet asked, following him.

"This is the *ground* floor." Grant said without stopping.

Violet knew he was irritated. "Ooh. Somebody's cranky," she said in a baby voice. "Somebody needs a nappy-wappy."

"Stuff it, Violet!" Grant barked.

"Stuff it? What is this, grade school?" She laughed as they reached the first floor.

Back down in the lobby, two figures strode through the entrance. No costumes this time, just their token black-on-black garments, and expensive pairs of sunglasses. Mr. Trafalgar and Mr. Crows had nothing to hide. They had their mission, and this time, it required no subtlety.

CHAPTER 73

Violet and Grant didn't wander through the museums as they had done in the past. They marched purposefully, Grant following the map in the pamphlet, and made their way quickly to the Dutch painting gallery.

They stopped in the center of the room and slowly scanned the dozen paintings on the walls. It didn't take much to find their quarry.

"Bingo!" Grant exclaimed. "That's obviously it."

Grant ran up to the painting. It wasn't very large, less than two feet in height. But its message was as clear as it can get.

Aert de Gelder's The Baptism of Christ was a richly golden-hued image. Seemingly framed in a desert landscape, gilded hills filled the background and foreground, several people gathered, dotting the terrain, as they watched the glowing image in the center. Huddled in the middle, John the Baptist stood over Jesus, his baptism the center of everyone's attention.

A powerful and brilliant beam of light filled the image, its focus on the child Jesus, but it is the source of the beam of light that drew in Grant and Violet.

High above Jesus and John, swirling in the sky, was a disc, a golden ovoid that seemed to spin in the atmosphere. In its center, a few bright spots, as if the engines kept it suspended. Four separate beams exited from the bottom of the disc, reaching the ground around Jesus, setting the desert afire in a blinding light.

"Holy…" Violet whispered.

"De Gelder is telling us they were present at Jesus' baptism. They watched over it, either protecting him or simply overseeing it. Perhaps they had already begun instilling him with their wonderful information." Grant spoke in reverent tones.

"Why is it that no one else sees this?" Violet asked. "Don't you think everyone would be talking about this stuff?"

Grant shook his head. "People see what they want to see, what they were taught to see. Things can be under your nose, everyday, and you'll never see it until something smacks you in the head."

"Well, call me smacked." Violet smiled.

"Okay, well enough of this. We have a mission here." Grant started looking around. There weren't any other patrons in the Dutch room, and Grant didn't hesitate to touch and feel the paintings frame and the wall around it. "The reliquary has to be here somewhere."

Violet watched as Grant felt all around the wall of the painting. He slid his fingers along the frame, inch by inch. Grant turned to Violet. "Go keep an eye out for tourists. I have to do some damage here." Grant pulled out his bent pocket knife.

Violet nodded and went to the doorway, she watched the hall as Grant stood hunched over, grunting in the corner, fumbling and struggling with something in front of him. *I bet that's a familiar scenario for him.* Violet laughed to herself.

"I got it!" Grant called out loudly.

Violet ran back. "Great! Keep it down," she hissed.

Grant opened the iron box and retrieved the scrolls. He unfurled the top scroll and his face fell.

1979

Op vergulde eik rijdt de gevleugelde boodschapper

Binnen de keyworn reliquery een geheime huiden

Ver onder de preekstoel van bittere kalk

Onze toekomst rust 'neath trap van tijd

AC7.7.12 GE4.9.18 PS37.1.2 PR30.29.13 RU2.8.13 LU16.4.6 EC1.10.11 DE28.68.9 PS35.3.7 PS147.1.6

"Well, it's in Dutch. And I don't read Dutch," he sighed heavily. "This puts a little damper on our travels. We're going to have to get it translated."

Violet reached out and took the scroll, she glanced over the ancient writing.

"Do not tell me, out of the blue, you can read Dutch." Grant laughed.

"No, Mr. Sarcasm. And don't be rude." Violet sneered at him. "I just wanted to look at it, is that okay?"

"Sorry. I'm a little frustrated." Grant said. "There's no point in reading the rest. It'll all be in Dutch." Grant shuffled off dourly.

Violet stared at the scroll, hoping that if she looked at it long enough the words would just transform into English. It wasn't happening. *Damn!* This couldn't be happening, not now, not after all they'd been through. Violet could feel tears welling up in her eyes.

Wow! She thought. *This has actually become important to me. I just wanted to make dad proud. So somehow, somewhere, wherever he was he'd know that I cared and that I wasn't a complete screw-up.*

"So we meet again!" a voice boomed from the doorway to the Dutch room.

Violet gasped and spun around, she heard Grant shriek from the other side of the gallery. Their eyes widened at the sight of the gun leveled on them.

"I'll be taking that." Mr. Trafalgar said to Violet, he took a few steps forward and snatched the scroll from her hands.

Mr. Crows stood behind his larger counterpart, wringing his hands anxiously, he eyed Violet and Grant hungrily. His head twitched as he glared at one, then the other.

"Let's see what this says." Mr. Trafalgar said, holding up the scroll. "What the Hell is this written in? I can't read this. This reads like a Tarentino script"

"It's Dutch." Grant blurted.

Violet shot Grant a nasty look. "Shut up! Don't help them with anything!"

"Sorry." he mumbled.

"That's okay, kids." Mr. Trafalgar laughed. "I'm sure the boss-man can translate it." He waved the gun in Grant's direction. "Come on over here, sunshine. We have business to attend to." Mr. Trafalgar smirked. Mr. Crows nervously laughed with him. "Well, I have good news, lady and, er, gentleman. We are heading back to America."

"Good, get going." Violet spat out, pointing toward the exit. "Don't let the door hit you in the…"

"Shut it!" Mr. Trafalgar barked. He looked over at Grant. "You may call the shots with your skinny little nerd boyfriend here, but I'm the dude with the gun. I call the shots and you all do what I say."

They are not going to let us live. Violet thought to herself. *These maniacs are going to kill us. And why not? They have everything they need from us. We led them here and now they're going to kill us and return home with what we found. Unless…*

Violet's hand shot out while Mr. Trafalgar was watching Grant cross the room. She grabbed the scrolls and took several steps back.

"What the?" Mr. Trafalgar yelled. "Okay, you stupid bitch. Give that back or I'll shoot you in the face!"

Violet ignored him, she stared intently at the first scroll. Over every word, she didn't know what it meant but she captured it in her mind's eye, tattooed it on her brain. Every letter, every number. Like an image. Not words, images. Take a mental picture. Like Grant did with his empty cameras.

"I said, give it back bitch." Mr. Trafalgar was red with rage now. "I swear to God I'll put a hole in your head."

Grant watched with terror. *What is she doing?* he thought. *She's going to get us killed. She's... oh, no! No, Violet, don't do what I think you're going to...*

Violet looked up at Mr. Trafalgar, a look of ferociousness in her eyes. "You... need... US!" she screamed then stuffed the first scroll in her mouth. She chewed and gnashed at it violently. Mr. Trafalgar barked an order and Mr. Crows leapt at Violet.

Mr. Crows landed a few feet from Violet, who fell backward in fear. She scrambled, like a crab, further away. She was chewing and chewing, her eyes watering.

"I'm going to cut you open to get that out!" Mr. Crows snickered, then leapt again, howling like a baboon.

Violet strained on the dry, ancient paper. It was wadded up into a large ball, there wasn't enough saliva in the world to break this dust ball down. She had no choice, she swallowed it whole.

Violet's eyes popped out of her head, a horrible noise emitting from her gaping mouth. She was choking! Water streamed down her reddening face.

"She's choking, you idiot!" Mr. Trafalgar yelled at Mr. Crows. "Tear open her throat and dig it out!"

Mr. Crows landed on Violet, he grabbed her by the neck. Before he could get his fingernails into her skin, Violet let out a loud gasp.

It was too late. She'd swallowed it.

With his hands still around her throat, Mr. Crows looked toward Mr. Trafalgar. "Do I still get to gut her?"

"You better not!" Violet rasped, her throat shredded. "That paper was hundreds of years old, you know damn well that it's ruined now. It's gone forever!"

Mr. Trafalgar rubbed his forehead. "That was really stupid, lady."

"Stupid?" Violet's voice sounded like gravel. "I memorized it. Now you can't kill us. You need what's in my head!"

"I hate to tell you this, sugarlips." Mr. Trafalgar waved the gun. "We weren't killing you anyway."

Violet's mouth squeaked. "Y-you weren't?"

"Nope. Orders were to bring you back."

"Oh."

"So I honestly do hope you memorized every freaking line of that scribble." Mr. Trafalgar leaned in close. "'Cause if you didn't, my little buddy here will get you alone in a room for a few hours. It'll feel like years with what he'll do to you."

"You'll never get away with this!" Violet yelled, hoping security or a passing tourist would hear and help.

"Ooh! Clichés! I like that." Mr. Trafalgar laughed. "I, *we*, can get away with anything. We're celebrities! We're famous. We are American royalty! We're unstoppable, just as OJ and Robert Blake proved. We can get away with murder. Besides, this is bigger than any of us. Bigger than you, me, my little buddy here, anybody out there that you're hoping will save you. I won't hesitate to shoot any of them if they interfere."

"You won't shoot us!" Violet said. "You said you were taking us with you. And you need what I memorized. If we walk out of here, what are you going to do?"

The four stood still. No one moving. They all eyed each other as thoughts whirled through each of them. Let's see what was going on in each of their thoughts...

Violet stared terrified at the gun pointed at her. She knew Mr. Trafalgar would pull the trigger if he had to. She knew she had no choice but to cooperate. She thought about her father, his bloodied, crumpled frame on the floor of the Met. She didn't want to let him down. Was this how it would end? Her being taken captive before she ever found out about her father's mysterious past and her heir to a secret knowledge from Jesus himself. And poor Grant. The young college professor who risked everything to help a woman on her quest for her past. He'd been so brave, so strong, so weird.

Grant was trying his best to keep from peeing himself. He was squeezing his thighs together to keep from releasing a bladderful of fear. As soon as the gun was pointed at him, however briefly, his body went rigid. His mind went blank. And he felt a white light encroaching on his vision. He could see nothing, nobody else in the room, he could only see the dull metal barrel of the gun. A tunnel vision of terror. He thought maybe he leaked a little. Hopefully it wouldn't show on the front of his pants.

Mr. Trafalgar's eyes scanned up and down Violet's athletic body. Boy, she's a looker. Got a nice, tight little body on her. Man, I sure could use a cigarette. Right after I kill this dweeb, I'm going to smoke. Speaking of the dweeb, aside from him cowering on the ground, he looks pretty good in those khaki pants. It accentuates his rump rather nicely. Right after I kill him and have a cigarette, I'll have another smoke.

Mr. Crows watched the three people facing off in the room. His thoughts wandered to killing puppies and sucking their blood and how that would keep him young forever. Oh and Pez, though he doesn't understand how those candies keep coming out of the plastic head, like magic, as though they were Jesus' basket of fish. Oh and how jumping makes him feel good and rain smells nice. Oh, and Oprah, that nice lady, I wonder what she'd taste like cooked. And lilies and moons and fudge in a shoe. Then his mind saw pinwheels. Clown hitting drums.

"Well, you're half right." Mr. Trafalgar grinned. "We do need you! But…" He paused for dramatic effect and then suddenly swung the gun toward Grant. "We don't need him! So if you don't want your boyfriend here to die, you'll do everything we say." He pointed the gun directly at Grant's forehead.

Grant's eyes narrowed. Time seemed to slow down. This was it, he had no choice but to act, Violet depended on him.

Grant moved with lightning speed, his fists and feet a blur. Like Bruce Lee, barely able to be caught on film, Grant flowed with strength and agility. He swung his fist around and grabbed the gun in Mr. Trafalgar's hand. The burly actor had no time to react, his jaw dropping in astonishment. Grant forced his opponent to point the gun to Grant's right as Mr. Trafalgar fired once. The bullet hit Mr. Crows in the chest. Mr. Crows fell backward, his eyes became empty, his mouth slack, he was dead before he hit the floor.

"Noooo!" Mr. Trafalgar screamed, his voice slowed down by the cool slow-motion effect of the battle. He turned to Grant, still wrestling for the gun. He brought up his left fist and clocked Grant in the chin. Grant reeled in pain but didn't lose his grip. The pain only fueled his anger and prowess.

Grant recovered from the hit in time to duck a second strike. Mr. Trafalgar was thrown off balance. Grant came around with a high roundhouse kick that landed directly on Mr. Trafalgar's face.

Mr. Trafalgar roared in pain, stumbling backward. "You son of a…" It was then Mr. Trafalgar realized he was no longer holding the gun. "Oh, crap."

Grant stood confidently, smiling. Time came back into its proper speed. "That's right fatboy. Now who's in charge here?" Grant glanced over at Violet, he couldn't be sure but she was looking at him different. Her eyes melted on him. That was it, she had just fallen in love with him. Nice.

Mr. Trafalgar smirked, his stance assuming more confidence. "You can't shoot me. You're not man enough to shoot another person." Mr. Trafalgar swatted dust off his black jacket and held it by the lapels. He acted as though he were fixing his jacket. But he had another gun just inside the jacket.

Grant cocked the gun, aimed it at Mr. Trafalgar, and smiled. "Try me." Grant hissed in his best Clint Eastwood. Which didn't sound like Clint Eastwood at all, but more like Ronald Reagan.

Mr. Trafalgar's hand was a blur. He grabbed his gun and aimed it at Grant in half of a second. A loud shot rang out.

Mr. Trafalgar stood with a shocked look on his face. He looked down at the red stain spreading across his chest. "Oh!" Mr. Trafalgar muttered. "Oh, man. That… that ain't cool."

"I'm not a nerd." Grant stated, blowing smoke from the muzzle of the gun.

Mr. Trafalgar fell to his knees, then collapsed forward, dead.

Violet ran to Grant and threw her arms around him. "Oh, Grant!" she said, her voice rich with emotion. She kissed him on the cheek. "Oh, Grant, Grant, Grant." she said louder. "Grant! Grant! GRANT!" Now she was yelling. *Why is Violet yelling?* Grant thought.

Violet was leaning over Grant, who was lying in a heap on the floor. He was smiling and mumbling, incoherent at first, but less slurred as seconds passed.

"I grabbed the gun. I shot them. I saved the day. I'm the hero." Grant spoke from his semi-coma. "Kisses. Kisses from Violet."

"No, Grant. You passed out and pissed yourself. You must have imagined all that other crap." Violet looked back up at Mr. Trafalgar, who was quite alive and still in possession of the gun with the still-alive Mr. Crows beside him. "He's okay. He passes out when he gets scared."

"He's alive because he fainted. I planned on shooting him there and then. I actually feel bad for the dork." Mr. Trafalgar grunted.

Violet lifted the woozy Grant to his feet. He was pale and pasty, at least more so than usual, and smiling very oddly at Violet.

Mr. Trafalgar nodded for Mr. Crows. "Get the shot. We have some flying to do." He waved the gun around toward Grant and Violet. "Let Mr. Crows here give you your shot, it's just a sedative to help pass the time. And no more funny stuff or I swear I *will* shoot the dork!"

Mr. Crows retrieved a hypodermic needle from his back pocket and primed it. He took a step toward Grant. Grant's eyes widened. Like a sack of potatoes, Grant crumbled to the floor, again, passed out. Violet sighed. "My hero."

Mr. Crows shrugged and stuck Grant with the needle anyway. He tossed the spent one away and got out another. He turned to Violet.

Violet shook her head. "No way. I don't like shots."

Mr. Crows snarled, his upper lip pulled back. She could have sworn she saw fangs. She squinted her eyes shut. "Okay, but make it fast!"

She felt a little prick then all went to black.

CHAPTER 74

It was a terribly long car ride back to the London International Airport, especially when your hands were tied behind your back and your mouth duct taped shut. Violet lay in the back of the limo while poor Grant was stuffed in the trunk. She felt bad for him but at the same time, didn't really want him lying on her or next to her in the back seat. He'd probably consider it a date. Plus, the front of his pants were soaking wet.

She had woken up rather quickly considering they weren't at the airport yet, which she figured couldn't have been more than two hours away. Her head hurt and her mouth was all cottony.

She could see her captors in the back of the limo with her. It was night now, and the passing street lights strobed over Mr. Trafalgar's visage as he sleepily sipped from a martini glass. Mr. Crows was curled up in a ball, apparently asleep, next to his larger friend. He must have been having a dream, his legs would kick sporadically, and he would whimper from time to time.

She assumed Mr. Trafalgar planned to fly his own plane, since in the press, he was known for piloting. She also assumed he was able to come and go without much or any security checks.

She, unfortunately, was right, and Mr. Trafalgar's limo pulled right up to his awaiting jet. Mr. Trafalgar gently awoke Mr. Crows, who yawned and stretched like a cat, before bouncing out of the limo. Violet feigned unconsciousness while the celebrities dragged her out and carried her aboard the jet unencumbered by legalities. She was unceremoniously dumped in a small room. Shortly after, Grant's slack carcass was dropped next to her.

Violet felt even worse for Grant once she saw him. His eyes were red rimmed and snot had run from his nostrils, over the duct tape, and caked on his chin. Violet was glad she had tape over her mouth. She would have laughed at the sight had she not felt so bad. And at least it looked like his pants were drying already.

They appeared to be in a small meeting room, wherein sat a round, oak table and a few leather chairs. A laptop connected to a digital projector sat on the table.

Mr. Crows stood over them a moment, growled, and then closed the door and locked them in, leaving them in the dark room.

Once her eyes adjusted, Violet was able to make out shapes in the room. Including the sack of potatoes she knew was Grant. Violet tried to whisper to Grant, but the duct tape made it impossible. She swung her feet around and kicked him. Nothing. She kicked him again. Grant's eyes fluttered. Violet hauled off and kicked him with everything she had. His eyes opened and the duct tape muffled his scream.

"Uh ne fuh!" He yelled through the tape.

Within minutes, they could hear the engines of the jet racing to life and soon they were moving along the tarmac.

Violet wiggled closer to Grant once they were in flight. She knew Mr. Trafalgar would most likely be busy piloting the entire trip and she really needed only to worry about Mr. Crows making unexpected visits to their room.

"Anf oo onfay?" Violet asked through the duct tape.

"Enf." Grant answered and Violet was pretty confident that it was a yes.

Violet started rubbing her duct tape on the carpeting, hoping to catch a corner of it. If she did, she might be able to peel it back. At least enough to communicate better.

Violet began rubbing her chin on the carpet and within two minutes felt the rug-burn kick in. "Neefus fushin kist!" she cursed, flipped sides and tried the other cheek.

"Tun ne uffer neek!" Grant laughed. "Nash wa neeshush woon nay!"

Violet glanced up at Grant furious. "Fuf uh!" She returned to her task and ignored the pain when she felt a bit of the tape catch. She squinted against the hot burn of the nylon carpet. Soon she had her corner free and she pushed the tape along until part of her mouth was exposed. Using her tongue, Violet pulled in the one corner and gnashed at it with her teeth. She soon pulled the entire piece of tape off her face. "Ahhh!" she gasped, spitting the tape onto the floor.

Her chin and cheeks were rosy with carpet burns. She looked up at Grant. "What did you say?" Then realized the futility of asking until his tape was also removed.

The question was: How to do it.

Or more importantly: How to do it without touching him.

Violet wiggled a little closer to Grant then gave him her most serious stare. "Okay, you little perv. The only way to get the tape off your mouth is for me to take it off with my mouth." Violet saw Grant's eyes light up. "See? That's why I'm hesitating. You're going to make this into something!"

Grant shook his head vehemently. "Nuf um nah!"

"You better not!" She warned him and writhed a bit closer. She began to lean in toward Grant but paused. She saw his eyes. His cheeks were flush and a trickle of sweat was running down his forehead. "Good God this sucks." she mumbled. "Grant, just close your frigging eyes! Can you do that much for me?"

Grant did so and it helped slightly. Violet gently reached out with her teeth, pulling her lips as far back as possible. She wanted to avoid as much skin-on-skin contact with Grant's sweaty, oily face as she was able. She couldn't feel the tape with her teeth so she was forced to search with her tongue.

I'm going to want to take an acid bath after this. Violet growled to herself.

Violet's tongue flitted over Grant's cheek and he rustled at the contact. She looked up at his eyes, which thankfully were still closed. But the torrent of sweat was really getting started. Violet hurried before the rivers of brine reached her tongue.

Violet moved her tongue faster and Grant giggled. She was about to abort, due to her intense nausea but finally found the corner. A waterfall of sweat was rushing her way. Niagra on Viagra. At the last second, she dove for the tape with her teeth and caught the corner. She threw her head back, tearing the tape from Grant's face.

"Yeeeooow!" he yelped.

Violet head-butted him, cutting his yelp short. "First, keep quiet!" she hissed. "Second, the head-butt is for being so gross!"

"Dang." Grant mumbled. "Sorry." He looked around. "Where are we?"

"We are on Jon Trafalgar's own jet. At least I'm pretty sure. And we are locked in what appears to be a small conference room."

Grant beamed. "This is so cool! We're on Jon Trafalgar's jet!"

Violet frowned. "Grant, this is really *not* cool, okay? We're in trouble here."

"Well, first things first. We have to get ourselves untied." Grant said. "Then, we have to get off the plane."

"Wow. You're brilliant." Violet scoffed. "You just solved our entire problem. You're my hero!"

Grant gave Violet a look. "Don't be wise. I was just assessing the situation."

"Yeah, okay."

Grant blew at a large drop of sweat hanging off the end of his nose. "Damn. I'm really soaked." Then he remembered his pants. "Oh, man."

Violet got shivers thinking about his level of sweatitude. *If he's that sweaty simply because I got close to his face, what would happen if a woman... Gah!* She didn't want to think any more. Erase! Erase! She wanted those thoughts permanently removed from her brain. But then it hit Violet. She started thinking about its benefits.

"Grant," she started. "What do you think the ropes on our hands are made of?"

Grant moved around a bit, feeling with his fingers. "Nylon. Definitely."

She couldn't believe she was doing this. "Do you think, if you were... sweaty enough, your hands that is, that you might be able to slip out of the ropes?"

"Um, well, sure. The nylon really doesn't absorb the sweat, it'd be more like a lubricant. I might be able to worm free. But how am I going to get *that* sweaty? The only way is when women get me all... Oh!" Grant blushed. "Oh! Oh, my."

Violet nodded. "Now, trust me when I say I really don't want to do this." She spoke sternly. "I *really* don't want to do this. *Really*. But it's the only way I can think of."

"Me too!" Grant replied a little too quickly.

Violet wiggled closer to Grant, her face right up to his. "Now work quickly, do *not* drag this out!"

"O-okay."

Thank God it's dark in here. Violet leaned in and kissed him. She could feel him shaking. The sweat from his nose rubbed onto her face. She pulled back and spoke in her best sexy voice. "Oh, Grant, you are so hot," she purred. "I want to eat you alive." She moved in again and tore into him, ramming her tongue into his mouth.

She swore she could taste Flintstone vitamins.

Grant was shaking like a leaf. She could hear his hands rustling behind his back. *Thank God they're tied* behind *his back!* She thought.

"Oh, Grant, you make me so hot." And then in her normal voice. "Are you anywhere yet?"

"Y-yeah, real close. Very close."

"I mean the rope. Sweating and all?"

"Um, yes. That too."

Violet returned to kissing Grant, she purred more, nuzzled his soaking wet neck.

Suddenly Grant howled like a monkey and Violet feared he orgasmed before he could get the ropes off.

"I got them!" Grant yelled out.

Thank you, God! Violet looked toward the ceiling.

Grant was panting heavily as he worked his remaining ropes off his hands. Violet rolled over so her back was to Grant.

"Come here and untie my ropes." Violet said.

"Wait. I can't."

"Why not? Don't play games, Grant, just get the Hell over here and untie me!" Violet began to get really angry.

"Just a minute!" Grant meekly argued. "I can't. I need a moment."

"Why the Hell not?"

"I-I, let's just say I'm not in a position to comfortably move about. Just yet."

"What are you talking about?"

"I got a woody."

Somebody help me. Violet sighed, thumping her head into the carpet.

CHAPTER 75

Grant was finally able to maneuver comfortably, he untied Violet, and once they turned the lights on, it was an awkward moment when they first met with their eyes.

Violet ended the awkwardness with a quick, "Stop looking at me like that or I'll throw you off this plane."

"Gotcha," Grant said, looking away.

They quickly began searching the room for anything they could use as a weapon or means to escape. While Violet searched the few drawers in the room, Grant went to work on the computer. After a few minutes he huffed in dissatisfaction.

"Unfortunately, this computer is either not set up for Internet access or they had the foresight to disconnect it."

Violet stood over him. "You're the tech geek, can't you hack your way into the main frame and discombobulate the thingers?"

"As technically accurate as that is, no. You can't hack into something if you're not wired in to anything." Grant pressed a button. "This is for viewing movies. Mr. Trafalgar has an editing suite on here." The projector came to life and images splashed into frame.

There were segments of car chases, alien spacecrafts shooting laser beams at people, and, of course, Mr. Trafalgar himself, running around with gun in hand, looking a little too old and out of shape to be playing the hero anymore.

"This is great!" Grant giggled. "We are getting to see his new movie before it's even finished!"

Violet smacked him on the back of the head. "Have you seen any of his other flicks?" Grant shook his head while rubbing where Violet had struck. "Don't get your hopes up that this one won't be as bad as the others. Come on, we have to figure out what we're going to do."

Grant turned off the movie and went back to the computer.

Mr. Trafalgar had just finished his Cohiba Torpedo cigar and was lighting a cigarette. The cockpit was filled with smoke, like a scene from a Cheech and Chong movie. He looked down at his little buddy, again curled up in a ball, and smiled. "The little fella is always tuckered out after a mission. He looks so cute and harmless when he's asleep."

Mr. Trafalgar grabbed a yard stick he always kept nearby. It was rough, splintered, and chewed upon. He gingerly reached out with it and nudged Mr. Crows.

Teeth gnashing and spittle flying, Mr. Crows awoke and had the yard stick in his mouth before Mr. Trafalgar could pull it back.

Mr. Crow's eyes seemed to find focus and, upon seeing his piloting companion, slowly released the yard stick.

"I dozed off." Mr. Crows sleepily said.

"Yes, you did little buddy. Sorry to disturb you but we're landing in about ten minutes. Go check on our guests and make sure they're ready for transport."

Mr. Crows nodded and pulled out two more hypodermics from his pocket. He stretched as he got up off the ground and shuffled his feet out of the cockpit. Mr. Trafalgar reached back and closed the door.

"So cute when they're sleepy." He blew out a puff of smoke.

The jet hit some turbulence and Grant's eyes fluttered. Violet caught him and shook him. "Don't you dare pass out, Grant!" she warned, shaking him harder.

"Ow!" Grant murmured. "Not so rough."

"I think we're landing. I can feel it in my ears. They won't pop."

Grant tilted his head. "Yeah, and the engine is decelerating."

They both leapt when they heard the lock to their room click. Violet dove for the light switch and Grant collapsed in a heap, passed out again.

Violet ran over and lifted Grant, she pulled him behind the door as it creaked open. Mr. Crows waddled in, wiping sleep out of his eyes. He paused upon seeing the nylon ropes scattered on the ground.

Mr. Crows looked behind the door. Violet, using Grant's limp body as a weapon, shoved the dead weight onto Mr. Crows.

Grant's ragdoll body took Mr. Crows down, the actor wrestling with the flopping, limp limbs, his hands slipping off the sweaty skin. He struggled but couldn't get a grip. The two hypodermic needles flew from his hand.

"Arrgg!" Mr. Crows growled. "I will kill you!"

Violet dove for the needles, scooping them up.

Mr. Crows rolled Grant off of him, his limp body falling between himself and Violet. She had the needles uncapped and reached over Grant, trying to stab Mr. Crows in the chest. Mr. Crows grabbed Grant by the ears and used his head as a shield, he dodged Violet's thrusts and parried the needles aside with Grant's sweaty melon.

Violet changed tactics and put one needle in each hand.

Mr. Crows saw the maneuver and smiled. "Smart for a dumb bitch," he hissed through clenched teeth.

"Well, you're... you're stupid, " Violet was out of breath. It was all she could come up with.. "Especially for an actor!"

Mr. Crows let out a battle cry and reached around Grant's head, grabbing Violet by the throat. He began to squeeze and Violet's eyes bulged.

She brought her hands in, stabbing the needles into his neck and depressed the plungers. Mr. Crows shoved her away. He rolled backward like a chimp and pulled out the needles. Grant fell to the ground, face forward, and landed on the floor with a sad thump.

"I will make your life a living Hell!" Mr. Crows screamed.

Violet laughed. "Sorry, I'm not going to be in your next fake marriage."

Violet lifted Grant's face off the ground.

Mr. Crows was spitting with rage, his eyes darting maniacally. He stepped forward and swung a shaking fist at Violet. She raised Grant, using him as a shield, and let him take the punch.

"Sorry." Violet whispered into Grant's ear.

Mr. Crows blinked his eyes. The sedative was taking effect. He swung again, this time his punch missing the Grant's face by inches. He stumbled backward, smacking into the wall. Mr. Crows slapped himself, trying to fight the drugs. He leaned against the wall and slowly slid to the ground. He was quickly passing out, but his stare never left Violet.

"I… will… kill…" Mr. Crows wheezed once and then was out.

Violet breathed out in relief. "Wow, I did it."

Then she remembered her friend, the human shield. She turned his face to hers. "Grant! Grant!" She lightly slapped him then immediately wiped her hand on the carpet. She decided to shake him instead. His head wobbled as though it were no longer connected, which might have been the case.

Grant coughed and his eyes fluttered.

"W-what happened?" Grant mumbled. He slowly opened his eyes and looked around the room. He gasped at the sight of the unconscious Mr. Crows. "What happened?!" he repeated.

"We did it!" Violet shook him some more, this time in triumph. "Mr. Crows is out for quite a while. One down, one to go!"

"W-we did it?" He sat up and felt his jaw. He winced at the shooting pain. "I don't remember anything."

"Oh, you were great!" Violet lied. "That monster came into the room and you jumped on him and wrestled him to the ground."

"I did?"

"You bet. While you kept him busy I grabbed the hypodermic needles and then he hit you. You fought back, had him real scared You took another hit or two and then I stuck him. You were a real tiger."

"I was?" Grant pushed himself up and momentarily steadied himself on the table. "I just wish I remembered it all. Or even some of it."

"Don't worry," Violet tapped the side of her head. "I got it all with my mental camera."

Grant laughed then cringed from the pain in his jaw.

The jet lurched slightly and the sound of rubber hitting tarmac at hundreds of miles an hour echoed through the plane.

"We're landing!" Violet said. "Hurry. Let's tie him up and see if he has any more needles on him."

"I'll tie, you find the needles. I can't take the sight of them."
Grant picked up the nylon ropes.

"Oh, I know." Violet laughed.

CHAPTER 76

Mr. Trafalgar opened the door to the cockpit and did a soft shoe dance across the main cabin. He had a pretty nice buzz going, thanks to his half a dozen martinis, and was happy this latest mission was near completion. And as much as he liked his little buddy, he was looking for some time off from babysitting him. And cleaning up the carnage left in his wake.

Speaking of the feral peanut, what was taking him so long?

Mr. Trafalgar scrunched out his cigarette on the floor of the cabin and approached the conference room. The door was closed. He tried the handle. Not locked. Odd. He turned the handle and pushed the door open, not stepping in. Lights were off. He leaned forward just enough to feel for the light switch. He found it and clicked on the lights.

Oh crap.

The unconscious Mr. Crows lay hogtied on the floor. His mouth open, his tongue hanging out.

Mr. Trafalgar stepped backward and turned to run back to the cockpit. He had taken the gun out and left it there, since when he was seated in his pilot's chair, it rubbed against his formidable belly. He spun around into the awaiting syringes in Violet's hands. She quickly jabbed both into his stomach.

"Ow! Man, that wasn't cool." Mr. Trafalgar looked down at the pair of needles hanging from his spare tire. "Really... not... coool." The actor stumbled backward and fell to his knees. "Man..."

Mr. Trafalgar did a belly flop onto the cabin floor.

Violet knelt down beside the celebrity and nudged him. No reaction. She grunted as she pushed him onto his side, exposing the arrows in his gut. She pulled out the hypodermics and tossed them.

Violet called out, "It's safe now, Grant. The needles have been used."

Grant ran from the bathroom in which they had been hiding. "Thank goodness. Ever since I was a kid I can't bare the sight of those dreadful things."

"Well, you don't have to worry, they're gone." Violet looked around the cabin. "We have to find something to tie him up with. Look for anything we can use."

Ten minutes later, after the exhausting task of rolling Mr. Trafalgar into the conference room, Violet and Grant opened the passenger door to the outside world. The door dropped and built in stairs unfolded as it did. Soon Grant and Violet were running across the tarmac in the early morning hours. The sun had not yet risen, but dull orange glow peaked along the west coast skyline.

"We have to find someone and get help," Violet whispered, looking out into the quiet hanger in which Mr. Trafalgar had parked them.

"I don't think that's a good idea." Grant argued.

"Why? These guys were willing to kill you. Who knows how many other people they've threatened or worse."

"Yes, but who's going to believe us?" Grant said. "Are we to drive to the police and say, 'Hey, guess what? Jon Trafalgar and Thom Crows are trying to kill us!' Is that what we should do?"

Violet's face twisted. "No. But then what?"

"I don't know." Grant looked around. "It's not quite day yet, but this looks like the Los Angeles International Airport. Makes sense that's where he would land."

"Why? Was he taking us to his house?" Violet laughed.

"No, but the Scientology Celebrity Center is in Hollywood, a few miles from LAX. I can only suspect that that is where they intended on taking us." Grant sighed. "I don't know anyone in California, do you?"

"No, I don't." Violet's shoulders slumped. "Maybe some Facebook friends."

"Ugh." Grant grimaced.

"Shut it."

"Well, that great idea aside, we need to find *someone*. Anyone that we can trust. Or more importantly, that'll believe us. Who would believe our story?" Grant patted the top of his head. "Think, darn it! Think!"

"Wait! Let me see your backpack." Violet reached to take it from Grant.

"No!" Grant pulled away. "I've got personal stuff in here."

"Hate to tell you, Grant, but I've already been through it. When you were sick earlier."

Grant's eyes widened. "What? Don't tell me you saw anything embarrassing?"

"Nothing. Now give it to me."

Grant handed over his precious backpack and Violet immediately dove in. She quickly pulled out a torn, beaten and stained book. She flipped through the pages. "Here it is. Don Brawn!"

"The author? The reclusive missing-for-over-a-decade man behind most of the Twelve lore?" Grant laughed. "You must be kidding. That book was written over thirty years ago. And he doesn't have his address in there. It's just been rumored he lives in the L.A. area."

"But it *does* say in the book he last was known to live in California! And we're in L.A. So at least are on the right part of the world for once. And he, out of anyone in the whole world, would believe us! And not to make you feel good about yourself, which I don't care to do, but if anyone can find him it's you, Grant."

"Thanks," Grant smiled. "I think."

"No prob."

"Well, I guess it's worth a try. At least we'd be away from here." Grant put his backpack on over his shoulders. "Los Angeles is tiny. How hard could it be to find Don Brawn in a small town like Los Angeles, who is only rumored to have lived there thirty years ago? Gosh, it'll be a piece of cake."

"I detect your sarcasm and do not find it helpful." Violet said.

Grant sniffed. "You realize that if Trafalgar had indeed intended on taking us to the celebrity center, then we're basically birds walking toward the cat's mouth. Or at least hovering near it."

"What choice do we have? No one else will believe us."

"You have me there." Grant said. "Was Mr. Brawn's photo taken outside, maybe we can start with that?"

"No. It's just him by some fireplace." Violet scanned the author's bio. "Not even a window. Just a painting on the wall, some books on a shelf behind him, and that's about it" Violet held up the battered hardcover for Grant to see.

"Well, Don Brawn is a master of riddles, symbols and clues. Maybe there's something there." Grant took the book from Violet and scanned the image. He was able to make out a few of the titles of the books that lined Don Brawn's shelf. The first book caught that his eye was titled, 'Entry point for extraterrestrials'. Grant smirked. "Well, I know what road he might live on. And it's not in L.A."

"What? That was quick!" Violet smiled widely. "How?"

"Well, the title of this first book here, 'Entry point for extraterrestrials' is an obvious giveaway. There is no such book."

"And?" Violet didn't quite follow.

"But what I do know is that's a famous quote. Don Brawn was quoting the French philosopher Jean Baudrillard, a suspected Twelvist himself, from his book 'America'."

"Okay, so what does it mean? We're not going to Roswell or something like that I hope."

"Nope. Jean Baudrillard said that the famous road Mulholland Drive was the entry point for extraterrestrials. I believe Don Brawn is giving his acolytes an opportunity to find him if they're worthy and knowledgeable."

"Aco-whats?"

"Students. Followers." Grant explained. "He's giving clues for the enlightened to find him."

"Great! So we're off to Mulholland Drive!" Violet was pleased. "Let's hail a taxi."

"Let's indeed." Grant mused, mulling it all over. "Maybe we *can* find him." Grant said with more confidence. "Let's get to Mulholland and on the way we'll see if anything else on the back of that book gives us any more information."

Violet took the book back. "We have to find him, he's our only hope." Violet said, looking at Don Brawn's photo on the back cover.

Don was a handsome man. At least he was then. With flowing hair, a wry grin and eyes that sparkled with brilliance. He wore a button down shirt and a tweed jacket with patches on the elbows. As any scholarly person would.

"Come on, Violet. Before our celebrity maniacs wake up." Grant took a step away from the hangar and Violet followed.

Though it was not yet full daylight they stuck to the sides of the hangars, hid behind luggage carriers, and crawled when workers drove or walked by. They didn't feel safe until they made their way into a terminal, using an employees' only door, and walked among the slowly growing number of morning commuters, travelers, and tourists.

They stopped briefly at an ATM and Violet took out some more money. For the first time she neither complained nor shot Grant a nasty look.

Once out front, Violet hailed a cab like an old pro. Having done so in half a dozen other cities, in two countries, she was feeling like she could hail a cab anywhere.

"Where to?" the driver asked, looking disinterested and in need of a shave.

"Hollywood, please. Mulholland Drive." Violet said, sliding over to allow Grant room to sit next to her. "Quickly please."

"You have a street number? Mulholland is kinda long." the man laughed.

"Um, let's just get there and we'll figure it out then. Thanks." Violet smiled.

"Okay, it's your ride." The driver shrugged and stepped on the gas. "So, you guys here as tourists?"

"No, not really." Violet shook her head.

"Let me guess, he's a writer of the next big blockbuster and you're the next glamorous starlet." the driver chuckled.

"Sorry. Wrong again." Violet stared out the window. *Please shut up.*

"That's good. 'Cuz you'd be doing porn in a month and he'd be flying home to live with his mom in no time."

"Okay, I'm sorry, but it's been a long night and we just need to get to Hollywood. Can you please just… drive?" Violet snapped.

"Jeez, okay, sorry." The driver waved his hand. "I was just making conversation. I see it all the time."

"Understood, but, long night... okay?"

"You got it." he answered with a smile, and then under his breath. "See you in porn." The driver sped south on Route 110.

CHAPTER 77

An hour after he was taken by surprise, Mr. Trafalgar awoke and found himself tied up and seated on the floor of the conference room. Luckily, his hands were bound not with the nylon rope they had used on Mr. Crows, but napkins, shoe laces, and even his own black tie. And they had to have been in a rush, or ridiculously nervous, because he was able to free himself with little effort.

Mr. Trafalgar eyed his little buddy, who was also awake. Sadly he was tied much better and even now struggled and strained against the ropes.

"Hold on, pal." Mr. Trafalgar lit a cigarette. "I'll be right with you."

He quickly pulled out his Blackberry and dialed. The phone on the other end rang once and was picked up.

"Go ahead." boomed the voice of Mr. Maystyne. He sounded as though he'd been expecting bad news. "Tell me you're here with them."

Mr. Trafalgar swallowed hard. "We have a problem."

CHAPTER 78

Violet and Grant sat hunched over the book, 'Holy Twelve, Holy Crap'. Though Violet knew she would probably be of no help, she couldn't resist wanting to be involved. This was like doing a crossword puzzle, which she was miserable at, or Sudoku, which she not only sucked at but couldn't even say the name correctly, but enjoyed attempting anyway.

Grant read off the other names of the books in the photo. "The book above 'Entry point for extraterrestrials' is 'A Dozen Pie'. That's an odd name."

"Shouldn't it be pies? Plural?" Violet added.

"One would think. The next one is 'My Toes Is' and the fourth is 'Der Poppart'."

"Do those mean anything to you?" Violet asked.

"Sadly, no. The fourth title rings with me but I can't quite place it. I'm hoping it'll just come to me." Grant sighed. "Anyway, I'm still stuck on the dozen pie title. Like you said, it should be pies."

"Maybe it's one pie cut into twelve pieces?" Violet offered.

"Possibly. But I don't think that references anything. I've tried anagrams. Basic codes. Even reversing it. Nothing."

"Gee," Violet was stumped, which really didn't take much. "Too bad you can't multiply a pie twelve times. Boy, that'd be a lot of pie to eat!"

Grant laughed. "Violet, you're a genius!"

"I am?"

"Yes, you are. It is pie, but not the food, it's the Greek letter! Pi!" Grant smacked himself in the head. "Of course, I should've thought of it!"

"Yeah, you're losing me. What are you talking about?"

"Pi, the sixteenth letter of the Greek alphabet. But as a mathematical constant it's an irrational real number whose value is approximately equal to 3.14159, which happens to be the ratio of a circle's circumference to its diameter in Euclidean geometry."

"Yup," Violet frowned. "I'm still sitting at the curb and the bus is gone."

"Me, too!" the cab driver called back to them.

Violet scowled. "Excuse me, just drive."

"Sheesh, sorry."

Grant continued. "So anyway, if you multiply Pi by twelve, you get…" Grant thought about it for a second. "37.699118!"

"Okay, and what do we do with that?" Violet was dizzy.

"I'm assuming that gives us our street address." Grant said.

"But that's awfully long for a street address. It has a period in it!" Violet said.

"Decimal point." Grant corrected her.

"Whatever! I doubt there is a street address like that."

Grant thought on that. "Well, if you remove the decimal point…"

"You still get a long-ass-number!" Violet finished.

Gran leaned forward. "Hey, driver. Do you know what are the street numbers on Mulholland like?"

"Oh, now you want to hear from me?" The cab driver rolled his eyes. "I told you, it's a long road. It practically extends from West Hollywood to Los Angeles."

"Shoot." Grant frowned. "Okay, do any of the numbers come close to 37699118?"

"You kidding? That number's ridiculous even for Hollywood standards." The cabbie laughed. "Why don't you round it up? You know, knock off a few numbers."

"Hmm. 37700? Is that an actual street number on Mulholland?"

"Too big. The numbers don't go above 20000." The driver offered.

Grant cursed. "It has to have something to do with the third book title. But what the Hell does *My Toes Is* supposed to mean? My Toes Is. My Toes Is."

Violet had remained quiet while Grant kept repeating the title. She was staring at the third book title. "Grant? Say it faster."

"Huh?" Grant paused.

"Say the title faster."

"My Toes Is. Mytoesis. Mytoesis."

"Isn't that a word. Mitosis. I remember that from science class. My teacher was really hot! He had the nicest butt."

"Violet, focus!"

"Sorry. Mitosis. Doesn't it suggest halves? Like cutting something in two?"

Grant took the book from Violet and reread the title. "Wow! That's brilliant! Violet, you're really becoming quite the helper here." He paused and look at her hard. "Who *are* you? And what have you done with the *real* Violet?" He laughed.

"I'm trying!" she said happily.

Grant quickly did the math. "So that's 18850. Driver? Does that sound right to you?"

"18850? Yeah, it could be. But that's back toward L.A. not in Hollywood or West Hollywood. That's further west on Mulholland."

"Well, if we have to go back, we go back." Grant forced a smile. "Back toward our killer celebs."

Violet returned the forced smile. Neither was happy knowing they were running back in the direction of the psychotic actors.

"No problem." The cab driver took the next jug handle to head back. "It's your fare, kids."

The cab zipped along Mulholland Drive, a winding hill-ridden road smattered with expensive mansions and private villas. They slowed down just catch their bearings and see what street number they were up to.

"That was 17250!" Violet called out. "We're getting close!"

"Yes, we are. It'll be on this side of the road." Grant stated.

Within minutes the car slowed to a stop in front of 18850 Mulholland Drive. The house was spectacular, built completely as though it grew out from the hill in which it stood. It was a tremendous Mediterranean Villa, complete with red shingles, tall archways and a terrace supported by columns overlooking the scenic valley. Vines grew up the sides and tall thin cyprus trees stood guard along the front. The mansion, despite its grandiose design and style, seemed uninviting and dark. Though its landscaping was current and sharp and the maintenance on the building crisp, the darkened, shuttered windows screamed for visitors to stay away.

"This is it." Grant fell solemn, staring up at the intimidating edifice "Now we get to see if we were on the right track or barking up an absurd tree."

"It's a beautiful mansion, but it's so... cold." Violet shuddered.

"I vote for right track." the cab driver offered.

"Thanks." Violet smiled as she counted out his fare. It pretty much wiped out her remaining money. Her bank account was empty, her charge card maxed, and she was left with $1.75. Not even enough for a cup of coffee in most places.

"You want I should wait?" the cab driver asked.

"No, really." Violet said. "We're out of money. If this isn't the place we're looking for, then we're hoofing it from here on."

The driver slipped Violet a piece of paper. "Tell you what, I'll take off, but I like you kids. If you need a lift, call my cell there. I'll throw you guys a freebie. Okay?"

Violet was stunned. "That is completely generous of you. Thank you."

"No problem. This was kinda fun. Not like my usual fare. Good luck you two!" The cab driver called out as he pulled away.

Violet and Grant waved to their new friend.

"Well, here we go." Grant said, fixing his jacket and attempting to wipe the collective dirt and dust from his khakis. At least they were non-wrinkle. And dry.

Violet attempted to fix her hair which, after almost two days and nights of running, sweating, hiding, wrestling, and most importantly, not showering, she felt as though a bird's nest was built upon her scalp. Her fingers snagged as she tried to run them through. "Screw it," she mumbled then adjusted her bra.

Grant raised a trembling fist and knocked, only once at first, and hesitated. Whether he expected the door to fly open, explode, or shoot him, his fear didn't manifest. So he knocked again, a little more firmly.

Suddenly a slat in the door slid open and two eyes peered out. "What?" A voice barked. "What are you selling?"

"Oh," Grant took a step backward, bumping into Violet. "We… we're not selling anything."

"Then what the Hell do you want?" The voice was already void of patience.

Violet felt like Dorothy before the Wizard of Oz.

"We w-would like to talk to D-don Brawn, sir, if we could, sir." Violet stuttered.

"Who?" The voice yelled. "Who the Hell are you talking about?"

Grant stepped forward and lifted the book. "Please, sir. We've traveled a very long way, we need to speak to Don Brawn. We're positive he lives here. We decoded his clues from the back of his book! We've found portions of the Twelve! We found proof of Jesus' relationship with aliens! We did it! And we're here! Don't we deserve the opportunity to at least talk to him?"

The eyes darted from Grant to Violet then back again. He hesitated.

At least he wasn't screaming at them. Yet.

"What's the password?" The voice asked.

"The what?" Grant asked. "The what? A password?" Grant turned to Violet. "We need a password? Nobody told us we needed a password."

"Calm down, Grant." Violet warned. "Maybe he'll give us a chance to…"

The slat closed.

"Or not." Violet frowned.

Grant threw himself at the door, hitting it with the palms of his hands. "No! No! What password? Come back here!"

The slat slid open again. The eyes looked disapprovingly on Grant.

Grant froze and looked up.

The voice asked again. "What is the password?"

Grant spoke quickly. "Please give us a chance. What password are you talking about? We need help!"

"No password, no entrance." The voice said and the slat shut again.

Grant's shoulders slumped. He turned to Violet. "We're done for. We're totally done for." Grant walked past Violet and stomped down the front walkway. Violet chased after him.

"Grant! Stop!" Violet cried. "We can't give up! We made it this far! You said it yourself, we came all this way, solved so many things, found ancient mysteries! We did it and we can do this! Don't give up on me now." Violet caught up and stopped him. "I need your help. I can't do this without you."

Grant stared at the ground. He shook his head. "I don't know, Violet. I'm running out of steam. My mind isn't working as well as it was."

"What are you talking about? Your mind has never been better!"

"How can you say that?"

"Grant, haven't you noticed? When was the last time you took a picture?"

Grant looked up at Violet.

"And when was the last time you did one of your OCD dances or weird things?"

Grant smiled as the realization dawned upon him.

"And your pills! Grant you haven't taken a pill in I don't know how long. Grant, don't you realize? Your mind has never been more focused, sharper!"

Grant's eyes looked into Violet's, then his smile faded. "You may be right about those things. I have been more focused. My odd little habits have lessened. But sharper? I don't think so." Grant held up Don Brawn's book. "Violet, the last two clues from this book's photo have pretty much been solved by you! I've been useless! It was you that read and solved them! You've become the brains here. We don't have a ghost of a chance if we... if we..."

Grant stopped mid-rant. He looked at the back cover again. "Der Poppart. Der Poppart!" Grant examined the photo. "Now I get it! I knew it sounded familiar! *Der Poppart*. That's a German word for a type of ghost called a 'rapper' or 'thumper'. And it's also the name for a goblin, the English translation being 'rattle ghost' but in German is 'rumpelgeist'. Which is another word for 'rattle stilt' which in German is 'rumpelstilt'. It's referencing the famous password from Rumpelstiltskin!"

"So what's the password?" Violet asked.

Grant turned and ran back to the front door, leaving Violet behind. She was smiling. He dashed up to the doorway of 18850 Mulholland Drive and pounded on the heavy oaken door. "I know the password! Hello? I said I know the password!"

The slat on the door slid open abruptly and Grant stopped knocking.

"Good for you, you know the password. It doesn't give you the right to be rude!" The voice reprimanded. "Now, what is the password?"

"Rumpelstiltskin!" Grant said firmly.

The eyes widened and stared at Grant for a few seconds.

The slat closed. Several locks could be heard clanking and opening, like a vault at Fort Knox. Soon, the thick wooden door swung wide, dust swirled, allowing Grant and Violet entrance. Grant hesitantly stepped in, followed by Violet. The door shut behind them with an ominous boom, they were shrouded in darkness. Suddenly a large chandelier overhead filled the foyer with light.

CHAPTER 79

"May I ask why you wish to speak to Mr. Brawn?" The man asked. Though seemingly in his fifties, he was an intimidating man, easily six and a half feet tall with broad shoulders. His thick, dark eyebrows hung from a protruding brow which cast a shadow over his lengthy and bent nose. He spoke with a heavy French accent. "I am Mr. Brett Hayer. You are obviously a very smart young man to have deciphered Mr. Brawn's clues on the back of his book." The man approached Grant and loomed over him.

"Well, Brett," Violet began.

"Mr. Hayer, to you," he interjected.

"Mr. Hayer." Violet slid in between them. "I helped! I helped solve the puzzles. Hello? I'm here, too!"

Mr. Hayer snorted derisively then returned his attention to Grant. "As I was saying young man…"

Violet slunk away and mumbled to herself. "Must be gay."

"Very smart indeed." Mr. Hayer continued. "But before I allow you to have court with Mr. Brawn, I need to understand the gibberish with which you assaulted my ears earlier."

Grant sighed. "I don't know where to begin. We, Violet and I," Grant swept his hand to include his traveling companion. "uh, I'm Grant, we've come so far. Her father was killed, protecting a secret that he seemed to have been guarding for some time. And before he died he left Violet a message, a quest of great importance. Which took us to Italy and the Vatican. Then to London. We found clues along the way and information about the Twelve. And we've found ancient reliquaries containing scrolls that taught us about some connection between God and aliens and Jesus."

Mr. Hayer broke into a loud and annoying laugh. "God and aliens? Well, that is quite a story. I'm not sure Mr. Brawn would waste his time…'

An intercom buzzed to life and a gravelly, wizened voice broke through the static. "Mr. Hayer! Stop antagonizing our guests!

It is obvious they are well informed and learned in the ways of the Twelve. They should be greeted with open arms, not treated like burglars. I will meet them outside of my study."

Mr. Hayer rolled his eyes.

"And don't roll your eyes at me, Mr. Hayer!" The intercom squawked.

"Yes, Mr. Brawn." Mr. Hayer forced a smile. He turned back to Grant and Violet. "Please, if you would, follow me."

Mr. Hayer walked them through the impressive hallways and rooms of the house. It was spotless and meticulously decorated with ancient art; paintings, ceramics and pottery, sculptures, even framed documents in other languages.

It was like a private museum. Even with the short time Violet had worked at the Met and with what she'd learned from Grant, she was able to appreciate the collection that lined the walls, halls, and shelves of Don Brawn's home.

"Please do not touch anything." Mr. Hayer said dryly and with no necessity.

"We're not stupid, frenchie." Violet spoke out of the side of her mouth.

Mr. Hayer paused briefly, thought for a moment, then continued on.

Grant whispered to Violet. "At least you're getting better at spotting accents."

They entered what looked like a second foyer with a large circular stairway, which they walked up. Huge portraits hung on the walls, light shone from a tremendous crystal chandelier that sparkled like diamonds. They quickly took another hallway and rounded a bend and found themselves face to face with Don Brawn.

The man looked timeless. He appeared as he did on the back of his book. He held an air of intelligence and benevolence. He smiled widely at his guests and, seeing the warmth of his demeanor, instantly put Violet and Grant at ease. He was certainly better than the icy and rude Mr. Hayer.

"Greetings, my dear friends." Don Brawn said, holding his arms wide. "Welcome to my humble abode. I hope that my assistant,

Mr. Hayer, didn't scare you in any way. He is a valuable person to have around despite his curt and gruff exterior."

"Well, he *is* French," Violet scoffed.

Mr. Hayer was about to reply when Don cut him off. "You have me there! Well, just call him Brett. He hates that!" He laughed. He then waved his assistant off, signaling him to leave. "Off you go, Frenchman." Don joked.

Brett's eyes glinted with anger and insult. He bit his lip and stormed down the hallway.

"He's so fun to joke with because he doesn't find anything funny!" Don wiped at tears of laughter in his eyes. "Especially when it's about him. Oh, he's a pisser!" He took a few deep breaths then composed himself. "Now, from what I gather, you two have had a very interesting few days. And seeing as how you're one of the few that have decoded my address from the back of my book, you've certainly earned my respect."

"There have been others to decipher it?" Grant asked, disappointed.

"Well, yes," Don patted Grant on the shoulder. He saw the look in Grant's eyes. "Don't feel any lesser of yourself. You are part of an elite group. Now this old hermit has had a few guests over the years since publishing my book, but if what I've heard is true, then you two may be the most accomplished of them all."

"Really?" Grant was shocked.

"Really!" Don continued. "Many have claimed to have found portions of the Twelve with little or no proof to back up their story. Others blindly run about digging holes in the ground, opening walls, destroying ancient relics and architecture, trying to find any one part of the Twelve. But you two, you have found what, two portions?"

"We found four, actually." Grant blushed, uncomfortable even making the claim.

"Four!" Don exclaimed. "Gadzooks! That is phenomenal. Good grief, four locations found!"

Violet stepped in. "Um, Mr. Brawn?"

"Don, little lady, please call me Don."

"Don, does this mean that… well, that it's true?" Violet paused. "I mean, you really believe all this stuff about, er, aliens and Jesus?"

Don smiled and his eyes twinkled. "My dear, of course I believe it. And so shall you." He turned to the large walnut doors behind him and swung them open. "Welcome to everything I know about the Twelve!"

The doors lead to a large room, tall windows allowed in generous sunlight that glinted off of walls of books, framed images, paintings, sculptures and statues, a myriad of maps and diagrams, stacks of scrolls and manuscripts. Suspended from chains were several reproductions of paintings, including many recognizable frescoes that both Grant and Violet had just seen in person, including the Sistine Chapel and The Annunciation. There were dozens of other large format prints hanging around the room. Each one with sticky notes attached, portions were circled and highlighted, and spotlights on certain sections. Violet and Grant's eyes swept the room, making an unsuccessful attempt to soak it all in.

"Holy…" Violet began.

"Crap!" Grant finished.

Don laughed uproariously. "Yes, indeed! Half the title of my book!" He ushered them with his hands. "Move along. Everyone on board. The train to enlightenment is leaving now. Come on! Come on!"

Violet and Grant shuffled in, their heads spinning around, trying to find a place to set their eyes. They were at risk of breaking their necks.

"I never thought I'd recognize any painting, never mind be able to tell you the artist." Violet admitted. "But there's Michelangelo's Creation of Eve. And there's the Glorification of the Eucharist!"

Grant beamed proudly. "See, Violet? I never doubted that you could handle all of this. I am so pleased with you."

"Thanks," Violet said. "But don't get all mushy on me, you little creep."

Don had worked his way to the middle of the room. "Violet, Grant," he began. "What you see about me is my life's work.

And what knowledge I've garnered since the publication of my book has more than quadrupled."

"Then why didn't you write another book?" Grant asked. "Or a new version of 'Holy Twelve, Holy Crap'?"

"Oh, my," Don shook his head ruefully. "When I put that book out, I was younger, more headstrong, and I had a vision. I thought I might change the world. I had dreams where upon publication I'd be hailed as a visionary, a brave warrior of the mind and spirit, the one who dared to bring to light an unknown truth. I thought the world would give me a hero's welcome." Don dropped into a chair and sighed. "But alas, that was not the case. Oh yes, my book sold in the millions, it made me very wealthy as you can see, but I was ostracized by the literary community. I was disdained by religious scholars. I was maligned and excommunicated by Christian churches. I was fodder for jokes. Smear campaigns were created by the Vatican to discredit me. My life fell into ruin. So I retreated to my house and have not left since."

Grant was stunned. "You've been here for over a decade?"

"Yes, and I have no interest in leaving. All I need is in this room. Anything else I need I hire others to do for me. I have contacts all over the world." Don stood up again and paced the room. "No, my work is here. My job is here, in this room, to analyze and study and sort through eons of history."

"That is so sad." Violet said, her eyes welling.

"Oh, do not shed a tear for me, my dear." Don looked around. "I have been very happy, nay, more than happy, spending my time in this room, with my collection. It is a simple way of life, but satisfying. As a great man once said, 'Simplicity is the ultimate sophistication.' And I believe in that."

"That's so true." Grant said. "What great man said that?"

"Da Vinci." Don replied.

"Arg!" Grant ground his teeth.

Violet laughed and, noticing Don's confusion to Grant's reaction, changed the subject. "So, can you tell me if Grant and I were on the right path? Were we really uncovering ancient secrets?"

Don moved over to Violet and moved stacks of books and papers from a pair of chairs, then sat on a nearby desk. "Have a seat my friends and tell me of your journey and I, in turn, will tell you everything I know. And who knows? By the end of this evening, we may all be the better for it."

Violet's rolled her eyes and fell into the seat. "Sheesh, where to begin?" She frowned, knowing exactly where to begin. It began with a moment she had yet to really deal with, she'd stuffed the loss and pain so far down she hadn't even thought about her father. She took a deep breath. "My father is… was… the curator for the Arms & Armor division of the Metropolitan Museum of Art. I worked with him there and two days ago… he was shot and killed."

"Oh, no." Don gasped, he was genuinely shocked. "I'm so sorry for your loss."

"Thank you." Violet continued, not wanting to dote on it. Violet began her story, not leaving out any details. When the timeline included Grant, they took turns telling the story. Don would look from one to the other; his enthusiasm and wonder grew with each adventure and discovery. His face held the expression of a child, sitting by a campfire, listening to amazing adventures of the old west. Nearly two hours passed as Violet and Grant spun their yarn, Don only interjected to ask pertinent and concerned questions, but never doubted their veracity. And by the time it was over, Don was speechless.

He took a few minutes to gather his thoughts. He stared off, rolling the information around his brain like a wine taster swishing a Cabernet in his mouth. Finally he breathed in slowly and deeply, "I envy the two of you." He smiled. "You have done so much. Things that I'd dreamed I was going to do but never accomplished." He slid off the desk and took a few steps. "But you've only skimmed the surface of the truth. Now allow me the honor of telling you what you were really discovering."

Violet and Grant exchanged glances, sharing the same thought. *Skimmed the surface? What we were really discovering?*

"The Twelve is just the tip of the iceberg. What the twelve represents is not simply information passed on to Jesus, but applicable sciences, psychologies, medicinal formulas and more. Hell, it even gives a recipe for goodness sake!"

"Recipes?" Violet laughed.

"Little known fact is that Colonel Sanders recipe for chicken is 11 herbs and spices and the chicken makes 12."

"Kentucky Fried Chicken?"

"You can't tell me it isn't delicious!"

"Well, no, I can't. I eat it frequently." Grant agreed. "But you can't tell me the colonel used the Twelve to make it? I mean, all portions of the Twelve have never been discovered."

"No, he didn't find every portion. Actually he found none. But he did pay a great deal of money and did a great deal of research to find a few of the ingredients in the alien's amazing chicken recipe. He kind of experimented to fill in the rest. And I'd say he did a rather fantastic job." Don rubbed his stomach. "Now I'm getting hungry."

"Me, too." Grant could hear his own stomach growling.

"I don't believe this." Violet shook her head. "I don't buy the recipe thing. Colonel Sanders was not cooking with an alien recipe."

Don sighed. "When you discovered the reliquaries and found the codes, did you see a small grouping of five or six numbers preceded by one or two letters?"

Grant thought about it. "Yes, I remember them. The first one was LE2.13.'

"Aha!" Don pointed at Grant. "Yes!" Don ran to one of many computer terminals and typed into it. A large screen came to life, an animated Bible flew onto the screen and pages flipped. The camera seemed to zoom into a section of print. "And that would translate as Leviticus, book 2, paragraph 13, and I quote, 'And every oblation of thy meat offering shalt season with salt; neither shall thou suffer the salt of the covenant of thy God to be lacking from thy meat offering; with all thine offerings thou shalt offer salt. What was the next one?"

"GE43.11" Grant said.

Don quickly typed into the computer again. The screen changed again. "Genesis, book 43, paragraph 11, and I quote, 'And their father Israel said unto them, If it must be now, do this; take of the best fruits in the land in your vessels, and carry down the man a present, a little balm, a little honey, spices, and myrrh, nuts and almonds. Ha! Bring it on!"

"CH1.23.29" Grant said, astounded. Even Violet was impressed.

Again Don typed and a paragraph was displayed.

"Chronicles 1, book 23, paragraph 29! 'Both for the shewbread, and for the fine flour for meat offering, and for the unleavened cakes, and for that which is baked in the pan, and for that which is fried, and for all manner of measure and size.' And there you have three ingredients of the sacred recipe of Jesus!"

Don danced around the computer, he typed in another series of letters and numbers. "I can give you the reference for which bird is the tastiest!" He said. "Deuteronomy! Gospel 14, paragraphs 10 through 20. 'Of all the birds ye shall eat. But these are they of which ye shall not eat: the eagle, and the ossifrage, and the osprey, And the glede, and the kite, and the vulture after his kind, and the owl, and the nighthawk, and the cuckow, and the hawk after his kind, the little owl, and the great owl, and the swan, and the pelican, and the gier eagle, and the cormorant, and the stork, and the heron after her kind, and the lapwing, and the bat. And every creeping thing that flieth is unclean unto you: they shall not be eaten. But of all clean fowls ye may eat!!!." Don had his hands raised in the air, poised, as if waiting for a round of 'Hallelujahs'.

Don left the computer and came back to his audience. "You see? There are some of the ingredients in KFC! And I believe the colonel got his hands on most of them!"

Violet shrugged. "Okay, I can almost sort of see that. I mean I did see those codes myself. But it's still kind of loony."

"And the last one, in Dutch. You said in the re-telling of your yarn that you memorized it, didn't you? Write it down for me would you? I can translate it for the most part." Don brought a pad and pen.

Violet looked away. "Um, er, well, I didn't."

"Didn't what?" Don froze.

"Didn't what?" Grant echoed, sliding to the edge of his chair.

"Uh, memorize it." Violet admitted.

"No!" Don cried. "What? Why?"

"They had a gun on us! They were going to kill us!" Violet defended herself. "Well, Grant at least. It was my only chance at leverage!"

Don dropped into another chair, without removing the stack of papers on it. "Then it's lost. Gone. Forever. An unseen portion of the Twelve. The totality of the Twelve will never be given to mankind. This is a sad day."

Grant looked at Violet with a broken heart. "But you said…"

"I'm sorry." Violet said quietly.

"Well, at least you have three other portions." Don turned to Grant. "May I have the honor to see the codes you found in the reliquaries?"

Grant shrunk in his seat. "Well, er, Jon Trafalgar took them from me."

"What?" Don screamed. "No, this is worse than I thought." Don hid his face in his hands. He sat still for several minutes before finally sitting upright. He looked from Violet to Grant. "Though this is tragic news indeed, it is not the end of the world. It is sad that those three portions have fallen into enemy hands." Don sprang up from his seat. "It is not a total loss! I have two new acolytes. A great deal more information. And the three portions taken by the Scientologists may be retrievable."

"Why *are* Scientology celebrities chasing us around the world?" Violet asked, glad for a change of subject.

"Oh, well, don't get me started!" Don whirled. "Too late! You did! That lunatic L. Ron Hubbard was a fanatical Twelvist gone awry! He was such a nice guy when he was writing science fiction. But when he first heard of the Twelve, it consumed him. He spent years searching for portions of the Twelve. He hired shady characters from across the globe to search out portions. There was one fanatical gun for hire that stood out back then…" Don paused and struggled to remember. "Ah, yes Barry Theete. That man was a vicious mercenary who would do anything for information on the Twelve. He aided Hubbard but backstabbed him. So Hubbard took what he had and ran with it. His pseudo-religion is based on what fractions of the Twelve he was able to force out of the weak. The rest of his religion is all his warped imagination. It was the Twelve that gave him the idea that an alien race is what propagated Earth in the first place. That is where Xenu and the Helatrobus race came from."

Violet laughed. "I knew Scientology sounded weird when I first heard about it."

"You have no idea, Violet. I feel so much for the poor souls who have been brainwashed and given their life savings to the foundation. Hubbard's wacky ideas and psycho-babble have fooled tens of thousands of people in need of guidance. There is no provable justification to Hubbard's claims and few who get involved in Scientology actually know how crazy the whole religion is until they are so psychologically entrenched in it and it is too late."

"What would happen if they did get their hands on the Twelve? I mean, what damage could anyone really do with it?" Violet asked.

"What damage?" Don's face paled. "Need I remind you of a little thing called World War II?"

"What?" Violet's forehead creased in disbelief. "What could the Twelve have to do with that?"

"It is pretty well known that the Thule Society was a powerful occult group in Germany prior to the war. It was also well known that their interest in the occult, including aliens, where they believed themselves to be from outer space. If my memory serves me correctly, they thought they were from the bright red sun Aldebaran in the Taurus constellation."

"Sounds like a bunch of fruitcakes."

"Maybe so. But these fruitcakes were pivotal in aiding Hitler with his oratory skills." Don said, then seeing Violet's blank look. "Speaking skills. It used to be speculated that the Thule Society used magic to make him the powerful leader he later became. But that is just silly. No, it was guidance from the Twelve that did it. Many consider the information they used was from as many as three or four portions of the Twelve that they had violently stolen from Twelvists. Hitler's interest in the occult also stemmed from his knowledge of the Twelve."

"You mean World War II could have been avoided if the Thule Society hadn't stolen portions of the Twelve?"

"Possibly," Don replied. "It may have happened anyway, but they certainly helped. The Thule Society were also said to be building their own spacecraft with partial plans they found within their portions. In fact, German manufacturers were the first to patent flying disc blueprints, coincidently in 1912. They had several failed versions of these discs, called Vril 1 and 2, from 1917 through 1925. Though they continued trying, it was unlikely they'd succeed in creating a working space craft, not with only portions of the information they needed."

"Flying saucers," Grant whispered in awe.

"Indeed, indeed!" Don cheered. "What do you think was going on at Area 51? Flying saucers. Plans and information we retrieved in defeating the Nazis! And when a ship crashed years later, who did the government conjure up to investigate, if not cover-up, the entire incident? The Majestic 12! What a coincidence, no? Truman purportedly put together a committee of great minds; scientists, generals, government suits, all men with connections to the Twelve, to orchestrate, initiate, over-see, and eventually cover-up, one of the greatest Twelvist experiments created and gone awry."

"Jeez." Violet shook her head. "What is this information? How could it apply to almost everything? Speaking skills, weapons, health, medicine, flight, even cooking!"

"Exactly!" Don clapped his hands together. "It *is* everything! Have you seen the code? Seen the actual portions?"

"Yes, but it's like a million numbers and letters."

"Absolutely! And if it is decoded, it shares with the reader information on just about everything. But it is in pieces! And those pieces alone can give anyone, good or bad, a jump start on whatever it is they wish to succeed at. Not as much as all of them together, obviously, but every portion can do great good and great evil. That is exactly why it needs to be kept out of the hands of the wicked."

There was a momentary ominous silence that fell upon the room.

Don smoothed out his tweed jacket. "Well, enough of my ranting. We have a castle to storm."

"A what to what?" Violet sat up in her chair.

"A castle to storm." Don said matter-of-factly. "I tell you, it'll feel good to get out again. It's been years."

"And where are we going?" Grant asked.

"To the Scientology Celebrity Center of course."

"What? Why?" Violet was shocked.

"My dear, they have taken the portions of the Twelve that you discovered. Are you really going to allow the enemy to walk away with such a powerful weapon?" Before anyone could respond Don stomped his foot. "Nay, I say!"

"Why on God's green Earth would Grant and I go to the center when they've been trying to kill us for the past two days? We barely escaped from them the first time. That's like the mouse walking into the cat's mouth."

"Because you want to keep God's green Earth green!" Don replied. "With the portions of the Twelve that Hubbard had before, and the portions that you two found, well, I dare not think what he could create, nay destroy, with that information."

"Hubbard?" Grant stood from his chair. "L. Ron Hubbard is dead. How could he do anything…"

"Dead? Ha!" Don chuckled. "Well, yes he is. But, there are stories that his brain is still alive. Attached to a machine!"

"And you believe that?" Violet scoffed.

"If you asked me fifty years ago that I'd believe that aliens shared information with Jesus, I'd have laughed. If you had asked me fifty years ago if a science fiction writer could create a religion followed by actors, I'd have laughed. These days, I am not so quick to laugh at the absurd."

Violet crossed her arms and sat back in her chair. "I don't know about this. How the Hell are we going to get in? We can't just walk up and say, 'Hi, we'd like to come in and look around.' Can we?"

"No, we can't." Don agreed. "They have very hi-tech surveillance; cameras, alarms, armed security. No, we need to create a distraction somehow. Sneak in. But how do we get past all that?"

"Maybe a fire scare? Wouldn't that empty the building?" Grant offered.

"Maybe, but they'd still have the doors locked and cameras running. No, we need to pull the plug on them. Shut them down for a minute or two."

"An EMP?" Grant bolted upright. "We can use an EMP!"

"Brilliant!" Don clapped his hands. "An E-bomb!"

"What the Hell is an EMP?" Violet asked.

"Electromagnetic Pulse." Grant explained. "If we set off an EMP bomb, the entire building would shut down for several minutes. They'd be in chaos and we'd be able to sneak in."

Don nodded. "It's perfect."

"A bomb?" Violet's eyes were wide. "You're going to set off a bomb?"

"There's no explosion. It's not that kind of bomb. It releases a powerful pulse of energy that shuts down all electrical equipment, including computers, cameras, everything!"

"You two are insane!" Violet scowled. "I regret ever getting you guys in the same room. And where do we get this bomb? I don't suppose Wal-Mart has them in stock this time of year."

Don turned to Grant, his eyes hoping for an answer.

Grant grinned. "I know where you can get almost anything in the world… Ebay!"

"Brilliant!" Don applauded and the two ran to a nearby computer. Violet sighed heavily and followed.

Within minutes Grant was on the site. He looked up at Don, who was standing over him. "Do you have an account?"

"Yes, I do." Don offered. "My username is… well.. sexytwelvist."

Violet stifled a giggle.

"Password?"

"Oh, you'll think I'm stupid for this. It's twelve."

"You really do have a one track mind." Violet wiped a tear of laughter from her eye.

"Okay, we're in." Grant tapped at the keyboard. "Let's see. Okay here we go. Wow! There's a whole bunch. Let's see if any biddings are ending soon. We want this baby as soon as possible." A few more taps on the keyboard. "Okay, here's one. Says it should take out a city block. The bidding ends in fifteen minutes."

"How much?" Don asked.

"I thought you were wealthy!" Violet knitted her eyebrows. "Because nobody better ask me for my wallet! I'm tapped out."

"I'm not concerned because of lack of funds." Don grimaced. "I have to make sure my PayPal account can handle it."

"$12,144." Grant said.

"What?!" Violet almost fainted.

"Get it!" Don said.

Twenty minutes later Grant pushed the chair back from the desk. "Okay, I'm having it delivered next day. So we have no choice but to wait until tomorrow."

Don straightened up. "Well, then we have some time to kill."

"Can you tell us more about Jesus' relationship with the aliens?" Grant asked.

Violet grumbled. "Yes, please, more lecturing and less eating or sleeping."

"We will dine and rest in good time, dear Violet." Don cleared his throat. "Now, after listening to your tale, it was obvious that you realized there was a relationship between God, Jesus, Mary and an alien race that was visiting Earth. But what you got wrong was that they were spectators. That they watched over Jesus and Mary. Or that they had communications with God."

"And the truth is?" Grant said with bated breath.

"God didn't co-exist with aliens. God was an alien. Or *the* alien, as it were." Don paused to let the expected looks occur. "In actuality, He was an entire race of aliens. And it gets better. Mary and Jesus weren't simply watched over by aliens. Well, they *were*, but for a reason. You see, Mary is probably the most famous alien abductee in history. Though few know that." He paused again, as if waiting for an explosive reaction. "And Jesus, the 'son of God', is the single most famous human/alien hybrid in all of time."

"What?" Violet cried out.

"Wow, that's so cool." Grant said.

"That is the underlying belief of all Twelvists. Jesus was imparted this wisdom because he was the 'son of God'. And he was , in a way, seeing how God was this higher form of intelligence and that they impregnated Mary via In Vitro fertilization." Don laughed. "Immaculate conception my ass! Ha! I always found it funny that Christians found that more believable than alien abduction."

"But where's the proof?" Violet asked.

"The proof? Look around you!" Don spun around. "Everything in here leads to that one single incontrovertible conclusion! Just look at your journey and the story it tells. Michelangelo's fresco of God, flying in the shape of a brain, creating man! The Annunciation of Mary, depicting a beam of light hurtling from an ovoid in the sky, penetrating her and causing her pain. DeGelder's The Baptism of Jesus, again aliens presided over the event, making sure all went well and that Jesus received his encoding. The Glorification of the Eucharist, showing Jesus and God, controlling advanced satellite technology. Had you traveled to the Visoki Decani monestary in Russia, you would have seen a fresco of Jesus' crucifixion, again presided over by two space craft, piloted by aliens." Don tapped the keyboard a few times and another image filled the screen.

"Oh my God!" Violet whispered. "That's amazing!"

"Damn skippy it is!" Don laughed. "Look at those cute little flying guys. When Jesus' body was placed inside the tomb after his crucifixion, his body disappeared. On the third day he rose again in fulfillment of the Scriptures. The aliens were with him every step of the way. They took him! Here's another."

Don quickly typed into his computer, producing another image.

"In the Svetitskhoveli Cathedral in Georgia..."

" The state of Georgia?" Violet interrupted.

"Um, no," Don frowned. "Georgia is its own country."

"You mean we lost a state?" Violet was baffled.

"Violet, dear, this Georgia is in Europe. It has nothing to do with our lovely American state. Please let me continue."

"Sorry."

"Anyway, this cathedral is in a little town called Mtskheta, which happens to be 12 miles northwest of the nation's capital of Tbilisi. And this lovely 17th century fresco clearly depicts UFOs hovering about on the day Jesus was crucified."

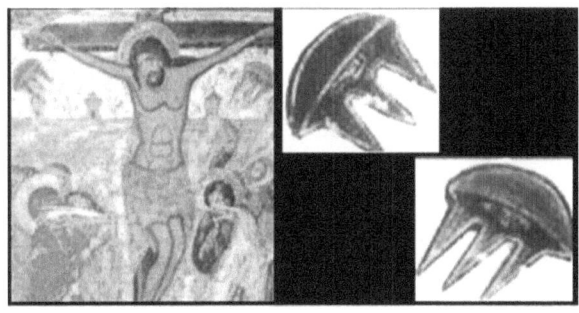

"Wow," Grant gazed at the image, which contained two floating discs, rays emanating from beneath, propelling the saucers up into the sky. The faces of the aliens can be seen in each UFO.

"That's nutty," said Violet.

"Heck," Don continued. "Mary's abduction is even in the Bible!"

"No, is it?" Violet couldn't wrap her mind around the idea.

"Yes, it is. In Luke chapter 1! The angel, Gabriel, comes to Mary and tells her that God will have her conceive his son. And Mary is scared of the messenger and doesn't understand what he is saying. It's a classic abduction! It is obvious that Gabriel was an alien and they abducted Mary and impregnated her and she held no memory of the event. The Bible has more references to aliens and UFOs than you can imagine. Take Job for instance. In Gospel 19, paragraph 15, it says 'They that dwell in mine house, and my maidens, count me for a stranger; for I am an alien in their sight.' That's another reference to visitations! It's all about perspective!"

Don stepped closer to his rapt listeners. "Do you really think that Jesus' resurrection is any more believable than the fact that, once dead, his creators took him home. Not to sound corny, but they beamed him. Isn't that just as ridiculous as God zapping him back up to Heaven?"

Violet thought about it for a moment. "I guess not."

"Aliens have been visiting us long before Jesus was born. He is not the first human/alien hybrid to have existed nor will he be the last. But he was certainly the most gifted, well known, and documented. The aliens have been tampering with this planet for eons. For all we know, it was them that added the special ingredients to the primordial soup that got mankind's ball rolling."

Grant chuckled to himself. "Mankind's ball."

Don ignored him. "They have tinkered with every stage of man's development. From the apes to the Neanderthals and on and on. The Incas, the Mayans, most of Eastern Europe have all documented ancient visitations by these 'gods'. Why do you think there are so many similarities between religions, between gods and deities, between our myths and legends. Because they all have the same source."

"Okay. Say this claptrap is all true. Why is this not in the Bible?" Violet asked.

"It *is* in the Bible. There are references to visitations, abductions, aliens and more. But it depends on your perspective. In ancient times, beings that appeared from the heavens were all called gods, or angels. Who's to say that it wasn't aliens. This has been discussed for centuries but the Vatican declares war on such blasphemy. They can't recant their doctrines and admit that their forefathers had it a little wrong."

"Where in the Bible?" Violet persisted.

"Job 19:15," Don stated. "I am an alien in their sight. Deuteronomy 4:19, And lest thou lift thine eyes up unto heaven, and when thou seest the sun, and the moon, and the stars, even all the host of heaven, shouldest be driven to worship them, and serve them, which the Lord thy God hath divided all nations under the whole heaven. Genesis 15:5, Look now toward heaven, and tell the stars, if thou be able to number them: and he said unto him, so shall thy be. Genesis 37:9, Behold, I have dreamed a dream more, and behold the sun and the moon and the eleven stars made obeisance to me. Judges 15:20, They fought from Heaven: the stars in their courses fought against Sisera. Job 22:12, Is not God in the height of heaven? And behold the height of the stars, how high they are." Don took a deep breath. "Just to name a few references. But it is not just about specific quotes that refer to space travel or visiting other planets, its occurrences, interactions, things that are amazing and seem to appear divine, but can actually also be credited to alien intervention."

"Like what?" Grant asked, getting more interested.

"Like the transfiguration of Jesus." Don replied. "The Transfiguration is a very clear account of a UFO visitation. Jesus, along with Peter, James and John travel to a mountaintop. Once there they are bathed in light, Jesus glowed like a sun. From seemingly nowhere, Elijah and Moses appear, as though teleported, and speak to Jesus. Then a bright cloud, or possibly a glowing alien spacecraft, appears and overshadows them. According to the Gospel of Luke, Jesus, Elijah and Moses enter the cloud. A voice booms from the cloud and talks to the men and the men fall to the ground terrified.

Then the cloud is gone, as are Elijah and Moses, and Jesus says to not speak of the event until after his death."

"And this rapture the Fundamentalists go on about. Isn't it amazing that it is so similar to abduction. Whooosh!" Don wiggled his fingers as if a cloud of smoke were exploding. "You're gone. Taken away by God. Zapped. Beamed up! The word itself, rapture, derived from Latin, means 'to be caught up, snatched away'. Rapture doesn't appear in the Bible itself, but instead what is used by Paul is harpazo, which is Greek, but holds the same definition."

"And what of these angels?" Don continued. "They're all over the Bible. Appearing here, beaming there. As I list their many abilities, I want you to think of all the countless descriptions we've heard in stories about aliens. Angels have been described in the Bible as bright, glowing people who terrify us with their presence. They can appear as humans or be undetected by humans and live among us. They appear in our dreams. They travel as though by lightning, or in explosions of light. They appear in our homes or floating above us." Don held his hands high for effect. He then lowered them and laughed. "Angels, indeed, they are brethren from another place! But not nirvana nor Kubla Khan nor Heaven. They are from another planet, solar system, perhaps another dimension altogether."

"Wow." Violet breathed out. "This is so… much."

"I apologize," Don said. "I have been exposed to this information little by little over my many years of research. I'm sure it's very overwhelming to learn this all in a few hours."

"Indeed." Grant agreed.

Don looked at his watch. "It is getting late and I'm sure you are hungry." He walked over to an intercom on the wall and hit a button. "Brett! Brett, you old escargot! We'll be eating in twenty so please set up dinner for three." He waited a few seconds then pressed the button again. "I know you can hear me, stop ignoring me!"

"Yes, Mr. Brawn." Brett finally replied dryly.

Don quickly pressed the button again. "And don't make that face at me!" He turned back to Violet and Grant. "We shall have a lovely meal and a good night's rest, and then tomorrow," Don raised his fist up in the air. "Tomorrow we fight!"

Violet and Grant exchanged an odd look. "Uh, okay." Violet said.

CHAPTER 80

Violet awoke the next morning to Grant's pasty face standing over her. He was shaking her, his voice as excited and giddy as a child on Christmas morning.

"Violet, get up!" Grant whispered loudly. "This is the big morning! Can you believe it? We're going to battle! We're going to storm the castle!"

Violet yawned, picked the crust from her eyes and wiped the white goo that had collected in the corners of her mouth. She had barely slept in two days and really needed at least a solid eight hours. It wasn't bad enough that Mr. Brawn had put them in the same room, but there had only been one bed. In this huge house? One room? Really? She was certain Grant had to have pulled Mr. Brawn aside and asked for a solid.

Before bedtime, Grant kept staring at her as though there was a chance in Hell they would actually share the bed, even after informing him that the floor looked like the perfect spot for him to sleep. In fact, what looked really comfy, Violet suggested, was the floor on the opposite side of the bed in the far corner of the large room, behind a dresser. Once the lights were out she could almost feel Grant's horniness emanating. Grant was talkative, like at a kid's sleepover party, where no one can fall asleep and someone keeps talking and everyone giggles. Except Violet didn't feel like giggling.

"This has been so great," Grant said in the darkness. "This adventure."

"Yeah, great," Violet mumbled. "Go to sleep."

"I really appreciate you taking me with you," he continued.

"It wasn't my idea. Go to sleep."

"I can't believe we're a part of this."

"Me either. Go to sleep."

"This is so exciting."

"Yep. Go to sleep."

"An EMP bomb. Wow!"

"Go to sleep."

That had gone on for quite a while and Violet had pretty much had enough when Grant asked her one final question.

"Did you really not memorize that poem."

Violet paused, not sure what to say. Then finally, "Grant, do you trust Don Brawn? I mean, what do we know about him? Other than he wrote a book."

"Of course I trust him, I guess. He's Don Brawn, right? The Twelve is the most important thing in his life."

"Yeah, so important he'd do anything to get the portions we found."

"Yeah, so?"

Violet shrugged, though she knew Grant couldn't see her. "Well, if it's important enough for Jon Trafalgar and Thom Crows to try and kill us for it… then what would Mr. Brawn do to get the same thing?"

"I don't know. I doubt he'd…" Grant sat up. "He wouldn't! Do you really think he'd kill us for the information? Not Don Brawn." Grant laid down again. "I'd never believe that. The man is a legend and a pioneer."

"Go to sleep, Grant." Violet pulled the covers up. "We have a lot to think about tomorrow."

"Goodnight, Violet."

"Goodnight, Grant."

She wasn't able to fall asleep until she heard Grant begin his litany of noises and she was certain he was out. Then sleep hit her fast and hard.

And now Grant was ruining her run at eight hours of sleep. She glanced over at the clock. It was 7:15. "Jeez, Grant!" Violet swatted at him. "Why do we have to get up this early? I need more sleep." She rolled over to face away from him.

"The EMP is being delivered first thing. We have to be ready."

Violet ignored him and suddenly he appeared in front of her on the other side of the bed. "Get up, get up, get up, get up!" Grant jumped up and down.

Violet groggily lifted her head. "How can you be so excited? You realize this is breaking hundreds of laws. We'll probably go to jail."

Grant laughed. "Ha! We're on a righteous mission here. We're the good guys. Besides, how many times in a lifetime do you get to deploy an EMP bomb and sneak into a Scientology Celebrity Center?"

"I had planned on never." Violet sat up and scratched the bird's nest that was once her hair. She noticed that Grant was not only completely dressed but had already showered, his hair was wet and forcefully combed back like a greaser. "Nice hair." she said as she swung her feet off the bed.

"Yeah, you too." Grant chuckled.

An hour later Grant, Violet and Don had finished a remarkable breakfast befitting a king. Brett had cooked for them a ridiculously complex buffet style breakfast of eggs, bacon, pancakes, waffles, fresh fruit, toast and a variety of jellies, juices, cereal and more. Brett himself served everyone, though with his expression of eternal constipation. He had poured their drinks, served the eggs hot off the frying pan, sprinkled powdered sugar on their waffles, and had even cut up Grant's fruit for him. He disappeared back into the kitchen with nary a word. Don wiped the maple syrup from his mouth with a napkin, cleared his throat, and laid out his plan.

"We'll take my Land Rover, with Brett driving, of course. It'll be big enough for all of us and the EMP. We'll park in the alley behind, detonate the bomb, and force our way in through a rear entrance."

"Sounds like a plan," Grant said gleefully.

"Sounds like suicide," Violet grumbled.

Don smiled at Violet. "I understand your trepidation, my dear. But you must remember, this is *your* right. Your birthright. The information that they now hold was not only literally stolen from you, but since it was passed on to you by your father, it has been stolen from generations of your predecessors. *And*, the fate of the world is now in our hands."

"Even if the Scientologists have eleven of the twelve portions, what can they really do with it?" Violet asked. "Don't they need all twelve? And now that the twelfth portion is lost forever, thanks to me, isn't there nothing to worry about?"

"Au contraire." Don wagged a finger at her. "Even with a few of the portions, look at what Hubbard accomplished. Or Hitler, and that was with only partial information. With eleven *complete* portions, who knows what monstrosities could come out of that place. Not only is it about having portions of the twelve, it is understanding them. And in the wrong hands, the information provided could do great harm. No, I'm afraid we have no choice but to extricate said portions from the hands of the enemy."

Don's speech was interrupted by a doorbell echoing through the hallways and into the dining room.

Grant shot up in his seat. "It's here!" he screeched.

"Stay seated, my excitable friend," Don said. "Brett will get it." As if on cue, Brett appeared from the kitchen and, with a sour puss on his face, walked down the hallway and down the stairs.

Brett slid open the panel in the front door and peered out. A delivery man in a brown UPS uniform stood waiting. On a dolly was a large cardboard box.

"Yes?" Brett asked.

The delivery man jumped, having not noticed the beady eyes glaring at him from the small opening in the door. "Jeez! I, uh, have a delivery for a Don Brawn."

"Just leave it there, thank you. I will retrieve it in a moment," Brett said.

"Gotta sign for it, buddy." The delivery man held up a clipboard. "I can't leave a box this big outside."

Brett huffed. "Fine, one moment." And he began opening the multiple locks and latches on the door.

Don was about to buzz Brett on the intercom to see what the holdup was when the frenchman entered the room. He looked more irritated than usual.

"Well, you blasted french fry, what took you so…" Don Brawn froze mid-sentence as two men entered behind Brett.

"I'm sorry, sir. They had a gun on me." Brett offered as Mr. Trafalgar pushed him ahead.

Mr. Trafalgar looked about the room, he stood in a very tight fitting polyester brown UPS uniform. It was obviously stolen from a much leaner man.

Mr. Crows stood growling behind his larger partner. He, too, was wearing a UPS uniform, but much better fitting. He scratched at the uncomfortable material and sneered. He was carrying a duffel bag.

"Well, isn't this a wonderful reunion?" Mr. Trafalgar glowed triumphantly. "I have come to complete previously unfinished business with Miss Violet Sterne and her weak little traveling partner."

"Hey!" Grant objected, then fainted when the gun pointed at him.

"That's what I thought." Mr. Trafalgar laughed. "And as a bonus I get to bring in the infamous Don Brawn. What a lovely day this is turning out to be." He pointed to Violet, Don and the unconscious Grant. "Tie their hands behind their backs," he said to Mr. Crows. "We've got to get back to the center, I need an auditing."

Mr. Crows retrieved several ropes and began trussing the trio. Grant came around, but remained groggy.

"And you are to leave me here?" Brett said, looking more irritated than scared.

"No, you're coming with us." Mr. Trafalgar said. "We need you to drive."

"Why me?" Brett argued. "Leave me here. You don't need me.

"Either you're coming or I'll shoot your face!"

"I'll drive," Brett replied.

"This is going so well." Mr. Trafalgar turned to Violet. "I'm surprised you're so quiet. I figured you'd be mouthing off to me. What's the matter? No wise cracks?"

"I'm too freaking tired." Violet grimaced as Mr. Crows tightened the ropes on her wrists. "I just wanted eight hours sleep."

"You'll have plenty of time to sleep when we're through with you." Mr. Trafalgar laughed. "If you're alive."

Suddenly a loud metal-on-bone collision rang out as Brett struck Mr. Trafalgar in the head with the frying pan he had used to serve the eggs. A leftover fried egg flew across the room and hit the unconscious Grant in the face. It slowly slid down over his closed eyes. Mr. Trafalgar went down with a booming thud and Brett scooped up the gun. He quickly pointed it at Mr. Crows.

"Hands where I can see them." Brett spat. "I'll shoot you. I'm French, you know I hate Americans."

Mr. Crows put up his hands and sneered, his upper lip revealing sharp canines.

Brett pointed to the trussed up trio around the table. "Untie them, quickly."

A few minutes later Mr. Crows was bound to his unconscious partner. He whimpered and licked at Mr. Trafalgar's face, trying to awaken him.

"That's really weird." Violet frowned.

"He's always been a pretty weird guy. Didn't you watch Oprah? Now we know just how much." Grant agreed.

Don rubbed at his wrists which were red from rope burn. "We mustn't waste any time. Brett, load the EMP into the Land Rover and bring it out of the garage."

Brett nodded and ran off.

"Mr. Crows," Don began. "Where are the scrolls that you took from Grant and gave to Mr. Trafalgar?"

"Die," Mr. Crows growled.

"Thank you," Don replied. "Someday I will, but until then where are the scrolls?"

"We don't have them." Mr. Crows laughed, it was reminiscent of a hyena. "You can search us but we don't have them."

"Where are they?" Don asked again.

"I'm not telling you!" Mr. Crows snapped.

Don pulled out a rolled up newspaper and smacked him on the snoot. "Bad!" he yelled at the actor. "Bad, Mr. Crows!"

Mr. Crows whined and looked down.

Don waved around the newspaper roll. "Now, again, where are the scrolls?"

Mr. Crows opened his mouth to say something but eyed the newspaper warily. He looked nervously around then slowly returned his gaze to Don. "We dropped them off at the Celebrity Center." He hung his head in shame.

"Where in the center?" Don was poised to strike with the paper again.

"What do you know about the center? You don't know the layout," Mr. Crows argued. "What difference does it make if I tell you where we dropped them off?"

"Just tell me and let me worry about that." Don held the paper up high, ready to strike.

"Fine. Third floor. Mechanical Gorilla Room." Mr. Crows resumed licking at Mr. Trafalgar's face. "Wake up, boss," he whimpered.

Don turned to Violet and Grant. "We must make haste. Surely, the center will be expecting them to bring us in. We must get there and break in ourselves before they realize anything is amiss."

Violet threw her hands up in frustration. "I can't believe we're going there! I mean, these guys were about to take us there at gunpoint. Do you think they were really going to have tea with us then let us go? If we go there, these maniacs will kill us!"

Don shrugged. "If you have a better idea to keep the enemy from taking over the world and destroying it, I'm all ears."

Grant nodded his agreement. "We have to, Violet. How many times do you get the chance to save the world?"

Violet sighed. "Fine. We're all a bunch of idiots."

"If it's any consolation," Don said. "We're heroic idiots."

A loud honk echoed in the front courtyard. Don ran to the window. "Brett is ready with the Land Rover. It's go time!"

Don and Grant ran out of the room with Violet grumbling behind them.

CHAPTER 81

Half an hour later, the Land Rover sat idling in front of the Scientology Celebrity Center in Hollywood. Violet was astounded when she saw the building. Though building was hardly a word to be used to describe this edifice. It was a castle.

Located at 5930 Franklin Avenue, this enormous structure was originally built in 1929 as a luxury hotel. Known then as The Manor Hotel, it reeked of opulence and wealth. Sadly, in 1992, this proud building was refurbished by the Church of Scientology and converted into an obnoxious Disneyesque monstrosity replete with restaurants, gardens, theaters, tall spires and a neon sign large enough to be seen from the moon. The obnoxious sign, that lit up Franklin Avenue from six stories above, read 'Church of Scientology Celebrity Center' and was as subtle as Kirstie Alley in a thong.

They had watched the front entrance building for several minutes and there was enough activity to make a simple walk-in the wrong method of entry. They drove around the large parking lot on the side of the building and parked more than once, each time using it to find a different angle on the side and back of the center. From their vantage point they could see the extensive flora, stone paths and fountains in The Garden. Violet gasped at the size of The Garden Pavillion, a tremendous 17th century French-style greenhouse that served as an auditorium and seated over 400 people. They watched as guests, with guides leading the way, walked through the extensive garden behind the gigantic building.

"This is so…" Violet looked for the proper word. "Excessive!"

"Don't forget, you *are* in Hollywood." Don reminded her. "Stars and their egos would never settle for less!"

"I don't see a way in," Grant said, getting back on track.

"Then the EMP will have to serve as a diversion." Don replied. "Once deployed, I'm hoping the center will be in chaos and we can slip in unnoticed."

"So the EMP will take out any alarms?" Violet said as Grant and Don slipped into the back of the Land Rover and tried to put the EMP together. Brett was outside the vehicle, keeping an eye out for police or scientologists. He was smoking like a typical angry Frenchmen.

"That's the plan." Grant said, he tossed a wire down angrily. "Why didn't they say there'd be assembly required!?"

"Patience, Grant." Don said. "There isn't that much to put together."

"And you're positive that's not going to blow up, right?" Violet asked nervously.

"Yes, Violet," Grant huffed. "You might feel a tingle, or vibration or energy in the air. Hell, your hair might get a little static-y. But that's about it."

"Okay, just checking." She crossed her arms, looking doubtful.

A few minutes later, Don shouted triumphantly. "Eureka! We've done it." He shook Grant's hand, felt the wetness, then wiped his own hand off on the floor of the Land Rover. "Good job, son. Now we can fire this baby up!"

Don opened the back of the Land Rover and all three of them climbed out. They stood at the back of the truck, as though at a tailgate party, crowded around the EMP. Don looked at Grant and Violet. "Here we go."

"Before you do," Violet blurted. "Mr. Brawn, I have to apologize."

"For what, my dear?"

"I lied to you." Violet looked at Grant. "And you, too."

Don smiled warmly. "About memorizing the code?"

Violet's eyes widened. "You knew?"

"Dear Violet, if there's one thing I'm good at it is reading people. I could tell you didn't trust me. And I knew you would tell me when you thought I had proven myself."

"So you're not mad?"

"Not at all." Don placed a friendly hand on her shoulder. "I knew it was safely tucked away in that beautiful head of yours. Once we regain possession of the other portions you and Grant discovered, we can get back to that."

Violet looked again to Grant. "Sorry, I didn't mean to lie to you."

"It's okay." Grant patted her shoulder.

Violet smacked his hand away. "It's not an excuse to touch me."

"Stupid Americans." Brett tossed his cigarette.

Don poised his thumb again over the 'on' switch. "Okay, *now* here we go!"

He flicked a switch and the control panel lit up. Violet could hear, no it was more like feel, a hum coming from the EMP. The feeling grew and her fingertips felt tingly. The lights blinked faster and faster as the energy in the air amplified.

Violet took a step backward.

Grant did as well.

So Violet took another two steps back.

Don stood where he was, his thumb poised above the detonation switch. The vibration of the EMP and the Land Rover had grown to a point where they feared it would draw attention. Don yelled out over the loud thrum. "Okay, and we go in three... two... and one!" Don flipped the switch.

Violet expected a loud noise. A boom. A bang. A flash of light. But was surprised to hear... nothing. The vibration died quickly. The parking lot was eerily quiet.

"Did it work?" Violet finally said.

From behind them, out on the corner of Franklin and North Bronson, they heard the tires of a car screeching, followed by a crash. Glass shattered. More tire screeches. More crashing. More glass shattering. A woman screamed. Someone yelled, "There's no power! The traffic light is out!" Then someone else, "God, help me! I'm bleeding." "Call an ambulance!" "I can't, my cell phone is dead!" "Mine, too!" "Dear God, what is happening!" "I can't feel my legs!" "I'm blind, I'm blind!" "Tell my mom I love her!"

Grant, Violet and Don looked at each other.

"I guess it worked." Grant said.

They looked at the celebrity center and saw that the obnoxious neon sign was off. Though it was daytime there were certain lights that normally remained on around the center, these too were no longer working.

"Quickly, we must get inside. I don't know how long the power will remain out!" Don dashed across the parking lot, Brett fell in behind him. Grant grabbed Violet by the hand and followed.

With the power out and mayhem ensuing on the streets outside, several of the Scientology employees came outside to see what was happening. Guests also stepped out, curiosity getting the better of them. At this point, it would be hard for anyone to know specifically who did or didn't belong inside the center.

Don found a utility door in the back of the building. It had a little picture of descending stairs on it.

"I think this leads to the basement," Don announced.

"You're brilliant," Brett sneered.

There was an electric keypad next to the door. None of its lights were on. Not only was the alarm disabled, but so was the electronic lock. Brett had brought a crowbar in case they needed to force their way in but he didn't need it. Don simply pulled on the handle and opened the door. Brett tossed the crowbar aside.

"Stay close together," Don whispered. "And act like you belong here."

"How do we do that?" Violet hissed.

"I'm not sure." Don answered. "Look confident, like you know what you're doing here and where you're going. If anyone asks, tell them you're going to the Mechanized Gorilla Room. If all else fails, try and look like you're brainwashed."

"That'll be easy for you." Grant joked to Violet.

She punched him in the shoulder. "Ow!" he cried out.

"Would you two stop it!" Don whispered harshly.

"Sorry." They replied in unison.

The stairs led down to another doorway, which indeed led to a basement hallway. But unlike any basement they had seen before. It looked more like a romantic walk along a rural Italian street. The floor was a beautiful terra cotta tile. The walls, painted in bright orange, had the appearance of short brick walls along the bottom. Growing from the brick walls was painted shrubbery. Faux windows, complete with blue shutters, covered the walls between doorways. Brass street lights, not working at the moment of course, lined the walls, adding the aura of a rustic town's cobblestone walk. They even placed a few potted trees along the way to add to the illusion.

"Damn." Violet whispered. "And this is just the basement?"

"Indeed," Don agreed. "Okay, let's find a way up."

They crept along quietly, Don trying certain doors that weren't clearly marked. A few were locked, others weren't. One door that he opened was a large storage room. It held shelves upon shelves of boxes, mostly containing files. Jars containing odd, floating artifacts also littered the room. Labels on them were written in a strange language.

"Let's go through here," Don whispered.

They each had a flashlight that Brett had handed out earlier. They maneuvered through the storage room along the lengthy and dusty shelves. Grant kept stopping and nosing through files.

"Stop that." Violet shoved him. "We don't have time for that."

Grant sighed and dropped the file. It read, 'Area 51 and Elvis'.

"Over here." Don called out.

He had found another door, again with an image of stairs on it. Don cracked it open and looked inside. It was a flight of stairs leading up. Single file with flashlights moving around like a spastic light show, the foursome went up the one flight of stairs. It came to a single door. Don again cracked it open and peered out.

Again the hallway was designed to look like an outdoor walkway in a quaint town. Stonework highlighted the corners, small spots of exposed faux brick showed through the painted walls. Potted plants littered the hall. Luckily the lobby was just down the hallway and enough light came in the windows as to remove the need for flashlights.

"It looks like a main hallway. I can see an elevator and what must be the lobby. There are people in the lobby but they're all watching the mayhem out on the street. Let's move!"

319

The four stooges dashed from the storage room, down the hall, and to the elevator. Don pressed the button. They waited for half a minute before Brett finally spoke up. "There's no power, twits."

"Damn it! You're right!" Don cursed through clenched teeth. "Okay, to the stairs!"

They ran across the hall and opened another door marked 'stairs'. They scrambled up the two flights and lined up outside of the third floor door. Don gathered them around.

"We do not know what sights we will see in here. No one who visits these areas ever speaks of what it holds. Scientologists are sworn to secrecy when exposed to the higher floors. So prepare yourself, for anything. No matter how bizarre, nor odd, nor frightening. Remain composed. Are we ready?" He looked from face to face.

"Yes!" Grant replied.

"I guess." Violet mumbled.

"I hate you Americans." Brett's face looked like he had just sucked a lemon.

Don paused, glaring at his manservant. "Remind me to get you help," he said to Brett. "Okay, here we go." Don swung the door open.

Gone was the rustic imagery of small village shopping. Here it was more like a hotel. The décor was beautiful, this floor was an earthy brown and green motif. The carpet was a deep green and red pattern that worked with the forest green and tan walls. The doors and trim were a serious mahogany. The color scheme was very rich and the detail beautiful.

"I expected it to be more, I don't know, space-like." Violet broke the silence.

"Me too." Grant agreed

"I as well." Don said.

"You Americans suck." Brett mumbled.

Don looked around, he shined his flashlight around the hallway. The doors were numbered, but there was no indication that the rooms had names. "This could take a while. We have no clue where the Mechanized Gorilla Room is."

"Well, I guess we'll just systematically work our way down the hall." Grant offered. "There can't be that many rooms on this floor."

"If we're lucky, we can find L. Ron Hubbard's office." Don said.

"He has an office here?" Violet asked. "From when he was alive?"

"No. He's never seen it." Don explained. "His office here was built after he died."

Violet frowned. "Why does a dead guy need an office?"

"You'll have to ask a scientologist." Don laughed. "Okay, let's get this started."

They each approached a door and attempted to open them. Grant's and Don's were locked. Violet opened hers and looked inside. She floated the beam of light around the room, then gasped.

CHAPTER 82

The room was entirely black save for a white circle in the center. There were no windows. It took a few seconds for Violet's eyes to adjust to the near darkness. Then she saw the man standing in the white circle, naked, with wires attached to every appendage. And we mean *every* appendage. The man seemed to be in a meditative state. Violet quickly closed the door.

"What was in there?" Grant whispered from down the hall.

"A naked guy," Violet rasped.

"Oh." Grant shrugged. "Brett? What about you?"

Brett opened his door, shone in his flashlight, and immediately closed it. He paused, as if trying to absorb what he'd seen. He opened it again, then closed it. Then he opened and closed it once again.

Don grimaced. "Brett you silly fondue-breath, what are you doing?"

Brett looked at the others. "I think you should all see this."

Don quickly walked down the hallway and joined Brett. Violet and Grant exchanged looks, then also met up at the door. Brett hesitated briefly, then opened the door. They all aimed their flashlights into the room. Grant fainted.

"Great Scott!" Don exclaimed.

"What the Hell is that?" Violet was shocked.

Before them was a large cylindrical tank, hooked up to large computers and machinery. Wires ran in and out of the tank. Computer screens filled the walls of the room as well as machines that looked more like they belonged in a hospital than in a celebrity center.

What was most disturbing was what was floating in the tank. A man's head.

"Could that be?" Don said, mostly to himself. He squinted his eyes. "But it is! It's the head of L. Ron Hubbard!"

"L. Ron Hubbard?" Violet gasped. "But he looks... dead."

The head floated lifelessly. Its eyes closed. Its mouth slack.

"He is *now*!" Don frowned. "Thanks to us. I dare say our EMP wiped out his support system."

Indeed it had. No computers hummed with activity. Print-out machines meant to show reports on his health lay silent. EKG meters showed no activity of brain function. The room was a large mausoleum, silent and gray.

"We killed him?" Violet sank down and knelt next to Grant's unconscious body. She looked up at Don. "But wouldn't they have a back-up generator or something?"

"It would appear that our bomb took care of that as well."

Don, Violet and Brett entered the room. They left the heap known as Grant lying in the hallway. They spread out and examined the machinery, the tank, and the morbid floating head of L. Ron Hubbard.

Violet tapped on the tank like a child does to a goldfish. "When did L. Ron Hubbard die?" she asked, then added. "Originally."

"In 1986." Don said as he picked up a small stack of computer printouts. He rifled through the pages, his jaw dropped in shock. "Violet, Brett, you must see this!"

Violet and Brett quickly joined him and looked over his shoulder. They added their flashlight beams to his to make viewing easier. "What is it?"

"It's the thoughts, I think, or even possibly the speaking of Mr. Hubbard himself."

"I don't get it." Violet said.

"Stupid Americans and their floating heads. Mon dieu!" Brett spat.

"Somehow, and I don't know how," Don stumbled, trying to find words. "These machines aren't just to keep the head of L. Ron Hubbard alive but it actually allows him to communicate."

"That's insane!" Violet looked back at the now dead head.

"It certainly is! Look at this, it seems to ramble a bit. If Mr. Hubbard was crazy before he died, then twenty years floating in a tank has pushed him over the edge. He's got new ideas for cleansing…" Don quickly switched to another printout. "Sorry, but that shouldn't be viewed by a lady. Okay, here's another one. He has an idea for a new book. You know, I always wondered how he could keep coming out with books after he died. And now I know!" Don flipped through a few more pages. "Oh, this is plain madness. It says here that he thinks Bigfoot is a collective field of negative energy caused by expelled protons from the human body once they've been cleaned using the E-meter. He thinks that this cryptozoological beast should be hunted down and kept in a stasis of electromagnetism and vanilla pudding, which in turn would finally cure bad pop music like Justin Bieber!"

"That's not such a bad idea." Violet agreed. "But it's still crazy. Everyone knows Bigfoot isn't real."

Don shot Violet a look. "If we had time, I'd explain how *she* is so very real and how *she* connects to the Twelve, but we don't!"

"She? Bigfoot is a she? No, don't tell me. I don't want to know," Violet decided.

"We must move on," Don announced. "Sad as this is. If anyone in the building is concerned for him then they will be coming in to check on him. And I really don't want to be around when they find him dead."

Violet returned to the hallway and knelt down to Grant. She lightly smacked his face. This was becoming a serious habit. He slowly came around. Brett had luckily closed the door to L. Ron's room.

"What happened?" Grant muttered as Violet helped him to his feet.

"You dropped like a sack of potatoes, G.I. Joe." Violet laughed.

"Did I see a,' Grant swallowed hard. "Floating head?"

"Yes, my brave little man. But it's gone now. We're moving along."

They quickly moved down the hallway to the next grouping of doors.

The foursome aligned with their own new set of doors. They each turned the doorknobs simultaneously.

Don's and Grant's were locked. Violet's was unlocked as was Brett's.

"Why don't I get an unlocked door?" Grant whined.

"Shush." Don warned. "Go ahead, Brett, take a look inside."

Brett wrinkled his nose in disdain, then swung his door open. He closed it and turned toward the others. "It is nothing. A closet."

Don turned his attention to Violet. "Go ahead, dear."

Violet opened her door and quickly pointed her light inside. The focus of her flashlight scanned the room, then she froze. The others watched in anticipation. She left the door open and faced them.

"I believe I found the Mechanical Gorilla Room," she announced.

Don and Grant rushed to join her. Brett took his time. They all peered into the room together.

Don looked around the room. It was an opulent room to say the least. From the murals painted on the ceiling, lit by a tremendous crystal chandelier. Polished walnut furniture ornately filled the room; desk, chaise lounge, multiple chairs, a grandfather clock, even a white grand piano. Carved wooden trim finished the edges of the brightly painted walls of cream and sienna. Mirrors and classical paintings filled in the empty spaces on the walls. Don was puzzled. "Why do you think... oh!"

Somehow he had missed the large mechanical gorilla in the northeast corner of the room. Standing at over 6 feet in height, it was wider than two people, and it was resting on its knuckles. Its face appeared angry, its lip curled up in a frozen snarl.

Don, Violet, Grant and Brett cautiously entered the office. Don and Grant wandered up to the gorilla. They stared up at its mammoth hairiness.

Violet walked around the room, absorbed in the beauty and detail of the majestic room. She slid her hand over the smooth furniture, tracing the carving and craftsmanship. She paused at the desk. "Oh shit!" She yelled to the others. "Guys, I found them! I found the other scrolls!"

Don, Grant and Brett dashed to her side.

They all stared down in amazement. Placed on the desk, rather haphazardly, were the scrolls. Violet carefully scooped them up and turned to Don. "Here you go, Mr. Brawn, I believe these are best left in your hands."

Don smiled. "Thank you, dear Violet. I will honor your trust and…" He stopped speaking when he noticed the gun pointing at him.

"I'm sorry, Mr. Brawn, but it is I that will be leaving with the scrolls." Brett said smiling wickedly.

CHAPTER 83

Don's face whitened. Violet's jaw dropped. Grant didn't pass out but peed in his pants for the second time in two days. Everyone looked at him with disgust.

"Sorry," he whimpered.

"Enough of this!" Brett snarled. "Hand me the scrolls!"

"Brett, how could you?" Don was genuinely saddened and hurt. "My trusted manservant. After all these years together…"

"All these years of what? Mocking me for being French?"

"I thought we were having fun," Don shrugged.

"You disgust me, you insipid Americans, with your fat stomachs and cocky self-righteousness."

Violet scowled. "I am not fat!"

"No, you are what we French like to call *dévergondée muette*!" Brett chuckled.

"What the Hell does that mean?" Violet looked to Grant.

"You don't want to know." Grant looked away.

Don broke up the argument. "But why, Brett? Why after nearly ten years of working together?"

"Because I am not Brett Hayer, you blind old fool!" The not-Brett-any-longer laughed. "For a man who has dedicated his life to solving puzzles, you would think that something as simple as an anagram would be easy. Ha! You are nothing!"

"An anagram?" Don rolled the information around. "You mean…?"

"Yes, I am Barry Theete! The French mercenary you so often speak of. The man who single handedly tracked down four carriers of the Twelve and painfully extracted the truth from them. I, Barry Theete, who cajoled Monsieur Hubbard and wheedled my way into his trust, it was I that found him portions of the Twelve. Well, I didn't find them as much as I ripped them from the cold dead hands of their protectors. Mr. Hubbard was so pleased, he funded my searches. Yes, I let him have them, but only briefly, I laughed as I took it all away from him. And it was I, Barry Theete, who befriended you ten years ago so I could stay close to someone who had the best odds of finding the remaining portions! You see it now, you stupid American? Brett Hayer is Barry Theete!"

"Oh! That wasn't what I was thinking." Don admitted. "I came up with something else. Never mind."

Violet shrugged her shoulders. "Barry Theete isn't a very scary name."

"Not really." Grant agreed, pants still wet. "Barry. Barry. Nope, not very scary."

"It doesn't matter!" Barry turned to Violet and waved the gun in her face. "Please hand me the scrolls, dear harlot. As Mr. Brawn can attest to my reputation, I will not hesitate to kill all of you."

The power then came back on. The room flooded with light. Grant's wet khakis were even more evident.

Barry cocked the pistol to accentuate his point. "Now, Madame Violet."

"Not so quick, man." a voice echoed from behind the mercenary.

Violet, Grant, Don and Barry all turned toward the entrance to the Mechanized Gorilla Room. Standing in the doorway, with a gun in each hand, stood Jon Trafalgar. Thom Crows crouched next to him, like a panther ready to strike.

"Not only do the scrolls *not* belong to you, but I owe you a little dance with a frying pan." Mr. Trafalgar's eyes gleamed, he was angry and volatile. A large lump was situated on his forehead above his right eye. It marred his Hollywood good looks. That didn't make him very happy. "So drop your little pea-shooter there, Jacque, and sit against the wall over there." He motioned to the empty wall next to the door.

Barry Theete never concerned himself with being outmanned, but he knew when he was outgunned. He tossed the .22 caliber aside and slowly lowered himself to the floor, his back to the wall.

Mr. Trafalgar handed one of the guns to Mr. Crows. "If he moves, shoot him. If he looks at you wrong, shoot him. But don't kill him. Save that for me." Then Mr. Trafalgar kicked Barry in the face for good measure, rendering him unconscious.

"Now cats and kittens," Mr. Trafalgar approached their group. "You can put those scrolls back down on the table and follow me. We're finally going to have that meeting you keep putting off. I'm going to introduce you to the big guy."

Don, Violet and Grant all looked at each other.

Don cleared his throat. "Do you mean… Mr. Hubbard?"

Mr. Trafalgar tilted his head. "How did you know he was *alive*? It doesn't matter. He'll know what to do with all of you. Especially you, Miss Sterne. He'll get that information right out of your head." Mr. Trafalgar made a loud sucking noise. "He'll pull your brain out if he has to!" Mr. Trafalgar noticed the odd looks on everyone's face. "What? What is it?"

All three exchanged glances.

"Do we tell…" Violet asked.

"No, we shouldn't…" Grant said.

"But, he'll find out…" Don added.

"He'll be mad…"

"He'll be more than that…"

"But, he'll shoot…"

"Probably will anyway…"

"Okay, you tell him…"

"No way, you…"

"No chance…"

"I feel faint…"

Mr. Trafalgar had had enough. "I've had enough!" he redundantly yelled. "What are all of you going on about? Tell me now or I'll shoot the geek in the face!"

"Well," Don began. "You see…"

Another voice boomed from the doorway. "Please put down the weapon, Mr. Trafalgar. Immediately!"

Mr. Trafalgar's eyes lit up and showed fear. He immediately recognized the voice. "Mr. Maystyne?"

CHAPTER 84

A man in a wheelchair, backlit by the light from the hall, was being rolled into the room by another man. With the bright lights of the hall behind him, the man's face was not clear at first. "Yes, my trusted servant. It is I, Mr. Maystyne. Please put down the weapon. There is no need for violence now. We are all here and we will settle this peacefully."

Mr. Trafalgar hesitated for only a moment before reholstering his weapon. Mr. Crows followed suit, mimicking his counterpart. Mr. Trafalgar smiled widely. "It is an honor to meet you, sir. I've been waiting for this opportunity for, like, ever!"

The man in the wheelchair was pushed into the light. Illuminating his face for everyone to see.

Violet nearly passed out. "Dad?"

Grant looked at Violet. "Dad!"

Don looked confused. "Dad. Whose dad?"

Violet burst into tears. "Dad, I thought you were…"

"Dead?" Randall laughed, but not in a warm-hearted manner. He laughed angrily. "Yes, well, you think a lot of incorrect things." He pointed to a chair. "Sit down, Violet, I will attend to you in a moment," he said sternly.

The not-so-deceased Randall Teodey rolled himself over to Mr. Trafalgar and Mr. Crows. Randall's bodyguard took point at the door of the room.

"You have served me well," Randall said, extending his hand. "Although your tactics are questionable and your ability to follow orders is tenuous at best. You did manage to pursue and corral our prey." Mr. Trafalgar took the hand offered and proudly shook it. Randall continued. "Even Mr. Crows did well, although I must admit I was nervous a few times there."

Violet interrupted suddenly. "Nervous? They tried to kill us! And it was you behind it? I can't believe…"

"Silence, Violet!" Randall shouted. "I will get to you!" He turned back to the pair of celebrities. "You have made me, my associates, and Scientology very happy. You are worthy of your reward." Randall waved his hand toward the door. "Follow my friend there. You are free from this obligation. Again I thank you."

The man standing guard at the door picked up the unconscious Barry Theete. The man removed the scrolls from Barry's grip and handed them to Randall before carrying him out of the room on his shoulder.

Mr. Trafalgar nodded and smiled widely. "You got it, sir! Well, it has been our privilege to work for you in this cause." Mr. Trafalgar turned to his little companion. "Well, buddy, it looks like our work here is done." He patted Mr. Crows on the head.

"Damn! I didn't get to kill that girl! She had it coming, too." Mr. Crows rubbed the toe of his shoe on the ground and shoved his hands in his pockets, pouting.

"Hey, I didn't get to kill the guy that smacked me with the frying pan."

"That's true." Mr. Crows nodded.

"Remember, there's always the next mission!" Mr. Trafalgar offered him. "Besides, you've got to get home."

"I'm not still married, am I?!" Mr. Crows was aghast.

"No way, skipparoo."

"God, girls are so icky." Mr. Crows pouted even more. "I'm trying to forget about that."

"I have a wife, too." Mr. Trafalgar reminded him.

"Oh, yeah. That's right. She's nice."

"She sure is. Keeps my house clean. Takes care of my kids."

"Kids?! Oh, God they make me nervous. They're like... small people! I don't like the way they look at me, all needy and stuff!"

"You have a daughter, don't forget." Mr. Trafalgar lit a cigarette.

"I have a kid?!" Mr. Crows was even more shocked. He thought about it briefly then smiled. "Well, at least I have someone to play with. Someone I can relate to."

"Just not too rough." Mr. Trafalgar warned. "You know how you get when you're carried away with playing." He put his hand on Mr. Crows shoulder and slowly led him from the room.

"Yeah. I won't get too rough." A dark look came over Mr. Crows' eyes. "But I bet the kid would taste great grilled!"

Mr. Trafalgar smacked Mr. Crows on the snout. "Hey! What'd I tell you? Do not eat the children! Do *not* eat your kid, nor my kids, nor anyone's' kids. Understand?"

Their voices echoed as they strolled out the door.

"Okay. Sorry," Mr. Crows apologized. "What about Brooke Shield's kids? Can I eat them?"

Mr. Trafalgar laughed. "I'll have to think about that one, peanut. Come on, I'll race you to the car."

"You got it!" Mr. Crows shouted with glee.

And they left, Mr. Crows running circles around Mr. Trafalgar.

CHAPTER 85

Randall casually flipped through the scrolls, then laughed. "A whole lot of nonsense and mayhem, over these scraps of paper."

Violet couldn't take anymore. "Dad, what is going on? Why did they call you Mr. Maystyne? Why are you alive? I thought you were shot and killed."

"Shot, yes. Killed, obviously not!" Randall pointed at Violet. "A man broke in to the museum, attempted to steal some artifacts and stumbled upon me whilst I was working. He panicked and shot me."

"A burglar?" Violet was stunned.

" You, dear, are a *moron*. If you took half a second to check my pulse, you would have known that." He frowned, the lines in his face deepening. "But then again, I guess you weren't taught that at your lesbian keg parties."

Grant's ears perked up. "Lesbian?" He looked at Violet in a whole new light. "Nice!" Grnat giggled. "Lesbian."

"Shut up, Grant." Violet growled. She looked back at her father. "But wasn't it an assassin? Someone trying to get your secrets?"

"Again, wrong." Randall said. "It was just a common thief. A thug."

Violet let the new information roll around her head. She shook in disbelief.

"As for Mr. Maystyne, that is a name I use when I hire certain individuals to do my dirty work." Randall laughed. "You don't think I made all my money as a curator, do you? The museum pays crap."

"What about the message you left me? The clues to the secret of the Twelve? The reference to Michelangelo?"

"My dear, I have kept the best tabs on you and your journey as I could, considering I was hospitalized with a bullet in my gut. If you had checked your messages at home, or turned on your cell phone, the police had been calling you all day. I had others trying to reach you the rest of the weekend."

"I wasn't allowed to listen to my messages at home." Violet glared at Grant. "And I lost my phone, so I couldn't answer it. But what about Grant here? Why did you need me to find him?"

Randall laughed heartily and Violet blushed. "Violet, that is *not* Grant Piosto."

Violet nearly passed out. *"What?"*

"That is Art Greekstek, a sixteen year old boy with more than a few mental issues. His parents have been worried sick over his disappearance. He has delusional episodes, schizophrenia, fugues, ADHD and a host of other issues. That is why he was in New York, his parents were taking him to specialists to help him deal with his problems. He is in dire need of his medications, which he has been off of for too long. You have already broken so many child endangerment laws by kidnapping him and taking him out of the country."

"Kidnapping?" Violet's head spun. "But... he said... I didn't kidnap... I thought..." She looked over at Grant.

Grant was blushing and he looked away sheepishly. "Sorry," he muttered.

She turned back to her father. "But he knew so much! I thought he *looked* young but he sounded like a professor."

"The boy is definitely a genius! There's very little he doesn't know about history and architecture. He is also absolutely crazy." Randall said. "He really is brilliant! But he is legally insane. He doesn't understand his actions, nor the repercussions of them. His mind is so deep and knowledgeable but fragmented." Randall continued. "The parents are filing some major lawsuits against you. Which is all the more reason to find the real Grant Piosto."

"Who is Grant Piosto?" Violet was on the verge of tears. "And why did you want me to find him?"

"Grant is a dear friend of mine. And a lawyer! Which is what you were going to need once the museum had started their lawsuit against you."

"Lawsuit? Why?"

"Did you think they wouldn't notice the missing Ancient Peruvian Gold and Diamond Earrings, Violet?"

Violet's face turned beat red. "I was going to return them! They were just for this party I was going to. I wanted to look good!"

Randall held up his hand to silence her. "Gerri Hender had told me the day before that you had pilfered them. She also told the Director of Operations. They were very upset with you. Not to mention you were a terrible employee to begin with. I was to fire you that morning and would have done so had I known you were in already. Probably looking at pornography on the Interwebs! But when I was shot, I didn't know if I was going to live or die but I wanted you to get a good lawyer. So I was trying to tell you to find Mr. Piosto. And now that you've kidnapped a minor and taken him on a worldwide spree, you'll definitely be needing him."

"No, this can't be!" Violet shook her head. "But what about Michelangelo and the Twelve?"

"Conspiracy nonsense! I am no Twelvist nor a carrier of sacred information from aliens and passed along by Jesus Christ. Do you hear how crazy that sounds?"

"But, Peter Boystead!"

"A school friend of Mr. Greekstek here. Not even from England!"

"I *knew* his accent was terrible. But what of Prince Shozich?"

"A homeless man who lingers around tourists traps looking for foolish Americans like you to get money. He listened in on your conversation and told you whatever you wanted to hear."

"But, Jon Trafalgar and Thom Crows? Dad, they're real! They're famous Scientologists and they knew of the Twelve!"

"They're also empty-headed, mindless actors. You won't find people more susceptible to following orders than actors. They need their heads filled for them, they can't do it themselves. I gave them a mission to follow and they did it. I needed them to believe in the same cause you were following otherwise they wouldn't have done it. And I needed people that were so famous they could literally do whatever they wanted and have no consequences for their actions. Celebrities are the perfect mercenaries! They are above the law!"

Randall shrugged."My only regret was not knowing how volatile Mr. Crows really was. Now *there* is a person with issues!"

"But why would you work with Scientologists?"

"I *am* a Scientologist!" Randall barked. "If you and I had one conversation that lasted more than 'hello' and 'goodbye' you might have known that."

"What about Mr. Brawn here?" She looked over at the author. "You're real, right? Please tell me you're real!"

Don Brawn nodded his head. "Yes, I am, Miss Sterne. And so is the Twelve. Your father is wrong."

Randall rolled up to Don. "Mr. Brawn you are higher than my daughter on the moron scale. You've dedicated your life to something so insipid, so ersatz, so ridiculous that I hate being in the same room as you. The drivel that you published all those years ago, putting crazy thoughts in people's heads about aliens and Jesus! You should be ashamed." Randall looked up at his daughter. "Mr. Brawn is real all right, Violet, a real charlatan. That is why he only wrote the one book."

"And made a lot of money!" Don blurted.

"Yes, you did, Mr. Brawn. But it doesn't validate your writing. Wealthy doesn't make your literature valid."

Violet didn't want to hear this anymore. "No, I can't accept this. So many people believing in it. Barry Theete, Mr. Brawn…"

"All wackos!" Randall cut her off.

"Hey, be nice." Don said under his breath.

"We found scrolls!" Violet shrieked. "We discovered ancient reliquaries with ancient scrolls in them! That can't be fake!"

Randall held up the scrolls. "You mean these?" Randall chuckled. "Well, to someone who wouldn't know an ancient artifact from a Taco Bell napkin, one might think they were real. People have been planting so-called artifacts throughout history. For instance The Donation of Constantine, or The Protocols of The Elders of Zion, some say the Shroud of Turin or the Dead Sea Scrolls. There's the Hitler Diaries, the Cardiff Giant, the Piltdown Man. The list goes on. Scientists and religious scholars spend as much time debunking hoaxes as they do unraveling true historical mysteries."

"Not real?" Violet didn't want to believe it.

"Violet," Randall continued. "Did you actually see this kid, Art or Grant or whatever you want to call him, did you see him get any of these scrolls out from their hiding places?"

"Yes," Violet paused. "No. No, I didn't. I was the lookout, or the distraction."

"Because they were never there!" Randall shook the scrolls in his hand. "He had them on himself the whole time!"

Violet shot Grant-now-Art a look. He frowned and shook his head. "Violet, that's not true. They *were* there!"

"Shut up!" Violet screamed. She looked back at her father. She needed more answers. "What about mom?" Violet asked.

"Your mom?" Randall repeated, surprised. "What about her?"

"Was she a Scientologist? Was she tied into all this with you?"

"Tied in? Tied in to all this?" Randall hesitated for a second, not seeing that sort of question coming. "No, you're mother was not a Scientologist."

"But she was abducted by aliens, wasn't she?!" Violet almost cried. "I remember that night! The lights, the gray men, her floating out of the room in the middle of the night! Why did you lie to me? Why did you cover that up?"

Her father again paused, but more out of utter surprise than anything else. "Aliens? Violet, where in the world did you get that idea? She wasn't abducted by aliens. You're poor dear mother was mentally unstable."

"Unstable?" Violet could barely say the word.

"She was crazy, Violet. Simply put, the woman was stone-cold nutty as a fruitcake. Your mother went through so many stages; paranoia, depression, schizophrenia, and in the end, suicidal."

"No," Violet whispered.

"That is why I never told you about that. I didn't want you to think it was hereditary. I wanted you to have only the few good memories of your mother."

"But the lights. The aliens."

"You're mother made one very serious last attempt at suicide in the middle of the night. If not for my inability to sleep deeply I would not have caught her in time. The lights you saw were police, and EMTs, and ambulances. Your mother holed herself up in the bathroom. It took an hour to get her out. She didn't float out of the house, she was rolled out on a gurney."

"But where is she? Where did she go?" Violet's eyes welled up.

"She was in an institution, Violet. For many years. We always hoped she'd recover. I made several visits every week to see her. I didn't tell you where I was going. I didn't want you to see her that way."

"That's what your secret meetings were?" Violet closed her eyes.

"Then, one night, even the doctors and staff couldn't stop your mother from ending it all." Randall cleared his throat, he himself pushing down the pain. "She ended it and all I wanted to do was spare you of that."

Violet was speechless.

"Violet, after all your screw-ups. After our years without talking. After you were academically removed from Vassar."

"I wasn't…" Violet protested. "I graduated!"

"I paid for that graduation, Violet." Randall said. "Of course, you wouldn't have noticed the new wing with my name on it being added to the library building. Anyway, after all the stupid things you've done, to me, despite me and in spite of me, like changing your last name, did you ever wonder why I never gave up on you? Did you ever wonder why I kept giving you chances and money and a job?"

"Because you love me?" Violet squeaked.

"Hell no!" Randall barked. "Because just before your mother ended her life, she made me promise to always look out for you. Your mother said you wouldn't be brilliant. She used to say you'd probably need special care and special education. She admitted dropping you on your head a few times."

"That explains a lot," Grant mumbled.

"And she made me promise," Randall continued. "To give you everything. Whether I approved of what you were doing or not. And even through the tattoos, the piercings, the charges for pot possession, the butch girlfriend you once had, I stuck it out. Because I made that promise."

Violet hung her head. "I can't believe… I mean, it doesn't… I feel faint."

Randall looked back to Don Brawn. "Sir, you are free to go. With my connections in the Scientology community I can have you leave without anyone pressing charges. Very serious charges I might add. So it is in your best interest to leave, do not come back, and do not discuss what took place. Am I understood?"

Don Brawn nodded. "I do. And though we disagree on what is or is not true, I will honor your wishes. Thank you, sir." Don began walking toward the exit.

"Wait!" Violet called out. "Charges? You mean like murder? We killed L. Ron Hubbard's floating head for God's sake! Don't walk out, Don. We can bust this wide open! We killed L. Ron!"

Randall looked from Don to Violet, then said. "Violet, there is no L. Ron head here. And if there was, it wasn't alive for it to be killed. Mr. Brawn is leaving."

Don Brawn frowned at Violet. "Sorry, Miss Sterne. I'm too old for jail." Don sighed heavily. " I didn't see a thing." A man met Don Brawn at the door and escorted him down the hallway.

Randall looked next to the not-Grant-anymore-but-now-known-as-Art. "Well, Art, my fried little friend, your parents are very worried about you. We have a ride waiting to take you to the airport."

Another man, dressed exactly as the others came in and waited next to Art. The young boy sighed then walked up to Violet. "I'm really sorry. It's just that when I saw you in the lobby of the Hilton, you were so beautiful, and in need of help, and I just wanted to have an adventure." His eyes pleaded with hers.

For the first time, Violet was actually able to see him as the young man he was. He wasn't a youthful-looking scholar, he was a teenager. A crazy teenager.

"Grant," she stumbled. "Art, whatever. Don't you dare…"

" You have to admit we had one heck of an adventure."

Violet stepped forward and cocked her fist, on the verge of striking him.

Art saw the fist and fainted into the arms of the man next to him.

Violet couldn't even find the display humorous. She sighed then turned back to her father. "Dad, I'm sorry. I screwed up."

"Yes, you did Violet," Randall agreed.

Violet knew it was all over. "Take me home."

EPILOGUE

Two days later, Violet sighed heavily as she sat on a bench in The American Courtyard of The Metropolitan Museum of Art. She was only a few yards away from where her father was "killed". He was recovering nicely from the gunshot, already starting to walk with crutches, but sadly he was not recovering from Violet's behavior and adventure from the past week.

She looked down at the small box at her feet. It held the few items that were actually hers from her desk. She had only a few minutes to retrieve her things, under supervision from Roy so as to make sure she didn't abscond with even more office supplies or thousand-year-old relics. Even now, as Violet sat in the courtyard one last time, Roy stood within view, keeping a watchful eye on her. *What was she going to steal here? A one-ton statue from one of the fountains?*

She had returned the Peruvian earrings, as she had planned to all along, but that didn't really help her situation. She had a court hearing at the end of the week and despite her father's anger, he had still hired the services of the real Grant Piosto, who was positive he could get her a minimum penalty of a fine and probation.

The fake Grant Piosto was now rejoined with his very worried family and was back on his medications. Though she was not allowed to talk to him or exchange any correspondence of any sort, Violet was informed via Art's lawyers to Violet's lawyers that the parent's were going to drop all charges. Art had spoken so highly of Violet and their travel had helped Art so much in coping with his multiple ailments, that the parents were actually partially thankful to her. Especially once they found out she hadn't had sex with him. Violet shivered at the thought.

With any luck, she'd be freed of any jail time. She was, after all, too dainty and delicate to go to jail. Yeah, right! She'd probably be the queen bee after a week.

But through all of this, it wasn't a complete loss, she came out with a wealth of experiences. Things she'd never dreamed she'd be able to do. Places she never thought she'd see, nor had she heard of most of them. She discovered she wasn't as dumb as she or others thought. She gained an appreciation for history, art, and architecture. She even quit smoking! Not to mention she memorized an entire poem in Dutch. Not that she knew what she'd memorized but it was like her brain worked for the first time in her life. It opened up and took a mental picture. As far as she knew, it was her first mental picture. She'd hoped there'd be more.

And then there was her father. If he ever forgave her, she'd gained new appreciation for her father and the fact that he was alive. She'd learned about her mother, and though it was a terrible tale, it was at least closure.

And yet, she still had a difficult time accepting that it wasn't true. The Twelve, Jesus and Mary and the aliens. Michelangelo and the secret code. Don Brawn and his novel. L. Ron Hubbard, Scientology and Xenu!

Was it a stretch? Damn straight it was. But it *was* all connected.

Don Brawn had gone into hiding. Violet had attempted to contact him but he had already changed addresses. His new location was as mysterious and hidden as any of the portions of the Twelve. She had hoped to reconvene their search, on the sly from her father of course, and continue scanning the globe for portions. But with Art under protective custody of his parents, and the restraining order they'd gotten against her, and with Don Brawn missing in action, Violet was alone. She couldn't do it by herself. She couldn't study the books, the maps, connect the dots and find the secrets. She couldn't do the research; spend hours studying old tomes, manuscripts and maps. She didn't know the history of religion, or science, or... much of anything. *Damn! She'd wasted her life.*

A small group of students trundled past Violet. They were looking at the statues and taking notes for school. They laughed and whispered and laughed again. Violet frowned. She *had* wasted her schooling, her education, everything!

She'd probably end up like her mother, she thought. That was a shocker. Loony as a... well, something loony. *I have to work on my metaphors.*

So her mother wasn't abducted, she was crazy. That would explain a lot about Violet. Her temper, her anger, her inability to concentrate, her obsessive oral fixation. *Damn, maybe I am crazy.*

She was crazy for listening to Grant-now-Art. She was crazy for believing that Mary was impregnated by aliens, that Jesus was a half-alien, and that her family were heirs to the equivalent of a historical and religious atom bomb. *Yep, she was crazy.*

Violet also figured she was crazy for attempting to find the next portion of the Twelve. Just last night she had contacted an online Dutch community and had the poem translated. For some stupid reason, she thought she'd be able to do it on her own. That she'd prove her father wrong, and prove to the world that she *was* somebody.

She ran the poem through her head again like she had all last night. She had it memorized. She smiled briefly. That was *two* things she'd memorized! She was proud that her mind, the very mind that she and others often questioned the capabilities of, had memorized not just the poem in Dutch, but the entire code that followed. Her mind had taken a picture, a mental picture, just as Grant-now-Art had said he did with his empty camera. She had had the poem translated, but didn't do anything with the code. That was her secret, her treasure, real or not, she was the keeper of the final portion. And that made her special.

The poem was beautiful. It sang to her. She enjoyed running it through her head ever since she'd had it translated.

> On gilded oak the winged herald rides,
> Within the keyworn reliquary a secret hides,
> Far below the pulpit of bitter lime,
> Our future rests 'neath stairs of time.

Violet breathed in deeply, something in there rang true. She didn't know what it was but she felt like she should know what it was referring to. Ha! Who was she kidding? She'd never figure it out. She wasn't educated like Don Brawn or her father. She wasn't insanely intelligent like Art Greekstek. She wasn't even as smart as Peter Boystead or whatever his real name was.

"Time to go and find a job," Violet sighed. She reached for her box on the floor. She stopped when a hand fell upon her shoulder, it was cold but gentle. It held her there for a second. A woman's voice, smooth and calming filled her ears.

"Yes, you can. You *are* special."

Violet's head spun around. "Who?" There was no one behind her. She stared in the direction beyond where the voice seemed to emanate. She saw the angel.

No! It couldn't be! Violet slowly rose to her feet, she slowly walked toward the northeast corner of the courtyard.

Violet approached the angel and stood below it. She gazed up at its wings, the flowing gown, the horn it was playing. Her head tilted, the angel, its platform, the carving, the stairs. It slowly fell into place. Now it all made sense.

Violet stood before the sculpture, *All Angels' Church Pulpit and Choir Rail.*

On gilded oak the winged herald rides!

The angel stood on a disc, a UFO shaped disc. It was unmistakable! The angel, riding the disc, stood flying above... a pulpit!

Far below the pulpit of bitter lime!

Bitter lime? It didn't make sense. Violet approached the plaque describing the sculpture. Violet nearly laughed aloud. The pulpit was made of limestone! Then she read the artist, Karl Bitter! Violet covered her mouth to obscure her widening smile. She was doing it! She was solving it. She went back a line.

Within a keyworn reliquary a secret hides.

She knew the secret would be here. But a keyworn reliquary? At least she knew what a reliquary was, thanks to Grant. I mean, Art. Keyworn! Violet looked all around the sculpture. Security guard Roy edged closer, not sure if Violet was going to attempt to steal this tremendously large and heavy sculpture.

Violet put her hands on her hips. Keyworn. Maybe it didn't refer to a key. What was that puzzle-thing Barry Theete referred to? An anagram? She knew that meant to switch the letters around. *God, how was she to do this?* Violet almost gave up. *No, I can't stop. I can do this.*

Wore. Won. Work. Krow? Wonk? No, not real words. Kon. Korn, good band but I don't think it's a word. Won. Own. Now. New. Violet paused. New! She had it. New York! *Of course, it's hidden in New York. Duh! I'm at the Met where my father worked and could watch over it every day.*

Violet walked to stand near the pulpit's stairs carved of bitter lime. She smiled. She'd done it.

Our future rests 'neath the stairs of time!

Our future. Violet repeated to herself. She thought about running to her father and telling him. She thought about telling the world. She thought about telling Fox 5 News! But a voice inside Violet told her not to. The world wasn't ready. It wasn't up to Violet to reveal this. It was up to the Twelvists. The true carriers of this fortune. The fate of the world rest in the hands of those that knew what they were doing.

Violet now knew what she needed to know. That it wasn't all in vain. That it wasn't bull. It was true! And no one, not her father, not anyone, would tell her otherwise. She now knew the truth. A truth she discovered! Her truth. And that was enough for her.

And now that she carried the final portion with her, in her mind, now that *she* was the final reliquary, she knew she was going to have a good life. She had a connection; to God, to Jesus, to the little green men from outer space, and to the number twelve. She was the chosen one. Well, not really the chosen one. It had fallen into her lap. Or had it? Could it have been fate? Destiny? It didn't matter. Not to Violet. For once in her life she felt special. She felt she stood out in a crowd whether the crowd knew it or not. Violet had become someone, if for anyone, for herself.

Suddenly Violet had a different outlook on life. If she could do this, she could do anything! Life was good. She'd get past all this ugly stuff. She had a great, bright future ahead of her. Violet looked up toward the heavens and smiled.

"Thanks, mom," she whispered.

Violet picked up her box of junk and walked out of the courtyard, her head held high, and a smile on her face.

ABOUT THE AUTHOR

Brian J. Orlowski was born at the crappy end of the 60's to an over-bearing father and a coddling mother and a wardrobe of plaid pants. He was considered a prodigy in his early years; a moniker he immediately set out to disprove with great success. His teenage years consisted of being fat, having a Kirk Cameron mullet, and wallowing in unpopularity.

An avid fanatic of all things film and television; Brian would write a great deal of nothing worth printing and has kept at it to this day. In the late 80's and early 90's, Brian became a stand-up comic and performed over a hundred times across the north New Jersey area with famous names like Uncle Floyd and, well, just Uncle Floyd. Brian almost received a degree in Fine Arts at the local community college and eked out a graduation from the prestigious Joe Kubert School of Cartooning and Graphic Arts.

Brian has been a graphic artist, technical artist, comic book colorist, multimedia specialist, web designer, video editor and throughout his tepid career always kept his dream of being a published and full-time working writer and cartoonist. He is a regular contributor to Girls & Corpses magazine and several other publications suffering from a lack of public awareness.

Brian still resides in the same town in New Jersey he grew up in and every day prays that he escapes before he dies. He lives at home with his wife, Anna, along with a large, stinky dog, Abigail, and an antisocial cat named Buddy. Every year Brian travels to the arctic to participate in the running of the lemmings. One day he hopes his dreams will be fulfilled, his career will skyrocket, his years of perseverance will pay off and prove his worth as a contributor to the art and horror community, and on that day a bus will hit him.